HARMONY BAY

DONNA —
MAY YOUR
LIFE BE
FILLED WITH
HARMONY!

HARMONY BAY

An adventurous slice of waterfront life where mystery surrounds history...

Tom Gahan

Outskirts Press, Inc.
Denver, Colorado

Outskirts Press, Inc.
http://www.outskirtspress.com

ISBN: 978-1-4327-6663-4

Library of Congress Control Number: 2010939595

Outskirts Press and the "OP" logo are trademarks belonging to Outskirts Press, Inc.

PRINTED IN THE UNITED STATES OF AMERICA

"Tom Gahan's first novel demonstrates his mastery of description. He layers the plight of a contemporary single parent with events of the American Revolution and weaves a tale that provides the essence of Harmony Bay…"

— Florence Gatto - Long Island Writers' Guild, author of *The Scent of Jasmine*

"Harmony Bay captures the scope of small town life…the way it should be."

— Jerry Schaefer - WRCN 103.9 FM

"Very impressive. Hats off to you, Mr. Gahan!"

— Deborah E. Gordon - Sarasota, Florida

"Wow! What an attention grabber…from the very first page Harmony Bay captured my attention and didn't let go…"

— Dominick J. Morreale, EdD - author of *The Legend of Benny*

"Harmony Bay, a warm-hearted place…a riveting, heart-warming story."

— Lisa A. Dabrowski - WLNG 92.1 FM, author of *The Hunting Poetess*

"Getting to know the delightful characters of Harmony Bay makes me want to walk down the beach with any one of them and call them friend…Well done."

— Caren Heacock - Southold, New York

"True escapism! …Tom Gahan brings a fictional world to life in Harmony Bay, conjuring up images of the past, interwoven with a present day tale. His intimate portrayal of the characters comes through in a style that brings the reader into their lives as if they were kin…"

— Craig Romain – Editor, Lost Island Media

"Harmony Bay uncovers the rich historical past of a small town through the eyes of newcomers...Detailed description laced with historical references gives the reader a feel for life in a bayside town..."

— Kathy Gemmell - Frederick, Maryland

"Very interesting book...I'm glad that we were able to provide some scientific background..."

— Emerson Hasbrouck - Program Director,
Cornell Cooperative Extension Marine Program

"From swashbuckling adventure to witty humor to romance, Harmony Bay covers all of the bases."

— Bob Mann – Tyler, Texas

For Christian
May your journey always be paved with harmony.

*A life in harmony with nature, the love of truth and virtue,
will purge the eyes to understanding her text.*
— Ralph Waldo Emerson

Acknowledgements:

To my sister Eileen—*Eileen* was the first word that I spoke as a toddler. I guess that's where it all began. Thank you for all of the words herein that you inspired and for always being a faithful fan.

Henry C. Tanck, thanks for steering me through four years of High School English. Somehow, it grew roots and sprouted.

Much thanks to Lori Derych for your encouraging advice; "*don't let this fall between the cracks.*" And, to Pat Rogers for coaching me to, "*write something every day.*" I managed to write enough on some days to finish Harmony Bay. Your advice spurred me on. Thanks also, to Joanie Schultz, for your support, kind words and cheering at the finish line.

Thanks to Jill Dougherty Warga for sharing the Pernundle story, Bob Spates, for your delightful discussions over good wine about "*each one, teach one,*" and to Rory MacNish and Joe Ciamaricone for the use of your wonderful names. I certainly couldn't make those up. Thank you, Rory, for educating me about shellfish, and Joe for the bits and pieces about fishing. Joe, your name lives on. May you rest in peace. Also, to Stan Sommers for your endless boating knowledge.

To Tommy Skinner, thank you, posthumously, old friend. The stories about Cappy, your courageous Newfie, live on.

Special thanks to Cornell Cooperative Extension's Kim Tetrault, Community Aquaculture Specialist for your aquaculture insight and to all of the men and women at the shellfish research programs on Long Island for their dedication to revive the bays. You are making a difference. To Scott Curatolo-Wagemann, Genetics Program Technician at Cornell, thank you for sharing your story about Shark Day.

Lastly, and mostly, thank you to my lovely wife Darla for your unconditional support and giving me the time and space to write. It is a generous and endearing expression of your love.

Chapter 1

He stood frozen with his feet welded to the ground as if held in place by an unearthly power.

James McDonough never imagined this new place held such terror. He thought everything to be afraid of was left behind in the city. The fear to go out in the world and— the fear to be alone. Born and raised in the city, he knew its network of narrow alleys and bustling streets well. James used to live in the Old Section, a haphazard matrix of crookedly aligned streets lined with two-story brownstones. *Old Section* seemed appropriate to him, not so much because of the aged shops and dwellings, but its inhabitants. Everyone on James' block seemed prehistoric. He took it in stride and relied on the senior citizenry for their daily greetings called out to him from their hand washed front steps. They provided the occasional dollar or two that he earned for running errands for them up to the shops on the boulevard. 156 Avenue C is where he had lived for all of his days and nights. His grandparents gave his mom their home when they moved to Florida. She and James lived with Gram and Gramps until the icy winter winds that whistled through the city sapped the warmth from their bones for the last time, making the final determination for the move south. Although he missed his grandparents, everything seemed okay on Avenue C. That was his world.

This was his first day in a new place and he feared it was his last. Only the nearby sun-bleached beach grass bowed in reaction to the February gusts. In spite of the bitter cold, James felt a searing heat race throughout his skinny frame. Adrenalin pushed his pulse, making him perspire beneath his down filled coat. Sweaty palms moistened his mittens, and worst of all, he felt tears begin to well in his eyes. The boy started to tremble, not from the cold, but from the horror before him. There were no shadows with the winter sun at its pinnacle. Everything appeared stark. Austere sand and sky were colorless. Dull red slats of snow fencing stood as pickets to the confrontation in sharp contrast to a scrim of decaying eelgrass and dirty snow. Drumming heartbeats in his ears blocked the sounds of coastal birds that wintered in the tidal wetlands behind him and erased the hushed lapping of smallish tide driven waves before him. At this very moment he wanted his mother, Gramps, or the ability to run. But not in that order. James had enough presence of mind to question if he should run if he could. He'd be overtaken in the first few yards and that would be the end of him.

It was an incredible beast. Soot black fur glistened in the midday sun. A watermelon head topped a massive and muscular frame. White, glistening teeth revealed themselves as the animal dropped its lower jaw. Its canines and incisors appeared even larger against the heavy, oily coat. The creature's front limbs were powerful and sturdy to support the substantial broad chest topped by solid shoulders. Hind legs were several times again thicker and more robust than the front. James had never seen anything like it in the city. It was huge. Now out on the coastal precipice of North America, James was certain he had encountered a bear. Welling tears started to trail down his stinging cheeks. He didn't cry out, but knew unless God or someone else intervened, he was a goner. A search party would never find his body. His mother would cry, being sorry that she traded the dangers of the Old Section for this sand bar and the marauding bears that roamed it looking for boys to eat.

The jackhammers in James' ears were loud enough to mask the sound of a distant voice calling from upwind. In the same instant, the hulking figure several yards in front of him reared up on its haunches and pawed the air with its enormous front feet. James had already slammed his eyes shut as an uncontrollable shaking replaced the tremor in his knees. While waiting for the monster to consume him—James pictured Mom, Gramps, and Gram.

Before closing his eyes James hadn't noticed the mop tail or the webbed toes on the animal and the barking didn't register with him as belonging to the bear before him. The voice that had been too far off and too diminished by his state of panic was becoming audible, calling out, "Angus, Angus!" James felt something on his shoulder that he was sure was either the hand of the angel of death, or the mouth of the bear grabbing him. Now right beside him, the husky but melodic voice was loud and clear saying, "Boy! Boy, it is okay. Angus, you rascal. Sit down and behave. It looks like you have scared this young man. Angus. Angus!" Before James fainted, his eyes flickered long enough to see a barrel-chested man wearing a red parka and a long white beard.

James awoke in the arms of the old man who gently placed him on the cold sand, supporting him like a reed of beach grass. Speaking in a low voice, the man's blue eyes were intense. "Well, lad, it looks like you have met Angus." His billowing whiskers were unable to hide the gentle smile that went along with words reassuring James that everything was going to be okay. "Hmmm, it looks like the winds have caused your eyes to tear a bit. I assure you, you will be all right. It happens to me all the time." He gave a knowing wink. "Welcome to Harmony Bay," he said.

Chapter 2

Surrounded by stacks of still unpacked liquor store boxes neatly piled three high on the linoleum floor, she quietly posed the question to herself, *good grief, what have I done?* Standing in the middle of the kitchen with hands on hips, she was sure the floor hadn't been washed since before she was born. Patterns in the flooring were indiscernible, masked by grime that had been well tread on over time. A fine residual coating of beach sand was on the floor adding to the mess. It had blown beneath the kitchen door where the weather sweep was missing. The ceiling was as nasty as the floor due to years of contact with nicotine and greasy smoke that billowed from the dilapidated stove.

Oh well, she mused, *buyer beware.* Dory found the cottage through an internet listing by a real estate agent. She wasn't buying the place, but was renting. Renting seemed a safer approach in case things didn't work out. It seemed like a good deal. Maybe that should have tipped her off—maybe it was too good. The ad read, *Beachfront cottage with sunny disposition. Easy access to all. Year round occupancy.* Dory phoned the agency and the agent e-mailed her photos of the place. Without a doubt, it seemed charming and peaceful enough. A screened front porch trimmed in green and ringed with beach roses offered a view of the bay. A red brick chimney rising up the north side betrayed the existence of the small fireplace in the living room. Two Adirondack chairs surrounded by potted red geraniums added to the welcome. Dory imagined herself in one of those chairs enjoying the sun and breeze on a Sunday afternoon. Set back from the bay, the place had a tidal creek around back that connected to the bay. Even with the crumbling one-lane asphalt strip known as North Road that served as a roadway in and out of the peninsula, it gave the illusion of being surrounded by water.

Dory noticed the creek's name on maps was shown as *Patriot's Creek.* She learned an interesting historical side note in the package of information sent by the Harmony Bay Chamber of Commerce. During the American Revolution, Patriots used the creek to sneak inland aboard whaleboats at night. With their oarlocks muffled with burlap, raiding parties were launched against the redcoat garrison at Harmony Bay. It was known during those times by its Indian name, Quahog Bay. The rebels caused mayhem by burning the hay stores of the British, letting the horses run free and setting fire to whatever other supplies they could find. Returning to their whaleboats before daybreak, they escaped with the tide, leaving the few British troops who remained seriously demoralized. Centuries later during prohibition, rumrunners took their catboats out to ships waiting outside the three-mile international boundary. There they picked up a hull full of liquor that was shipped up from the Caribbean or down from Canada. Catboats were well disguised as pleasure crafters. Their shallow draft, large capacity and ease of handling made them ideal for the smugglers who could move up the creek with the load of alcohol from the seagoing ship and meet trucks waiting on the beach that disappeared up into the hills as soon as the transfer was made. Every Fourth of July, Harmony Bay had an enactment of the whaleboat raids with young baymen entering in the festivities. To date, no one had thought about a reenactment of smuggling Jamaican rum.

The realtor's pictures also showed a dinghy alongside the house stored upside down on sawhorses just waiting to be the host for a bit of fun. She thought about how James would like that and how they could row and have all sorts of fun that was never possible before in the city's Old Section.

Dory had only ever known the city. She was born in the city and grew up there watching the changes of the seasons and in the inhabitants. That section of the city housed many immigrant Irish and Italian families, but evolved to host many other ethnicities. Dory represented the third generation living on Avenue C and waved goodbye to her parents when they shipped out to Florida. Although they spoke by phone and exchanged cards at every holiday, it wasn't the same as them being there. Dory figured she and James could visit eventually. That might have to be some time in the distant future due to allowable time off at her new job. Dory hoped her parents could hold on until then. She didn't want to admit that she was sensitive to their mounting years.

Dory twirled her jet-black curls between her fingers. She tried not to give in to the overwhelming feeling generated by the formidable cleaning job ahead. It was her intent to make her home livable to her standards and wondered where to begin. Given that they had to eat and sleep, she instinctively knew the kitchen and the bedrooms had to be the first order of business. The living room had to wait. When she arrived, Dory had the movers stack all the boxes in the kitchen thinking it might be easier. Now she had to move all of those boxes into the living room except for the ones containing kitchen utensils and supplies. Cooking supply boxes got stacked on the kitchen table, counters and chairs. The other boxes were placed neatly along the living room walls and a few were placed on the cold fieldstone in front of the fireplace.

In each drawer and cabinet she wasn't surprised to see the same messiness that decorated the room. Dory figured the refrigerator should come first. Once cleaned, it would offer an airtight storage space for food and whatever else needed protection from the presently hostile atmosphere. Dory removed all the shelves, drawers and bins from the refrigerator, filled the bathtub with hot, soapy water, and deposited each item into it. She felt she couldn't wait for the reward of a hot, bubbly bath herself once the place was tolerable. She shuddered, and then laughed, wondering how far in the future that was going to be. Dory washed down the appliance inside and out with ammonia water, grimacing each time she rinsed the washcloth and watched the oily water swirl down the drain. After that, she wiped it down with water and white vinegar, found a light bulb that fit, and rooted through one of the packed boxes to find a picture of James. She placed it dead center on the now sparkling white enameled door with a magnet that looked like a bumblebee. "Ah—Bee-utiful," she said, and allowed herself a giggle.

Dory set about washing out the drawers and cabinets with Murphy's soap, scrubbing each of them with a stiff wood handled brush until all traces of grime were gone. She hadn't unpacked the radio or CD player yet. She alternately hummed or sang to no one other than herself to make the time pass and to take her mind off the monotonous work. One by one, each cabinet and drawer came clean from the efforts of her long and slender fingers and manicured but unpainted fingernails, protected from the cleaning solutions by rubber gloves cuffed midway up her forearms. Dory pondered how best to attack the floor. She carefully swept up the sand and shoved a rolled up towel into the opening under the door to prevent any more windblown sand from entering. Next, she filled the scrub pail with hot water and added a cup full of non-sudsing ammonia. Although she was certain the drafty house had more than enough natural ventilation, she opened a couple of windows and felt the February chill pour through the kitchen. Slopping on the steamy liquid in a push-pull motion, the entire floor was covered in short order. She noticed how much of it had spilled on her running shoes and began to realize the wetness on her toes. She figured she'd take a break to change into some dry socks and allow the solvents to dissolve some of the greasy dirt.

Leaning against the wall and holding the mop like a sentry, she daydreamed through green eyes and watched the steam create a lazy haze on the floor. She was pulled from her daze and back into the surrounds of Harmony Bay by a loud knock at the kitchen door.

Chapter 3

Dory opened the kitchen door and was startled by the appearance of a very large man with a long, white beard that parted to reveal a wide smile and glistening teeth. An equally strange, enormous, jet-black, slobbering dog, wagged its tail as it stood beside him. They accompanied her son.

"Greetings," the man said. "We found this young man on the beach." He filled the doorway with a chuckle. "Angus and I thought we would walk him home and introduce ourselves. Welcome to Harmony Bay." On cue, the dog sat and lifted a paw while cocking his head. "Go ahead and shake. He is very friendly," he said, extending his own hand. "Billy is the name."

Dory looked at James, and then Billy, and finally kneeling before the dog, took his gritty paw in her gloved hand. Now standing and removing the rubber gloves, she graciously extended her hand to Billy, noting the disparity in the sizes of the two extremities.

"How do you do? Call me, Dory," she said. She snapped her head to the side to fling her long dark tresses back over her shoulder. "Won't you come in?"

"Only for a minute. I can see that you are busy with chores. I wanted to make sure that your son made it to the door okay. He got the wind knocked out of him a bit."

"Yes, this is my son, James," Dory replied. She gave the boy a hug that he tried to retreat from. "Are you okay, honey?"

"Yeah, I'm fine," James said.

"Well then, fine it is. We need to head into the village and stock up on some groceries," she said.

"Know where it is? Right down by the firehouse," Billy interjected.

Dory told Billy about how she came to Harmony Bay to work at the library and was already familiar with the layout of the town from her previous scouting missions.

"Very well then. Angus and I will be running along. We will be around if you need something, just give a call," Billy said, giving a crisp salute. Billy and Angus turned and left.

Dory and James loaded themselves into the car. It still had a couple of boxes containing keepsakes on the back seat that needed to be moved into the house. Dory felt she didn't want to leave these to the movers, fearing the items might break. They trundled along the shore road beneath the swollen nimbus clouds while James fiddled with the radio, twirling the dial back and forth scanning for music. Dory began to wonder about this man named Billy. *Who was he? Where did he live? Was he dangerous?* His last words to, *just give a call,* echoed in her mind. He left no phone number. *Where was she supposed to call?* Those thoughts left her as James began to tell about his encounter with Angus on the shoreline.

"You know, Mom, until Billy came along, I thought that big dog was a black bear," he said.

"What made you think Angus was a bear?" Dory questioned.

"When I found out we were moving to the country, I was sure we'd come across all kinds of wild animals. I figured it was a bear. He's as big as a bear. What else was I supposed to think?"

"Were you scared?"

"Nah." James wasn't telling the truth.

"We're out in the wilderness now. I guess we'll see all kinds of stuff." If Dory was concerned about wild animals, she kept it to herself.

Winter threw flotsam in a haphazard fashion on the path of the narrow road. They were not obstacles, but served as reminders to Dory of her new surroundings in a coastal community. Harmony Bay's all encompassing quiet and lack of hurried, crowded streets pleased her, giving an immediate calming effect. A charming community that included a profusion of kindhearted individuals awaited them with its spirited deep-sea fishermen on the commercial boats, shopkeepers whose bayside businesses had been handed down from one generation to the next, professionals who sometimes bartered for services, and a wealth of everyday folks who befriended newcomers. The town had strong historical roots. Visits by pirates, habitation by Native Americans and occupation by British redcoats decorated its past. It was a collage of early American history memorialized in white clapboard, gray cedar shakes and red brick.

Mother and son journeyed on, across the rickety bridge then on past the marinas, the boat yards and tackle shops. Entering the town, they passed the spanking white church with a sign on the lawn proclaiming Reverend Roger Simvasten, Pastor, founded 1715. Dory grinned as she wondered whether the church or its pastor got started in 1715. The steeple soared above the array of one and two story antique shops, the sweet shop, Hirsch's Hardware, the bank, a barbershop, Shea's Bakery, Aldo's Pizzeria, and the post office.

Dory swung the car into the grocery parking lot and parked near the front door. A hand painted wood placard above the entrance simply stated, *Dzjankowski's*. That was all anyone needed to know. People had been coming to the market for well over 100 years. There were no signs proclaiming what was on sale or announcing anything else for that matter. Stepping from the warm car and through the short corridor of February air, Dory and James entered the store. Although small, the store had a wide variety and enough quantity of everything a small village could demand. Dory was taken in by the quaintness of it all. She marveled at the natural wood floors and the old-fashioned iron, industrial light fixtures dangling above. Every counter gleamed, the windows sparkled, and aromas were layered from aisle to aisle, enticing buyers to add the scents to their cart. Fruits and vegetables painted a tapestry of unending colors while meat cases had a plentiful supply of beef, pork, poultry and lamb. Dory later learned there was no fish counter because Dzjankowski's wouldn't impede on the local seafood shops that only had finfish and shellfish to sell in order to make a living. It was all so much smaller than the supermarket in the city, but all wonderful to Dory as she pushed the undersized shopping cart through the market.

Mr. Dzjankowski, wearing a faded green canvas apron, walked slowly as he rounded the cash register to meet and greet the newest inhabitants of Harmony Bay. He had a pencil tucked behind one ear. "Call me Jank. Everybody in town does. It's a lot shorter and easier to remember," he said.

"Well, I'm delighted," Dory said. Grabbing James by the hood of his coat, she yanked him around and placed him in front of her. "This is my son James. Come Monday, I'll be starting over at the library."

"Eeee-yup, replacing Mrs. Bell, are you?" the grocer said. "She's a great woman. Sorry to see her retire. Guess we'll be seeing her around town, though. Her family has been around Harmony Bay for generations." He shoved his hands in his pockets.

Dory was a bit startled that he knew this information before she even started her new job. Dzjankowski noticed the perplexed look on her face. He offered from below his bushy brows, round wire-framed eyeglasses, and from between his chin and brushy moustache, "In a small town like Harmony Bay, everybody keeps track of what's going on." For him it was only being neighborly and it was good for business.

"Oh my, I'm sorry, Mr. Dzjankowski. I'm Dorothy McDonough," she said.

"Eee-yup, I know that. I was part of the crew who hired you for the library. I sit on the library board." Dory felt a little more relieved when she realized Dzjankowski wasn't using psychic powers to identify her.

"I'm sure everyone who walks through your door for the first time must tell you of your striking resemblance to…"

Dzjankowski cut her off in mid-sentenced and finished the statement in a loud, theatrical voice. "A professional historian, naturalist, explorer, hunter, author, and Rough Rider. The twenty-sixth president of the United States, the youngest man to hold the office and the last man in the White House to have a moustache. Yes, just bully! I get that all time."

Laughter filled the scented air at the far end of the store. Not a shrill laughter, it was womanly and rich in tone. Dory turned to see a matronly woman coming down the aisle with her shopping cart. She was short and thick bodied. Her fully gray hair was tied in a bun atop her head. Her brown eyes danced.

"Oh, Jank! Don't you ever get tired of your little skit?" the woman said. "Of course you don't. There's plenty of history in Harmony Bay and you're part of it you old coot." Turning to Dory she held up both hands. "Welcome to Harmony Bay."

"Aren't you just adorable," she said, and cradled Dory's face with her hands. Dory now began to realize it was a custom and ritual among the locals. She was never welcomed by so many in such a short time.

"I'm Angelina Verdi," she said. "I live outside the village near the marinas that you passed on the way in."

Dory found the woman to be delightful. They chatted for a while, with Dory expressing her excitement about her new job at the library. "I knit, and sew wares for the local tourist shops. Occasionally, I do a little housekeeping during the season too," Angelina said.

Dory trusted in her new friend. "I'm looking for someone to look after James when it's my turn to work on Saturday at the library," Dory said. "And I need someone on the weekdays that I have to work late. Otherwise—James will be home alone. Most days he can come to the library after school and do his homework there and wait until I'm finished."

"What about your husband?" Angelina asked. A somber look replaced Dory's smile. Dory explained in a measured voice, "I lost my husband in the war nine years ago and my parents retired and moved south. Now it's only me and my son."

Angelina understood the hardships of being a widow and told Dory so. "I'm a widow, too. I lost my husband to the sea. I have no grandchil-dren—so I make everyone in Harmony Bay part of my family." She held up a finger. "I know the perfect person to look after James," Angelina said.

"Who?" Dory asked. Puzzlement washed over her face.

"Me! Capisce?"

"Really?" Dory questioned. "I don't know if I could afford your ser-vices. I'm going to look for a second job once the tourist season kicks in. That should help."

"Mamma mia! Let's not worry about it right now. We'll work it out later. It will be a pleasure to have this young man around," Angelina said as she hugged Dory.

The two exchanged phone numbers while Jank observed from behind the counter with his arms folded across his apron, nodding with approval. "Yes, yes. Fine additions to Harmony Bay. Very fine additions," he said under his breath.

On the way out of town, Dory decided to stop at the hardware store to pick up some picture hooks and a few more cleaning supplies. Pulling the car up to the curb, James was the first to exit and dashed into the shop. Much like the grocery, the hardware store exhibited an unassuming hand-carved wooden sign above the entrance stating the case for the establishment, *Hirsch's Hardware*. Outside in front of the store various goods awaited new owners. Snow blowers, doghouses, garbage cans and wheelbarrows all rested on the porch away from the elements.

Once inside Hirsch's, the contents of the labyrinth of narrow aisles with creaking, dusty floors amazed James. Dory immediately noticed the difference in ambiance between Dzjankowski's market and this place, which had seen as many years, but showed its age. Sharing space under a common roof were: spools of rope, chain and wire, cast iron frying pans, overflowing bins of plumbing parts made of copper or brass, switches, outlets and electrical plugs skewered on pegboard displays proclaiming their value to the do-it-yourself electrician, lengths of plastic piping and copper tubing lying in racks, garden implements hanging on the wall beside carpenter's tools, cardboard trays in racks that held every imaginable nut, bolt or screw with a label and drawing of its contents. Chainsaws, along with block and tackles, hung from the rafters with crab traps and clam rakes wearing cobweb veils. A menagerie of wares that could satisfy the every need of homeowner and professional alike, regardless of their trade, were organized in no certain order. Dory squeezed through the clutter, found the small section of picture hanging hardware and made a few selections.

She could hear James' sneakers making progress through the store, his location betrayed by the squeaking floorboards. The telltale noises stopped. Dory called out and asked where he was.

"Over here, Mom. Look what I found," he replied.

James was in awe. He found what would normally be called the sporting goods department in a larger store. Standing upright in a crate with wooden dividers were fishing rods of various lengths and styles. Each was purposeful for catching the type of fish that swam the bay and beyond. James fingered each one and then looked at each package containing iridescent lures, buck tail jigs and rubber worms. Fishing reels were stacked separately on a shelf allowing the angler to the match rod with reel. He wanted to know all about these things now that he lived on the water and could use them.

Dory appeared behind him. "Tell me, what did you find?" she asked.

"Fishing stuff and it's way cool. Can I get a fishing pole, Mom? Please, can I?"

"Well," Dory said, "your birthday is coming up in a few weeks. Maybe then. Besides, it's so cold out right now I'm sure the only thing you might catch is a frozen fish." James continued to plead to no avail. Dory knew she was on a tight budget and couldn't afford the luxury of an unwarranted gift. In her heart, she wanted to do something for James. She wasn't sure how their relocation was going to affect him. She went about her business of gathering steel-wool soap pads and a powder to remove the rust stains from the porcelain fixtures in the bathroom and kitchen of their new home. James continued to ogle at the fascinating assortment of fishing tackle.

After completing her selections, she made her way to the counter at the back of the store. A young man with closely cropped hair stood behind it. Dory estimated the muscular man was about her own age. His demeanor was calm and unobtrusive. He spoke in rural way. "Welcome to da neighbo'hood an our fine, fine lie berry. Glad y'all stopped by Hirsch's amazin' house o' hardware an o' sorted sundries," he said.

Dory was taken aback. She wondered if everybody in town knew her business.

Dory asked the clerk how he knew who she was. He told her tourists never buy picture hooks because they were never around long enough to hang a picture. More to the point, the season was months away and no city folk came to Hirsch's in the dead of winter. He continued on, "Looks to me like ya got all da signs of a movin' in person. An, I hear yesta day we was gittin' a replacement for Mrs. Bell at da lie berry. A young woman who was at a lie berry in da city. So I'm thinkin' to myself that's you. Winton Hector at yo' service. Y'all kin call me Winton, or y'all kin call me Mr. Hector, or y'all kin call me Winton Hector, which eva one y'all think fits best."

"Yes, that's me," Dory said as she began to blush. His unsolicited introduction aside, Dory took a liking to him, if for nothing else, his bucolic tone and its delivery. "Dorothy McDonough. It's a pleasure to meet you. The boy who is glued to the fishing department is my son James." Dory reached across the counter and shook his outstretched hand. "But please—call me Dory."

"Lenny. Hey, Mistuh Hirsch! C'mon up heeya. There's somebody I want ya to meet," Winton called out to thin air. An older man shuffled from the back room folding a newspaper as he filled the doorway. "This is our new lie berryin', Dory McDonough."

"Hello there. I'm Lenny Hirsch, pleased to meet you." The portly Mr. Hirsch wore blue denim coveralls, pens and pencils bristled from the top pockets. Fastened to a loop at his midsection was a ring of keys. Salt and pepper hair topped his head along with similarly colored bushy brows. Giving a slight bow, he flipped the newspaper on the counter and stretched his hand across it. Dory graciously accepted it.

"As you may have already determined, I run this old collection of everything useful and useless. My family's been at this location for about 120 years. If there's anything you need, or something that needs fixing, Winton or I have probably seen it or done it a dozen or more times already. Don't be afraid to ask…advice is free."

Dory called out for James, instructing him to join her at the back of the disheveled store. James made his way by leapfrogging through the maze and hopped up to the counter. "Hey there, young man," Hirsch said. "Welcome to Harmony Bay. Say hello to Winton Hector."

"Nice to meet you," James said.

"Nice to meet ya too, buddy. Interested in fishin' are ya?" Winton said. He reached over the counter to shake hands.

"But—I don't know how to fish," James said. The corners of his mouth turned down. Hirsch chortled at this remark and told James there were sure to be more than enough people who could teach him how to fish the waters of Harmony Bay.

"Might ya'all be interested in learnin' how to play some gee tar too—or do ya'll already know how to do that?" Winton asked.

"I don't have a fishing pole or a guitar," James snapped. The frustration was beginning to overtake him.

Winton went about telling James and Dory that he gave beginner's guitar lessons to young people at the library after school on Tuesdays. The lessons were free through the library. Winton wasn't concerned about James' lack of a guitar. He told James he had a few and would be happy to lend one to James to get started on.

"Well, that's a very generous offer, Mr. Hector. I don't know that we could accept," Dory said.

Winton shot back quickly. "It's only jes a loan. If James takes a likin' to it, we can work somethin' out down da road. If not, no worries. Ya'll already be at the lie berry, so ya can check his progress if ya'll like. The school bus drops off da kids at the lie berry. Then ya kin drive him home afta he's done."

The continued outpouring of warmth and hospitality from their new friends and neighbors astonished Dory. This was something she never experienced in the city where everyone was only concerned about themselves as they bustled from one seemingly unimportant errand to another insignificant one. Nobody ever took the time to introduce themselves, shake a hand, or be neighborly. It was a good feeling to own. She was always a little apprehensive about meeting new people, not so much about meeting them, but having a relationship with them. The feeling of being welcomed was exhilarating and Dory delighted in it. She figured it was better to let go of her old fears and trepidations and roll with it. It was good to be appreciated for being herself and who she was.

Dory returned to the conversation. "James, is that something you'd like to try?" She hoped he'd say yes because she was determined to get him involved in as many activities as possible so he could make new friends. She and James agreed that he'd always have to at least try new things. If he didn't succeed, or truly didn't like it, she wouldn't force him to continue. Something such as music or art might be a good complement to Little League baseball, or perhaps, fishing. Dory prayed daily for guidance in raising her son on her own. She wouldn't be the first woman to do it and knew she certainly wouldn't be the last.

"Yeah, I'll give it a try," James said. He took a giant hop across the floor. His insistence on learning how to fish spilled out in rapid-fire talk. The adults all laughed and nodded their heads. Yes, James would learn how to fish. She suggested that he should first read about what he was anticipating catching. Dory asked for a duplicate house key to be made and opened her handbag to pay for her purchases. Hirsch held up his hands in protest.

"Let's just say that this is on us as a housewarming present," he said.

Dory hesitated then began her own objection. She was overruled by the insistence of the hardware man. She bowed her head slightly, "Thank you very much," Dory said. "You're very generous."

Hirsch handed Dory's key to Winton. Dory noticed Winton walked with a pronounced limp as he headed toward the key cutting machine. Winton whistled an unknown tune as he reproduced the key. He finished the job by snapping on a brightly colored key tag promoting Hirsch's Hardware. Dory felt for the young man and wondered what had happened to him to produce such a shuffle.

From the corner of his eye he saw, or sensed, Dory's appraisal of his disability.

"Oh yeah, da leg thang," he said. Winton stamped the prosthetic leg several times to punctuate his words. "Lost it to da war courtesy of our Uncle Sam." Shifting uneasily, Dory was immediately embarrassed. The man reassured her. "Hey, no worries— I git by jes fine."

Dory and James exited the hardware store. Pushing open the wood framed door with full-length glass, they emerged into the last gasps of afternoon and the smell of coming snow. Once outside, James spoke, "Too bad about Mr. Hector's leg. Huh, Mom?"

"Yes, it is too bad. How difficult for him," Dory said. A wave of wartime memories flooded into her thoughts.

"Seems like he's doing okay," James said. After climbing into the car, Dory turned on the headlights and flipped the heater fan switch to max. The car made a u-turn and headed back out through the village past the sun dangling in the western sky supported by the hilltops and past their new friends and acquaintances.

Chapter 4

The adventurous twosome spent the next couple of weeks getting used to their new surroundings. Dory started her new position at the Harmony Bay Library as a reference librarian. James joined his class at Harmony Bay Elementary School. Dory felt very much at ease at the library. Her coworkers were all friendly and lacked the cattiness of the employees at her former job in the city. It was a pleasure to work there. Dory actually looked forward to each day at the red brick, well-windowed building. However, she didn't relish the thought of sending James off to school in a new environment without friends or siblings. Dory intuitively knew—for the long term, this was a far better life for James and he'd adapt. She felt James was outgoing enough to make new friends soon.

Her boss, Mrs. Lanscome the library director, was a peach as Dory described her. Everyone in town knew Mrs. Lanscome, although, it wasn't difficult given the size of Harmony Bay. Some knew her as the library lady, some as head of the Garden Club and others for her powerful soprano voice in the church choir. In her senior years, she still had the energy of a woman forty years her junior. Always first in the door at the library and last to leave, her calendar was always full. She liked it that way.

Margaret Eleanor Lanscome, or Mel as her close friends and family called her, kept her hair in a fashionable, yet businesslike style. She still maintained the honeyed blond tone of her youthful days. No one in Harmony Bay had ever seen her wear anything other than a dress or a skirt. Even for gardening, or the most casual affairs, it was never pants.

"I am a lady first and I shall always present myself like a lady," the elder member of the bay's aristocracy would say. Like her coiffure, she maintained a trendy level of dress. Her footwear was always stylish. She always wore high heels. At work those shoes were her trademark, offering a staccato teletype of her location on the library's terrazzo floors. Mrs. Lanscome always spoke in a pinched, high-pitched voice. It gave her an air of arrogance. In actuality, she was not like that at all. When she asked patrons how they or their families were, she was always truly sincere and concerned.

Her husband Fred was a retired science professor from the university up west. Fred gave his social butterfly wife as much room as she needed. He was content to fish, enjoying the golden years at their bay front home.

Instead of James riding the bus, Dory decided to drive him to school the first few days until he got his whereabouts. Dropping James off for the start of school was going to get her to her job early since his classes started an hour before the library opened. She figured she could use the time wisely to organize her desk. It would give her the freedom of a few moments to enjoy a cup of coffee and read the Harmony Bay Gazette.

Dory and James arrived at the school far in advance of the bell on the first day so she and James could both meet his new teacher, Miss Donnelly. James liked her. Sensing his apprehensions, she was very kind to him.

"Here's your cubicle to stow your stuff," Miss Donnelly explained. "That will eliminate you having to carry home books that we aren't using for homework. I don't give a lot of homework, but whatever I assign, I expect to be handed in on time." She showed him where to hang his coat in the back of the classroom. "I think you are now the tallest boy in my classroom." She patted the top of his dark chestnut hair. "We'll have to check that later."

"Me? The tallest? Really?"

"Probably so. I see your mom is very tall."

"My dad was, too."

"I see," Miss Donnelly said. "Have a look around the room while I chitchat with your mom."

James investigated the classroom's aquarium with tropical fish and terrariums containing lizards and turtles. He looked at student artwork stapled to something called the reward board. It included the last vestiges of Ground Hog's Day and Valentine's Day greetings. He examined the assortment of plants stretching for the attention of the sun's rays that beamed through the easterly facing windows, the blue cast of the fluorescent lamps and the muted translucence of the skylights. James noticed right away how much friendlier the atmosphere in the room was than at his old school. Here, there were no security guards at the front doors. You could walk in without a confrontation. It was a departure from the metal detectors and near prison-like treatment he was accustomed to at his school in the Old Section in the city.

Dory and Miss Donnelly chatted at the teacher's desk while James roamed the room. Dory filled her in on her son's history and his behavior.

"James can be very quiet at times," Dory said. "Don't take it as disinterest or disrespect. He's just absorbing everything there is to learn."

"I see," Miss Donnelly said.

"Actually, if given the chance, he's as rambunctious as any other boy his age."

"Rambunctious is fine. I can handle that."

"If he gets out of line—don't hesitate to call me."

"That's refreshing. Some parents don't want to take responsibility for discipline."

"He's a good kid. I don't think you'll have any trouble. James really loves books and reading. With my job—I'm delighted."

"Ahh, the sorcerer's apprentice?" They both laughed.

"I guess. You need to challenge James with higher-level materials."

"I agree. I've seen James' transcripts. His reading level and comprehension skills are astonishing." The adults said their goodbyes and the teacher invited her new student to take a seat beside her desk.

"Do you like animals, James?" Miss Donnelly asked. James replied he did and admitted he really didn't have a lot of experience with them. "What else are you interested in? What are your favorite subjects—do you like to read?"

"Yeah, I like to read," James said. His enthusiasm was painted on his face in a wide smile. "I'm glad my mom works at the library."

"Hmmm," Miss Donnelly said. She leaned her head back, closed her eyes and placed the tips of her index fingers on her temples. "I see that you went to Coolidge Elementary and used to live on Avenue C. Am I correct?"

"Gee, yeah. How did you know, Miss Donnelly?"

"Hmmm, guess what? I went to Coolidge too! I grew up on Avenue E near the train station!" She threw her hands in the air for emphasis. "Let's see. You like animals and you're a good reader... I have something for you. It might be a little scary. Some parts are sad. We can talk about that if you want. But—if you stick with it, there's a good ending."

"Oh?" he said. She reached into her desk drawer and pulled out a package wrapped in brown paper.

"This is for you. Welcome to Harmony Bay Elementary," she said. James accepted the gift and noticed a card tucked beneath the string surrounding it. "Well, go ahead."

James opened the envelope containing the card that simply said, *Welcome*. Inside the card the sentiment continued in blue ink, *Welcome to our Fifth Grade Class*. Beneath the neatly scripted words were the names of every student in Miss Donnelly's class written in their own hand. James didn't know what to say and turned to Miss Donnelly with wide eyes. He slid his spindly fingers below the string and removed it along with the brown paper covering. The package contained a stout, hard covered book. The profile of a wolf was pictured below the title *White Fang* and above the author's name, Jack London.

"Is this a library book?" he asked, now cradling the book on his lap.

"No, James It's yours to keep. Enjoy it."

James' head spun with a foreign feeling. Never before had anybody, except for his mother and grandparents, done something nice like this for him before. James locked his gaze on the woman's soft blue eyes and smiled.

"Thank you, Miss Donnelly," he said.

"Oh, you're welcome, James. Let's get you set up with your new desk." The bell announcing the day's commencement rang. "I put you up here by me until you get the chance to make friends with some of the other kids."

James noticed Miss Donnelly was moving around the room like an athlete in her cross-trainer shoes. Her auburn hair was pulled back and held in place with a simple clip. The teacher's perfect posture filled the doorway. Each child entered her room and she greeted them by name. James could see how much they loved her. Arriving in ones and twos, they each acknowledged her and went to their desks, which were formed in a U shape with the open end facing the front of the room. James, sitting to his teacher's left, enjoyed a panoramic view of the U and its occupants.

Maureen Donnelly was now in her third year of teaching at Harmony Bay Elementary. It was the first teaching job for her. After finishing college and her Master's Degree with honors, she welcomed the opportunity to come to the small waterside town. She realized, as James had, it was an extreme contrast to living in the city. She cherished the opportunities to run on the beach with her mischievous dog. Miss Donnelly lived close to the village in an apartment in one of the old, stately Victorian homes off Bay Road. When the weather permitted, or she didn't have an armload of work to carry, she'd ride her bicycle to the school. After experiencing two muggings in the city, she decided to expand her job search to rural communities. Offering peace and security, Harmony Bay filled the bill perfectly. Quickly becoming one of the most honored members of the community, everybody from cops to store clerks looked after Maureen Donnelly. The teacher had some distant relatives in the area, so she was accepted as family. Her parents convinced her to get a dog for protection. Miss Donnelly chose a golden retriever and named her Riley. She was a good watchdog, but was far from ferocious. Riley was the village clown who rolled over and played dead or sat up and begged for a stranger. Whether Maureen was on the beach or a bike, Riley followed her everywhere.

Dave at the auto repair shop kept a box of milk bone biscuits on hand. He always tossed one to Riley who would catch it in mid-flight whenever she passed by with her master. Dave Small's repair shop was as whimsical as the rest of the town. The sign over the garage's roll-up door stated, *Dave Small Auto Repair and We Fix Big Ones Too*. After a very short time at Harmony Bay, Maureen Donnelly realized she probably didn't need canine protection. Nevertheless, she loved Riley for the companionship that she provided.

Once they were all settled in their seats, the PA speaker in the room crackled through the murmurs with an announcement to stand for the pledge of allegiance. Newsy messages and a recitation of the day's cafeteria lunch menu followed as the children took their seats. At the conclusion of the messages delivered through the scratchy loudspeaker Miss Donnelly said, "We have one more announcement. Please everybody get up on your feet and welcome our new class member, James, with a round of applause." James remained seated. Twenty-two children stood facing James and clapped energetically as he shifted nervously in his seat. When the noise subsided, Miss Donnelly instructed the students to introduce themselves one by one to James. Each did, along with cordial, welcoming words.

The class consisted of sons and daughters of fishermen, bankers, preachers, shopkeepers, baymen, village employees, power company workers, police officers, waitresses, nurses, telephone linemen, teachers, mechanics and a librarian.

James once again experienced the same dizzying feeling he felt while receiving the gifted book. Overwhelmed by the attention, he could feel the warmth in his face as the blood rushed to his cheeks. He asked himself how this could all be possible. At first, he rebelled against the idea of moving away from the only home he knew. Now, kids who seemed eager to be his friend surrounded him. James thanked them all and sat down at his desk flush faced, hoping nobody noticed. Miss Donnelly gave him a thumbs up.

Throughout his first days, James became more intimately acquainted with his classmates. Steven was a know-it-all and told everybody his opinion whether it was asked for or not. Steven made it clear to everyone in the room that he was at the top of the order in scoring the highest on quizzes and exams. Katie, often absorbed by the classroom computer, gathered James under her own undeveloped wing. She delighted in showing him everything about the school and making introductions. Like James, Katie was quiet and shy. Although, she bubbled enthusiastically from within about the things she liked. Raymond was a wild kid. James sensed it, electing to keep his distance from the recalcitrant boy. Regardless, Raymond seemed to force his way into James' life. Peter was the class artist and always had the best drawings, specializing in caricatures of his friends. Each day rolled into the next for James. Each morning he eagerly awaited the opportunity to go to school to be with his friends and learn new things from Miss Donnelly.

Chapter 5

Dory decided to shop during her lunch hour for some needs for her new home. She knew James never had the patience for such mundane missions. She looked forward to enjoying the opportunity to get out, stretch her legs, and get a breath of fresh air. The weather was cold yet clear. She opted to walk to Hirsch's Hardware a few blocks away. Strolling on the uneven sidewalks and hop scotching over the occasional snow patch from last week's storm, reminded her of her childhood and cautioned herself to stop on neither a crack nor a line in order to protect the health of her mother's back. In her mind she repeated the children's phrases. *Step on a line break your mother's spine, step on a crack you'll break her back.* How dreary, she thought. What could ever encourage a child to harbor such evil feelings toward their mother?

Clomping up the front steps of Hirsch's, she crossed the short wood plank porch with its array of snow shovels, rock salt products and ladders. She opened the door, which responded with the jingling of its alerting sleigh bells. Dory met a blast of warm air causing her to unwrap her scarf and open the buttons of her heavy woolen Navy pea coat. She stuffed her mittens in her pockets. Wandering farther toward the back of the store, she exchanged greetings with Winton. "Good afta noon Missus McDonough," Winton said. "Y'all need some help?"

"Thank you, Winton, I'm going to browse for a bit first," she said.

"Take all o' the time ya needs," Winton advised her. "I's be right they-uh if ya needs assistin'."

"Thank you," she said again. "Please, call me Dory." In the background, a radio played the local station with its annoying deejay who extended his morning show into the lunchtime hours, filling the air with a feeble feed of sorely outdated tunes and static.

Dory walked the dusty, cluttered aisles, glancing through the house wares, the home goods, the small appliances and gadgets, which only brought to mind how many things she needed around the house. They'd have to wait because of her precarious budget. She planned to take a second part-time job a couple of days each week once the tourists and summer residents filled the town. Dory worked her way through college with waitress jobs. She felt it was something that could put some extra cash in her pocket and allow her a few small luxuries. It would be a hardship for James to be with someone else for those hours. He needed to bear with it until they got over the financial hump. Today was for necessities and Dory picked out a white switch cover to fill the void around the kitchen light switch. She selected a roll of heavy, clear three-inch wide vinyl tape to seal some of the drafts around the windows. Finally, she began to search for some curtain rods. She wanted to sew curtains to offer privacy and abate the winter's chill before it entered the house. Dory began to make her way toward the cash register at the back counter after finding the curtain hardware. These were all projects she could do and she was glad that she could. Her father was always very patient with her in instructing her on how to use tools. Dory was grateful for that. She was as independent as she could be and was always willing to try anything, but was wise enough to know when something fell beyond her grasp. Of course, these were small tasks and that was okay. On larger projects, she figured she'd cross those bridges as they came along.

Dory meandered past the fishing section, remembering how it enthralled James a couple of weeks earlier. Eyeing the fishing poles with cork handles and brightly colored threads wrapped around various sized line guides and at the ferrules that joined the sections together, the same questions that coursed through James' mind crossed her own. There was a variety of rod styles, endless choices of hooks and peripheral accessories. Dory contemplated if now was a good time for her to pick out a birthday present for James. It wasn't often that she had the opportunity to shop by herself and create a surprise for him. She eyed the fishing tackle and their price tags guessing how much it was all going to cost, what was the right thing to get, and most of all, if it was beyond her budget. Since Winton was busy at the back of the store, she certainly wasn't going to bother him with this. Besides, she felt totally out of her game and didn't want to appear ignorant. The menagerie of gear baffled her and she thought about opting for something practical like a new sweater. She cradled her purchases in her arm and lifted a spin casting rod and reel combination from the sectioned wooden box, being careful not to knock anything over with its seven-foot length. Dory let out an audible *humpf* and stepped back, absorbing the whole picture of outdoor gear before her.

Deep in thought about the fishing tackle, Dory didn't hear the floor creaking behind her that would have given notice of another person's presence. Jolted from her daydream by stepping backward into another person unexpectedly, Dory dropped the fishing rod along with all of her selections, which landed with their own assortment of noises. The clatter was followed by man's voice.

"*Whoa!*" he said.

Mortified by her actions, Dory was now back-to-back with a stranger in the crowded aisle. Both man and woman spun and turned face to face with equally startled expressions. The embarrassment initially brought out the worst in her.

"Whoa *yourself,*" Dory said. She said it in an acerbic way that was not her style. "Oh, I'm so sorry," she said and began to stoop down to pick up the clutter.

"Well, hey now, going fishing are you?" he said. Dory turned crimson from embarrassment and the anger that she now aimed toward herself.

"No, not me. This is for my son, I think."

"You think you have a son or you think he's going fishing?"

Dory was now outraged by the crass comment from someone she didn't know. *All the nerve,* she thought while glaring at him. *Questioning if I know whether I have a son?*

She began to size him up. Standing a hair over six feet tall, he was sandy haired with no signs of thinning or gray, a broad forehead and a strong jaw. Wire-framed glasses surrounding blue-gray eyes were perched on a straight nose with narrow nostrils. He was a sturdy man in good physical condition. Dory suspected he was some sort of tradesman given his apparel of khaki pants and denim shirt. Despite the cold weather, or because of the warmth of the hardware store, he only wore a red, down-filled vest as his overcoat. She noticed even though his clothes were frayed, they were clean. Being close enough to him, she detected that he smelled clean as well. Not perfumed, only the fresh smell of soap.

He addressed the awkward confrontation in a friendly voice. "No, please, allow me. I should have been paying more attention to where I was going." He knelt down and gathered up Dory's purchases and the fishing pole. "Nice rod," he said.

"Oh, is it? I wouldn't know." Now she was even more humiliated after having made such a rude comment to this person when the fault was obviously hers.

"Sure is. Probably the perfect set-up for whatever swims around here, at least in the bay—that is," the man said, lifting the rod to a forty-five degree angle with a muscled hand. He flicked its tip slightly with his wrist. "Your son will have a lot of fun with this."

"Well, it's a little more expensive than I'd planned on. But after all, it is for his birthday."

"Ah, hey, I understand," he said and then smiled. "The way I've always sort of looked at it is, make investments in good books, quality musical instruments, and good fishing gear. They all give you something back. Although, about buying it, that's for you to decide." Dory liked his philosophy. Sensing an intelligence and sensitivity that wasn't evident earlier, she started to warm up to him slightly.

"Are you a fisherman?"

"Sort of."

"One of the commercial boats?"

"No. Nothing like that. But I am out on the bay somewhere most days. Almost never venture out to the deep waters, though."

Now Dory was puzzled. With the way he was dressed, she took him to be some sort of an electrician or carpenter. On the other hand, perhaps, he ran some sort of boat business, or one of the marinas. From his manner of speech and his comment about books she sensed he was well educated.

"Well, I suppose then, since you recommend it, I'll be taking that fishing rod," Dory said.

"How old will he be?"

"He turns ten next week." The flush drained from her face and was replaced by a slight smile.

"Hey now, that's great. Fishing is a good pastime for a boy. It teaches patience, a love of the outdoors—and respect for nature. He'll need some hooks, a few sinkers and some bobbins. They're not too expensive. Flounder seasons starts in a few weeks. That's a good place for him to begin. He'll need something to keep all his stuff together too," he said. He plucked the packages of flounder hooks from their hanger and pointed to the tackle boxes. Now Dory began to worry. Things were adding up fast. Nevertheless, she was advised a moment ago—it was a healthy activity and a good investment. She figured what the heck; birthdays and Christmas only come once a year.

"Okay then," she said, "sounds good."

Dory picked out a green plastic tackle box. It opened to reveal a pair of compartments for fishing gadgets and a deep well in the center for larger items.

"Let me give you a hand," he said. Only because she was inundated with items did she agree and willingly let him carry the rod and reel along with his selections of tackle to the back of the store.

"Thank you very much for your help," Dory said as he placed the items on the counter. "Not a problem. Good luck wrapping the present— and with the fishing." He walked toward the door and gave a slight wave to Hirsch and Winton.

It occurred to Dory that the shopping trip turned out to be a little more than she anticipated and wondered how she was going to return to the library carrying all of the stuff. She exchanged greetings with Hirsch who stood in the doorway to the stockroom with his hands on his hips.

"Did ya'll find everythin' ya'll was lookin' fo'?" asked Winton.

"I believe I did," she said.

Winton carefully wrote out each item on a sales slip. He spoke without looking up. "Is dis here gear fo' dat fine young man o'yours?"

"Sure is. I think he'll be very happy," Dory said. She glanced at a stack of flyers on the counter announcing early registration for spring Little League.

"It's a great program," Winton said. She hadn't noticed him observing her and was a little startled by his remark. She folded the green paper, placed it in her handbag and pulled out her wallet to pay for her purchases.

"Thank you, Winton. I'm sure James will be looking forward to it. By the way, may I ask you to hold the fishing things aside here until next week? If I bring it home, I have no idea where I could hide it until his birthday."

Winton let out a whoop and began singing *Happy Birthday* in a fine tenor tone. "Sho' enuf, dat's not a problem a' tall. I'll tag it with yo name on it and keep it right heeya wit me."

Dory trusted Winton and Hirsch; they seemed to be respectable community pillars. "Say guys, there's been an old guy coming around the house with big white beard who goes by the name, Billy," she said. "Last weekend he arrived on a big white horse. That certainly had my son's attention. He also has a giant black dog. He seems nice enough. But, uh, do you know anything about him? How should I say this…is he *okay?*"

Hirsch and Winton turned to each other and laughed heartily. "Billy, okay?" asked Hirsch. "He's been here longer than the hills. Everybody loves him and he's about the nicest guy on the coast. There isn't anything that he wouldn't do for anybody. Believe me Miss Dory, you have nothing to worry about with Billy. I can vouch for him personally, he's a good man." She was relieved. She was really only interested in protecting her son. It was hard to sort out all of these new people.

"Yep," Winton said, "Billy, Chloe and Angus. What a trio, they surely are da big three o' Harmony Bay."

"I agree," Dory said. "The three of them are bigger than life. I do love that horse, though. She's beautiful."

—◦◖〗♪〖◗◦—

It wasn't an unusual sight around the bay or in the hills to see Billy atop Chloe with Angus trailing behind. At seventeen hands high, the white mare was more of a workhorse than a racer. The three relied on each other in a symbiotic relationship for companionship during the long winters, and in practical matters, they supported one another. Billy supplied the food and the animals performed chores. The only place Chloe could remember living was on Pencil Hill at Billy's. It didn't matter that there were no other horses as friends. There was no loneliness. Chloe was content to serve Billy in what ever he needed her to do. Besides, Angus visited the stable every day.

It was only the other day that Billy put on her saddle. With Angus in tow, they trotted along North Road to visit James and Dory. There was snow on the ground that freshened the air and the senses. Cold weather didn't bother Chloe at all. With her winter coat she rather enjoyed it as compared to the summers, which although balmy, could deliver smothering humidity.

A horse seemed out of place to many in the fishing town, but Chloe could trace her lineage back to a time when her ancestors pulled wagons laden with finfish, crustaceans and shellfish caught from Harmony Bay to the inland markets. Chloe loved to work. Even more, she loved to please Billy. Whether dragging trees felled for firewood or pulling the plow to till his overly large garden, it was all very acceptable to her and he treated her very well for her efforts. The horse was tireless and looked forward to working every day, the new tasks that were in store and the rewards that came afterward, usually carrots or apples. Chloe got additional exercise by carrying her jocular master around the village. Billy didn't always rely on her for transportation. He had his nearly antique red pickup truck. It was as indefatigable as the mare.

Another usual sight around town was to see Billy behind the wheel of the truck with his benevolent dog in the bed. Angus hung his head over the side, gulping air and drooling continually. When they pulled up to a stop sign or reached their destination, Billy never worried about Angus taking off after another dog or disturbing the peace with his baritone bark. He was obedient and loving of Billy and always was at his side on their adventures. During times when Billy was working the garden, chopping wood or fabricating things in the woodshop it was another matter. Then the dog would wander off on adventures of his own, visiting the shoreline, or the other animals in the deep woods behind the cabin. Occasionally, he stopped by a summer resident's home where he was well known—hoping for a treat. He always came home, called by his inner clock, when it was time for his supper. Angus always considered a friend of Billy's a friend of his. Since everybody on the bay knew and liked the man, the dog was in good company. If Angus recognized a human was well liked by Billy, he protected that outsider like they were family. The animal had an innate sense about humans. Sometimes he intuitively knew when a human was not sincerely a friend or was dishonest. At those times, he took a few steps back from Billy, out of the arm reach of the suspect, but always nearby enough to protect his master if need be. The dog felt this way about Edmund "Fishhook" Cutsciko, the villainous landlord who cheated poor people on their rent and took advantage of them by not fixing their rental homes. Financially, he was the wealthiest man on the whole bay, but had very few honest friends. Whenever Billy encountered Cutsciko, he would be outwardly cordial and gracious. However, the dog always deliberately stepped back and allowed himself a low, deep-throated growl.

⸺◦⟨⟨⟨⟨⟨ʃ⟩⟩⟩⟩⟩◦⸺

Dory emerged into the brisk afternoon, buttoned her coat, rewrapped her scarf around her neck and pulled her mittens from her pockets as seagulls rose from their resting places to circle overhead. Her nervous excitement about the purchase of the fishing equipment started to fade as she questioned if she went over the budget. The words of the stranger filtered back into her mind. She tightly clutched her brown paper bag of hardware purchases and by the time she reached the library steps, she reassured herself.

She deposited the package beside her desk then went to the coatroom to hang up her things. All the while, a nagging feeling enveloped her. The stranger in the store was the only person she had met from the community who didn't outwardly introduce himself. He was nice enough, to be sure. Perhaps he wasn't from the area or he was shy. Or, given his initial remark, maybe he wasn't socially adept. He also seemed a little mysterious about what he did for a living. Then Dory thought she was possibly being a little too nosy and—it wasn't really any of her business. After all, come to think of it, she hadn't introduced herself to him either. She felt she really should have been a little more thankful given the amount of time the man spent helping her.

Dory put her thoughts aside as a patron who needed assistance approached her. James' school bus would arrive in a few hours. Dory had signed him up for the after school program at the library in which the kids went downstairs to the public room for a snack. Afterward, high school student volunteers helped them with their homework. In exchange, the high school kids received tutoring and help with essay and term paper writing from approved adult mentors in the community. Behind her desk was a large colorful wall poster proclaiming Harmony Bay's mentoring program. It showed two hands reaching toward each other above the boldly painted words, *Each One, Teach One*. With each passing day, Dory fell deeper in love with the town and its people. She now knew— she and James landed in the right place.

Chapter 6

It was Saturday morning. The sun was up and there was no wind, making the March day one of those that gives a sneak preview of spring. James finished all of his homework the day before. He was now free to do the things boys do on a weekend. It was his mom's day to work at the library so it was only he and Mrs. Verdi at his house.

Angelina prepared James his favorite breakfast, pancakes and bacon. He gulped down the buttermilk pancakes and the curly, crisp Canadian bacon as though he hadn't eaten in a week, then washed down the mouthfuls of food with ice-cold orange juice. James liked Mrs. Verdi. She always seemed to know exactly what he needed to make him happy, but was always tough when she needed to be. In a sort of carrot and stick relationship, James knew if he stayed in line the good things like pancakes and bacon were going to keep flowing.

Angelina made small talk about how beautiful the weather was today and how the crocuses would be up soon, then the daffodils. She lived on Harmony Bay almost her entire life. She became accustomed to the rigors of winter here, but always had the wonderful spring, summer and early autumn months to look forward to. Her voice wafted through the sunny kitchen. James politely half listened while daydreaming about what to do for the day.

James had his new baseball and glove that Billy gave him for his birthday and as a welcome present to Harmony Bay. Dory felt it was far too generous. Billy insisted, telling her Angus, Chloe and he were giving it jointly. Therefore, he felt he was only one third responsible.

Billy told her a proper baseball glove was one of the necessary tools for growing up and no boy should be without one. His logic prevailed and Dory could no longer argue. James was thrilled with the acquisition. In his room he'd lie on his bed and place the glove over his face, inhaling the rich smell of leather. The ball was an official Major League Baseball hardball. He never had one of his own. His only experience with them was during his brief foray into the church sponsored Little League in his old neighborhood. He tried to count the stitches in the ball several times, having heard that every pro-baseball had an exact number of stitches. A number he couldn't recall. Each time he counted, James became frustrated when he lost his starting place. Now the glove and ball sat on his shelf over his bed like a trophy.

James wondered if Angus might be around today, which could be a lot of fun. They might go exploring along the canal bank at low tide where there was always something interesting that nature or man had deposited. How awesome it would be, he thought, if they discovered an Indian arrowhead or the imprinted fossils or bones of some prehistoric animal. Also to consider for the day's itinerary was the brand new fishing pole and tackle box that his mom gave him for his birthday. She told him as soon as the weather warmed up they'd take the rowboat out and try their hand at fishing. James liked that idea. He envisioned himself coming home with a boatload of fish. Mom would cook it up and be so proud of him for the catch.

"Flounder season officially starts on St. Patrick's Day," Mr. Hirsch told him during a visit to the hardware store. "That's around the time the bottom feeders wake up after their hibernation in the mud flats and start looking for food." James reasoned that St. Patrick's Day had been the week before and today was the warmest day since he arrived at Harmony Bay. Maybe fishing was an option. Mom was at work and wouldn't be home until late afternoon. He couldn't take the rowboat out by himself, but maybe there would be fish in the creek or across the street at the beach. He figured he could test his casting skills there.

Angelina asked if he wanted more juice as James returned from his daydream. His subconscious reply was in the form of a loud burp.

"James!" she said.

"Oops. No thank you," was James' only reply.

"Well then, get your coat on. Go enjoy the outside. It's nice out."

"Sounds good to me."

James placed his plate and glass in the old cast-iron sink and proceeded to his room. He searched under his bed for his sneakers, found them and put them on as he squatted on the floor. He leapt up in one bound and was on his bed. Reaching for his baseball glove and ball, he grabbed them, pirouetted, raised his hands over his head like a victorious pitcher and hopped to the floor. Three giant steps vaulted him out of the room and into the hall where he almost collided with Mrs. Verdi.

"See you later," he said.

"Don't go too far." Her words faded as he continued his animated kangaroo hops toward the coat rack behind the battered kitchen door. He put on his down coat, zipped it up, and exited via the kitchen door. It closed with a slam.

James burst into the cool, bright sunlight and inhaled the salty air. He ran to the back of the house to check the creek to see if the tide was in. It was. *Darn*, James murmured. Although it was still winter, low tide always revealed some kind of weird critter carcasses. Either the empty shells of crabs from last season or something the gulls had left behind. *Oh well*, he thought. *The tide changes twice a day. Maybe later there may be some adventuring to do*. In the brief spit of sand behind the house, he tossed the ball high in the air practicing catching pop flies. After the third throw, the ball drifted and bounced on the roof, rolling down the green asphalt shingles to the front of the house. James feared it would get stuck on the roof and ran to the front to look for his prized baseball. He rounded the corner and arrived in front of the porch to see Angus standing there with his tail wagging and with James' ball in his mouth.

Billy often let Angus roam the bays and the beaches by himself. He never felt the cold in the winter and didn't mind a bit if he got wet. His thick oily coat offered amazing protection. James asked Billy why the dog didn't run away. Billy told him everyone on Harmony Bay knew Angus, so you are never really lost when you have your friends around. Anyway—Angus knew when and where his dinner was served. Why would he take off? All in all, Angus had an easy life as a four-legged beach bum.

James commanded Angus to drop the ball. The big dog willingly obliged with his tail still wagging furiously. "Yuck," he said, picking up the slimy baseball now dripping with dog saliva. "Oh well, not much I can do about it now. At least there are no teeth marks. C'mon boy!" James ran full speed across the front yard and the narrow asphalt lane to the beach, popping the ball in and out of his glove as he ran with Angus in hot pursuit. Angus' pace, breathing heavily and letting out the occasional woof of approval for the opportunity for company and play, was more like clumsy bounding than running. In the wide-open space of the beach and without the obstacles of roofs, James continued his pop fly rehearsals.

On a perfect morning that breathes warmth and new life into everything, a boy and a dog had the world at their feet. They danced around in the sand alternately hooting and barking. There was no one on the beach as far as the eye could see and there were no commercial boats on the bay within sight. Pleasure crafters were still months away. James was in the *new world*, as his mom called it, a short time and hadn't made any close friends yet at school. Only the polite hellos to the new kid. James was okay with that. On days like this, it was hard to imagine a better place to be.

He had a warm feeling about this place and the people he already met, although most of them were grownups. The adults treated him like a celebrity. James didn't realize it was the tendency of Harmony Bay inhabitants to extend their welcome and hospitality to all newcomers. New folks that didn't cause trouble and acted neighborly were always treated hospitably. With no siblings, and no other family close enough to see regularly, it pleased him that he had a newly acquired extended family. James didn't really think of people like Billy, Mrs. Verdi, Miss Donnelly, or Mrs. Lanscome, or Lenny, Winton or Mr. Dzjankowski as every day people. James put them up on their respective pedestals with a reverence usually reserved for aunts or uncles. He could now readily do without the hustle and bustle of Avenue C, or the anxieties he felt there. He never did get homesick for that place; there was nothing to miss. Harmony Bay was a far better place to be for making new friends. That would take a little time. He knew, due to his shyness, it might take a little longer than it should. Sometimes he felt awkward with people and wasn't always sure what to say until he knew them better. His mom told him not to worry about it, saying he wasn't shy—just quiet. Even Dory questioned whether *quiet* was the right term. When James was in full play mode, he could be anything but quiet. If the topic suited him, he could ramble on.

James continued his underhand throws into the air. Angus watched each ascent and descent giving almost a nodding appearance as he followed the flight. "Pop fly to center field," James called out. "I got it!" he hollered to himself. Angus barked loud enough in response to startle James and make him take his eyes off the ball. James glanced toward the noise. He returned his gaze skyward and was momentarily blinded by an eyeful of dazzling, late winter sun. Still scanning for the ball—all he could see was spots. The next thing he felt was the smack and a stinging sensation as the baseball beaned him square on the nose. Sunspots gave way to a total white-out of vision. The words *ouch* formed on his lips and tried to make their way out of his throat. James put his ungloved hand to his nose to inspect for damage and realized a warm wetness on his scrawny fingers. Angus turned his head to the side and let out a cry of his own, mimicking the boy's sign of distress. He then pushed up along side James to give him something to lean on. Not knowing if his nose was broken, James didn't know what to do other than follow his first instinct and run for home. While in a fast trot, he covered his nose with his bare hand, leaving the offending ball behind, which Angus retrieved from the sand. Together they retraced their steps to the back door of the house. James flung the door open with blood streaming from his nostrils and called out for Angelina. The blood, and the lightheadedness overtaking him, added to the drama of the moment.

"Mamma mia—what happened? Don't drip blood on the floors, I just finished washing them."

James wasn't thrilled with the woman's seemingly uncaring off-hand remark. Little did he know, that she being older and far wiser, used the tactic to distract him for the moment.

"Is it broken?" he asked. Angelina told James to tilt his head back and gently pulled his hand away.

"How did it happen?" she said.

"Is it broken?" he repeated.

Mrs. Verdi assured him he was fine and he would certainly live, but still wanted to know how it happened.

"I hit myself in the nose with the ball." Angelina rolled her eyes and shook her head from side to side. She pulled the chair out from the kitchen table and made him sit down while she got a bag of frozen peas from the freezer and wrapped it in a tea towel.

"Trust me—in fifteen minutes you'll be as good as new and be ready to go back to spring training. Let the ice work. And let me get you cleaned up," she said.

His baseball glove never came off his left hand while James held the frozen peas in place. She washed his face and hand with a warm soapy washcloth, all the while humming some tune that was unfamiliar to James.

"Why don't we give the glove a rest too?" she asked. He squeezed the glove with his armpit and pulled his hand free.

"Hey, my ball! I left it on the beach—." Angelina reassured him there was nobody else around and the seagulls weren't interested in playing baseball. She couldn't say it fast enough as James bolted up from the chair and pulled the kitchen door open to reveal Angus lying patiently outside in a sphinx position, the ball on the ground in front of him protected by his huge paws.

Chapter 7

James was determined to make the best of the day. After giving it some thought, he determined that chasing pop fly balls should be put on hold for the moment. Or, perhaps at least until he garnered more courage. Angus and James shuffled aimlessly along the beach investigating what was along the high-tide line. Angus did the detective work with his nose while James occasionally got on all fours to thoroughly examine the marine life trapped in the sand. The exposure to the remains of bivalves and crustaceans started James wondering about what else lived in the surf. He knew the commercial fishermen were bringing in their catches of cod and now was the time winter flounder started to stir. He wondered about sharks. Ferocious Great Whites were surely in the waters farther out. He had seen other sharks in the city aquarium and learned that some could come close to shore. With those thoughts in mind he intensified his efforts hoping to find shark teeth along the beach. After what seemed like an eternity, James called off the search. He was getting bored and needed a new distraction.

The rowboat was stored upside down behind the house with its oars neatly tucked underneath it. James became inspired to undertake a serious adventure. He knew he needed to have Mom, Billy, or an adult around if he was going to take the boat out. That wasn't going to happen any time soon since the water was still freezing cold, even colder than he realized. A person in the water at the bay's mid-March water temperature would only survive about ten or fifteen minutes. James considered the possibilities. If he could right the boat, he could probably push it to the tidal creek behind the house. Once at the water's edge, he figured he could get in the boat, and by using the oars, push himself out into the creek without getting his feet wet. He could stay in the creek where they'd be safe and not venture around the point into the bay. Angus could come along to keep him company. Of course, he thought, what was the point of the expedition if it didn't have a purpose and concluded that catching some flounder would be perfect. His mother would be so proud of him for his catch. She'd cook the fish and they'd have a dinner that she didn't have to go to the market to buy.

James knew stealth was necessary to avoid Mrs. Verdi. With coyote steps, he tiptoed onto the front porch, retrieved his new fishing pole and tackle box and held the screen door as it closed so it wouldn't slam. Ducking below the kitchen window as he passed, he made his way around the back of the house to the boat.

He lifted one side of the boat with all of his might. The slight downward slope away from him gave a little extra leverage. After a few tries, he got the gunwale all the way up. With the opposite side of the boat now resting on the sand. James, along with Angus, scurried to the other side, reached up and pulled down, causing the hull to land with a soft thud. The dog scooted out of the way, wagging his tail as he gave a soft bark of approval. At the stern, James placed the rod and tackle box in the well-seasoned boat. Fortunately, the boat was lined up perfectly for direct entry into the water. He pushed with all of his weight, his sneakers digging deeply into the soft sand. The keel and hull offered very little resistance and the downhill slide surprised James. The boat moved forward easily.

James, Angus and the rowboat all made it to the water. The outgoing tide drained the wetlands behind them and the current teased the peeling white paint on the bow. James hopped in and called to Angus to join him. Angus effortlessly leapt over the transom and James directed him to sit in the bow. Taking one of the oars, James stood up, pushing off in a Gondolieri like fashion. It took several tries to move the weight of the boat, Angus and himself, but they were now floating freely on the water. James was delighted. A secret mission was pulled off perfectly. He figured out how to undo the hasps on the oarlocks and dropped an oar into each one. The oar handles felt rough in his hands. He reached into his down parka pockets for his gloves. Even with the sunshine, it was still very cold. He dipped the blades into the water without comprehending how much coordination it was going to take to move forward. Alternately, each oar took small nips at the top of the water and sprayed them aft. James adjusted the angle of his oars and they lunged forward into the creek.

Angus took it all in with great amusement. After all, the dog thought, *if not on dry land, where better for him to be than on the water?* His tail continued to wag as he let out an intermittent gravelly rumble. He watched the laughing gulls circling them. Occasionally, a male tossed back his head as he landed and let out a call to attract a mate. The dog observed the loitering golden eye ducks, the mallards that stayed through the winter, the westerly breezes that stroked the plumes of phragmites and blond cord grass, and the tidal swirls of water that were carrying the boat, its contents and the water of the creek toward the bay. This twice-a-day occurrence was crucial to life and existence at Harmony Bay. Flounder, bluefish, and many other small fry incubated in the tidal marshes and later move out into open water. The incoming tide carried nutrients for the hatchery and the outflow later carried new and precious life toward the bay.

Angus instinctively knew that this was all a part of the cycle of life, the annual death and rebirth of the bay, and that somehow, he was part of it all. He heard the humans talk about God, how they thanked God for all that had been created and for the beauty and bounty of nature. Angus agreed. He never met God, but felt he'd like to. God, in his estimation, was brilliant. God was surely a power far greater than any human or animal. God had drawn this complex plan where everything worked together perfectly. If it was God who was responsible for it all, then so be it. He would accept that—for there was no other explanation. He knew God should be obeyed and respected, the same way dogs obeyed and respected their human masters.

Angus watched the shoreline drift by, growing farther and farther away. He enjoyed the warmth of the sun on his large shoulders as he drooled and sporadically licked the salty air from his nose. All was good with him.

James was too taken up with the initial success of his mission to realize how far and fast the current was pushing them. He didn't panic. In his opinion, the safety of the shoreline was only a few short oar strokes away. *Time to fish*, he thought. Not having any live bait, James took out one of the red rubber worms from his tackle box and a hook from the plastic package labeled *Snelled Flounder Hooks – Size 10*. Removing his gloves, he put the loop of the leader line onto the snap swivel at the end of his monofilament fishing line. He added a beefy lead sinker to carry the whole works to the bottom.

The bench seat in the rowboat served as his workbench. He pierced the artificial worm with the business end of the hook. "Ready to go," he said aloud. James placed the tip of the rod over the side and undid the catch on the reel, letting the hook, line and sinker find its way to the bottom. He wondered how long it would take for his first bite, how big the fish would be, and again questioned the time it might take for him to catch his prize. After a while, he grew weary. James reeled in the line for an inspection to see if everything was in place. It was. Satisfied, he let the line pay out again.

He speculated whether he could actually see the bottom and the fish below. James stood up holding onto the amidships gunwale and gripped the rod between his legs. This stance, with his feet together, greatly upset his ability to balance and absorb the pitch of the boat from the intermittent soft swells. The dog joined him alongside the starboard edge of the boat, placing his paws on the weathered frame, mimicking James' posture. They both peered down into the foamy green water. James once again thought about sharks and if they could be this close to the beach. The harder James stared, searching for life or his untouched hook, the less he concentrated on his surroundings.

He leaned over farther. A rogue swell rolling from port to starboard, rocked the boat, which was already canted at a steep angle from the combined weight of the dog and boy, forcing it over on its keel. The laws of gravity and physics prevailed, pitching the occupants of the dinghy overboard into the frigid water.

James gasped from the sudden shock of cold water. Swallowing salt water, he coughed violently. The salt stung his eyes and blurred his vision. His heavy overcoat, jeans, sweatshirt and sneakers were saturated, pulling him down below the surface. He continued gasping and flailing.

Resurfacing, the boy felt himself losing the battle and most certainly knew the shoreline was too far away. Delirium overcame him in a matter of moments as the cold sucked the life from his body. He pictured his mother and felt himself saying he was sorry this happened. He called out for God's help, but didn't have enough time to think about his demise. The light dimmed. He began spiraling downward toward the darkness.

The last thing James consciously recalled was being gripped by the shoulder and pulled through the water. Again, his head broke the surface and he gulped in cold air. *A shark—* he screamed inside his head. *I'm being eaten by a shark!* In the same instant, James came to a vague realization that the other life form in the water with him was Angus. With frozen, shivering hands, he reached around the dog's neck and clasped them together, clinging on for his fleeting life.

Angus' ancestry and decades of training to rescue humans in the maritime was bred into his genetic code. He knew precisely what he had to do. Billy had told Angus a story about Angus' forefather, a Newfoundland Dog in the 1830s, who saved over 100 Irish immigrants in Nova Scotia from the wreck of the brig *Dispatch.* Swimming through the treacherous seas with a chunk of wood, which the survivors attached a rope to; the heroic dog towed the rope to shore. This allowed rescuers to set up a Breeches Buoy and haul the stranded sailors ashore one by one.

The animal's webbed feet paddled feverishly beneath the surface in the Newfoundland retriever's unique down-and-out breaststroke pattern. His head stayed above the water and he kept his focus on the beach. Well insulated with his waterproof, double-layered coat, he didn't feel the cold the way James did. James hanging around his throat didn't represent a challenge for Angus at all. He easily outweighed the boy by more than 120 pounds. His immense musculature and extra lung capacity was developed for strength and stamina to plow through rough seas and strong currents. He could swim for hours without tiring. This was a game for Angus and he was overjoyed to exhibit his lifesaving skills in the surf. It wasn't often that he got to play this role.

Within twenty feet of the beach, James stopped convulsing and slipped into an indifferent hypothermic stupor. He lost his grip. Angus was unfazed. Gently grasping the hood of James' coat with his teeth, he picked up his pace toward shore. Once his paws touched the bottom, he maintained his grip on the coat and walked backward, dragging James to land. Pulling James onto the safety of the sand, Angus sniffed the boy's face. After giving it several licks, he left James' limp body amid the beach clutter.

He flew to the front porch of the cottage where he smashed against the frame of the outer screen door, bursting it open with a loud thump that allowed him into the screened porch and access to the front door. Angus relentlessly pounded the front door with prizefighter blows. At the same time, he barked and howled with all of his might.

The ferocity of the dog's cries alarmed Angelina as she rushed to the front door. She opened the door to the front porch as a soaking wet mass of dripping black fur spilled headlong into the entryway.

"Angus, for heaven's sake! What are you doing?" Angelina shrieked. What's with this incessant barking?"

His tail did not wag, but hung lifelessly as he scrambled wildly to his feet leaving a puddle of seawater and drool. He turned and ran back out the door he had just entered, stopped and turned on the porch, letting out more frantic cries and yelps. He repeated the act of entering, leaving, and yapping several times, becoming more animated and histrionic each time. Angelina stood with her hands on her hips, not knowing what to make of the unusual behavior. Angus was always docile and quite well mannered. Angus finally launched from the house entirely. Several yards from the porch door, he faced the location on the shore where James' limp body was. He barked loudly and alternately bowed the front of his body.

Instantly it all came together for Angelina. "James!" she cried out. With that single exclamation, Angus bolted toward James with Angelina in anxious pursuit.

Chapter 8

Angelina covered the distance from the front yard to James in moments. Understandably, Angus made the trip across the sandy divide far in advance of her arrival. She knelt beside James. Propping up his wet head, she looked for signs of life. Using her thumb and index finger, she pried open an eyelid and saw his eye roll back in his head. James then opened his eyes to mere slits while his lean frame continued to shake. Through pursed lips he uttered a single word in a weak, gargled voice. "*Cold.*"

Angelina now stooped behind James and slid her arms up and under his, locking her hands together across his chest. Her stocky build easily hefted him up as she stood. She began to drag him backward across the beach toward the kitchen door and the warmth of the cottage. His heels left parallel furrows in the sand. Angus walked along side, staying out of the way, but near enough to be in a role to protect and serve. He licked James' hand from time to time. At the kitchen door, Angelina gently lowered James to the ground while reaching behind her for the doorknob. She twisted the knob and shoved the door open. Angelina cleared the kitchen table with a broad sweep of her arm and lifted James onto the edge. Laying him down carefully, she darted to the kitchen wall phone and punched in the number for the Harmony Bay Fire Department, which was plastered on the phone in red and white along with the instructions to dial it in an emergency.

"Harmony Bay Fire Department," a dispatcher answered.

Angelina spoke in a hurried voice. "Yes, this is Angelina Verdi. I'm out at Dory McDonough's. The new librarian's place at the end of North Road. Her son James fell into the creek. He almost drowned. He needs help. Send the ambulance right now! Hurry. *Please* hurry!"

"Okay, we're on our way. Is he breathing?" asked the other voice.

"Yes, but he's blue, and is only semiconscious," she said.

An alarm sounded at the firehouse and the call went out on the radio to all available volunteers and was relayed to the Harmony Bay police. The dispatcher spoke into the mic in an authoritative voice. "Attention all hands. Attention E.R.U. team, respond to base. Male, age ten, hypothermia—possible coma. First responders report directly to the scene." With the message, he gave the location on North Road and the community came together.

Police Chief Dooley heard the call on his police scanner while parked in front of Hirsch's Hardware chatting with Lenny Hirsch. Hirsch leaned on the police car's open window with both elbows. "Hirsch, see if you can find Doc Tollenson and get him out there," the gravel voiced chief said. It came out more like an order than a request. Dooley flipped switches activating the red flashing lights on the roof, dropped the cruiser into gear and put the throttle down to the floor. Tires spun up a cloud of gritty dust as he headed the car out of town toward North Road. He keyed the mic of the two-way and spoke, "Roger that, Luke. Dooley here. Unit 0-1. I'm on my way."

Although Dooley had more years as a cop than he cared to recall, he could never get used to it when a child was in trouble. It went right to his heart. Harmony Bay always had its fair share of water accidents that included tourists injured by doing crazy stuff out where they shouldn't be, capsized sailboats, boat collisions and the occasional drowning. It was all on par for Harmony Bay and he took it in stride, but not when a kid's life was at risk. He gripped the wheel, tripped the siren, gunned the engine and drove as fast as he dared. Dooley didn't know what to expect. He picked up the mic again. "H-Q this is Dooley. Send one of the four-wheel-drive beach units out to the scene. Do you copy, Luke?"

"Roger that, Chief. I'm on it," Luke radioed back. "Do you want me to alert the Coast Guard for a helicopter air-lift?"

"Yeah. Call them—ask them to keep a chopper on stand-by until the EMT's know what we're dealing with."

Within minutes, volunteers from the medical team assembled at the firehouse and boarded the ambulance. First to arrive was Susan, brunette and pleasant, she was a volunteer emergency team nurse who worked as the school nurse at the high school during the week. Chester, an EMT who was decorated by the Coast Guard for his life-saving heroics, ran over from the post office. He began to check the gear aboard the ambulance and snapped a stethoscope around his neck. Frank the driver, a phone company retiree, slid behind the steering wheel, turned the key and the diesel clattered to life. The firehouse's overhead door reached its peak, bathing the berth in yellow light. Each crewmember fastened their seat belts and the cube-shaped Harmony Bay Emergency Response Unit rolled out with lights and sirens blazing. It shattered the quiet of the little village on an off-season Saturday afternoon. Frank spoke into the radio mic, "Attention all units. E-R-U in route to North Road incident."

Harmony Bay was far from major population centers and their related inland facilities. Volunteering was a way of life in the town and everyone contributed to the degree they could. It ensured everything got done. Neighbors relied on neighbors for the essential elements of the community that included the Ambulance Corps, the Fire Department and the Bay Patrol.

With urgency, but without a sense of panic, Angelina went to Dory's bedroom. She pulled the down comforter, with its blue and white stitch work mosaic, off the bed and returned to the kitchen. She turned every burner on the gas stove and set the oven to high. Now bending over James, who was lying prostrate on the oak table, she began to peel the waterlogged clothes from him and dropped them on the floor. First the sneakers and socks. Then the coat, followed by the sweatshirt and finally the jeans. Doubling the comforter over, she placed it over him. Her hands gently continued their work of removing his underwear beneath the warming surround of the quilt. A halo of warmth generated by the stove enveloped the two. Angelina prayed for the ambulance to arrive quickly. Angela sighed in relief when she heard the faint sound of a siren in the distance.

Dooley arrived and stormed through the front porch door, calling out as he made his way to the back of the cottage. In the next breath he cursed Fishhook Cutsciko, the landlord, for what he must be charging in rent to the occupants for the rundown place.

"Hey Angie," the chief said, wrapping his arm around her, "you okay?"

Hey now. Grazie. I'm fine, Chief," she replied. "But he's in rough shape." Barely audible gasps coming from James' throat were the only sign of life. Dooley felt the boy's forehead with the back of his hand.

"Geez, Angie. Okay, the med crew is right behind me. They train for this sort of thing— they'll be here any minute." Chief Dooley had no sooner said the words and the emergency crew arrived.

Susan and Chester came to the boy's side and went to work. Susan took his pulse while Chester the EMT extracted a specialized digital thermometer from his belly pack. The thermometer analyzed James' critical core temperature.

"Rate forty and thready," Susan reported.

"We've got a cold one. Core temp eighty-eight," Chester said. "Let's get him outta here—stat! Chief, have Frank back up to the kitchen door and help him get out the gurney. Have him radio County General. Tell them what we've got, and that we're on our way," Chester commanded. Dooley stood behind the red and white mammoth box and directed Frank to the kitchen entrance. The chief held his hands apart so Frank could see the approximate distance in his rearview mirror. The back-up alarm chirped madly.

Two Harmony Bay cops arrived in a four-wheel-drive truck along with Doc Tollenson and other members of the volunteer fire department who responded to the scene. They snapped into action, helping Susan and Chester lift James onto the stretcher then into the ambulance. The team worked carefully. They knew a sudden jolt could set off a fatal arrhythmia.

"Chief," one of the officers said, "Bay Patrol spotted an empty rowboat adrift. Most likely it was the one with the boy and the dog. The wind is carrying it toward open water. I told Bay Patrol to secure it and tow it to the beach. We'll retrieve it from there and drag it with the beach patrol unit back here to the cottage."

"Okay," Chief Dooley said, "are we sure this was the only kid in the boat?"

"Not sure, Chief."

"Then get out there and start looking!" Dooley screamed. "Call Bay

Patrol and the Coast Guard. Have them get a chopper up. Order a full grid sweep of the area. Tell them I said so. Radio Luke. Tell him to call the firehouse and get some more guys out here." The veins on Dooley's forehead bulged. "I'm not taking any chances. It could be a while until this kid is conscious enough to talk."

It was agreed that Angelina would ride with Chief Dooley and Doc Tollenson would ride in the ambulance and monitor James' condition. Doors slammed shut and the caravan headed toward town on North Road. After passing through town, they turned west heading inland toward the only hospital some thirty minutes away from the peninsula.

Dooley radioed headquarters. "Get someone over to the library to round up the mother and take her out to County General Hospital. Handle it delicately. That's an order."

Chief Dooley ordered the cops to block the only two intersections through town to allow them unhindered progress to the hospital. Additional volunteer firemen were sent to the intersections at Bay Street and Main Street to stop traffic to clear the artery to the county road.

Sheryl, Harmony Bay's only female police officer, was at the police station when the call came through. She volunteered to go to the library and break the news to Dory. Sheryl entered the library through the back door and went directly to the reference desk where Dory was seated.

"Mrs. McDonough, there's been a little mishap. It involves your son," Sheryl said in a calm, clear voice. "He's okay, but they are taking him to the emergency room to get checked out." Dory bolted out of her chair and rounded the desk.

"Oh, dear God, what happened?"

"Come with me, Mrs. McDonough, I'll drive you out there," Sheryl said.

"Oh, that's okay, I can take myself there," Dory shot back.

"I understand, m'am. But I'm under orders from the chief to give you professional personalized service. And that's exactly what I'm going to do. He doesn't want you driving if you're upset. Roland is a volunteer fireman who works over at Shea's Bakery. He'll follow us in your car."

"Tell me what's happened to James," Dory demanded.

"We can talk on the way."

Dory and Sheryl arrived at the hospital with the convoy of the ambulance, the chief's car, Roland in Dory's car and another vehicle driven by a volunteer to be on standby if someone needed a ride back to town before the others. Dory leapt from Sheryl's car and raced to the back doors of the emergency vehicle. Its rear doors opened. There in the dim light she could see her son's face covered with an oxygen mask. Dory's knees buckled. Sheryl and Dooley shored her up on either side. The chief was the first to speak, "Let's get out of their way and let them do their work. We'll see him inside."

White coated nurses met the stretcher at the door and wheeled James directly to a curtained bay. They replaced the gray, scratchy wool blanket from the ambulance with a cotton sheet. It wasn't much softer than the blanket. James was still too delirious to notice. Like the volunteer crew, the hospital staff was well versed in treating hypothermia and exposure to the northern climate.

To monitor James' weak heartbeat, stethoscopes were applied to his chest, and then electrocardiogram electrodes were taped in place. They followed the color code for each point. Red on right with black above and green on the left with white above. A doctor placed a mask over James' face that administered oxygen warmed to 108 degrees. A nurse started an intravenous line. It pumped out James' blood, warmed it through a heated filter, added oxygen, and then returned it to his body.

James awoke after a painfully long time. Dazed at first, he began to focus on the cluster of doctors and nurses, Angelina Verdi, Chief Dooley, Doc Tollenson, Nurse Susan, Chester the EMT and finally, his mom. His green eyes continued to flicker in response to the bright overhead lights. He gave a slight smile that was reflected by everyone around him. They all broke into grins.

"He's going to be fine," the doctor said.

"Praise God," Dory replied. "Well son, I think we have a lot of people to thank…beginning with Mrs. Verdi for rescuing you." Dory nodded toward Angelina.

"No— it was Angus," James blurted from behind the oxygen mask. In turn, each adult shot puzzled glances back and forth across the emergency room bed.

"Angus?" the chief questioned.

"Yeah, Angus swam me home," James said and began to fade off to a light fog.

"That's right," Angelina said. "I found James up on the beach. The dog must have dragged him there. Angus saved his life."

"Well, my goodness," Dory said. "I do believe there will be a few big steaks in that dog's future." Everyone chuckled then lowered their eyes as Dory thanked each one with warm words and hugs.

Chapter 9

The weeks since James' near drowning passed and Dory regained her confidence in leaving him with Angelina. He had scared himself half to death, so Dory felt he wasn't likely to try another stunt any time soon. She discussed some new guidelines with Angelina for keeping an eye on him, but still felt guilty about not being there. Dory was the sole breadwinner and had to go to work. Her finances were ravaged from the expense of moving, car repairs and mammoth heating bills that were much higher than she had anticipated. During her lunch break she scoured the help wanted ads looking for an additional part-time job close to home to supplement her income. Dory skimmed through the positions listed in the Harmony Bay Gazette newspaper. Her eye caught an ad that simply read, *Molly's, wait staff, apply in person after 2 PM.*

Dory heard people mention Molly's. Although, she never had seen a sign on a restaurant that said *Molly's*. She decided to ask Mrs. Lanscome if she knew where Molly's Restaurant was.

"Sure do," Mrs. Lanscome said. "It's right down the street."

Puzzled by the response, Dory asked, "Exactly where down the street is it?" Mrs. Lanscome laughed at the inquiry.

"Dory, everybody on the bay, dry land and sea alike, knows the Bay Front Restaurant is commonly referred to as Molly's. It's the name of the proprietor, Molly McDuff."

Molly's was at the edge of the water facing the pleasure craft marina and adjacent to the boatyard of commercial fishers. The front dining room and the bar were built on pilings that jutted them out over the water. Windows surrounded by gray weathered shingles afforded a view in every direction.

Perfect, Dory thought. It was only blocks from the library. After Mrs. Lanscome left her desk, Dory printed out a copy of her resume and work experience. She asked Mrs. Lanscome if she could take a late lunch to visit Molly's to see if the job was still available and if she was acceptable for the position. A little before two o'clock Dory reapplied her lipstick and checked her hair, choosing to walk the short distance rather than drive. She was thankful the winds were calm today so she wouldn't become a wind-blown mess by the time she arrived. Dory was a little anxious about applying for the job. She took into account that she was very much an outsider who had only been on the bay for a couple of months and wondered if they were only looking to hire a local. However, she began to recall how warmly many of the townspeople had welcomed her. Perhaps this would be more of the same.

Dory walked the four blocks on the uneven sidewalks that were pushed up by immense tree roots. She stepped up onto the planking skirting the water and passed the slight aroma of diesel fuel. A gaggle of Canada geese scattered as she approached. Arriving at precisely two, she entered the empty restaurant.

The Bay Front Restaurant had been in Molly's family for generations and served a wide variety of patrons and their tastes. The doors opened in the predawn to serve up breakfast for the charter boat clients and their crews, a lively mix of salty veteran baymen, and deep-water boat crews. By six o'clock, the place was a clatter of coffee cups mingling with the smell of bacon, salt air and vigorous conversations about the day's upcoming events. Right before noon during the season, the tables filled with tourists, day-trippers from up inland and summer residents who came to Molly's for the seafood lunch specials from the local waters. Dinner began at five o'clock when the charters returned and the ravenous baymen were done for the day. An assortment of locals and visitors combined to enjoy the day's catch, or what hadn't sold at lunch. Spirited arguments could always be found around the bar. Many of those animated discussions about the size of the fish that got away, or how good or bad their luck was, carried late into the evening. On weekend evenings young adults gathered to socialize at Molly's. Some did their own trolling while listening to the occasional solo musician performing in the far corner where the tables were cleared and moved to the side. Every day the schedule and the process repeated itself. The only change came at the turn of the seasons when Molly's capacity swelled or shrank.

It was a demanding job to manage the place and Molly ran it like no one else could. Round-faced and ruddy, she was as tough as some of her customers. She had ankles as thick as her knees, a bear grip handshake from decades of shucking clams and oysters and a back and shoulders strong enough to lift a full beer keg or bushel of clams over her head without effort. Along with all of her rugged traits, she had a heart of gold. Now middle aged, and never married, she had been running the restaurant since leaving college in her late teens when her father took sick and couldn't keep up the pace anymore. The balance of her family made a living off the water: clamers, lobstermen, anglers, and charter boat captains. It worked out well for Molly. With a fresh catch arriving daily directly off the boats, she didn't have to haggle with middlemen and purveyors whose product quality and freshness could be questioned. Her younger brother Liam, an excellent chef, worked the kitchen. Molly paid his way through culinary school and they both enjoyed the benefit.

They didn't worry about reviews in fancy travel magazines or city newspapers. Molly's was a place unto itself where folks enjoyed the waterfront ambiance along with great food. Satisfaction guaranteed. Slow times were never a worry except for in the dead of winter when they actually enjoyed the break from the hectic summer season. Business might be slow during January and February, but Molly vowed not to lay off the full time regulars. She found busy work for them to fill the hours. Easter week always seemed to signal the start of the high season. Even if the weather was still cold, people would begin to venture out of hibernation and Molly's Bay Front was always a good place to start. If sunny skies and mild temperatures brought an early break to late winter's clutches, the restaurant was swamped with an early rush.

Dory walked up to the bar where an aproned Molly slid freshly washed wine glasses into the overhead rack. "Hello," Dory said. "I'm here to apply for the wait staff position. Who should I speak with?"

"Ahoy! That would be me," Molly bellowed. She thrust her hefty hand across the bar toward Dory. "Pleased to meet you. Molly McDuff is the name. Proprietor, sometimes chief cook and bottle washer. You're that new gal at the library, yes?"

"Yes, that would be *me*," Dory said. She tried to hand her resume and work history to the woman.

"Ah, hey now, that's not necessary. Got any waitressing experience?"

"Well, yes. During college I worked as a waitress and hostess to help pay my way through school."

"Okay, swell. Anybody Mel Lanscome hired is fine with me. You've already passed the test. The job is yours if you want it. And, as pretty as you are, you'll be good for business— if not your tip cup. I'm figuring you're looking for something nights or weekends to fit in with your library job? Besides, maybe you can recommend me a few good books while you're here."

Dory was flustered and blushed from the woman's sudden approval and remarks. She graciously accepted the position.

"You want coffee? Eat lunch yet? Molly said.

"Yes and no," Dory answered.

Molly gave a puzzled look and produced a mug of coffee along with a creamer and sugar. She pulled a pencil from behind her ear and said, "What'll it be? This is probably the first and last time I'll ever be waiting on you." Dory was taken aback by the generous offer as Molly shoved a lunch menu toward her.

"Liam is still in the kitchen. Pick whatever you want." Dory stared at the menu while all sorts of thoughts raced around in her head. She didn't expect things to go so smoothly.

"May I have a bowl of the clam chowder?" she asked.

"Gee whiz—you're a cheap date. That's all you want?" A little embarrassed by the comment Dory shook her head yes. Molly disappeared into the kitchen through the swinging door. Dory took account of the place. There were tables lined up against each green curtain-framed, six-over-six window that looked out to the gulls on the water. Each was readied for the dinner shift with a red and white checked tablecloth and the perfunctory array of condiment containers. The thick tables, mostly with two and four places and a few with six, featured heavy, mismatched wooden chairs. They were practical, but didn't look too comfortable.

Some tables had one or more legs shimmed with oddities to accommodate the rolling floors. Paintings of bay scenes by local artists hung next to fishing paraphernalia, haphazardly decorating the walls in a nautical theme. A rowboat was hung upside down from the vaulted ceiling. Inside the boat, a clam rake, oars, crab trap buoys and line were secured to defy gravity. Harpoons, gaff hooks, long silent ships bells, signal flags, an aging nautical map of the coast, and a board displaying sailing knots all added to the ambiance. A gas-fired fireplace with an intricately carved mantel that helped the aged heating system in the off-season months lined the back wall. Prominently mounted above the polished golden teak mantle a ship's figurehead, a beautiful blue-eyed young woman with elegant blond tresses that eddied around her shoulders, gazed out into the rear dining room. Immaculate floors that saw generations of grit, spills, and swabbings, were very wide planks of straight-grained mahogany, owning weathered subtle hues of grays, browns and purples ranging from plum to mauve. Dory's eyes fell on a small sign suspended by a nail above the ornate brass cash register that said, *A Small Town is Like a Big Family*.

That's it! Dory said to herself. *That's what I'm feeling*. Never having had the luxury of a big family, let alone siblings, she let the concept flow through her body. It gave her goose bumps. Billy, Angelina, Mrs. Lanscome, the library employees, Chief Dooley, Jank, Hirsh, Winton Hector, Dave Small, Maureen Donnelly, the firehouse volunteers, and everyone she met in her new town, including Angus and Chloe, treated her like a member of the family. That was never the case back in the city. People were distant. They kept to themselves by living inside their own individual cocoons of personal space. City people never reached out to a stranger and shuttered the windows of their souls to intrusions. All of the feelings made Dory's eyes tear for a moment as a lump began to form in her throat.

Molly reemerged and gestured toward a table. She carried a tray containing a bowl of steaming chowder, freshly baked bread, a cup of coleslaw, pickles, and a mountain of macaroni and cheese.

"Oh my," Dory said when the food was served, "you shouldn't have gone through all of this trouble. I could never finish all of this."

"Careful, it's hot. I thought I'd put out some side snacks," Molly said. "No trouble at all. When you're done, we'll make up a nice to-go package for that boy of yours. What does he like?" Again, Dory was taken with yet another random act of kindness.

"Fortunately—and unfortunately, he eats everything and anything. He's like a junkyard dog," Dory said. "He goes through groceries in a jiffy. I guess it's normal for a growing boy. I'm glad he's not a picky eater."

"Without a doubt—it's normal," Molly said. "For the most part, I raised my younger brother Liam from a pup. That boy could eat. Our mother passed away when he was young and dad was always busy with the restaurant while we were growing up."

Dory spooned up the chowder. "Molly, this is delicious. No wonder this place is so busy."

"Give the compliments to Liam. He's responsible," Molly said. Peering over her soupspoon, Dory went on to admire the beautiful floors of her restaurant.

"Yep. Well hey, there's a story that goes along with those floorboards. And some of the other parts of this old place too," Molly said. Her raucous laugh filled the air. "Over 150 years ago, a beautiful four master, the schooner *Jeni Lyn*, went up on the rocks out by England Point during an unexpected brutal nor'easter. All hands were saved. But most all of them made it to the beach. They were banged up and bloodied from tumbling in the boulders and surf. Somehow, the shipwrecked sailors managed to get around to the protected cove on the lee side of the point and got a fire going. That kept them from freezing to death. At the same time—it sent a signal here. The next morning, some brave Harmony fishermen were finally able to launch a rescue party. They landed at the cove and rescued the crew. By then a lot of them were in very bad shape from their wounds and exposure. They had to be carried aboard the fishing boats." Molly looked out the restaurant window. Her thoughts wandered.

"Come to think of it… hey now, y'know Doc Tollenson?" Molly asked. "His great-great grandfather was first mate aboard the *Jeni Lyn*. He settled here and the rest is history. Story goes on to say that they tried everything to refloat the *Jeni Lyn* and free 'er up when the weather cleared. Her hull was too badly smashed up by some of those ledges out there. She listed over and began to settle in the sand. Before they scuttled her, they salvaged everything they could. These floors were from the top deck of that ship and many of the timbers in the frame of the Bay Front are from her bulkheads and whatever else they could scavenge. The teak in the mantle back there is from the captain's quarters." Molly jerked her thumb toward the back room. "That pretty little thing above the fireplace is based on Jeni Lyn herself. She was the ship owner's daughter. According to the legend, the crew remembered Jeni was the last thing they saw as they abandoned ship. So, she sort of became their lucky charm. If you go have a look you'll see thirteen stars carved in the front of the mantel, a star for each hand that was aboard, with Jeni still watching over them. Through the ages a lot of young men proposed marriage to their girl while sitting beneath Jeni hoping for good luck. The fireplace used to burn wood, but it's a little too crazy at times to deal with that. It got modernized years ago. It was switched to gas."

Molly slapped the tabletop and stood up. "Come have a look behind the bar," she said. "There's a trap door there. It was used during prohibition to sneak booze in here that was delivered by smuggler boats at low tide. This place is so far from anyplace I don't think the Federal agents wanted to be bothered coming out here to check— especially in the winter. There's hundreds of stories that go with this place. After a while you'll learn them all. Tourists love to hear that stuff. If Jeni Lyn or the walls could talk I'm sure you'd learn even more."

Dory decided she liked Molly's forthright and honest way of talking. She decided to open up to her, even if only a little, going on to explain how her husband was lost in the war shortly after James was born. "Actually, I still wasn't much more than a kid myself at the time. When things became difficult we moved in with my parents," Dory said. "I was able to return to college and earn my Library Science degree. And later, my Master's degree."

Dory explained she wasn't resentful or angry about the loss of her husband, or being a single parent. It was just the way it was meant to be. She wasn't happy about it, but didn't complain. She accepted it as God's will. Calamity in her life forced her to move forward, attempting and accomplishing things she never thought possible. Accordingly, she was trying to make the best of her limitations. Above all, she learned how to be brave. Some things were unpredictable. Whatever happened to her and James on this spit of sand was their destiny. Not being afraid of hard work, getting her hands dirty, or hardships, she felt she could slightly alter her course through perseverance. Dory's mom and dad raised her with a strong work ethic and the priorities of God, family and country. Figuring she had everything in perspective, she instilled these same values on her son. She hoped if not now, that at some point, it would all make sense to him and serve him well. Time would tell.

"Sure—I'm lonely at times," Dory said. "I haven't really thought about being in a relationship." She didn't let those feelings bother her to the point of distraction. Dory continued, "Married life, as brief as it was, was bliss. My place is in the here and now with my son. When we lived in the city, mom and dad could watch James. For fun, I went on a few casual dates. Moving to Harmony Bay erased all of those relations." Dory shifted in her seat and lowered her voice. "I never considered anything for the long term. Being a widow with a young kid—I wasn't sure how attractive that made me to the opposite sex. Parenting and survival is the main thing now. That's just the way it is. Someday, things may change as James gets a little older—or maybe not." Molly shook her head up and down in agreement. "For right now," Dory said, "I'm not going to consider sharing my life with anyone who didn't treat my son like his own."

They talked about how things worked at the restaurant. Dory agreed to come on Thursday after work for training. She could start on Saturday morning because she only worked one Saturday each month at the library and would work one dinner shift for Molly during the week.

Molly gave Dory the dress code, "Wear whatever you want to be comfortable. Folks will figure out that you work here by the apron. It's a dead giveaway."

Dory said she'd call Angelina when she got home to make sure she had coverage for James. At the mention of Angelina Verdi's name, Molly's eyebrows shot up. "Angelina's husband was partners in a commercial fishing boat with my uncle Mike. It was a long time ago," Molly said. "Uncle Mike and Adamo Verdi were lost, along with their boat, the *Liberty Belle*, to the deep in a nor'easter. It was a November gale far up the coast. Mike and Adamo were well-seasoned experienced seaman. It didn't matter much—." Her voice trailed off.

When matched against mountainous seventy-foot seas and merciless 100 mile per hour winds, anything could happen. The warnings came too late. The diesels weren't strong enough to outrun the storm; the seventy-eight foot boat was a mere bobbin. There were no witnesses and no survivors. It was anyone's guess as to what actually happened. A ruthless rogue wave could have swamped the *Liberty Belle* before any lifeboats could be launched. Even if they were, the chances of survival at sea were almost nil.

These accidents occurred along the coast, but in Harmony Bay, the loss of Mike and Adamo pierced a hole in the heart of the community. They were lost to an unforgiving mistress that snapped men, boats and dreams like matchsticks, and turned fisherman into martyrs. The two men were loved and respected by all who knew them. Crewmen aboard the *Liberty Belle* were not as lucky as the hands on the *Jeni Lyn*. Compared to the sea, regardless of its vastness, the bay was a welcome haven. Dory never knew disasters like these. She wasn't shipwrecked, but events in her life washed her up on the beach called the peninsula of Harmony Bay.

While discussing what hours she could work, Dory glanced at the clock and realized she'd be overdue from her lunch break. The librarian thanked Molly profusely, stood up, and moved toward the door where she stopped, turned and said a final goodbye. There was a bounce in her step as she returned to the library, a gait produced by the warm feeling of the chowder and the open conversation with Molly.

Dory covered almost two blocks when she heard Molly's booming voice behind her. Molly was at full speed, or at least as much speed as her stocky legs could produce, calling out to Dory and cradling a bulging bag. The brown paper bag was stenciled in green to give the appearance of being covered in fishnet while red letters boldly proclaimed on its front: *The Bay Front Restaurant—Grog and Victuals—The Best Seafood Anywhere.* Molly was thoroughly out of breath by the time she caught up to her new waitress.

"Hey, you forgot this. It's for that boy of yours. There's two slices of blueberry pie in there too. One for each of ya. You didn't stick around for desert."

"Oh Molly, how thoughtful of you. Thank you so much. I'm sure

James will love this. You are too generous," Dory said as she gave the panting woman a hug. "I'll see you on Thursday at five."

Dory breezed through the next couple of days, finding herself back at Molly's on Thursday. It was old hat for Dory. She learned the ropes in short order. Since it was only for training she didn't have to stay until closing to set the tables for the morning's breakfast shift. Welcoming the opportunity to scoot early, she arrived home well before it was James' bedtime. Dory tucked him in, kissed his forehead and said goodnight.

In Saturday's predawn Dory would have welcomed the opportunity to spend some more time between the blankets. She shook her head to loosen the dream strings, placed both bare feet on the cold floor and then into slippers. Before she headed to the kitchen to start a pot of coffee, she wrapped herself in a bathrobe. *Angelina will be here soon*, she thought. *What the heck. Life is short, coffee is cheap. Enjoy both.* She opted to make a full pot to share.

When the coffee finished perking, she reached for her favorite cup and wondered what the day would bring. While taking the first invigorating sips of coffee, Dory walked out onto the front porch that screened in last night's chill. There was a warm orange and red glow low in the sky like radiant embers in a fireplace. Within the next few moments the distant horizon released its hold and the sunflower showed its fiery head. Petals at first, then the full bloom of a brilliant sunrise announced the start of the day. Dory, fortified and warmed by the contents of her now almost empty cup, reflected on how blessed she was to be here to witness it all. Her spell was broken by the arrival of Angelina. Dory retreated to the kitchen and opened the door, welcoming her with a hug.

"Good grief, you're early," Dory said.

"Ah, hey now, no worries," Angelina said. Her brown eyes were wide and bright. "An old gal like me doesn't sleep much. Thought I'd get over here early. Didn't want to hold you up. It being your first day and all. I'll put breakfast up for the champ as soon as he rolls out of bed."

Dory arrived at the Bay Front restaurant and greeted Molly and the other staff members. Still being early in the season, it was a relatively quiet morning according to Molly. She always seemed to take everything in stride. Molly handed Dory an apron and pointed across the mahogany decking to the table by the front window facing east.

"There's your first victim," Molly said, "go get 'em." Dory squinted into the sunlight at the table where the lone customer sat with his back to her. Molly tied Dory's apron strings behind her and gave her a little push. Dory approached somewhat timidly— which was unusual for her. Dory rounded the table. With her back now toward the sun, she stood and faced the customer. She did a double take when she realized who sat alone at the table.

"Good morning, my name is Dory. Would you care for coffee?" she said and extracted an order pad from her apron pocket.

"First day?" the man asked.

"Yes— it is."

"Coffee sounds good. Hold the cream and sugar. How's your son doing? Quite the accident he had. Lucky thing that dog was with him," the stranger from the hardware store said.

"Oh, he's fine. Thank you for asking. Yes, he was lucky to have the dog, Mrs. Verdi, the police department, the fire department, and all those people who helped him. Thank goodness the fishing rod and reel you picked out for him didn't go overboard." Now Dory's antennae was fully up and her radar was scanning this individual who she initially thought was rude to her in Hirsch's hardware store. *She wondered, how did he know about the accident and that James was her son? Surely it was a small community, but did everybody know everything? Was this guy some kind of stalker?* Then her eye caught the glint of the sun off the bronze cash register. It reflected upward, illuminating the small sign. It reminded her, *A Small Town is Like a Big Family.*

Yes, Dory thought. *Without a doubt, this is what it's all about.* It wasn't about gossip. It was neighborly concerns and sharing the community news. With his face now lit fully by the morning glare, she began to notice things about him that she hadn't before. His eyes were much bluer and his hair a bit longer and blonder than she recalled. His face held a pleasant kindness that matched the calm nature of his voice. Calloused hands were tipped by long ringless fingers. Sort of good looking, she thought.

"Fishing today?" Dory said. She hoped to continue the small talk. It was her only table.

"Nope. I'll be working on the old *Sea Horse* to get her ready for the season. Trying to take advantage of the next couple of warm days."

"Let me grab your coffee."

Dory returned with a coffee pot, turned over the cup at the upper right corner of his place setting and filled it. With order pad now in hand, she placed the coffee pot on the table. "So, what can I get you?" she asked.

"Three eggs over easy, double order of bacon, stack of pancakes. Definitely home fries and large OJ. Oh, and could I please have some blueberry syrup for the pancakes?"

Dory's eyes widened as she scribbled his order on her pad. Noticing her reaction, he reassured her that he didn't eat like this everyday, which altered the bewildered look on her face. She returned with two plates of food and slid them in front of the man. "Must be hungry," she said.

"Sure am. I was shipwrecked here and I haven't eaten in weeks," he said. He flashed the librarian a smile and gave a wink. Dory laughed openly at the silly joke and left him alone to eat.

Other customers began to filter in and Dory took her turn with the wait staff serving them. She saw that he finished and asked if there was anything else he might like. Although, she could not imagine how he could eat another morsel. He gave the international sign for the check by making a flicking motion with his hand, as if he was holding a pen. Dory went to the register and tallied his bill. She thanked him, wished him a wonderful day and placed the check face down before him.

"I certainly will. I'm off to a great start," he said. He flipped several bills on top of the tab. "Nice to see you again. It's all good. I don't need any change. By the way. Do you give service just as good over at the library?"

Caught off guard by the remark, Dory felt herself blush. "Well I sure hope so," she answered.

Dory counted the wrinkled bills on the table twice after he departed and shook her head in disbelief. He remained an enigma to her. Sure, he was handsome, well spoken, polite, self-assured and obviously generous. The man left a ten-dollar tip.

Chapter 10

Every time the heat kicked on at the library, the mobile above the circulation desk started its sluggish rotation. Dory wasn't sure if it was planned that way or it just happened. The carved wooden fishes that represented the sea creatures of the region's aquatic food chain started their endless, crazy chase, never catching each other. Each of the licorice-eyed fish, which were recreated by a local artist, were anatomically correct in every detail. When it was conceived, the whirling sculpture created a scandal. The artist was paid a very hefty sum by the library for his work. Hard working locals thought it was far beyond excessive; the arts community thought it wasn't enough. Harmony Bay's library board had a fair share of artsy-craftsy members who were acquaintances of the fledgling wood carver. His name was now public knowledge by way of the polished bronze plaque beneath the dangling sculpture commemorating him and his work. They pushed through the vote for the expenditure in short order. The community responded with letters of outrage to the editor. Artists, mainly considered aloof, snobby elitists by the blue-collars, retorted that public art was vital for society. Those who worked the waters with aching backs and calloused hands argued spending hardearned dollars to pay taxes for phony finfish was beyond wasteful. They felt the money could have been better spent by replenishing the library's books. After all, that was the business the library was supposed to be in. Some old timers guffawed the artwork was idiotic. They said not all of the depicted species swam together at the same time. Dory remained diplomatic. She knew better than to enter into those discussions, but noted the mobile gave a completely new meaning to the word *circulation* desk. Nonetheless, in the final analysis, the fish culled from the forest pursued each other through the air every day at the whim of the thermostat.

Dory glanced at the clock noticing it was almost three. James would be dropped off soon by the school bus for his group guitar lesson with Winton Hector. It was time for her turn, along with Mrs. Lanscome, to staff the desk underneath the circling fish while other employees took their coffee break. From her desk in the reference department, Dory moved toward the main entrance. She passed a group of boisterous teens chatting on their cell phones.

Mrs. Lanscome shushed them, pointing to the sign that forbade cell phone use in the library. She then pointed at the guilty and gave a single word command, "*Outside!*" Rather than being driven out into the drizzle the offenders opted to holster their phones. They moved along quietly, waving at Dory McDonough, their favorite librarian. Harmony Bay's teenage girls knew that Dory would always go out of her way to help them with assignments. And, she took the time to give compliments or constructive criticism about their outfits. More importantly, Dory helped them research the colleges that were recommended by the girl's guidance counselors. They were high school students who were at the library for after school help from a number of mentors, mostly retired folks like Fred Lanscome. "She's so cool," a teenage girl with hair the color of recently split golden oak said and motioned toward Dory. "She's so awesome. Maybe she'll help *me* pick out a college."

A school bus pulled up in front of the main entrance and unloaded James and six other children from Harmony Bay Elementary School. Each struggled beneath backpacks and rain slickers. James finally scurried in the door. He gave his mother a hello and a goodbye all in one breath and trotted to the community room. Dory wondered how his day was. *What was new? Any homework? Any new friends?* It would all have to wait until later.

Dory got busy scanning in the barcodes of a pile of returned books. Each book made a lively chirp as it passed through the red scanning beam, signaling the library patron had returned the book on time. Methodically, she flipped open each book at the back cover. Chirp, chirp, chirp. Without missing a beat, and without looking up, Dory grasped three more books that were placed in front of her. She placed the first of the trio under the laser. The machine emitted an audible, irritating *aaaant*.

"I'm sorry, this book is overdue," Dory said. Still not looking up, she noticed the label stated the book was part of the inter-county library lending system. She started the process on the next book. Again, the machine produced the unpleasant sound.

"Yeah, I know. I got shipwrecked and couldn't get 'em back in time."

Dory looked up for the first time and saw it was the fishing advisor from Hirsh's Hardware, who was also her first customer at Molly's last Saturday. She eyed him up and down. He looked altogether different wearing a light blue button down oxford shirt with sleeves rolled half way up his forearm, a loosely knotted gold and navy stripped club tie, casual khaki chino pants slightly in need of ironing, Sperry top-sider shoes and no raincoat. His hair was shagged and moppish. The computer monitor told her the patron's name and address, Jacob Kane with a Harmony Bay Post Office box.

"Well, Mr. Kane, I see you're indebted to the library for the princely sum of seventy-five cents."

"Glad to pay it and glad it was a short ship wreck. The charges could have swelled to at least a dollar."

"Yes, welcome back. Molly's and the library would have both lost a customer if you hadn't returned."

"Funny thing about those wrecks. You never know where you'll turn up," he said. Dory smiled as he pulled a dollar bill from his pocket and placed it on the counter.

"Thank you, Mr. Kane. Do you want your change, in small bills, or large?" She winked. They both laughed.

"Just call me Jake."

"Okay, Jake." Dory decided to make a bold move that was a little out of her comfort zone. "You're looking mighty sharp today," she said.

"Oh—these old things? It's just a little outfit I threw together."

The librarian rolled her eyes in an exaggerated fashion at his self-effacing joke, but giggled anyway. *So*, she thought, letting her mind wander, *Mr. Jake Kane, the man of many disguises. Intriguing. What is he doing here on a Tuesday afternoon? He surely isn't wearing the uni-*

form of the Harmony Bay working class today.

Dory rang up the charge on the register and skimmed the quarter change back across the counter.

"Don't spend it all in one place. You're account is all up to date. Now the library police won't be looking for you," she advised.

He winked back and said, "I'm a slow reader, so maybe they will. See you soon." She looked at the books he returned. They were scientific technical books about oceanography, marine biology and advanced calculus. She was even more surprised when he left the counter to join the group of high school kids filing into the conference room.

"I see you've met our scientist," Mrs. Lanscome said to Dory.

"Scientist?"

"Yes, without a doubt. A marine biologist. Rather a fine man. Very good looking too—don't you think?"

"Well, uh, yes. I really don't know."

"Harmony Bay is very proud of him. He's such a big help with the kids."

"Hmmm...tell me more."

Even though they were alone at the desk, Mrs. Lanscome lowered her voice and leaned toward Dory. "Jake Kane started coming out here for the summers as a kid along with his sister and their folks. It seems like it was only yesterday. Anyway, Jake became extremely interested in the stuff in the waters here. He went to college, graduated and became a scientist. A marine biologist. He spent some time in the Caribbean after school, worked his way up the coast and landed back here. He works here now in conjunction with the university studying the brown algae tides and temperatures that affect the shellfish catch. Over the years, the beds became depleted because of the brown tides. It really hurt many people here financially. As you already know, the town literally lives off the bay." Mel Lanscome craned her neck to check on the high school students who now hovered around the entrance to the community room. She held her index finger up to her lips. "He worked through the university to develop a program to re-seed the bay and bring back the shellfish population. Other scientists are working on a cure for the brown blooms. During the summer months, you'll see he has student interns who he works with out here."

The library director stacked returned books then continued. "Jake lives alone aboard an old houseboat down at the marina. He seems content with that. And he has that big old former lobster boat the *Sea Horse* that he uses for his work. Fred tells me he has it outfitted with all sorts of electronic gear. I don't think he goes out past the point much. Then again, not many do unless they're going out for tuna or sharks.

Jake never married, or at least, hasn't married yet. It was a sad story. There was a girl in his life, his college sweetheart. They were engaged some twelve or thirteen years ago. Abigail, yes, Gail. That was her name. They were madly in love with each other. After college, she decided to see the world a little and try to improve it while she was out there. She was on a humanitarian mission. Haiti, I think it was. The plane was small, it went down in the ocean—no one survived." Mrs. Lanscome looked at Dory, who was running books through the scanner, to see if she still had her attention. "When Jake got the news, understandably he was devastated. It was a Saturday morning. He went to Molly's and sat by the window alone. It took him a long time to deal with it. He thinks he's over it, but it's easy to see that he's still not. Fred, the baymen and the others rallied around him and pulled him through. However, every Saturday ever since that fateful day, he's returned to Molly's to sit at the same table alone. Sort of his tradition. Maybe he thinks about a lot of things as he looks out over the bay. Don't know why he hasn't landed another catch yet. I just don't know. Although... there's been a few nibbles over the years."

Mrs. Lanscome let Dory absorb the words. "We're lucky to have him here at the library. He and Fred mentor the kids in science and math and help them with their college applications. Some of these kids are the first ones in their family to attend college. Jake is a little more well rounded in science. Fred is a little sharper on the math."

"Not when it comes to leaving a tip," Dory quipped.

Puzzle pieces cascaded together for Dory. Now she felt a little ashamed of herself for prejudging the guy. Moreover, she understood the long path it took to heal a broken heart. Dory continued her thought process. *Hmmm, an intellectual and forthright member of the community.* She couldn't decide if living on the houseboat was eccentric or if he really needed to be that close to the water. Him sitting at the table alone every Saturday was romantic, but he really needed to move on. The thought caught her by surprise as she recognized herself in the same situation.

"Dorothy? Are you still with me?"

She snapped out of her trance of deep contemplation. "Sorry, Mrs. Lanscome."

"You okay, dear?"

"Sure, never better."

"Anyway, quite the guy. Don't you think?"

"Interesting, to say the least."

"Yes, we most often see him in church on Sunday, usually in the off-season. During the summer, I think his work, and supervising those college kids, keeps him tied up on Sunday mornings. I'm sure the Lord takes it all into account. Still, it's kind of sad to see him there by himself all the time."

It was all coming together for Dory. Mrs. Lanscome was obviously trying to set her up with this eligible bachelor. It also occurred to her why Molly had her wait on Jake's table. It was okay with her. They were only looking out for her best interests. If they didn't think Jake Kane was a good man, and a possible good match for her, they never would've brought it up. Surely there was no harm done as far as she was concerned. Dory was a little surprised at herself that she felt put out when she learned about him being busy on Sundays, her only day off. In her opinion, the jury was still out, but the verdict could be turned in any minute. Dory considered that maybe she should start going to church more often.

With coffee break time finished for Shirley and Louise, they returned to their posts at the front desk to manage the ebb and flood of books under the watchful eyes of the fish. James emerged from the community room beaming from ear to ear. A black guitar case was slung over his shoulder. His backpack dragged on the floor behind him as Dory returned to her desk.

"You're done early. What have you got there?" she asked.

"My backpack."

"No, over your shoulder."

"A guitar."

"Whose guitar?"

"It belongs to Mr. Hector."

"Why do you have it?" Questioning James was becoming a full time job.

"To practice with. He loaned it to me to take home so I could practice."

"I see. Take good care of it and don't let it out of your sight while you're here."

"Okay, Mom."

"You should make him a thank you card."

"Okay, Mom."

"Got homework?"

"Yep."

"Anything new?"

"Nope."

"Go over to the study area and do your homework. When you're finished, you can go on the computers. Leave the guitar here with me until it's time to go. Okay?"

"Okay."

Dory was glad that the library had computers for James to use. They didn't have one at home. Although the internet wasn't the same as books, it did offer opportunities for learning. She realized computers were an essential tool in today's world. Anybody who wasn't proficient in their use would be left behind. Dory took several computer courses in college and was now recognizing the value of that knowledge in her work. Never considering herself a computer wizard, she knew more than enough to stay on top of the kids. Library pages kept a close eye on the kids to make sure they didn't surf past the filters to something inappropriate. Still, she always made it a point to check the browsing history while the kids were still there.

Work was finished for the day. Dory logged off of her terminal, put her things away in her desk and went looking for James with the guitar slung over her shoulder. She found him in the computer room engrossed in a video presentation about the actions of tectonic plates.

"Time to head home, buddy," she said. James didn't resist as he sometimes did. He was hungry and wanted to get home to dinner.

"Hungry?" Dory asked

"Very."

"Did you have a snack?"

"Yup."

Dory knew it was going to be a while until they got home. With no leftovers available to pop in the microwave, dinner wouldn't be early.

"I have a great idea," she said.

"What?"

"Let's celebrate! As of today, we've been here two months. I say we go straight to Aldo's and have pizza. What do you think?"

James didn't need a second invitation or convincing. He was already headed to the front door with his mother in casual pursuit. Dory rounded the bend and entered the lobby to see Jake Kane by the main entrance chatting happily with Maureen Donnelly. *What was this all about?* she wondered. Dory approached, trying to overhear their conversation.

"Sure, any weekend, any time. Just let me know," Jake said.

"Thanks, Jake. I'd love to take you up on the offer," replied the smiling schoolteacher.

Dory's heart sank as she listened to the exchange. She decided maybe Miss Donnelly wasn't all that cute or athletic. She was jealous.

Jake was the first to notice Dory. "I didn't know you played the guitar," he said.

"I don't. It's for James."

"I didn't know James plays the guitar."

"Well, he doesn't. At least not yet."

Miss Donnelly excused herself, leaving with a cheery goodbye. "I'm late for my yoga class in the community room," she said.

"What a great teacher. She's very good with the kids," Jake said.

"I've heard the same about you," Dory said.

Jake sheepishly put his hands in his pockets. "Well, I'm glad to help these kids out if I can. It's the least I can do. You know, like the sign says—*Each one, Teach one.*"

"So tell me, how *is* Miss Donnelly?" Dory said, and raised an eyebrow.

"Oh, she's okay. She asked about borrowing my kayak. I told her no problem. I never use it. It's sitting out behind Fred Lanscome's garage.

I told her she could use it anytime—she should just let me know in case somebody else wanted to borrow it. I get these crazy college kids out here for the summers and sometimes it's best to keep them busy. You can't get in much trouble in a kayak. And they burn up a lot of energy." Jake leaned against the wall while his hands imitated paddling a kayak.

"I tell you what... if you and your son want to take it out, that's fine with me. It's a two-man ocean kayak. Just promise me he'll have a life vest on." Dory noticed he was speaking more rapidly than she had ever heard before. He seemed a little excited. "You can put in right from Fred's backyard. He doesn't mind a bit. I think he likes people stopping by. It keeps Mrs. Lanscome out of his hair for a little while, what little he has."

"Thank you, that's very generous of you," Dory said.

"No problem at all. I hear you're great with the kids, too."

"Thank you." Now it was Dory's turn to be sheepish. "Let me go feed this kid before he implodes." The three headed to the door. Jake stopped to check the community bulletin board.

The day's drizzle became a steady evening rain as they made their way to their cars. Dory placed the guitar in the back seat then got in and turned the key. Click, click, click was the only response as the starter solenoid tried to complete the connection with too little voltage.

She had left the lights on.

"Oh no," she said to James and rested her forehead on the steering wheel. "I am not a ditz." She repeated it over and over. "I may be overworked and run ragged, but I'm not a ditz." James didn't seem to care. She tried the key again; the clicks came farther apart and stopped. A red Jeep pulled up along side just as she was about to go back out into the rain and return to the library for help. It was a canvassed topped two-seater with heavy-duty all-terrain tires and fog lamps mounted below the front bumper. Dory rolled down her window to see Jake sticking his head out of the Jeep's window.

"Hey Lady, did you call for road service?" Jake said.

"I think the battery is dead."

"No worries. These things happen. Jake's road service will get you going. Stay in the car."

"It's raining!"

"It's only water."

Dory was mortified. He exited his vehicle coatless. The man was getting soaked. She tried to protest his action to no avail. Dory turned to James. "You have your slicker on. See if you can help him. He's getting drenched." James thought this was a novel idea and hopped out of the car.

Jake removed his tie, threw it in the front passenger seat of the Jeep and got back in. He pulled it up nose to nose with the dead car, left his engine running and set the parking brake. James stood beside him as he opened the hoods of both cars. Jake went to the rear of the Jeep and lifted the rear hatch, extracting a snakelike set of bright orange jumper cables with two red clamps and two black clamps. Returning to the front of his vehicle, he asked James if he ever jump-started a car before. James replied he hadn't.

"Okay, here's how you do it," Jake said.

"You got to remember safety comes first when you do this. You leave the jumper car running. Next, take the red cable and attach it to the positive post. And—don't stick your head in the fan. Sometimes it will be marked with red. If not—it'll have a plus sign or say *pos*. You always do positive first. Anyway, it's always the bigger post. Make sure you've got a good connection. Then you go and clamp the other end onto the dead car. Like this. Then you go back to your jumper car and clamp on the black cable to the negative post. Okay, here's where the safety stuff comes in. Okay, you with me?"

"Yeah, okay."

"Take the other black clamp and attach it to the engine block of the dead car. You might get a little spark. Don't worry about it. Just means you've got everything hooked up. Don't hook up to the dead car negative battery post, because if you get a spark over there, it's not good. You could get an explosion. Got it? Here take the clamp."

Jake pointed to an engine manifold bolt where James should make the connection. James used two hands to open the heavy-duty jaw and snapped it on the bolt. It caused a little spark as he made the connection. James flinched.

"Okay, there's your spark. Perfect. You're all hooked up. Go in the Jeep and rev the motor a little."

"Who me?"

"Yeah you, Mr. Mechanic."

James scurried to the driver's door and hopped in. His foot barely reached the gas pedal, which he eventually stabbed, causing the engine to race wildly.

"Hey, not so much!" Jake hollered. "Okay, Dory—try it now."

James let up on the gas. Dory turned her key and the engine sprang to life. Jake removed the positive cable clamp from her car and the idle speed of the Jeep returned to normal. He stood by her window as he coiled up the orange snakes.

"I am so very grateful," she said. "You're sopping wet. I'm sorry I don't have a towel or a blanket or something dry for you. Are you going to be all right?"

"No problem, I'm good. Glad I could help." Jake said. His eyes were still bright behind his rain-spattered glasses. His hair was like matted straw. "Keep the motor running for about fifteen minutes. You'll be okay. I'll have somebody check up on you to make sure you got home all right."

"We were headed to Aldo's," Dory said, trying to deliver a subtle hint.

"Let her run for fifteen minutes and shut the lights off," he said. "You might want to have Dave Small test the battery tomorrow."

"I am not a ditz. Honest." She felt it was the least she could say in light of the fact that Jake was waterlogged.

"Hey, don't worry about it. It happens to everybody. At least you weren't shipwrecked."

James exited the Jeep and Jake shook his hand. "Good job, my man. Thanks for the help. Give me five." Jake said. The two slapped hands in mid-air.

"Hey you're welcome. That was fun. That's a cool Jeep. How fast does it go? "

Dory thanked him again, rolled up her window and rolled out of the parking lot. Her windshield wipers slapped out a steady beat as she and James turned down the narrow street toward Aldo's pizza.

From inside the warmth of the Jeep, Jake dialed Harmony Bay's police headquarters on his cell phone. He reached his friend, Luke Hewes, the dispatcher. "Hey Lukey, 'ol buddy. Yeah… it's Jake. I need your help on something."

"Hey there, clam man, what 'er you up ta?"

"Hey, Bozo. Just finished helping out that new library lady. She had a dead battery. I think everything is okay now."

"Okay, Jake, what can I do for *you?*"

"I thought maybe one of your boys could take a ride out on North Road in the next hour or so in between donut breaks to make sure she didn't get stranded."

"Say please."

"Okay, *please*. And, please tell me this isn't going to cost me a bucket of steamers and two beers at Molly's."

"Hey, no problem, clam man. We'll take care of it. We're here to protect and serve. I'll get somebody out there."

"Thanks. How about we go out and try for some stripers in a couple of weeks?"

"Sounds good. Mamma does love her striped bass. Let me get back to work."

"Work?" Jake laughed. "Hey Luke, don't strain yourself. Catch up with you soon. Thanks."

Jake shifted into first, let out the clutch… and headed for dry clothes.

Chapter 11

Spring rains charged with ozone brought freshness to the air. Dory welcomed the arrival of the daffodils that dabbed the first colors of spring's palette on the landscape. Tree buds that would soon explode into emerald canopies began to thicken. Leaden clouds, the remnant of the ephemeral storm, now slid from west to east across the bay and out to sea where they met the rising sun. Early morning showers now gave way to a glorious day. She drank it all in on the way to the library for another day's work.

She had stopped at Dave Small's repair shop to have her car's battery tested as Jake had suggested. After performing an open circuit voltage test and a load test, Dave asserted that the battery probably had one more hard winter left in it, much to her delight. "Don't leave the lights on. Next time you may not be so lucky to have a Good Samaritan nearby who's willing to stand in the rain," Dave said.

Morning quickly became afternoon. James would be delivered to the library along with an influx of other students. He arrived last, as usual, straggling behind the others. Since the day blossomed into a sun-drenched delight, James arrived with his raincoat stuffed into his backpack. Mrs. Lanscome greeted him as he swung the front door open. "Good afternoon, James McDonough."

"Hi, Mrs. Lanscome."

"You don't seem too chipper, skipper. What's the matter?"

"Oh, nothing."

"Well, why don't you go see your mom? I know it will make *her* happy."

"Yes, Mrs. Lanscome." James took exaggerated giant steps across the floor toward his mother's desk, placing a foot in the center of each large floor tile. Dory noted his dour mood when he arrived.

"You don't seem like your pleasant self today."

"I guess I'm bored."

"Right. I see. How unfortunate for you. Anything I can do for you?"

"Nope."

"Hmm, I have an idea. Would you like to run an errand for me?"

"Okay. Where?" James responded without enthusiasm.

"I need some things at the drugstore. Since the weather is so beautiful, I thought you might like the chance to be outside. You know, take a walk there."

"Okay. What do you need?"

"Here, I'll write a list, but I'll also call ahead to Kelly's Pharmacy and let them know what brands I want. They'll find them for you. Okay?"

"Okay, sure."

Dory pulled a twenty-dollar bill from her purse. She handed it and the shopping list, which showed toothpaste, shampoo, and a box of facial tissue, to her son. "Stuff it deep in your pocket," she instructed him. James complied. "Okay, you know where Mr. Kelly's is. Stay on the sidewalk and bring back the change. And— by the way, pick out a candy bar for yourself while you're there."

"Yes!" James shouted. He held both arms up in a touchdown signal.

"Shush. You're in the library."

James picked up a short branch as he headed down the street, dragging it along the white picket fences along the way. The boy was delighted to hear the rat-tat-tat as it plucked each picket and post. He observed the rainbows in the large street puddles created by oils dripped from various passing vehicles and decided to eradicate their delicate patterns by jumping from the curb, landing feet first in the pool's epicenter. After a few attacks he thought the better of it, recalling his mother's warning to stay out of the street. Crying gulls that traced figure eights in the briny wind alighted in the puddles that James recently vacated. They pecked the dirty water hoping to find something edible.

He arrived at the pharmacy. Its sign dangled from black iron chains beneath the eave of the white clapboard building, proudly declaring,

Harmony Bay Pharmacy & Compounders, Established 1895, Daniel Kelly RPh, Proprietor. James swung the door open wide. Mr. Kelly stood directly in his path.

"Ah, hello, James, we've been expecting you," Mr. Kelly said.

James was startled, recoiling slightly, as he replied. "Hello, Mr. Kelly. Did my mom call?"

"Yes, she did. I have everything all ready for you. Although, I understand that you need to make a selection for yourself."

James looked at the rack of chocolate bars and assorted candies and became frustrated by his inability to come to an immediate decision. He picked one up. Then placing it down, he chose another. This process repeated itself over and over until he settled on one that assured the consumer that there was heavenly dark chocolate and peanuts in every bite. James paid with the twenty. Mr. Kelly thanked him for his purchase. James thanked him for the change and put it in his pocket.

He left the drugstore, impulsively deciding to take a circuitous route back to the library that took him past Hirsch's Hardware and the other village shops. He ate the chocolate bar as he walked. James approached the hardware store and saw Billy's flare side pickup parked in front with its hood open. Billy and Winton were leaning on the red, bulbous front fenders, peering into the engine compartment. James walked up to the front bumper between the two men. "Well good afternoon, young man," Billy said.

"Hey, James, wut's happenin'?" Winton said.

"What are you looking at?" James asked in reply.

Billy spoke first, using his clipped and proper enunciation, "My vehicle was very hard to start today, James. Once I did getting it going, it ran very poorly. It had no, how do you say it? *Oomph.*" Lenny Hirsch joined them at curbside. Standing with hands on hips, he greeted James.

"Hello, James, good to see you out in the sunshine."

Winton entered the conversation. "Billy, looks like y'all got some problems," he said. "Mebe moisture up under da distributor cap from all da fog an rain we been havin'. I be right back." Winton went into the hardware store, returning a few minutes later with two different size screwdrivers, a hammer, a roll of gray duct tape, a spray can of WD40 and a rag.

He twisted out the distributor cap hold down screws with the longer screwdriver. When Winton picked up the black plastic cap and turned it upside down, the coil wire that was plugged into its center fell free. "There's problem numba one. Loose coil why-uh." Winton continued to examine the underside of the cap, noticing tiny water droplets. "Here's problem numba two, Billy. You got condensation trapped up in there." He sprayed WD40 into the cap and wiped it dry with the rag. Now using the smaller screwdriver, Winton pried back the ignition breaker point and let it snap shut. "Here's problem numba three; you points is all closed up."

Winton whistled as he went about his work. His audience looked on. Taking the duct tape and tearing off a short length, he jammed the coil wire back in its tower and wrapped the tape around the boot, securing it in place.

He took a break for a moment to stretch and straighten his back. Winton told Hirsch, "Bump it over till I say okay." Hirsch obliged. Reaching in, he turned the key. The engine turned over once, then twice. Winton called out, "Hold on!" He saw the breaker-point rubbing block now rested on the high point of the distributor cam lobe. "Anybody got a match book?" The onlookers looked at each other and then rummaged through their pockets hoping one might appear there. In unison they said, "No."

"Okay den, anybody got anythin' *about* as thick as a match book cova?" Lenny Hirsch offered him a Hirsch's Hardware business card. Winton nodded and snatched it away. Once again leaning over the fender, Winton bent the card into an L shape and inserted its edge in-between the ignition points. With his other hand, he deftly manipulated the setscrew tension for the points, adjusting the distance between them to the thickness of the card. When he was satisfied, he tightened the setscrew. His whistling now increasing in volume and tempo. He reattached the distributor cap and closed the hood. Turning to James he asked, "Where ya headed to?"

"Back to the library."

"Okay, let's go fo' a test drive."

"You're all done?"

"Yep."

"With only a screwdriver, a hammer, duct tape, WD40 and a rag?"

"Yep. Back when things was simple you could fix stuff with a hamma an a screwdriver. And—whateva needed to be stuck togetha y'all just used duct tape and if it needed un-stickin' ya used WD40. Today we can save da hamma for bangin' nails."

Hirsch added, "Everything used to be simple in the good old days. A man's word was worth something. Around here that still holds true in most cases." Billy stroked his beard and nodded in agreement as James and Winton got in the truck. Billy unknowingly dispensed wisdom or conveyed a thought by the simple act of stroking his beard.

———

A grandfather or great-grandfather figure for some, and without doubt, a Santa figure for others, Billy was a puzzle with as many pieces and twists as a bag of pretzels. He wore the hats of outdoorsman, farmer, fisherman, carver, craftsman, erudite closet intellectual and philosophizer. Billy never showed raw outward emotion, therefore, some folks often mistook his quiet nature for weakness. Following an unconventional dress code known only to himself, he was polite and properly mannered to the extreme. Although he was kindly and sensitive, wise and all knowing, Billy was physically powerful enough to split hefty lengths of firewood clean through with the single blow of an axe. It was common lore that years ago, while shoeing a horse's rear hoof, it became impatient—or annoyed, giving Billy a kick. Billy walked to the front of the animal and clocked him with a closed fist. The horse shook off the blow and humbly lowered his head. He never gave his farrier a hard time again.

His recluse nature, and living a frugal hermitic life on Pencil Hill, caused great speculation about his identity. Even though, everybody loved Billy and always asked him for his opinion. After hearing an advice seeker's question, he would stroke his snowy whiskers and make a statement without supplying an answer. The inquirer then usually wondered why he hadn't thought of the evident solution himself. Nobody knew how old he was or if he was ever married. And nobody ever asked.

The truck started with the first turn of the key and ran smoothly. Winton rolled down the window and told Billy, "Stop by Dave Small's tomorra'. Git him to fix yo'self up wit a new distributor cap an sparkin' plug wires. Y'all should be peachy-keen afta dat."

"Peachy-keen?" inquired Billy. "I see. Is that me or my vehicle?"

Winton laughed as he shifted into first gear and let out the clutch. James watched Winton depress the clutch pedal and pull the gearshift from first to second. He was amazed how well Winton could manipulate the pedal with his prosthetic leg.

"This has a stick shift like Jake's Jeep. My mom's car has a per-nundle," he said.

"A wut…? A pernundle?"

"Yeah, down there it says, P-R-N-D-L. Per nun dle," James remarked and pointed to the shift knob.

"Yep, it works pretty much da same as Jake's," Winton said. He downshifted for a stop sign. "Jes think of it as a big 'ol letta H on da floor." With the clutch in, he pushed the shifter to first. "Heeya's first gear. Dat's fo gittin' started. When you need to go a little faster, ya pull it straight back an it's in sccond, cross dat H an push foe wahd and y'all's in third fo highway drivin'. I don't know dat Billy uses third too much any mo'. Pull it straight back from there an, in this buggy, it's reverse." Winton demonstrated all of the positions and then left the stick shift in neutral. "Righ' heeya in da middle, where da H crosses, is neutral. Ya can't git in no trouble there. But, if y'all is on a hill, an y'all is in neutral an ya don't step on da brakes—ya'll will roll. Heeya, feel where neutral is."

"Who, *me*?"

"Anybody else in here— 'cept you an' me?"

"Uh, no," he said. James jiggled the shifter as Winton had done.

"Okay, heeya we go. I'm gonna do da clutch pedal an you is gonna shift." James shook his head in disbelief. "Each time you shift you hafta push in da clutch pedal. When ya'll are fixin'to let that clutch pedal up—

ya feels a lil' viber ation. Dat's when ya know yo at the point to let er out nice an easy. Ya gotta let er slip a little or yo gonna buck. Okay, first gear!" Winton placed his hand over James' for emphasis, pushing it from neutral toward the dashboard. Firmly planted in first, Winton released the clutch pedal and they started to roll. "Now, second!" he said, pulling James' hand and the shifter straight back. They repeated this maneuver at several stop signs. Actually, it was the same stop signs as they went in circles around the block. Winton pulled up in front of the red brick library to drop James off. "Say hey, there's yo first drivin' lesson," he said. "When y'all fixin' to park, ya push in the clutch an slip 'er into first, then shut off da motor. If y'all let up on da clutch before shuttin' off da motor—yo gonna have a bronkin' buck on yo hands. If yo on a hill—pull back on this here hand brake too so's ya don't roll."

"Wow, really? That was fun! Can we do it again?"

"Well, mebe 'notha time. Don't tell Billy you was drivin' his truck. And, mebe wait a while til ya tell yo moma ya was drivin'."

"That's a deal. How long should I wait?"

"Hmm, I'd say wait till you's 'bout—twenty-one. *Okay*? Gimme five."

Dory noticed an improvement in James' disposition when he returned to the library. "I see a walk on a nice day and a candy bar put a smile back on your face," she said.

"I was learning how to fix cars."

"Really? You've been learning a lot about cars the last couple of days. Well, that could come in handy." Dory watched as James' appearance slowly became serious again.

"What's wrong James?"

"I miss Gram and Gramps."

"I do too."

"Will they come to visit?"

"Being retired, they're on a tight budget. I don't know how soon they could come up."

"Gramps would like it here. You know, with the fishing and all."

"You're right about that. Let's call them when we get home and say hello."

"Sounds good."

"We still have a few minutes before I can leave. In the meantime, go on the computer and make them up a nice card. They'll like that."

"Maybe we can go visit them?"

"I'd love to. But it will be a little while until we're able to."

"I understand."

James left for the computer room. Dory looked up from her desk to see Jake Kane standing before her.

Chapter 12

"Hi, Dory. I heard your car's battery passed with flying colors," Jake said.

"Yes, thank you for your help last evening. That was very kind of you." Again, Dory contemplated how Jake knew everything that went on in town.

"Wasn't a problem. At least we got you going."

"Oh, and thank you for teaching James about the battery jumping thing. It's always good to know how. Is there something I can help you with Mr. Kane?" Dory asked in a demure, humble tone.

"Truth is, I don't have your phone number. Since you're new to the bay, you're not in the phone book. I really didn't want to bother you at work."

"So, what's up?"

"Well—I'd like to invite you to celebrate Shark Day with me this Saturday evening."

"*Shark Day?*"

"Yeah, it's a tradition."

Dory ran the term Shark Day through her head. She hadn't seen anything on the bulletin board about it or in the Harmony Bay Gazette's community calendar. She decided to proceed cautiously.

"Well, how does one celebrate Shark Day?"

"Uh—I was thinking of a movie and a special dinner."

"Are you asking me out on a date?" Dory felt herself beginning to blush.

"Sure, if you want to call it that. Otherwise, let's just call it a Shark Day celebration with the pleasure of your company. Unless of course, you'll be tied up with washing your hair." Jake motioned to the contents of the Kelly's Pharmacy bag that had spilled out onto her desk.

"Oh, excuse me," she said, pushing the toiletries back in the bag. Dory raised her eyebrows. "I do have my son to worry about. I'll have to see if my sitter is available."

"Not to worry. Ol' Jake has secured the child tending services of ol' Billy himself."

"Billy?" Dory didn't know whether to laugh or groan. "Has he ever done this before?"

"Billy has probably looked after half of the kids on the bay at one time or another—including *me*."

"Then I suppose he comes with a good reference."

"Yeah—just pull out a few of those old classic black and white DVD movies like *Mr. Smith Goes to Washington*, or *Casablanca* for Billy to watch after James goes to bed. You have 'em in stock here. Billy loves that stuff. And, oh yeah, he'll fix dinner for James. The price is right. We barter favors and stuff back and forth all the time. He likes his payment in scallops."

"James likes classics. We watch them together."

"Perfect. Invitation accepted? I'm thinking we should do this early. You know, catch an early show up west."

"Might he like a book?" Dory's mind was elsewhere. She was still startled about unexpectedly being asked out.

"He's read a million of 'em. You know, not having a TV and all."

Dory absentmindedly coiled her raven hair around her fingers while Jake waited with anticipation for an answer. "Yes, early would be good. I do have to work at Molly's on Saturday morning. What time are we thinking of?" she said.

"I'll pick you up at five. Casual is fine. I'm thinking jeans and a sweater for me." He added his comment hastily in case Dory was about to change her mind.

"Well thank you, Mr. Kane. This is a lovely invitation. Do you know where we live?" Dory now showed a faint, dry smile.

"Sure—out at the end of the peninsula. I know the area well."

"Maybe I should meet you here so you won't have to drive all the way out there."

"Won't hear of it. Jake's limo service is scheduled for a pick up on North Road at 17:00 hours."

"Will you be at Molly's for breakfast Saturday?"

"Yeah, unless I get shipwrecked."

After he left, Dory Googled Shark Day along with Harmony Bay and a few other keywords. Nothing. Shark tournaments in August yes, but nothing about celebrating Shark Day or nothing under Saturday's date combined with sharks. *Well, he can be a little zany sometimes*, Dory reflected. It was puzzling, but she'd have to wait until Saturday to find out more. She was getting jittery and didn't know why. That wasn't like her.

—◄▰▰▰◊▰▰▰►—

James dialed the phone as his mother recited the number. A women's voice answered on the third ring. "Gram, it's me, James."

"What a pleasant surprise. How *are* you?"

"I'm good. When are you coming to visit?" Dory shot him a reprimanding glance.

"Well, James, we'd like to come soon. But… it *is* a big trip for us."

"Gramps would like it here. There's boats and fishing."

"Yes, I know. I've heard all about it. I've been getting your cards, too."

The exchange went on for a few more minutes before James asked, "Do you want to talk to Mom?"

Satisfied that things were well with Gram and Gramps, he handed Dory the receiver. "James, put the TV on—I won't be long with Gram," Dory said. Mother and daughter exchanged greetings, family news and talked about the weather.

"You sound happy, Dory."

"Things are a little hectic…but good. A local asked me out for this Saturday evening."

"Ah ha, I thought so. I can hear it in your voice. He must be a nice guy."

"He is. He's a scientist who works here on the water. A real gentleman, a sturdy man. People speak highly of him."

"Any special plans?"

"Yes, it's a Shark Day celebration —I think."

"Shark Day—?"

"That's what *I* said."

"Call me Sunday and tell me all about it."

※

When the week dwindled down to Friday, Dory went to the library's DVD inventory and checked out copies of *To Kill a Mockingbird* featuring Gregory Peck and *The Maltese Falcon* with Humphrey Bogart as Sam Spade. She also selected a movie for James.

Friday became Saturday morning, which saw Dory arrive a little earlier than usual at Molly's. Even so, already seated at his usual spot was her solitary diner. Without bothering to ask, she approached Jake's table with a full pot of coffee.

"Good morning, sir. My name is Dory. I will be your server this morning. Coffee— yes?" They looked at each other for the duration of more than several heartbeats before he answered.

"Yes, please," he said. Snatching up the mug in its upside down position, Dory began to pour without taking her eyes off him.

"No!" Jake shouted as he jumped up from his seat. At the same instant Dory realized she had never turned the cup over to its upright position before pouring. Once the hot liquid hit her hand, porcelain and steaming coffee plummeted to the floor.

"Oh my God," she said over the clatter. "Don't you dare laugh."

He countered facetiously, "Clean-up on aisle six."

"I am *so* sorry. I feel like such an idiot."

"Are you okay?" Jake asked.

"I'm fine. Let me clean this up and get a clean apron."

"Let me help you." Jake was on his knees mopping the spilled coffee with his napkin.

"I should be doing that. I'll get in trouble."

"No you won't. I promise."

"*Please, Jake, no.*"

"Okay, all cleaned up. Only casualty is one coffee cup. Life goes on."

"Thank you. I am an idiot."

"No you're not. Stop saying that. It was an accident. Promise me we'll laugh about this later," Jake said.

"Okay. It's a deal."

After a new apron and a new cup, this time properly filled, Jake polished off his usual hearty Saturday morning meal. And, as usual, over tipped. The morning rolled quickly into the afternoon.

Promptly at five, Jake's Jeep crunched over the crushed seashells in the driveway. He was pleased to see Billy's truck already parked out front. Angus was lying in the sand by the front porch door. Jake patted Angus on the head then knocked on the outer screen door, called out, and then entered the porch. Jake stood on the porch as James opened the inner door to the home, which released a delicious aroma. "Billy is making us spaghetti for dinner. Want to eat here?" James asked.

"Sorry, buddy. Some other time, there's other plans for tonight. To tell you the truth, it sure smells good. Maybe we should… " Jake's voice trailed off when Dory entered the living room.

She looked stunning in a casual sort of way. Her ensemble included a long denim skirt with a single row of buttons up the front and a hemline just below her knee, brown leather boots with a fashionable heel, heather mock turtleneck, and a dove gray velvet jacket. Dory carefully did her dark hair in a French braid. Judicious application of lipstick, eye makeup, simple dangling silver earrings, and a thin silver necklace complimented her features.

Jake eyed his date up and down. "Wow, you look marvelous."

"Thank you. Sometimes a girl can't be too careful about what she wears on Shark Day." If James blurted out that she glommed more than half of her outfit from the racks of the Good Will store back in the city, Dory would have fainted.

"Gee, I think I'm underdressed," Jake said.

"You said casual. You look fine," Dory said. She did like the way he looked in a pullover crewneck fishermen's knit sweater and only slightly faded fitted blue jeans. "James, come give mommy a hug. You and Billy have a nice evening. I have my cell phone on. If you need me, call me. Be good."

"No problem, Mom. Have a good time." James uttered as he hugged his mother and then scooted off.

Jake opened the Jeep's passenger door, holding it open for Dory he said, "We'll be heading up west for the movie."

"What about the theater in town?"

"It isn't very nice. We'll go up west to the state-of-the-art theater. I want you to enjoy yourself *and* I want you to still speak to me after the show."

"It's that bad?" Jake slid into the driver's seat, shifted into reverse and crunched back out of the driveway.

"Yeah. Your feet stick to the floor and the seats can give you head lice."

"Eewh."

"It's a shame," Jake explained as he aimed south on North Road. "We were supposed to have a beautiful new multiplex on that land on the edge of the village. It was supposed to be built by a developer with no costs to the town. It's the property with the vacant buildings on it."

"Yes, I know where you mean. It's not far from the library. What happened?"

"Correct. The mayor's brother owns the theater in the village and he wasn't in on the new deal. If a new movie house comes in, he's finished. As it stands now, most townies make the sixty mile round-trip for movies."

"If the public isn't supporting the mayor's brother's movie house, why isn't he finished already?"

"Good question. At the moment, I'm not sure what the answer is."

The land flattened as they left the upheavals of the coastal moraine. After the forty-minute drive through the countryside highlighted by polite conversation about how the rest of their days went, the couple arrived at the cinema. Shark Day did not come up, primarily because Dory didn't bring it up. Jake purchased two tickets then offered Dory popcorn and the usual assortment of snacks. She declined, telling Jake it would spoil her appetite. She didn't want to disappoint him at dinner. The two arrived early enough at the first run romantic comedy to get good seats in the theater. It eventually sold out.

An unexpected spattering from a spring shower greeted their exit from the theater. Cars sped through the parking lot with flapping wipers. Dory impulsively and unconsciously reached her left hand to his right. Clasping his hand, it felt warm, dry and strong. Surprising herself by her action, she thought about retracting her hand, but chose to keep her grasp. Unfazed by the drops, and surprised by Dory's unexpected hold, Jake escorted her hand-in-hand to the Jeep.

Trusting Jake's judgment, Dory didn't question where the next stop was. Lively review of the movie made the return ride to Harmony Bay pleasant. A three quarter moon began its ascent as the passing shower abated. Returning to town, Jake pulled up in front of Molly's. *How unoriginal*, Dory mused. Dory stopped her thought in mid-process. After all, it was his invitation and she was happy to have a nice evening out with grown-up conversation.

"Gee, look at this place. Never been here before," she teased.

"It's part of the tradition."

"Your tradition for first dates, or for Shark Day?"

"Oh, for Shark Day. For first dates the usual tradition is the local flick house then pizza at Aldo's."

"Oh, I see." Dory didn't know whether or not to be flattered.

Still being the off-season, the restaurant was only half-full. Candles glittered on the tables, light chatter and laughter filled the room. At Jake's request, the hostess showed them to a private booth in the rear dining room off the u-shaped bar. She took their drink orders, an imported beer for him, a Pinot Grigio for her. She told them their waitress, Kaelin, would be with them shortly.

Dory excused herself for the ladies room. Jake took the opportunity to visit the bar where he fist bumped the bartender who burst out in laughter, "Clam-mon! Hello, Mon!"

"Hey, Kenny. How you been?" Jake said.

"Everything be cook n' curry."

"That's great. Haven't seen you in a while."

"No problem, Mon. I see you here wit dat fine, fine lady. Irie!"

"Yeah, we're here to celebrate Shark Day."

Usually very animated, Kenny, with sharp, chiseled features that provided a paradox to his melodic voice, became very quiet as he let the words sink in. His skin shone like polished anthracite. He broke into a broad toothy smile when he spoke. "Ya Mon, Shark Day. Good reason to celebrate. You an dee lady, first round is on me. No problem, Mon."

Returning to the table simultaneously, Dory asked what he was up to.

"Oh, that's Kenny Clarke, an old friend from below the Tropic of Cancer. Just saying hello to the crazy Jamaican."

"I heard you two talking about Shark Day. Okay, I'll bite—no pun intended. What's with Shark Day?"

"Right. Your beverage is compliments of Kenny, in celebration of Shark Day, that is." Dory was growing tired of the shark charade.

"Remind me to thank him." Kaelin delivered the drinks and left two menus with an invitation to let her know when they were ready to order.

"Are you sure you want to hear about this?" Jake asked. She rolled her eyes. "Okay, okay, all right, I'll tell you," he said.

Jake first looked down into the flickering candle and then set his gaze on the candle's reflection in her eyes as he began his tale. "Right out of college I had the opportunity to do research in the Caribbean. My fiancé was doing some save the world work down that way. I figured there might be an easy opportunity for us to spend some time together. Maybe meet at one of the islands. There were seven of us, including Kenny Clarke, aboard a research vessel. It was partially sponsored by NOAA. That's the National Oceanic and Atmospheric Administration."

"Yes, I know. Go on."

"It was a joint venture with NOAA's National Marine Fisheries Service and a few Banana Republic governments. Half of us were studying climate change, tropical depressions and hurricane patterns. The rest of us were studying and tagging fish. We were tagging big fishies that follow the warm Gulf Stream water as part of a sustainable fish for food program. Also, we were researching climatic action on bivalves. That was my gig. Actually, we were trying to see if it affected all wildlife from

Hatteras to Nova Scotia." Dory nodded. She understood.

"You were tagging sharks?"

"No actually, but you're getting warm."

"So, I'm scuba diving looking for specimens, then it happened."

"What happened?"

"I was probing the bottom and I got attacked by a shark."

"You mean on today's date? This is like an anniversary? What kind of shark was it?"

"Yeah, Shark Day is my annual celebration of surviving it. It was a shark with a lot of teeth. Does it really matter what kind it was?" Jake chuckled.

"I'm sorry. I didn't mean to be insensitive."

"It's okay. My sister sends me a funny shark card every year. Anyway, it was a Caribbean reef shark that I startled. They're usually not aggressive. Sometimes they hide in caves or lie on the bottom waiting for prey. I guess he was about six or seven feet long. Even a two-foot shark can inflict a lot of damage. Chances of a shark attacking a human is around one in five million. You have a better chance of getting struck by lightning."

"That's awful. You must have been scared to death."

"I didn't have time to be scared. My dive partner had already left for the surface. I kept trying to punch Mr. Shark in the head, but you know how everything moves in slow motion underwater. I was finally able to keep jabbing my thumb in his big, black eye. He didn't like that and swam off. It was too late. By that time he had shredded me up pretty good."

"Oh my God, Jake. I am so sorry." Dory bit her lip and looked down into her wine.

"I knew I was in bad shape. Sharks can smell one part of mammal blood in up to 100 million parts of water. I didn't want his friends jumping on the buffet line. I knew somehow I had to get back on the boat."

Dory leaned forward in her seat and blinked away tears. "What happened next?"

"Even though we were in less than twenty feet of water, I wasn't able to swim. And I was starting to panic. What I didn't know was that Kenny Clarke," Jake pointed his thumb toward the bar, "saw the whole thing go down. At that depth, the water is still crystal clear. Kenny grabbed a snorkel mask and a spear gun—then fearlessly jumped overboard. I looked up and saw him coming toward me. I was able to detach my weight belt, which started me slowly floating up in a trail of blood." Dory grimaced as she took a deep breath. "Kenny swims down, drops the spear gun and hooks his arm around me. I took off my air supply mouthpiece and gave it to him to get a lung full of fresh air. He dragged my chum producing body to the surface. By then, the rest of the crew was at the gunnels and hauled me up on deck. Kenny put himself at tremendous risk to save me. In reality, he was only on board as a ship's mate and cook."

"Jake, that's incredible. You're lucky to be alive."

"There's a little more to the story about me and crazy Kenny if you want to hear it."

"Sure, go ahead. It's all right."

"Kenny was not only the cook, but was the best on board at first aid stuff. Kenny's parents were healers; his father was a doctor and Kenny's mom was a nurse. That's probably how he knew a lot of first aid stuff. Remember, he's more than a few years younger than me. So at the time— he was really only a kid. They pulled up the anchor and hauled out of there with me leaking my innards all over the deck. On the way to port, they got the authorities on the radio. Kenny took command of the situation, applied a tourniquet to my leg, and used compression to stop the bleeding in my side. There were a few other love bites, but they weren't life threatening. An ambulance met us at the dock and rushed me to a Jamaican hospital. *That* scared me. Kenny was on board the ambulance, never taking his focus off the tourniquet the whole time."

"That is amazing."

Jake took another sip of his beer. "So…we arrived at the hospital. And who's there? Kenny's father, Doctor Clarke. I underestimated the situation. His old man was a skilled surgeon and patched me up real well. After I was discharged, I still wasn't in any kind of shape to take care of myself. So, Kenny picked me up at the hospital and took me to their home where his mom, his sisters and him took care of me. Really a lovely place on a hill overlooking the ocean."

"How did Kenny end up here at Molly's in Harmony Bay?"

"Right. Well, Kenny didn't want to pursue a medical career. His folks told him they didn't care what he did as long as he went to college. He could go wherever he wanted to go, they didn't mind. Kenny didn't see a bright future in Jamaica.

It was around then I wanted to come back north. I found out that a wealthy guy was looking for a crew to sail his yacht up the coast and deliver it to his yacht club up near here. So, I'm thinking, wow— a free ride home. Especially because I was really broke. He hired me on and I needed a crew so I made a deal with Kenny—who's a hell of a good sailor—and his family."

"Which was?"

"Kenny would come with me to America and I would get him into a college. While he was here, he could stay with me and I would look after him. It was the least I could do to return the favor. Kenny went to school and got a business degree. He now owns a highly lucrative charter sailboat business. You know, sightseeing tours by sail, sunset cruises, special occasion charters, that sort of stuff. He rakes it in. The tourists love Captain Kenny."

"Sounds romantic."

"He's an excellent sailor. If you look behind the bar, those sailing trophies are his. He tends bar here in the off-season to help the cold months pass more quickly. Oh, and he's a great bartender too. Quite a character. We'll have to get you and James out on his boat some day. He's made Harmony Bay his home. I sponsored his citizenship a couple of years ago."

"What a great story. *You* are amazing."

They drained their glasses as Kaelin returned to take their dinner order. Jake said, "Let's do away with the menu. Please tell Liam Jake is here."

"Yes, Mr. Kane, I'd be happy to do that. I'll do it right away." Dory sensed Jake knew the teenage waitress, but didn't inquire. After all, everybody knew everybody here.

Liam arrived at their table wearing a traditional chef's jacket. He and Jake exchanged handshakes. "Good evening, Jake. Good to see you."

"Hey, Liam, how are you? Allow me to introduce Dory McDonough."

"I'm charmed," the chef said as he stretched his hand toward her.

"Know what today is, Liam?" Jake asked.

"It's Saturday."

"No, knucklehead. It's Shark Day, and we're celebrating."

"Ah yes, today *is* the day."

"You clown. You already knew that," Jake said.

"Tell me, Dory, do you enjoy seafood?" Liam asked.

"Yes, I like it very much."

"Have you ever eaten Mako Shark?"

"I don't think I have. I'm told it's very good."

"I've prepared a special dish for this evening for you and Jake. *Mako Poivre*. If you don't care for it, you can send it back. I won't be offended. It's Mako Shark seasoned with a variety of ground peppercorns then sautéed in butter. The fish is served with a sauce prepared from shallots, cream, cognac and veal glaze. I serve local farm fresh roasted asparagus and new potatoes done in a vinaigrette of olive oil and rosemary. I pair a Cabernet Franc with this dish."

"That sounds delightful. My mouth is watering."

"Okay then—Mako for two it is," Liam said and left the table.

"I used to go out in season during the late summer," Jake said, "hook a shark, and keep it in Liam's freezer. Now I leave the work up to the charter boats and Liam preserves a few shark steaks for the occasion."

"A little vengeful are we?" she asked.

"I guess you could say that. It's my feeble attempt to cover a bad experience with some gallows humor."

"It's not *fresh* fish?"

"Almost never is. Most of the stuff you see in the markets, swordfish and such, was hooked months ago out in the middle of the North Atlantic. They pack it in ice after it comes out of the water and it stays iced until you see it. If you want fresh fish, wait down on the dock for the charter boats to come in, find a pin-hooker, or… buy a fishing rod." Dory felt stupid for asking the question, so she was hesitant when she asked what a *pin-hooker* was. "Oh, sorry, those are guys who fish for sport. They keep some of the catch for themselves and the rest they sell to fish markets or restaurants for *pin money*. Thus the term, pin-hooker." Dory was relieved by the explanation.

Dining on their specially prepared meal and sipping red wine, they explored each other's thoughts about past episodes in their lives. Dory told him about her love of her work, American History, good books, romance movies, Christmas and that she'd love to have a garden some day.

"The library surely is the best place for a book lover to work. You'd be interested in the important part that Harmony Bay played in early American History. And *everybody* loves Christmas," Jake said.

Dory told him about the chain of events that led to her late husband's death. Her husband volunteered to fly on a mission to rescue soldiers pinned down in battle. She detailed how they shot down his helicopter before they reached the landing zone, with no one surviving the crash. Jake asked why she didn't remarry. "I've spent all of my time and energy focusing on my son. I don't know if the knights are into charging out to save a damsel with a kid attached. Besides, the right guy hasn't come along to rescue me from the fire breathing dragons," she said.

"That's ridiculous."

"Are you saying I shouldn't be selective about a mate?"

"No, that you think your kid is stopping someone from being interested in you. You're not the first young, single mother there's ever been."

"Thank you for thinking that."

Dory then asked Jake why an eligible bachelor such as himself was still walking around unattached. He unfolded the story of how his fiancée's plane went down in the ocean and how it took him years to get over the pain.

"She must have been very special. It's hard to let go, isn't it," Dory said.

"Yeah, she was special. But that was a long time ago. I've let go and moved on as they say."

She knew otherwise from Mrs. Lanscome's explanation and his self-imposed solitary confinement at Saturday breakfasts. "But, you're still single."

"Over the last few years my work has kept me busy. There's been a few different women, nobody special. I haven't heard the call of a stranded princess from a castle tower." They both laughed.

"Tell me more about your work," she said.

"I grow oysters, and clams, and scallops. Then I teach other folks how to do it."

"Interesting. So, you're sort of a farmer?"

"I think I'm some sort of scientist."

"Oh. The fringe benefits must be fantastic!"

"Yeah, but it's like working in a donut shop. After a while—there's just so many can you eat."

"Please, elaborate."

"It's easier to show you than tell you. Why don't you and James come by the lab next Sunday? I can show you how it all works. Does he like science?"

"A laboratory in Harmony Bay?"

"Yeah, you wouldn't know it to look at it."

"Yes, James does like science."

"How about eating shellfish?"

"He's not a picky eater. He eats everything. That sounds like an interesting day."

They finished up with coffee and a decadent chocolate desert. Dory pulled her handbag onto the table. "Let me help with this," she said.

"It's all taken care of. We should go. It's getting late," Jake said. Dory protested to no avail.

Jake's Jeep turned away from the village and headed toward Dory's house. "Let's have some fun. Hold on," he said. Jake pointed the vehicle off North Road and onto the beach. He put the vehicle in four-wheel drive and gunned it in the direction of the water. They bounced over the sand while small waves teased the beach. Jake and Dory sped along, skirting the high water mark in front of dozens of empty beach houses.

"Aren't we on these people's property?" she asked.

"Not at all. From the high water mark on the beach, out to the international limit line is public property. It's owned by everybody in the country."

"Wow. Great country—huh?"

Only the dunes and an evening sky punctuated by stars bore witness to their travels.

Chapter 13

Dory and James went to the waterfront at the edge of the village. Dory found the address based on Jake's description of the building without any trouble. Long ago, the weathered wooden building served as a sail maker's shop. Now it housed a laboratory that was capable of growing millions of shellfish each year. They waited in the car outside the deserted building. It was desolate on a dull, dreary Sunday afternoon. Early spring still had neither brought warmth to the bay, nor did it burn off the overcast. Jake was overdue and James, growing impatient, decided to try the door and kick stones around the parking lot. The door remained shut, although James managed to rearrange a lot of stones.

Jake announced his arrival with a toot of the Jeep's horn. Dory and James joined him at the entrance door. Jake juggled a cardboard box. "Hey, good afternoon. Hope I didn't keep you waiting too long. Here, hold this," he said to James.

"We wondered where you were, Mr. Kane. You're usually very punctual," Dory said.

"Yeah, I stopped and picked up some coffees for us. It's damp today, isn't it? I had to wait for them to brew a new pot. Then, Ben Hathaway, the Bay Constable was bending my ear—you know how that is. Coffee is in the box and there's a hot chocolate in there for you, Mr. James." Jake keyed the rusty lock.

"Very thoughtful of you. Say thank you, James," Dory said. "What did the constable want?"

"Seems Hathaway snagged a couple of guys taking clams in a restricted area," Jake said. He flipped on the entryway light switch with his elbow. "I know it's been tough on these guys the last couple of years, but we're working as fast as we can to turn things around."

"It's hard to be patient when you're hungry and have bills to pay."

"Yeah, you're right. It's a big bay and they were being lazy. They could have worked the bottom somewhere else. Like in a legal space. You know what I mean?"

"Okay, but I understand their frustration."

"They were taking shellfish from a restricted, polluted area. So who are they really harming?" Jake answered the question himself. "The people who end up eating them."

"Oh, I see your point."

Jake moved farther into the capacious building, flicking more switches as he went, bathing dozens of coffin shaped troughs in cold, buzzing, fluorescent light. The place was a labyrinth of tubing, pipes, wiring and vats of viridescent algae. Motors hummed as the endless array of pipes and pulsing tubes spewed bubbles and foam into the tanks.

"This is where it all begins," Jake said.

"Wow, this is way cool," James remarked. He stuck his fingers into a water tank while he babbled on.

"Very impressive," Dory added.

"Let me show you around," Jake continued. "First thing we have to do is get the mollusk conditioned for reproduction. Like spa treatment. The breeders get fed a diet of high octane, high performance green algae that gets grown here in the lab. The algae is packed with all kinds of super nutrients. That puts the clams in peak condition when it's time to do their thing."

"What thing?" James asked.

"We keep the ladies and gentlemen isolated in their own, separate comfy troughs. When we think they're at their prime, we combine them in this little vacation resort tank over here," Jake said. He walked toward a fiberglass tank infused with bubbles. "We turn up the heat so they think it's spring. Then we turn down the lights and put on soft music to get them in the mood."

"Really?" Dory said.

"It works for people doesn't it?"

"I guess so."

"Then—abracadabra! Take a look at this." Jake popped a VCR tape into a player and switched on a TV monitor. It showed two clams submerged in a spawning tank. Footage of female clams spewing thousands of eggs and male clams releasing fertilizing sperm came into view. "Here you're looking through a microscope at the miracle of life being recreated. It's time-elapsed. You can now see the cell division, each cell doubling in size then doubling again."

"I guess the low lights and mood music works, huh?" Dory said.

"Yeah, but also, all of the ladies and gentlemen are clustered together in a perfect environment with no predators. That causes the spawning and survival rates to go up exponentially. Let me show you what they look like a few weeks after this when they are still in their itsy-bitsy stage."

"Itsy-bitsy?" Dory quizzed. A puzzled expression covered her face.

"Yeah, it's an industry term," Jake said. "It's a little bigger than teeny-weeny." Jake led Dory and James to a long, low tank with a fine mesh false bottom that was constantly flooded from a gurgling hose. Jake said to them, "After the stork arrives, the animals morph from the larval stage to the juvenile spat stage. In here, they're still being flooded with high-grade algae food. Put out your hands." They obliged with palms faced up. Jake plunged his hand into the spume and grabbed tiny seashells, not much bigger than an asterisk. He placed a few in each of their hands.

"They're so cute," Dory remarked. She peered into her hand to examine the minuscule scallops. "How many of these can you hatch?"

"It's not a question of how many. We could produce tens of millions. The problem is, these things keep getting bigger every day. We're limited by the size of the operation here and the manpower to move 'em around. The whole process is labor intensive. Sure, these little guys are itsy-bitsy now, but what do you do when they all get to around this stage." Jake walked to yet another row of brine-filled troughs containing hard shell clams. He reached in and pulled out a hockey puck size clam.

"I see your point," Dory said. "Do you grow cocktail sauce here, too?"

"Anyway, after the spat stage, they spend some time in these downweller tanks. The downwellers constantly flow nutrients over them and carry waste products out the bottom. Sort of like a coffee percolator. Liquid goes in the top, the animals consume it, then waste flows through the mesh and out the bottom. Shellfish growers use wellers to force feed nutrient-rich oxygenated water to the juveniles. That gets 'em growing quicker and trains them to always want to eat. You have to remember— there's no predators in there, so the survival rate is extremely high. The quicker they grow, the quicker they can be set out in the lantern nets."

Jake picked up a scallop the size of a quarter from one of the bins. "You see this little guy; see those weird stripes on his shell? These are called skunks. We genetically alter these guys and it gives them those markings. If you come across a skunk out there on the bay, you know it came from here. Eventually, some of these will cross breed with the wild stocks." Jake tossed the scallop back into the bin. "So over time, many more will be striped. Something else we do here is genetically enhance shellfish to be immune to juvenile clam disease. That helps improve their chances too. And just like the skunks, those enhanced clams will carry their immunity over to wild stocks."

Dory interjected, "So, you're playing God?"

"No, not at all," Jake said. "We're taking something that already exists in nature and making it available in a broader sense. And—undoing some of the mess that man created. Once these animals are planted, that's pretty much where they will stay for the rest of their lives… give or take. Scallops can swim. They can get around pretty good, clams can move slightly." Jake checked one of the gauges above a tank and tapped it with his knuckle. He turned a valve, allowing water to surge into the half-empty container. "A hurricane or something can move them all out around the bay. For the genetic transfers to take place, we still have to rely on the tides and currents to do some of the work. We can measure the progress by counting skunks and see what the increase is from year to year by percentage. First year scallops are called bugs. We count the bugs, too. The number of bugs is a usually a good indicator of what the crop will be next year. Low tech, but it works."

"I'm sorry I interrupted. Go on," Dory said. She was delighted by Jake's ability to explain the process.

"From the hatchery, we move the shellfish to lantern nets on the long-lines supported by buoys. There they mature and grow on the goodness of the bay. Putting the spat in the dangling lantern nets creates mass concentrations of scallops. This greatly improves the chances of spawning. The wild stocks became too depleted by the brown tides to allow a high enough rate of concentration for reproduction. Some bugs from the hatchery get planted directly in places like Patriot's Creek or bay beds. I'll take you out on the boat to the long lines and show you the rest of the process…once the weather warms up."

"How soon will that be," James asked.

"Soon enough, I'm sure," Jake answered.

"James, we shouldn't be impatient and bother Mr. Kane about this, okay?" his mother said.

"Okay, Mom. If we go on the boat, can we go fishing? Where's the good fishing?"

"We'll have to ask."

Jake explained, "Here we go. Harmony Bay is sort of shaped like the letter C, but like it was written by somebody with a shaky hand. At the top point of the C where you start to write is England Point. If you continue around to about the halfway point, that's where *your* house is. A little farther along and you're right here where you're standing. Keep going to the end-point of the C and that's La Plage de Sable Rouge. The open space between the points in the C is called Osprey's Gut. That's where the best fishing is, but the water can be rough when the tide runs."

"Osprey's guts?" James asked, followed by an uncertain look.

"No, no, a gut is a narrow opening where water drains through. I guess it got the Osprey name because lots of birds fish out there. Small fish get tossed around in the rough surf and they're easy pickins' for the birds. Where there's little wiggling fish, the big fishies aren't far behind." James slipped the splinter of information in the back of his brain. Jake continued, "When the tide goes out, the whole bay gets sucked through the gut. When the tide comes in through the gut, the current hits the prevailing westerly winds and it stacks the water up. If you add a storm, a nor'easter, or a hurricane, the waves are high and the current so strong out there… you're way better off on dry land. England Point has some wicked good fishing spots. So does La Plage de Sable Rouge. It's only accessible by boat, though. The only way to get out to the beach at the end of the C by land is on foot over the rocks. It's really only safe at low tide. Even then, it's a slippery trip. If you slide on the barnacles it'll scrape you up something awful." Dory thought about the story of the *Jeni Lyn* running up on the ledges in a nor'easter.

James asked another question. "La Plage de Sable Rouge. That's a funny name. Where did that name come from?"

"It means— *The Red Sand Beach.* Those rocks lining the coast at Sable Rouge are high in iron ore content and other minerals. Over the centuries, the surf pulverizes the rocks and the iron in 'em stains the sand red."

"Oh, okay. Why is it hard to say?"

"A French pirate, a ruthless buccaneer named Francois deBois, gave it that name eons ago."

"Pirates?"

"Yeah, pirates. Legend is—they took prisoners ashore there for torture and execution. The sound of the ocean drowned out their screams. And—some of that sand *still* caries the stains of their blood. If the pirates were trying to squeeze a story out of a guy, like where he buried his treasure, they took him ashore at low tide and buried him up to his gills below the high tide mark. The tide would start creepin' in and they told the prisoner he'd be dug out if he gave up the location of the loot. If he didn't he'd be a goner. I don't know how many guys squealed—or how many guys drowned." Dory shuddered at the thought and wondered if James would have nightmares.

"Wow. Buried treasure?"

"Could be. Sneaky pirates were always hidin' stuff. Harmony Bay was a good place. They could get to the beaches with a small boat."

"No way."

Mustering a pirate voice Jake said, "Aaarrgh! *Yes* way, laddie. I wouldn't be kiddin' you."

"Jake, speaking of buried treasures," Dory said, "did Hathaway take those baymen out to La Plage de Sable Rouge?"

"Nah. He made those guys dump the clams back overboard and let 'em off with a stern warning. Hathaway told them if he caught 'em again he'd turn them over to Chief Dooley."

"That was nice of Hathaway," she said.

"Yeah, times are tough enough for everybody. They have families to support and they weren't going to be able to do it if they were in the cross bar hotel. I hope those two jokers learned their lesson. Funny thing is— an adult clam filters about a gallon of water per hour and takes out the impurities. With thousands of clams at work, nature might have cleaned up the water eventually if they would've just left things alone."

Looking down into the pool of shellfish Dory said, "Can the shellfish eat and eliminate brown tide?"

"Well yes and no. They do eat the brown algae, but that's not the whole problem. The algae bloom happens fast, and it's enormous, so it consumes all of the oxygen in the water and blocks out the sunlight from the eelgrass. Eelgrass is the incubator for all sorts of stuff out there. Scallops need to attach to something after they're spawned. Eelgrass beds offer the perfect environment. So, the fish die, and plant life dies. Their decomposition pushes the nitrogen level to beyond toxic." Jake showed them samples of eelgrass growing in an aquarium.

"Dredging and development of the shoreline has wiped out eelgrass, too," Jake said. "Eelgrass is interesting stuff. It's the unsung hero of the bay. In the old days, people harvested cartloads of eelgrass wrack to use for mulch in their gardens or pack it around their house's foundation for insulation. It's loaded with silica, which makes it fireproof. It's a lot safer than dry hay or leaves."

"Okay then, what causes the brown tide?"

"Some folks believe the algae bloom is caused by human influence— high nitrogen lawn fertilizers, road runoff and such. While I'll agree that none of that stuff is good for the environment, along with pesticides, antifouling hull paints and other stuff that causes different problems—I don't buy that it's the root of the problem. A couple of guys came here a few years ago and made grandiose statements to the press that they identified the culprits that sparked the brown tide as fertilizer and road runoff. The flaw was—it wasn't based on any scientific study or experiments. It was only a hypothesis they were promoting."

"Well then, Jake, where does it come from?"

"*Nature*, Dory. It all comes from nature. Although brown algae isn't indigenous to this area, it's seen all around the planet. It's a lower life form species that has probably been around since just after the dawn of time. Old timers in these parts recall brown tide long before lawns were being artificially greened up or there were enough roads or cars to have any runoff. They called it *coffee water*. The bay water looked like somebody dumped coffee in it. Locals didn't put two and two together to recognize the scallops, which only live for two years anyway, would be wiped out two years later. You see, the scallops didn't live long enough to spawn in their second year."

"I see. Are you sure brown tides weren't caused by those scruffy guys the pirates buried up to their necks out on La Plage de Sable Rouge?" James cracked up at the joke. In turn, Jake and Dory laughed at James' reaction.

"Uh, Dory, did you and James have any dinner plans for this evening?" Jake said.

"Well, no, not really. We ate a big breakfast. I didn't know how long we'd be here at the lab. I figured I'd wing it."

"I'm sure he's getting hungry. It's not much of a Sunday dinner, but I'd like to invite you and James to Aldo's for pizza, or maybe pasta with clam sauce for you?"

"Pizza sounds good. I think I'll stick with that. I've gotten way too much information about clams today."

"Ye're joshin' me. Obviously you've never tried Aldo's marinara clam sauce."

Chapter 14

Maureen Donnelly pulled her car in front of the peninsula cottage with two bikes on a rack. One was a brand new mountain bike. The other an off-road bike as well, although worn, was well polished. Worn, not due to a lack of maintenance, but because of its age. It was Saturday and Dory's turn to cover at the library. James bounded out of the house to greet his teacher.

"Mom called and told me to stick around because you were coming," James said.

"That's good, James. How are you? I saw your mom and discussed an idea with her. She told me you didn't have a bicycle. I got a new bike and have my old one as a spare. I thought you might like to have it. I can only ride one at a time."

"Wow. Thank you, Miss Donnelly."

"I stopped by Dave Small's repair shop. He lowered the seat a bit. I hope it's okay." James tried on the bike. It fit his lanky legs perfectly.

"And it's a mountain bike!"

"Yes, James. It'll come in handy around here. A lot of the roads aren't paved up through the hills. The ones that are paved are usually covered with sand."

James looked it over. The green bike had eighteen speeds, aggressively treaded all-terrain tires, dual drink bottle holders and a rack on the back to carry his gear. James never had a bike like this. Actually, he never owned a bike at all. In the city, it wasn't practical. There was no place in the brownstone to store one and outside, even if locked up, a thief would always be tempted.

He stands watch at the stop for the bus that takes his grandson and a few other kids to Coolidge Elementary School. It is cold. Gramps rubs his hands together. Propped against a nearby building, he readjusts the muffler around his neck. It is Gramp's turn in the rotation to be the adult guardian. "You can't be too careful," he told his wife.

The city is growing ugly. Vile characters happen by every so often. Hop heads, junkies if you will, who are willing and able to hustle a kid out of their lunch money. A grownup on guard is good policy. Gramps doesn't mind, it is only one morning each week. He welcomes the opportunity to spend more time with his grandson. Besides, he likes the other kids who gather there. They all call him Gramps.

Impromptu games of tag break out among the children. *It's a good outlet*, Gramps thought. *Let them burn off a little energy; they need that.* Today it distracts them from being cold until the bus arrives. Gramps leans against the wall of the public housing apartment and watches its door open. A rawboned punk with pallid eyes exits and lets the door slam behind him. He sits on the tenement steps. *Gee*, Gramps thinks, *tough day to be sitting on cold cement.* Gramps doesn't let it bother him. James' bus will be here in a few minutes and he can head home. One child after the other races past—chasing their prey in a make-believe world. The young man on the steps lights a cigarette. *That's why*, Gramps realizes. *He's come outside for a butt. His old lady doesn't want him smoking in the apartment.*

Blue smoke from his lips blends with the morning air as he puffs. Gramps is close enough to smell it. Kids are now dancing on the sidewalk in their own private production as a street skell, ragged, blowsy-faced and unshaven, approaches the smoker. He sniffs and rubs his nose with the back of his bare hand, then spits on the sidewalk. He sits next to the man on the scrubbed cement stoop. Gramps hears their voices increase in volume, hoping the kids don't hear the expletives and gutter talk that mix with the smoke. Conversation turns to debate and then to a broiling argument. They both rise to their feet.

"Come over here kids," Gramps commands. They are motionless, hypnotized by the sudden outburst.

Push turns to shove and the two unsavory characters tumble down the steps onto the sidewalk, pummeling each other until climaxing in a stalemate. "I didn't cheat cha. I ain't neva shorted ya, man—not even once. Neva," says the man who came from the building.

The street low-life challenges him. "You think you're smart? You think you're so freakin' smart? It's the last time— the last time I'm tellin' you. You never learn..." the assailant's words trail off. He pulls a large caliber revolver from under his thick coat. Waving it back and forth, he barely aims. The shot leaves a black hole between the sallow eyes. Blood and gray matter spray the steps where the two men sat moments ago.

There are witnesses, Gramps and six children from the Coolidge school, including James. It is more than anybody should have witnessed—it is far too much. It doesn't matter. Another drug deal gone bad. The shooter disappears like the smoke from the cigarette and the barrel of his gun.

Screaming, sobbing, confusion—Gramps hugging James. Sirens, police cars, one ambulance, crime scene tape and footage on the six o'clock news. Mug shots, line-ups, obnoxious reporters, endless questions, followed by sleepless nights. It is *all* far too much.

—⌇⌇⌇ʃ⌇⌇⌇—

"James, go put on your team shirt. Grab your hat and glove. I'm taking you to Little League. We're giving Mrs. Verdi a break," Miss Donnelly said. James obeyed. He returned outside, walked to her car and opened the door. "No, James, we're going by bike." James' only response was a questioning look. "It's a great day for a ride. It will be an adventure. Here, put this on," she said, handing him a bike helmet.

James clamped his glove and cap in the rack on the back of his bike.

It was a safe ride down North Road. The only oncoming traffic was a few joggers and other bicycles. Seagulls loitering on the roadside were the only obstacles. They scattered as Miss Donnelly and James approached. Miss Donnelly led the way over North Bridge, turned right on the dirt road, and then over a culvert pipe carrying water to Patriot's Creek. James knew the road went up Pencil Hill and wound its way to Billy's house.

"Where are we going?" James asked, hoping they were going to visit Billy.

"We have some time to kill before you have to be at baseball. I thought we'd take a look at the pond. It's beautiful this time of year," Miss Donnelly said. She dismounted from her bike. "We'll have to hike in from here."

She pointed out blooming American Elderberry bushes. "These produce an edible berry. You can make pies from them," she said. Traveling further on the path, she directed James' attention to certain wild plants by pointing her toes, "Here's the purple leaves of the Eastern Skunk Cabbage, these are white Canada Mayflowers, this strange looking plant is called Jack in-the-Pulpit. Those over there with the pretty pink flowers are called Lady's Slipper." James was astounded. Not far from the sights and sounds of the bay was a woodland paradise teaming with amazing plants. They arrived at a clearing that revealed the pond. "This is Mill Pond. It's fresh water fed by underground springs. In the rainy months, it really swells up. It dumps into Patriot's Creek through the drainage pipe we crossed on the road. There's all sorts of cool stuff here."

"You'd never know it's here. It's hidden," James whispered.

"Yes, that's what's kept it so special."

"I don't see a mill. Why is it called Mill Pond?"

"Hundreds of years ago there was a sluice right where that drain pipe is. It drove a mill wheel. Mill Pond sits a little higher in elevation than the bay. So, pond water rushed down with enough force to turn the wheel. It was a key location. In colonial times, the mill house was the tallest building for hundreds of miles around. People could deliver grain right up to the mill by coming up the creek in small boats. It was much easier than trying to come over land. In those days, roads were nothing more than twisty, rutted cart paths." Miss Donnelly stooped down to pick a wildflower then continued.

"Having a mill was essential for the success—and the survival of the settlement. During the dry months, every man and boy was ordered to dig a ditch by hand from Ezra's Pond to the Mill Pond to help fill it."

"Hey, that was slave labor," James commented. He tossed a stone into the pond.

"It's almost a quarter mile away." She pointed west between the trees toward the other pond. "In the winter months, blocks of ice where cut from the pond with giant saws to fill people's icehouses. Animals in the area still rely on Mill Pond for fresh water."

James thought about the primitive nature of it all. "Back then those guys were troglodytes," he said.

"Troglodytes? That's a big word for someone your age. They were pretty smart troglodytes. Yes, smart cavemen. It was very archaic, but it all worked."

"What happened to the mill?"

"It was torched by the British forces during the Revolutionary War. They said it was a stronghold for American Patriots and *Sons of Liberty* activities. There's a lot of history in these hills."

"Why didn't it get rebuilt?"

"That's a good question, James. By the time the war ended in 1783, all of the big white oaks used for timbers to build the mill were gone. The land was stripped of all large hardwood trees and sent to England to make furniture. The white oaks, because of their strength, were used to build ships. Smaller oak trees, and the remnants of the larger ones, were used to make barrel staves. Smaller trees were used for firewood. Everything was used. It was considered a sin to waste anything." Miss Donnelly motioned toward the bay. "Over there, barges were floated up on the bay beaches at high tide and pulled inland by horses."

"Can we get going?" James asked.

"Hang on for a minute," the teacher said, "this is an important lesson. They could do it here at Harmony Bay because of the flat, sandy beaches. When the tide went out, the barges were sitting high and dry on the beach. The lumber that was loaded on and the barge was floated back out on the rising tide where it met the mother ship to transfer its cargo."

He took in the serenity and beauty of it all. At the water's edge he watched a large turtle plunge in from a half submerged log. He noticed deer tracks in the soft dirt and imagined animals coming to the pond to drink. On his left he caught a glimpse of what was unmistakably a tree house nestled in the boughs of an immense maple tree. A crude wooden ladder, made with branches nailed to the trunk, led up to it. A rope swing, dangling from one of the branches extended out over the water.

"Look up there Miss Donnelly, it's a tree fort."

"Sure is, James. It's too bad the tree was damaged to make that tree house. As a sapling, it witnessed men digging the ditch from the bay, ice being cut and the American Revolution being fought." James was intrigued by the tree house, but felt badly about the tree.

"Okay, we can get going now," she said. They retraced their steps to the bikes and pedaled the remainder of the way into the village. James' legs, which were usually tireless, ached by the time they arrived at the high school's ball field.

Baseball filled a void in James' life. Every spring, just like the dandelions, Little League arrived on schedule. On Harmony Bay, baseball was a worthwhile distraction for boys and grownups alike. It occupied the blank spaces on Saturday afternoons. Wednesday evenings were reserved for practice, which neatly split the week in half. James loved the game.

James played right field. "It's too boring," he often complained. He wanted to be an infielder, most certainly a shortstop. Stanley Dzjankowski, the grocer, was his coach. Jank saw the grumble in James' attitude when he handed out position assignments for today's game. He pulled the boy aside.

"Now listen here, son. I need you and those long legs out there to cover the field. *And*, I need that strong arm of yours to make the throw to third all the way from the outfield. That is… if somebody is lucky enough to make it that far. Got it?"

"Yes sir, Mr. Dzjankowski," James said. Harmony Bay Little Leaguers played on the high school field. Although the pitching rubber was moved toward home to the Little League regulation distance of forty-six feet, covering the outfield was a daunting task for the younger players. For ten-year-olds, clearing the outfield fence from home plate was only dreamed about. All of the other Little League rules applied. Harmony Bay didn't have the land, or the budget, to build a regulation size Little League field.

"Good boy. On top of that—Babe Ruth played right field—he had 714 lifetime home runs. He didn't let that position stand in his way."

"Yes sir, Mr. Dzjankowski. Where am I batting?"

"Because you are showing such good team spirit you'll bat in the fourth spot today. Yes, my boy—you're batting clean-up." The coach's confidence in his hitting ability took James by surprise.

"Thank you, Mr. Dzjankowski." James couldn't contain his enthusiasm and ran out to right field.

His first at bat produced an inning ending double play grounder to second base. On his next turn at the plate, after being walked, James was thrown out attempting to steal second. Defensively, he covered the outfield well. It was now the bottom of the sixth with a tied score as James' team came to bat. James was up third in the inning. The opposing pitcher struck out two in a row before James entered the batter's box. Bottom of the sixth, tie score, two away. His mouth dried. He clenched the bat. The first pitch came in high and tight inside, almost catching the visor of James' batting helmet, knocking him backward into the dust. The sidelines gasped.

Dzjankowski charged from the bench running to James' side, "That was uncalled for!" he screamed at the umpire. The umpire removed his protective facemask and asked James if he was okay.

"Yeah, sure, I'm alright." James stood up and asked for time out.

Nodding his head, the umpire told him, "Go ahead, son, take your time." The ump turned to Coach Dzjankowski. "I don't know that it was intentional," he said. Dzjankowski glared at the umpire.

"Don't let it happen again. If there's any more chin music—you run him." He jerked his thumb toward the pitcher's mound. "Understand?" Jank said.

James stepped back from the plate. He brushed himself off and looked toward the pitcher. "Hey give me your best stuff—just put it over the plate—then we'll see who's better," he shouted. The pitcher glowered and kicked the rubber.

"Yeah, you'll see real soon. We're not playing for a tie," the pitcher said.

"Shut up and play baseball," James called back. His peripheral vision captured something behind the backstop he hadn't seen earlier. Jake and

Billy stood alongside Miss Donnelly.

"That'll be enough, boys," the umpire said. "Just simmer down." He motioned James back to the batter's box.

"Focus, James," Jake said.

"No homework on Monday if you get a hit," Miss Donnelly said.

"Play your game, not his. Keep your eye on the ball, James. Do your best. I know that you can do it," Billy called out.

The pitcher wound up and fired it in. Crossing the plate slightly above his knees, James took a savage cut and missed. Pitch number three came in low and away. James made contact and fouled it off. With the count now at one ball and two strikes, the pitcher snickered. James heard Billy's voice again, "Keep your eye on the ball. Do your best."

On the mound, the pitcher planned to put everything into what he believed would be his third strike. After an impressive windup he released a fat pitch. The ball whistled in dead center over the plate and belt high. James leveled the bat and swung hard. A loud crack accompanied the connection, followed by the roar of his teammates and the cheers of Jake, Billy and Miss Donnelly. The ball cleared the outfielder's up stretched glove and the centerfield fence. It went to a place rarely visited when a Little Leaguer was at bat.

Mr. Dzjankowski and his bench emptied onto the field after James rounded third and headed home.

Jake was the first to reach him. "Atta boy," he said and delivered a fist bump.

"A magnificent feat of skill if I ever did see one, young man. Yes, indeed," Billy said.

"James, I am so proud of you. I can't wait to tell your mom," Miss Donnelly added.

"Thank you Jake. Thank you Billy. Thank you Miss Donnelly," James said. He danced in the dust and waved his cap overhead with his team whooping and thumping his back.

"A walk-off home run. *Fantastic*! James—I think this calls for victory hot dogs and Cokes. My treat," Miss Donnelly said.

James slept well that night. He liked being a hero.

Chapter 15

Angus sat on the bluff overlooking his splendid domain. It included the salt marsh with its tidal pools, the creek, beach, bay, and behind him, the shoreline woodlands robust with spring color. Closest to the base of the hill, where freshwater that trickled down from the inland pond merged with brine in the marsh, a male red-winged blackbird perched on a cattail calling out *conk-la-ree*! Angus observed the Menhaden fish breaking the water's surface in the creek. Ospreys circled above the fish on their nearly six-foot wingspans, occasionally hovering above an intended victim. They unleashed their staccato calls before striking feet first. Brilliant white egrets quietly stalked prey in the marsh on their black stilt legs. Blue herons erupted from the reeds, emitting raspy barks as they flapped back to their treetop colony. He watched herring gulls drop shellfish on North Road from altitude to crack them open. Farther out in the bay, cormorants sat atop rocks drying their wings. In the distance, clouds met the indiscernible horizon, a mere smudge line of haze with no boundaries. A few summer resident sunbathers relaxed on the white sand of the bay, oblivious to nature's show all around them. They seemed quite safe to Angus. Nobody was venturing into water deeper than their waist and there were no young children for him to keep an eye on. To his back were the woods and all of the birds and mammals that lived there. Dark green wild shadblow, now full of ripe, dark purple berries, provided a feast for the birds. Critters and ground birds were sheltered in the thick bramble-habitat of a variety of wild rosa rogusa. They relied on its rose hips to survive the winter. Native raspberries and blackberries tangled in an intricate web. Oaks provided acorns for the squirrels. Patches of Christmas ferns and Bracken ferns littered the forest floor in between cedars, red maples, honey locusts and fragrant summersweet. Harmless snakes, toads and colorful box turtles slithered, hopped and crawled through the matted carpet of last autumn's leaf fall, while beneath the surface, moles burrowed in the earth and shared space with roots and insects. From these subterranean tunnels to the tops of the tallest tree, life was abundant and unstoppable.

This season the heat arrived early. It was certainly more oppressive than Angus could remember. The stifling humidity made him feel slow and lethargic, suppressing any desire for physical activity. Air, with the consistency of moisture-laden gauze, swathed the beachfront. It invaded every pore. He thought back to his puppyhood and forward to the present. He could never recall being this uncomfortable. His thick double-layered coat that helped him stay warm in winter's icy water now added to his misery. He thought it was far better to sit in the shade and snooze rather than trekking up and down the hills or being out at the beach in the blazing sun. In the early morning's dew, he had made the rounds of his kingdom, checking the usual haunts and their inhabitants. Deer, raccoons, squirrels, rabbits, chipmunks, red fox, opossums, ground hogs and all of the birds learned long ago not to fear Angus. He meant them no harm and they learned to respect him. Angus did not need them to survive, so he happily coexisted with them. Occasionally, he served as their defender by keeping order among the living things of the woodlands. Being large enough to take on any animal that existed in his protectorate, the presence of his bulk served as a silent peacekeeper to extinguish any chaos before it occurred. He knew this was his role and the animals understood and accepted it. As the largest force, he also had responsibilities not to overextend his authority. Angus lived the life of a benevolent authoritarian protecting the innocent and helpless.

The waters were another matter. There was only so much he could do as a land animal. Nonetheless, he patrolled the beaches to keep everything in order. Gulls, terns, sandpipers and plovers had the rights to the debris jettisoned on the high-water line where the surf disgorged its lifeless occupants as food sources for the birds. Carcasses of horseshoe crabs, fiddler crabs, blue crabs, green crabs, rock crabs, mollusks, a variety of gritty bivalves and an occasional finfish littered the shore after the exit of the tide, much to the delight of the scavengers. In lean times, a raccoon or opossum might visit the beach under the cover of darkness. Angus let it happen. The balance of nature provided enough for all of them. Now in the prime of his life, age brought wisdom to Angus and he took everything into consideration. Wisdom was something that only came with age. It required the combination of knowledge, experience, intuition, facets of common sense and trial and error. There were many trials in his life. Without realizing it, each one played a role in shaping the being he was today. Every matter, circumstance and season was a trial that contained a lesson to be learned. He had no school to attend. Therefore, his knowledge was based on what his internal chemistry provided and the experiences of everyday life.

Some animals did things impulsively based on their natural instincts. At times, Angus did too. Now, he knew the value of not rushing to judgment in matters that involved putting his body at risk. With purebred pedigree from exceptional lineage, the dog's pride also played a part in his behavior. He never wanted to make himself look foolish. Not like the mongrels that fought among themselves, barked for no apparent reason, and at times, drove their masters crazy. Angus was always positioned to be reticent and act responsibly.

He drooled, licked his nose and breathed in hurried, panting breaths. He shifted his bulk, arose and moved to the deep shade of an elderly sweet-scented honey locust. The dog used his baseball mitt paws to scallop a shallow gully in the damp earth and moss. Lowering himself into the cooling earth, he kept his drooping brown eyes focused on the beach. He began to contemplate many things.

After listening to numerous human conversations and the faceless, scentless voices on the radio, there was a lot he didn't understand. Angus had heard terrible stories about humans killing each other, but not for survival or for food. He heard about parents who hurt their young or abandoned them, even though the offspring had done nothing wrong and were perfectly healthy. There were things called crime and stealing for something called personal gain that he knew nothing about. These were all things that pained him greatly. Humans bought food at markets and didn't have to hunt for sustenance. They knew how to make fire and had heated dwellings, so they didn't have to fight the elements or migrate to warmer surroundings. Water flowed freely from their faucets. Therefore, they never had to wait for rain to quench their thirst. Humans had it very easy. It made Angus wonder why they brought so much hurt on each other when it wasn't necessary. Couldn't they just use all of their magical powers to look after each other?

Three white butterflies waltzed in front of his nose while he licked his front paws. The distraction took his reflections in another direction. One thing he could not comprehend was the existence of bugs. They destroyed the garden and made Billy cuss. Fleas and ticks were his only enemies. They were no fun at all. Angus saw the purpose in most animals, but insects, except for the friendly honeybees pollinating the garden and bugs that fed the birds, bewildered him. Aside from the garden, carpenter ants and termites ate Billy's home, mosquitoes bit him during the night and gave him a terrible itch, deer ticks made humans very sick with disease and brown recluse spiders lived in the firewood pile ready to deal out a sickening, if not deadly, bite if disturbed. There were other culprits. Angus saw the damage the aphids did to Mrs. Lanscome's rose garden and the treachery the slugs imparted on her succulent hostas. These marauding acts left Mrs. Lanscome upset to the point of hysteria.

As much as he didn't like the bugs, he liked the birds. They didn't bother any other animals. Woodland songbirds filled the air with wonderful sounds each spring that lasted until the leaves changed color. Baltimore orioles delivered clear, loud songs from the treetops, sparrows twittered, catbirds mewed. Mourning doves cooed and even the woodpecker's hammering was enjoyable. This wasn't the case for the shore birds. Gulls made annoying sounds with their constant heckling, *cagh-cawing*. The terns screamed, geese honked and the ducks quacked incessantly. Besides, the birds of the forest were much nicer to look at. Brilliant reds of the cardinals and woodpeckers, yellows of the orioles and finches, and colorful blue jays all created a new picture every day. Angus figured he'd think more about this later and rolled over, enjoying the coolness of the soft humus on his back. He flicked his paws skyward toward the birds and dozed off.

Harmony Bay was different from the far away places on the radio. Folks, with a few exceptions, knew how to be neighborly and caring.

Angus didn't know why it was that way here or why he had the good fortune to live at Harmony Bay. He didn't know anything about luck, but figured he was here for a purpose. Even if he wasn't sure what that purpose was, he'd do his best to fulfill it. For him, it came down to doing what he felt in his heart was the right thing at the right time with love, obedience, and helpfulness. In his heart, he knew how to be neighborly and caring and thought it best to lead by example. His life was fully immersed in the culture of the place. He had set down his own roots and became part of it. Everyone knew him by name. Calling to him, Harmony Bay folks doled out pats to his head and warmly scratched him behind his ears. He liked it this way.

Temperatures began to fall along with the sun as it dropped toward the hazy strawberry horizon. The dog awoke, yawned once, then twice, and then again. He hoisted up his hindquarters and assumed a bowing position that allowed himself to stretch lavishly. His pendant ears perked up with the noise of people splashing and laughing in the surf. Well rested, he stood on all fours, stretched again and wagged his brushy tail. It was cool enough now and Angus scrambled down the hill through the fading swelter. Taking a shortcut, he plunged into the creek and swam across to the opposite bank. He clawed his way up the slippery embankment and scooted across North Road, the last obstacle between him and the bay beach. Angus sprinted across the sand and launched into the high tide, creating bubbly foam in his wake. He continued out to James' friend Katie who was the person furthest from shore.

Angus felt compelled to carry Katie, who was merely enjoying herself, to shore even though she was a good swimmer. She was not in danger at all. Katie treaded water and greeted Angus who paddled around her in tightening circles. To avoid his churning paws, Katie got along side the dog and threw her arms over his back. She knew his game and accepted the ride to ankle depth where he shook his fur frantically to dry himself. Angus responded to Katie's animated melodramatic hugs with a wagging tail and returned to the water for another faux victim. The charade was over.

The dog exited the water for the last time, dripping from every ebony hair. Angus shook his body once, then again. He was panting heavily, but wagged his tail with as much vigor as before. In his humble opinion, his job was finished for the time being. He took great delight in doing it with a bonus of making humans happy. Tomorrow another day would dawn that might be cooler or rainy. No matter what the weather was, Angus would keep watch over Harmony Bay.

Dusk brought a swarm of mosquitoes from the marshes, chasing humans, regardless of size or age, from the beach. With his internal clock telling him to return home for dinner, Angus retraced his steps across the beach and the road. Rather than walking on the hot asphalt of North Road to cross the creek on North Bridge, he once again dove into the creek separating him from the marsh and the bluffs. He passed a raft of mallards, and at the other bank, a wary green heron stabbing at small fish in the muddy shallows with its long beak. Zigzagging up the face of the steep bluff through the dune grass and past the sumacs, he took the long and winding path through the stands of maples, scrub oaks and patches of ferns interlaced with poison ivy. Finally arriving at the fragrant cedars, he made his way up Pencil Hill—returning to home and master.

Chapter 16

Dory and James started their usual morning routine. After dropping James off at school, she'd continue to the library and start her day at a leisurely pace. The school year was almost finished and their routine would change soon. With the early heat spell still on, Dory and James literally steamed toward town. Steam billowed from under the hood of her car as the temperature gauge pegged itself in the red zone.

Now what? she wondered, and pulled to the side of the road. Looking at the puddle of hot, bright green liquid beneath the car, they knew it couldn't be good. An eye-watering cloud met Dory as she opened the hood. James pointed to the radiator hose hissing vapor like a serpent.

"Gee, Mom, if I had duct tape, I could fix it," James said. Dory was startled at his remark, not being quite sure why James made the inference for a duct tape fix or where he got the mechanical knowledge.

"You've become very much the Mr. Fix-it, haven't you?" she said. Dave Small's repair shop was closer than trying to make it to the library, or back home. She decided to wait until the temperature came down a bit and then limp to the repair shop. The longer she waited, the more her anxiety grew about what the newest unexpected expense would be.

When she turned the key the engine started without trouble. They drove with the windows down and the air conditioner off. Dory pulled into Dave's lot and the steam appeared again. Dave walked out to the car as he wiped his hands with a rag. "Mornin', Miss Dorothy. Mornin', James. Looks like you're the latest victim of this brutal heat we've been having," the mechanic said. "Pop the hood—let's have a look."

"It's the hose. It's split," James said.

Dave put the rag over the radiator cap and cautioned them to stand back. He loosened the cap a quarter turn, which released violent bubbling noises from the radiator. The hissing reached a crescendo. After a few minutes, the chaos under the hood was reduced to a slow, steady drip on the bluestone gravel below. Dave pushed his baseball cap back and wiped the sweat from his forehead with his forearm. "Miss Dorothy, I've got some good news and some bad news," Dave said.

"Okay, don't keep me in suspense. Give me the bad news first."

"I can't fix your car today."

"Oh, I'm sorry. You're busy and I didn't make an appointment."

"Nah, that's not it. You can drop by here any time you need to. We'll always squeeze you in. The problem is, I don't have the part to fix it. It has to come from up inland. If I order it now, it won't be here 'till tomorrow."

"Okay, that's not too bad. What's the good news?"

"You only blew a radiator hose. A hose and a gallon of antifreeze is all you need. I'll check it over real good, the radiator, thermostat and all. I don't think you did any other damage. Don't even fret about the labor. It'll only take me ten minutes to put the hose on and fill the radiator. All's it's going to take is a screwdriver. This all isn't going to cost much." Dory sighed in relief. James' ears perked up. It was a step beyond duct tape, but still fixable with only a screwdriver. Winton was right.

"Thank you, Dave. Thank you, very much."

"No problem, Miss Dorothy. Only being neighborly. Being fair and honest is what keeps me in business."

"You set a good example. Can I ask you a favor?"

"Sure."

"Please call me Dory."

"Sure, that's an easy one, Miss Dorothy." Dory let it go.

"I'll call the library and ask someone to come get us."

"Don't bother. I'm headed up that way. I'll drop James off at the school and you at the library. Today I'll line you up a ride home after work. Tomorrow, when the car is ready, we'll drop it off down at the library. You can settle up whenever it's convenient for you. Hop in the tow truck."

At the end of the day Dory was surprised to see Winton Hector walk into the library. There were no guitar lessons today. Normally he was at the hardware store at this hour. He approached her desk. "G'afta noon, Dory. Dave asked me ta swing by an gather ya'll up. I'm yo ride home." Dory was concerned. She knew Winton didn't own a car and she wasn't sure, due to his disability, how well he could drive.

"All right then, Winton, let me gather my things and find James."

"I borrowed Billy's truck an was fixin' ta run some errands. I stopped by Dave's wit a delivree from Mistuh Hirsch an' I see yo car is there. Dave tol' me what was happenin' an' asked me ta collect y'all up an' take ya ta home."

Winton, James and Dory squeezed in to the cab of the pickup. James sat in the middle. They snaked their way out of the village on Bay Road, past the stately Victorian painted ladies with their finery of flowering shadblow, locusts, trellised roses and synthetically greened lawns. James asked Winton if he always lived in Harmony Bay.

"Nah, not always," Winton said. "I grew up way down south. Way back in da woods. My family lived dare fo as long as anyone kin rememba. There was ten of us in one house. My daddy was a share croppa, so's was his daddy befo him. Tobacca mostly. I wanted out o there. I wanted somethin' betta—so I joined da military an got my leg shot off. Kinda funny, y'know. Day had me workin' in da motor pool fixin' trucks an stuff. Every thin' was cool. Jest peachy-keen. Then they sends me ova to da war ta drive one o' dem big ten wheelas. Had me drivin' it righ' inta da battle zone. We gets pinned down by da' enemy. Dey sent a helicopta ta rescue us, but it got shot down." Dory stiffened at the words.

Could that helicopter be the same one her husband was aboard? What a coincidence that would be, she posited to herself.

"Anyways, I finally gets rescued an dey ships me to da Veterans hospital up noth near Catacoot. I was a long ways from home. Dat's where I met Mistuh Hirsch. He was visitin' an ol' friend who was in the same room as me. We gots ta talkin'. I was in a real bad way. Mistuh Hirsch got to know me a bit. He'd visit his ol' army buddy an talk to me, bring me stuff ta read. Den his buddy passed on— but he keeps on visitin' me. Tells me ta stop feelin' sorry fo' myself an dat God helps doze dat helps demselfs. I laid in that hospital recouperatin' for a long time an it really got me ta thinkin'. Anyways, dey fix me up wit dis here leg an gets me walkin' agin. I's gots a purple heart an was due ta be discharged from da army soon. Mistuh Hirsch comes a callin'— he offa's me a job at his hardware sto' an a place to stay till I kin git myself on track. Y'know, nice an organized an' all. Now everyday I thanks da good Lord 'cause I coulda jest died out dare in da middle o' no place. Hamony Bay is a good place y'know. Everybody looks afta each otha. Every place should be like dat. I's got me a nice lil' place o' my own an I bin savin' up fo' a car or a truck or sumpin'. Once I do dat, I'm gonna take a drive an visit my momma. Itsa a long ride. I think I'm gonna git me one o' them cars wit a pernundle." He poked James with an elbow.

"A pernundle? What's that?" Dory asked. James and Winton laughed at the question.

"Dory, It's always bin righ' unda yo nose," Winton said.

Winton eased the truck to a stop at a crosswalk. "Okay now, James. Let's see if ya kin shift me from first ta second." Winton started forward and as he pushed in the clutch, James pulled back on the gearshift.

"James, where did you learn how to do that?" his mother asked. She was now not only amazed at Winton's mastery of his disability, but of James' knowledge of a standard shift.

"On the internet." He elbowed Winton in the ribs and tried not to laugh.

Her son was growing up a lot faster than she thought. In another ten years or so he'd be finished with college and off on his own. She hoped the days would pass slowly.

Chapter 17

Today Jake was taking Dory and James on an excursion around the bay to show them more about his work with shellfish. Afterward, Jake's plan was to cruise the *Sea Horse* up past La Plage de Sable Rouge and across Osprey's Gut, do a little fishing with them, the on to England Point.

Dory and James arrived as the lab's parking lot as Jake was maneuvering the *Sea Horse* up to the floating dock where bay water slapped against barnacle covered pilings leaving a filigree of white lace. Classic rock music blared from weatherproof speakers aboard the boat. She had filled a cooler with sandwiches and soft drinks. Straining under the weight of its contents, she carried it along with their two backpacks to the dock. James unloaded his fishing rod and tackle box from the car and followed his mother down the gangway.

After nosing in against the fenders of the boat slip, Jake knocked the *Sea Horse* down to a low idle and shifted to neutral. He threw a bowline with a looped end to James. "Wrap it around that cleat," Jake ordered. He pointed to the pitted, tarnished hardware bolted to the dock. The aft line went to Dory with the same instructions. Jake leapt over the gunwale, landing squarely on the dock. He secured the boat in the slip with the spring line.

"That's an awful lot of boat for one man," Dory said.

"That'll change as soon you two jump on board. I filled the gas tanks, topped off the fresh water, emptied the head, checked the oil and cleaned the windshield. We're ready to go. I'll be right back—don't leave without me," Jake said. A grin covered his face.

To thoroughly warm the engine, Jake left the boat idling. The *Sea Horse,* which was once a lobster boat, now served as a science research vessel. Ironically, now its work might help lobster populations that it once harvested. Framed in oak and planked with cedar, its wooden hull was painted white. A short bow deck preceded a small wheelhouse. Behind the wheelhouse was a wide-open aft deck that offered workspace and storage for lobster pots. The wooden *Sea Horse* was one of a dying breed. With its powerful diesel, it could reach a top speed of perhaps twenty-five knots. She was one of the quickest working boats on the bay. Jake never pushed it that hard. He respected the boat's age and avoided unnecessary consumption of fuel. Today, a good cruising speed would be twelve knots. Plenty fast enough for a leisurely cruise, but slow enough to keep the RPM's in an economic range. A small crane-like winch with a swiveling boom hung off the starboard side. Secured below the gunwales were fish gaffs, a boat hook, clam rakes, oyster tongs and long-handled fishnets. In the cockpit sat state-of-the art electronic equipment, VHF and single-sideband radio, LORAN, GPS, and Doppler radar. Alongside were displays showing water temperature and depth, and—an elaborate stereo system. Like its skipper, everything on board was well worn, but clean and orderly. Today three blue canvas chairs sat on the aft deck.

Jake jogged down the dock and disappeared into the lab building. He came out a few minutes later carrying a galvanized pail. "What's in the bucket," Dory asked.

"It's bait. Menhaden, or bunker, as it's usually called. We'll try for some bluefish— they've been running pretty good lately. They're a lot of fun on the line. Even a two-pounder puts up a nice fight."

Jake loaded the bucket of bait, cooler, backpacks and James' fishing tackle on board. He then helped Dory over the side by holding out both of his hands for her to hold. James was apprehensive about the space between the dock and the boat. The gap grew and shrank as the boat rose and fell. Jake heaved on the spring line to decrease the distance, then hoisted James up off the dock in a single motion, depositing him on the deck.

Once settled in, Jake gave the housekeeping instructions for the boat, including where garbage was stowed, how the head, located up in the bow worked, and where James and Dory should stow their gear. Then it was time for the safety drill. He showed where the lifejackets were kept, pointed out the life saving ring with its line attached, and showed them the emergency inflatable life raft.

"All you have to do is pull this ring and the raft will inflate automatically. It's over-kill, but it keeps the insurance company and the school happy," Jake said. The last stop on the orientation tour was the radio console. "If I get snatched up by a flying saucer, or a pirate ship, punch this orange button. It sends out an automatic emergency signal with our exact location. The Bay Patrol and the Coast Guard *will* come. If it's dark, there's emergency waterproof lanterns and signal flares in this box. Jake rapped the wooden box to emphasize his point. We're going to have a smooth cruise, but as your captain, I am required to inform my crew."

James was in awe of it all. It was all new and exciting. He turned his baseball cap backward on his head and yelled out, "Full speed ahead!"

Herring gulls stalked the *Sea Horse* as Jake gently nudged the gearshift into reverse and backed her out into the channel. Spinning the wheel hard, she ventured south along the coast leaving a broad, v-shaped, foamy wake for the birds to follow.

"Let me show you what we're going out to take a look at," Jake said and held up a circular contraption three feet in length. It had five compartments wrapped in green mesh. On the outside were sturdy black nylon lines grasping the baskets at several intervals. These lines joined at the top where Jake held them. "This is a lantern net that I told you about in the lab. You saw the spat we grew. Those get placed in these baskets and are put out in the creeks to grow. Lantern nets are hung on a long-line that's stretched between two anchored buoys. About twenty lantern nets dangle from each line. Every once in a while you have to yank 'em up to clean off the trespassers like sea squirts, crabs, and the muck. It's messy work. The tide is out. We can look at some now in the deeper water. The *Sea Horse* won't have enough draft to make it farther in there. Folks usually use flat bottomed barges to service the long-lines."

The *Sea Horse* rounded a bend and entered a protected creek where cord grass marched into the water. Jake cut the engine, letting the boat drift up to a series of parallel lines connecting white buoys, each twenty feet in length. It was quiet, the stillness only broken by splashing bunker.

Jake used a gaff hook to pull up one of the buoys. As he had explained, a lantern net, heavy with hundreds of small oysters, hung from the line. The lantern net was out of the water long enough for James and Dory to catch a glimpse. "You can see why we use the crane to crank these up," Jake said. "These nets keep the brood stock safe from predators."

"What kind of predators?" James asked.

"Blue crabs, green crabs, mud crabs, and horseshoe crabs. Also, whelk, even though they have those fancy conical spiraling shells, are deadly to clams. Moon snails will eat a perfect hole in a clam's shell. Sometimes you'll see those clamshells on the beach. Looks like somebody bored a hole in 'em with a drill press. Starfish wrap their legs around the shell and pull the clam open. Skates feed on them too. We've got all of them here in the bay. Scallops only live for two years. You have to hope they get to the spawning stage before something else eats them." Jake wiped his hands dry with a towel.

"I guess everybody likes clams," James remarked.

"Here's where it gets interesting. We handle a lot of these nets—which is very labor intensive. So, we started an aquaculture program here with community volunteers. We supply one hundred thousand seed clams to people who want to help grow shellfish. They pay a small fee. It helps cover the cost of education and training. If they don't have waterfront property, we'll set them up in a space like this where they can tend the lines. Volunteers have to agree to never sell what they produce."

"The clams they raise are put out in the wild seeding program?" Dory asked.

"That's a good question. The answer is yes and no. Anybody who grows the clams, oysters, or scallops, is entitled to keep as many as they want for their personal consumption. It's a big commitment—they deserve some reward. The rest of the batch goes to the seeding program, which we manage. We work with baymen and the DEC to get a feel for what areas need seeding the most and what areas could produce the most yield." Jake slid the hook back into the rack.

"Fred Lanscome, Kenny Clarke, your teacher Miss Donnelly, Roland Rutledge at Shea's Bakery, Buzzy the postmaster, even Pastor Simvasten all grow shellfish for the program. Hey, James—maybe next year you'll want to put a few lines out behind your house in Patriot's Creek."

"Hey, Mom, could we do that, *please?*" James asked, pacing in the confined space of the aft deck.

"If Mr. Kane thinks it's something you could handle, we can look into it. It sounds like fun. And—I wouldn't mind a few fresh clams once in a while."

Jake re-fired the engine. Slipping the boat into gear, the screw propelled them away from the creek with crying gulls once again in pursuit. He pointed the boat east toward La Plage de Sable Rouge. Dory was delighted. It was all simple, yet so enjoyable. The only noise that betrayed their presence was the sound of the diesel and the churning prop. Dory looked back at the creek they just came from. Farther to the right, the docks and village of Harmony Bay dwindled away. They were now clear of all marker buoys and pleasure craft.

"Okay James, time for you to take the wheel," Jake called out over the steady throb of the engine.

"You're going to let me drive?"

"You betcha. You're the first mate today. The captain needs a break."

"How will I know where to go?"

"Here's your compass." Jake pointed to the black and white globe above the wheel. "Keep her lined up on E. If you start drifting toward N, turn the wheel a little to the right—that's starboard. If you see the S coming into view, turn the wheel a little to port."

"I can't see over the wheel." Jake took an empty plastic bin and flipped it over.

"Here stand on this."

James squinted. "Yup, I can see now."

"Okay—keep it lined up on the E. You'll be right on target for La Plage de Sable Rouge. That's the bottom point of the C I told you about. Stay on the lookout for other boats and stuff in the water. Holler if you see something."

"How long will it take to get there?"

"It's about a fourteen mile trip. We're already out about two miles and cruising at a little under twelve knots—we'll be there in about an hour. Today's adventure will take us on a triangular route. We head east to Sable Rogue, then north to Osprey's Gut to fish. That route will take us past England Point to go swimming. At the end of the day it's a straight shot west to get back home." Keeping watch on the horizon, Dory and Jake stood behind James. Jake knew he could set the autopilot, but thought it was better for James to learn dead reckoning and navigation skills. Jake's eyes occasionally scanned the radar and the engine's gauges.

Jake produced a thermos of coffee and two mugs, turned to Dory and said, "Hey, it's my turn to serve." Being mindful of the undulating deck, Jake didn't fill them all the way. Although, the *Sea Horse* was big enough, so the small swells sliding under her hull probably wouldn't spill the coffee if he did fill the mugs completely. Dory curled her hands around the cup and told him the coffee tasted good. It was a welcome relief from the salty spray. "Here. Hold this," Dory said. She handed Jake her cup. She went below and returned with a brown paper bag. "I made these this morning." The aroma from the bag was intense enough to overpower the smell of the bay. Dory opened the bag and pulled out a cinnamon bun iced in creamy white. "Here ya go, Cap'n. Something to swab up your coffee with." Jake took a bite and chewed slowly.

"Aw— man, this is delicious." He licked the icing from his fingertips and spoke with a full mouth. "If you keep bringing stuff like this aboard I'll have to make you the full-time galley slave."

"Beg your pardon, Cap'n? Galley slave? I was thinking more along the lines of *Her Admiralty.*" Dory's joke, and Jake's puzzled expression, made her smile. James asked for a cinnamon bun. "Not till ye're done drivin', matey James. You'll get the wheel sticky."

"C'mon, Mom. They're good."

"Tell you what," Jake said as he shot a glance toward Dory. "Once your mom finishes her coffee, we'll have her take the wheel and you can chow down."

"Oh, I've been upgraded from galley slave?"

"Actually, on the long-liner fishing boats out at sea, the cook takes the helm to give the captain a chance to eat. It's sort of nautical multitasking."

"Who better to multitask than a woman?"

"Aye-aye."

Now more than half way across the bay, Dory took the wheel. The wind picked up as the *Sea Horse* bounded in the foamy waves. Salty spray dampened the boat and its crew.

"Okay—got your sea legs?" Jake asked and slid behind her.

"It's getting a little rough out here, isn't it?"

"Yeah, it does that a little past the midway point. We get some freaky winds out here. It'll settle down in a little bit. Wave sizes are determined by three things, wind speed, time and distance, or *fetch* as it's called. Water temperature and low atmospheric pressure can add to the mix. Cold water is denser and doesn't rise up as easily. Wind speed is how fast the air is moving, time is determined by how long that wind is blowing over an open body of water. Fetch is the last determining factor. Wave height, or lack of height, is limited by how long and how fast the air moves over a distance. The reason you could never get truly monster waves on the bay is because there isn't enough distance for everything to build up—not enough fetch. Even if you had winds blowing for a week, they wouldn't have the fetch.

The reason it's a little rougher out here is because the westerlies are pushing the waves over ten miles of open water. On the other hand, out in the open ocean, waves can develop and build over hundreds, or even thousands, of miles. During a nor' easter or hurricane, waves in the ocean of seventy feet or more aren't uncommon. Once the waves start to grind on the shallow slope of the bay bottom, they're done. Sort of the same way coral reefs knock down waves." The *Sea Horse* forged on effortlessly as the lower point of the C came into view.

"Where am I heading?" Dory said. A sudden large swell of the following sea caused her knees to buckle as the deck rose and then dropped abruptly. Jake reached around Dory on both sides, steadying the wheel, her hands, then her shoulders. Jake knew the hull could handle the water, but he didn't want to chance the additional pressure of seawater flowing up the exhaust ports and flooding the engine. He cracked opened the throttle slightly to keep ahead of the green water that rolled under the stern and lurched the vessel forward. "Hang on, James!" Dory called out. James braced himself in his seat as he bit down on his third cinnamon bun. James found the whole ordeal amusing.

Jake hunched over and spoke directly in her ear, "Look straight across. Do you see that lighthouse just to the left of the bow?"

Dory, fully aware of their closeness, squinted. "Yes I can make it out."

"All right, do you see that radio tower off the starboard at about two o'clock?"

"Do I have to wait until two o'clock? It's not even lunchtime," she said playfully. Dory tightened her grip on the wheel to adjust for the pitching of the deck, letting go only to brush her hair away from her eyes.

Jake feigned a laugh. "Uh, right. Do you see the radio tower off the starboard bow—that's your *right*."

"Yes. Yes, I can see it now."

"Okay—you're doing good. Keep the lighthouse on your left and the radio tower on your right. You'll be fairly well lined up on Sable Rouge. We'll make the final course adjustments as we get closer." Within a few more minutes they could plainly see the red rocks of Sable Rouge.

Exactly as Jake predicted, the water flattened as they approached the beach. "I'll take it from here. It gets a little tricky on the next leg. There's a lot of big rocks in these parts," Jake said. "You both did great." A hundred yards from shore Jake swung the bow north, slipped the boat into neutral and idled down the engine. The diesel quieted to a burble low enough to hear the surf breaking on the beach.

Dory was shaken. "*It gets a little tricky on the next leg?* What would you call that *last* leg?" Dory asked if she and James should put on life jackets.

"Everything is fine," Jake answered. "It seems scary, but those swells are only little speed bumps is all." Jake took a pair of binoculars from the console in the wheelhouse as they drifted off shore and went aft to the starboard gunwale. "Here, take a look at the sand." He handed the glasses to James. "Yeah, it *is* red. Wow, you were right." In turn, James handed them to his mother. "Hmmm—it's low tide isn't it?" she said.

"Yeah, dead low," Jake said.

"Graveyard dead." Dory continued peering at the beach through the binoculars. "Hmmm—I think I see a pirate on shore buried up to his chin." James cracked up.

Jake returned to the wheel with Dory and James beside him in the cockpit. Easing the throttle up, Jake began the traverse across Osprey's Gut while keeping an eye on the depth indicator. The wide-open seas were to their right, the entire bay to their left. The water was choppy with green moguls as far as the eye could see. Sea birds of every description swarmed about. Jake pointed to an osprey circling overhead.

"Osprey's are unusual birds," he said. "Their name is from the Latin word *ossifragus*, which means *a bone breaker*. In some places they're called sea hawks. Ospreys are the only birds that can completely submerge themselves when they dive into the water and still be able to fly away with their prey. By comparison, bald eagles are limited to plucking fish from the surface of the water as they fly by." Jake squinted and shaded his eyes to follow the circling birds. "The Osprey has closable nostrils to keep water out of its beak during dives, and backward-facing barbs on the talons, which help hold its catch. Ospreys are also the only birds that can hover above a target for a few moments before they dive. They first spot their fish from about thirty, up to about one hundred feet above the water." The circling osprey hovered and dove.

"Ospreys have an opposable toe. It can face forward or backward. While the bird is perched, it usually has three toes facing front and one in back. When an Osprey catches a fish, it positions its feet and toes with two toes on either side of the fish, one foot ahead of the other. The head of the fish faces forward in an aerodynamic position for flying through the air. Osprey's diet is almost entirely fish," Jake explained.

The ledges of England Point loomed ahead. Jake altered his northerly course slightly to the west toward the bay. With her bow into the wind, the *Sea Horse* settled down. "Okay—here's the plan," he said.

"We'll take a little break, gear up, and get our lines ready here. Once we're all set, I'm going to nose out into the Gut. The tide is shifting in now. We're going to let the tide current carry us over the fish as we drift back toward the bay."

"How do we know there's fish there?" James asked.

"Well, if the birds are fishing—it's a good sign," Jake answered. "We'll rig up for blues, but you never can tell *what* you might catch. Fish run in cycles. Go and ask any of the old timers."

"You mean like Billy?"

"Yeah, Billy will remember. He can tell you about the days when bluefish were so thick you could walk on their backs to cross the bay. Other years there were none to be found. Atlantic salmon, halibut and cod were plentiful out there." He pointed over his shoulder toward the open sea. "Boats came in loaded down with so much fish the water was up to their scuppers. Halibut and cod got fished out. Wild Atlantic salmon are almost extinct. Atlantic salmon sold today are all farm raised. Mostly because of the factory ships. They used to come in from foreign countries when we only had a three-mile territorial limit. Those ships sucked up every living thing from the waters— they'd leave a virtual desert behind them. Their bottom trawling destroyed habitats along the coast. Swordfish in the North Atlantic, which are long-line caught, are making a comeback since catch regulations were put on them."

"The way we're fishing—is that bad for the fish?"

"The only way to truly protect the waters and everything living in them is to never take anything out and don't put anything in that doesn't belong there—like pollution. But it's not practical. Fishermen have to make a living. If you follow the laws for only taking fish above the keeper size and the bag limit, everything will be okay. That's how the striped bass population was able to make a comeback. Although, a lot of work still needs to be done on controlling pollution in areas where bass spawn."

Jake knelt down as he set up James' rod with a wire leader and a large hook. After tying on the hook and leader, he skewered a chunk of bunker on the hook. He looked up at James and said, "If blues are feeding today, they'll bite anything. We could use anything for bait. We could even use an old Barbie doll and they'd bite it."

"Can I fish now?"

"Wait till we set up the drift. Be patient for a few more minutes." Jake turned the boat 180 degrees and headed east toward the ocean. Once in the middle of the Gut he turned west again, lowered the engine speed to idle and put the boat in neutral. He called James to the starboard side of the stern, had him lower his bait into the water and showed him how to set the drag on the reel. The boat began to drift west on the incoming tide, moving at about three knots. Dory decided to stay out of the sun under the protection of the wheelhouse. "Call me if you catch something," Jake told him and went to join Dory.

"This will keep him busy for a while," Jake said as he leaned up against the console.

"He does get impatient." Dory now applied sunblock to the fair skin of her face and exposed parts.

"He'll be fine. I guarantee it."

"Whoa!" James called out. His rod doubled over.

Jake didn't want to see James' rod and reel get pulled overboard. Jake said, "Step back from the stern and start cranking him in." The line played out, zigzagging in the choppy water as James cranked as hard as he could. Jake wasn't sure what was hooked, but it gave James a workout. The fish tired before James did. Jake stood by with the gaff and a net. James could see the silver sides flashing as the fish circled in the water. Jake reached over the stern and hand hauled the fish in the last few feet, dropping it on the deck. The four-pound bluefish slapped on the deck, flipping and flopping, its razor teeth biting the air.

"Don't touch him, James. They can take a finger off. I'll get the hook. Looks like you've guaranteed us dinner."

"What did I catch?" James was jigging on the deck in celebration.

"He's a blue, and a good size one at that. Eh?" Jake tossed a rag over the fish. Holding it down with his foot, he used a pair of pliers to extract the hook. "Some folks don't like to eat blues—but I've got a great way of grillin' him. You'll like it." Dory produced a camera and had James, Jake and the fish pose for posterity.

"Honey, you were fantastic!" Dory said.

"Mom, can I keep fishing?"

"I think so. It's up to Mr. Kane."

"Aren't you going to fish?"

"I'm leaving them all for you." She wasn't about to admit that everything she knew about fishing could fit in a thimble.

"Fishing is what we're here for," Jake said. "I'll put him in the cooler and let's get you baited up again. Let's get the line down a little more and see what you can catch this time. We've drifted a good distance. Let me put her back out in the Gut again." He hooked another piece of bunker on the hook and snapped on an extra lead sinker. Jake returned to the controls and brought the boat around again for another float. James repeated the process and took his position at the stern. Jake and Dory gazed across the water at England Point. Dory asked how England Point got its name.

Jake raked his fingers through his sandy hair. "Take a look at that ridge way up there," he said while pointing to the steep cliffs. Her eyes followed his direction up to the long, narrow hilltop. "Legend is—on a clear day you can see England from up there," he said. Dory groaned.

"C'mon now—I'm not that gullible." She snapped a picture of the peak.

"Well, that's the story. There's a little more romance to it than that."

As they gazed over the water and hills a bloodcurdling scream shattered the late morning air. Spinning aft, they saw James scurrying back from the transom and a large, dark fin slowly knifing through the water. The fin passed the stern and turned west coming alongside the *Sea Horse*. "*Oh my God*! They're never going to believe this at the library," Dory said, and clicked off one picture after another of the slow moving shape. She closed her lips in a thin line. The animal swimming just below the surface was easily more than half the length of the boat.

"A sh sh shark!" James said. Still clutching his rod, he now stood slack jawed in the center of the aft deck.

"Everybody calm down!" Jake shouted. "It's a basking shark. It's harmless."

"Look at the size of that thing," Dory countered.

"I'd put it a little over twenty-five feet long. They'll grow to about thirty, thirty-five feet, which is a good size considering they only eat microscopic stuff. The largest specimen ever accurately measured got itself trapped in a herring net up in the Bay of Fundy in 1851. It was over forty feet long and weighed an estimated nineteen tons. The only shark that's bigger is the whale shark."

"Microscopic stuff?"

"Yeah—zooplankton mostly, along with some invertebrates and small fish. Basking sharks are filter feeders. They feed by filtering the water as they swim. That's why they have that huge mouth, and little teeth. An adult basking shark will filter up to two-thousand gallons of seawater per hour. Basking sharks migrate to follow the plankton. Tagging and satellite tracking have shown they swim thousands of miles during the winter months to locate plankton blooms."

"Amazing. Do they live around here?"

"Not really in the bay. A twenty-five footer, about five thousand pounds, washed up on the Town Beach a few years back. It really freaked out the tourists. They called me down there. We took tissue samples, but we never did determine the cause of death. It didn't have any outward signs of injury. It wasn't old age. Like I said, they max out at thirty-five feet."

"I *knew* there were sharks here. What did they do with the one that washed up?" James asked.

"It was so big it had to be cut into pieces to be hauled away. What a stinky mess. The seagulls were the only happy ones."

"Ewe—gross!" James' nose wrinkled up in distaste and he pinched it between his thumb and forefinger.

"Did you know sharks and buffaloes are the only two animals known that don't get cancer? This animal was probably following a food trail that was washing in with the tide, or maybe it's a mom looking for a place to have her babies. Basking sharks enter shallow coastal waters to give birth. It's not unusual for them to check out boats. Maybe it's only here to have a look at us." James shot Jake a questioning look.

Jake continued, "From the mid 1940's up until 1970 the Canadian government tried to eradicate them. They were considered a nuisance on the fishing grounds of the Canadian Pacific coast. It's now listed as threatened and is a fully protected species in the North Atlantic and other places. Let's leave it alone. How's your hook doing, James?" James completely forgot about his line that was dragging along the bottom with its added weight. "Reel it in. Maybe something stole your bait."

James began to crank his line in rapidly. The rod tip twitched as the sinker bumped along the bottom. Suddenly the rod arched over then returned to its upright position with the slackened line floating on the water. James thought he had missed his chance on the bite. Curious, he drew in the line, which became increasing taught, then straightened, pulling line from his reel. The drag sang out in protest. "Looks like you got one!" Dory called from her seat. "Keep him coming."

Jake readied himself again with the gaff. He recognized the streamlined silver body in the water with longitudinal dark stripes from behind its gills to the base of its tail and switched to the net. "Striped bass on the line!" Jake sang out. Dory applauded.

"You're a lucky guy," Jake said. "Striped bass are nocturnal feeders. This guy was probably just moseying along the bottom looking for a snack after a nap and happened on your bait. He's a nice size, but he's not a keeper."

"I can't take him home?" James said. The disappointment turned down the corners of his mouth.

"Sorry, not this one. He's too short. In 2007, striped bass were designated a protected game fish by the federal government—he's below keeper size. Have your mom take a picture then we'll put him back in and let him swim for another year."

"Kind of a big fish to be too small," Dory said.

"Yeah—a keeper has to be at least twenty-eight inches," Jake replied. He removed the hook and held the fish up to lines measured off on the gunwale. "This handsome fella comes in a little shy of two-feet. Believe me, I like bass better than lobster. If we could keep him we would." Jake showed James how to hold the fish by the gill slit. "Striped bass are what are known as *anadromous*. That means they go from salt water to fresh water to spawn. The success of stripers repopulating every year depends on a variety of conditions including water salinity, temperature, turbulence, pollution and what's available to eat. They mostly feed on small fish like your bunker bait, but bass also take lobsters, crabs, clams and mussels. Striped bass will live up to thirty years old and grow to over 100 pounds. Although, smaller ones make for much better eating." James' catch was heavy enough to make his skinny arm sag for the photo op.

"Okay, back he goes," Jake ordered. James flipped his fish overboard.

James' run of beginner's luck continued. He bagged two more sizeable bluefish in rapid succession. One of them weighed seven pounds. Jake stopped the fishing activities. "We're not going to take home more than we can use. There's already more than enough for dinner."

"Hey Mom, what if we invite company? We could have a barbeque at our house," James said.

"Who would you like to invite?" she said.

"How about calling Mrs. Verdi and Billy, Winton Hector, and maybe Miss Donnelly."

"Miss Donnelly?" her voice trailed off. "Well, okay—I'll call as soon as I can get cell service." She bristled at having to invite the redheaded Miss Donnelly, Harmony Bay's most eligible bachelorette. Dory kept the feeling to herself and let it evaporate. It was James' request and Maureen

Donnelly had been very generous and kind to him.

"I'll do the grilling. Since Billy doesn't have a phone I'll see if I can round him up once we get back," Jake said.

Dory was becoming excited at the prospect of entertaining with an impromptu dinner party with Jake Kane and a few friends. "Speaking of food, you guys must be starving. I'm sure those cinnamon buns wore off a long time ago." Dory went below and pulled out the cooler.

"Why don't we hold off for a few minutes," Jake said. "I'll get the boat over to some flat water so you don't get seasick while you eat. Plus, it's a good place for swimming. Did you bring your swimsuits like I told you?" Dory and James nodded they did.

Chapter 18

Jake steered into a tranquil, protected nook a thousand yards north of England Point. It was breathtaking. Notched into the sheer cliffs climbing from the bay, the shallows provided quiet pools in front of short sand beaches for stilting snowy egrets. He slipped past the gigantic boulders ringing the sanctuary on its outer periphery. Small waves rode up their faces and sucked back down between their barnacle-coated gaps, then flowed out to the bay. Once beyond the outer boundary, he killed the engine and let the vessel's momentum carry it farther. The birds didn't seem troubled by the arrival of the boat.

"Jake, it's beautiful here," Dory said. She clicked pictures of the cliffs, the egrets and the humpback maze of the rocks they had passed through. "It's like a whole other world."

"It's called Carroll's Landing," Jake said, then headed forward to set the anchor.

"Let's eat lunch," James said.

"I hope you guys washed all of that fish guck off your hands," she said, opening the cooler and distributing soft drinks and sandwiches. "The captain eats first— here, Jake." She handed him a sandwich and a Coke. "So, another place out here with a name. Carroll's Landing?"

"Yeah," Jake replied, "some hermit fisherman in the mid 1700's named Christian Carroll had a fishing shack on that beach. I guess he wanted to be the first guy on the fish in Osprey's Gut when the tides flowed. Maybe he was a recluse who liked the scenery—I don't know, but his name stuck."

"He must have been kind of fearless and resourceful living out here by himself." Dory imagined living on the beach protected from the ocean by the rock wall behind it.

"Story is—when it wasn't a good day for fishing, Christian Carroll was out on the point scavenging stuff from shipwrecks and digging around for buried treasure. He must have had some kind of impact on Harmony Bay, or Quahog Bay as it was known back then."

"What makes you say that?" Dory said and then gave a baffled look.

"Put your thinking cap on, Dory— do you know Carroll Way? It's a narrow street that crosses Bay Road in the village. It leads right down to the water and lines up directly with Carroll's Landing."

"Oh yes, now that I think about it a little, I do know it."

"Back in those days, there were very few inhabitants of Quahog Bay. The name must have had something to do with him."

"Pretty awesome," James chimed in. "Having a landing *and* a street named after you."

"Who knows," Dory said, "maybe he was more than a lonely fisherman. It might be interesting to look into. It will be fun to research. I wonder what he might have found among the wrecks." The three of them sat on the deck chairs that Jake set out, ate their lunch and exchanged theories about Christian Carroll.

"Here's another local tidbit," Jake said. "You know the story about the *Jeni Lyn* crashing into the ledges at England Point, right?" Dory and James nodded in unison. "And you know the crew got rescued by Harmony baymen?" They continued to nod. "Those stranded sailors got rescued right off this beach." Jake pointed toward the shore, now only about one-hundred feet away. "The fire they set was right up against that rock face." Jake rubbed his belly in satisfaction and thanked his guests profusely for the meal. "Okay, James—go below and put on your swimsuit. After your lunch goes down we can take a swim."

Dory gathered up the empty cans and lunch wrappings. She closed up the cooler and told James to lug it below with him, and then faced Jake. "Does the galley slave get to swim, Captain?"

"That's entirely up to you."

"You're not going to make me walk the plank are you?"

"Eh, no."

"Well then, as soon as James comes up, I'll go down and change." James came to the wheelhouse wearing his swimsuit and swimming goggles. Dory pushed past Jake. At the top of the companionway she looked back over her shoulder. "No peeking," she said. She opted for her more modest one-piece swimsuit. She wriggled into it in the cramped confines of the head, checking herself in the mirror one last time. Her body wasn't very different from what it was during her college days. Dory was confident enough in her figure to wear a more revealing two-piece, but she didn't want to give Jake the wrong impression. She picked up the pile of clothes James had left on the floor and made her way above deck.

Jake was startled when Dory returned. Her appearance caused him to gasp slightly. Dory's shiny hair, drawn back tightly in a single plaited ponytail, contrasted strongly with her porcelain skin. Delicate tendrils at her temples, not caught up in the braid, danced in the intermittent breeze. A halo of sunlight bounced off her shoulders and the top of her head. Statuesque, she could have easily graced the pages of *Sports Illustrated's* swimsuit edition. The top of her long legs met a solid blue Speedo, cut high at the outer thighs, very much like the ones worn by competition swimmers. Clinging, it accentuated every curve. Jake caught himself looking for far too long. His imagination blocked out all other thoughts.

Dory methodically applied waterproof sunscreen to James. "All righty then, crew—time to go overboard," Jake said. Jake carried a cumbersome wooden ladder to the port side that now faced the beach. He hooked it over the gunwale and dropped the steps into the water. "Ladies first," he said with a pronounced bow.

"You're not going to throw me overboard are you?"

"Did you want me to?"

"No, I can throw myself overboard."

"Earlier you asked about life-preservers for you and James, do you want them? Can you swim?" James doubled over with laughter. Jake once again took it as only an adolescent response. "Dory, are you sure you don't want a life vest?"

Dory stepped over the side and stood on the ladder's top step, facing inboard with aplomb. In response to Jake's question she asked, "What's the depth here, skipper?"

Jake held the life preserver and glanced at the depth gauge. "Uh—two fathoms—about twelve feet."

"Any big rocks down there?" Her knees were now completely bent; her hands grasped the top of the ladder rails.

"Nah. It's a sandy bottom from here all the way in. Water temp is seventy-two degrees if you want to know."

Her response cut his words short. "Perfect."

Dory launched herself into the air. Once airborne, she tucked her chin to her chest, pulled her legs up and wrapped her arms around her lower legs, drawing her thighs tightly to her belly. Now at full altitude, she straightened and entered the water cleanly, having executed a perfect back-flip. The dive was exhilarating, the cool water refreshing. Dory surfaced, treading water. "C'mon in buddy—the water's fine," she called out to James. Standing on the ladder's top step, he cannon-balled in, only inches from his mother. "Oh! You little wise guy," Dory shrieked as the ensuing wave caught her in the face. Jake stood with one hand on his hip and the other holding up the flotation devices.

"I guess you don't need these, eh?"

"Eighteen years at the YMCA pool. About seven for James. I think we'll be okay."

Jake tossed his glasses on the console, kicked off his deck shoes and stripped off his shirt. For the first time Dory saw the cruel, serrated, purple shark bite scars tattooed below his ribcage. In Dory's eyes it didn't detract from his appeal one bit. He stepped up on the gunwale and dove in holding a blue mesh sack. He broke the surface between James and Dory.

"Dory, that was some dive. You been practicing?" Jake said.

"Well, actually—no. I'm a bit rusty."

"Can you two make it to the beach?"

"Piece of cake. What's with the bag?"

"It's for treasure hunting."

The three struck out for shore. It was an easy swim in the buoyant, seaweed-free, salt water. In less than half of the distance, Jake and Dory could touch the bottom. For James, it took a few more strokes. Once out of the water Jake said, "Let me show you a couple of things. Not too many people know about this." Even though they were all dripping wet, they were not cold. There was no breeze in the sheltered cove, the water was warm, and the sun melted any tinge of discomfort they may have felt. Jake led them to the rock wall, forty feet in height, which acted as the backdrop for the beach. There was an opening to a small cave at the base, its entrance well camouflaged by boulders.

Jake continued, "It would make sense that Mr. Carroll spent his time there during the more brutal weather. He probably would've made some sort of door from driftwood and lined the interior of the cave with dried eelgrass. He'd be as snug as a bug in there. I also think that's where the survivors from the *Jeni Lyn* spent the night. At least the badly injured ones did. It's big enough in there to hold over a dozen men. The cliffs protected them from the easterly winds. That night it was likely pouring buckets. Down low in this nook, it was probably dead calm. Inside the cave they could've gotten a small fire started with a flint then moved it outside to build a signal fire once the rain let up. Let me show you something." Jake steered James away from the cave entrance. "We don't have flashlights with us. I've been in there. It's just rocks—not much to see. Walk this way."

A mere twenty feet to the left of the cave entrance and twenty feet off the ground, an outcropping of rock jutted several feet out from the vertical face. The stone below the overhang showed obvious evidence of charring. "I believe this is where Christian Carroll smoked some of his catch in the mid 1700's and a hundred years later the sailors built a driftwood fire here big enough to be seen across the bay."

"This is amazing. A lot of local history evolved from here," Dory said.

"But wait—there's more," Jake said. "Have a look at this." Jake doubled back past the cave entrance to where the stone became smoother. Clearly carved into the wall was a C, a foot in height. An identical C, below and to the right of the upper C, overlapped it creating a sort of monogram. "He left his mark. Colonial graffiti."

"It looks like a sign, kind of like an advertisement. Like CC lives here," Dory offered. "Time was valuable for survival in those days. It had to be spent gathering food and fuel, *and* making a living. I wonder what prompted him to do it." Jake traced the carvings with his finger. "I don't think it was done for vanity— especially living out here alone."

Intrigued, Dory felt there were things about Christian Carroll they didn't know.

"Who left his mark?" James said.

"CC—Christian Carroll," Jake responded.

"Wow. Way cool. How'd you know it was him?"

"How many guys with the initials CC do you think were in this hideaway long enough to chisel their initials into solid rock?"

"I guess you're right." James looked at the mesh bag in Jake's hand. "When are we going treasure hunting?"

"How about right now?"

"Where do we go?"

"There's treasure buried all over the beach." James did a double-take from Jake to the waterline and back again.

"Let's go!" James raced toward the water as Jake and Dory followed casually behind.

"Hmm … I think I know what you're up to, Tom Sawyer."

"Aw c'mon, this will be fun."

"You and James go ahead. I'm going beachcombing."

James joined Jake in the first couple of inches of water that met the beach. Jake dug his toes into the sand. It was the consistency of wet cement. After a moment, he stopped, bent over and scooped a large clam from its hiding place.

"Wow. That's all you have to do to get a clam?" James now mimicked Jakes actions.

"Yep, sometimes they give themselves away with a few telltale bubbles. Nobody ever comes out here, so this beach is loaded with shellfish." James stabbed his toes at bubbles coming from the wet sand and was rewarded with his first clam. Jake and James continued the process, placing the mollusks in the bag in rapid succession. "Hey we better stop now. We've got more than enough for dinner." Dory took a walk to the far end of the cove and returned after they had tallied four dozen.

"Jake, look what I found," she said. Dory held out an empty scallop shell its cupped side facing upward.

Without his eyeglasses, Jake squinted down at the shell. "Yeah, that's a scallop shell. Good to see them out here."

"Look closer." She flipped the shell over in her hand. Lifting it up to his face, it revealed ridges decorated with distinct, dark stripes. "Is this what I think it is—a *skunk*?" she said.

"Holy mackerel. We did it! The lab spat grew and crossbred with wild stock. We've never, ever seeded any scallops way out here. The tides and winds carried the young critters clear across the bay!"

"Congratulations, clam-father." Dory eyed the large sack of clams lying in the water. "How are you going to get them back out to the boat?"

"Stick with ol' Jakey boy. I'll come up with something. Let's go." Jake waded out with the sack of clams, his head spinning. A great day had just become perfect. All the years of hard work were showing results sooner than he imagined. "Wait here with the appetizer course. I'll be right back," Jake said when they got to waist deep water. He swam toward the *Sea Horse*. Dory had no idea what he planned to do. She stood in the water with the clam bag at her feet. Jake boarded the boat and was back in the water a moment later with two life vests. He returned to the waist deep water.

"No really, we'll be fine. We can swim it from here. It's very chivalrous, but not necessary," Dory said. She looked at the two blaze orange vests. Each now had an additional mountaineering carabiner clip attached to their D rings. Jake reached down and pulled the clam bag to the surface. He snatched the webbing of the bag with the carabiners. The bag now dangled in the water suspended between the two vests. Dory burst out laughing.

"Chivalry isn't dead. I wasn't going to make you swim back carrying a sack of clams," Jake said and pushed the floating clam bar forward. He pushed until his feet no longer touched bottom, then kicked his legs while holding the vests in front of him. The three swam to the *Sea Horse*. Arriving at the boat, they dragged themselves up the ladder, pleasantly tired from the day's activities.

"Okay, you two are going to be in command while I clean the catch of the day. In the meanwhile, let's have some snacks," Jake said. Producing a clam knife, he shucked open a half dozen clams. He handed a raw clam to Dory who sucked up the contents of the shell. "Will you eat one, James?"

"I'll try it," James said. Passing another clam to James, he slurped it down.

"Like it?" James shook his head up and down vigorously.

Jake stopped opening clams for a moment and said, "People like you are good for business—you'll keep shellfish prices up. Eat up before the gulls come and snatch 'em. We'll save the rest for this evening's barbeque."

"Oh that reminds me," Dory said. Reaching into her backpack, she pulled out her cell phone and flipped it open. Seeing she had service, she scrolled down the address book. Stopping at Angelina's number, she pressed call. Dory extended the invitation and did the same with Maureen Donnelly and Winton Hector. "Okay, everybody's in. Maureen is bringing beer. Angelina has some fresh basil and mozzarella. She'll pick up some tomatoes to go with that. Winton said he'll stop by Shea's Bakery and bring dessert. I'll stop by George's farm stand to pick up corn and stuff to make a salad."

Jake lifted a three-foot long plank, walled in on three sides to a height of four inches. In each wall, scuppers vented the long flat surface along with a series of one-inch holes drilled through the board. Extending below the board were two legs. Jake inserted them into corresponding brackets on the port gunwale that allowed the board to cantilever out over the water. Remaining barefoot, Dory pulled on a pair of shorts and a windbreaker over her swimsuit. "What do you need me to do, Captain?"

"You and James can go forward and aweigh anchor. You'll see the pegs on the foredeck where the anchor line gets wrapped. I'm sure you'd rather not be at this end of the boat."

Jake went about the business of cleaning the fish on the board hanging over the side. First, he removed the head and tossed it overboard. Then running his filleting knife deep into the gut, he made a lateral incision working from back to front. Scooping out the innards, Jake threw these into the water. Scraping the pocket clean, the job on this fish was done. James appeared at his elbow as he pulled another bluefish from the storage well. "James, do you want to give it a try?" He declined, electing to observe rather than operate. James looked up at Jake the whole time, admiring everything about him. With all three fish cleaned, Jake pulled a bucket of seawater on board. He poured the bucket over the cleaning table, rinsing the remnants of guts and gore through the drainage scuppers.

Dory sat on one of the deck chairs watching Jake with James at his side. James never experienced another man in his mom's life. With Jake, she could see everything was good. However, she decided she'd ask her son about that at some time in the future. Jake pulled the cleaning board from its mounts and stowed it away. He turned to James, "Good thing we stopped at three fish, eh? Otherwise, you'd have kept me cleaning fish all night. We'll be back at the dock in an hour, why don't you and your mom relax while we set sail for home."

Dory and James slouched in the deck chairs with their feet propped up on the transom. Dory sat soaking up the sun as she gazed at the cove, the swooping gulls and the towering cliff above it, then off to the right to the peak of England Point. Jake started the engine and eased the boat between the rocks. Dory looked at the chair to her right and saw James was already asleep. Dory turned his baseball cap around to shade his face and put her windbreaker over him to block the sun. She pulled herself up from the chair and took up a position beside Jake. "Like some company, Captain Kane?"

"Sure," he said, "I thought you'd be back there taking a break."

"Well, I was, but James is sleeping—I didn't want to leave you alone."

Now next to Jake, she leaned her back up against the forward bulkhead, looking back at the birds and England Point receding in her view. "Jake, tell me, you said there was more romance to the story about England Point."

"Yeah, well okay…" Jake said, "let me see if I can remember the whole story. Back in the 1600's over in England, there were these two young kids in love, Nehemiah and Priscilla. Nehemiah was a groom on a big country estate over there, who in addition to brushing horses, could play the flute fairly well. Priscilla was the daughter of the quasi-royal estate owner, Lord Falsipents. Anyway, Lord Fancy Pants gets wind of the romance between his daughter and a lowly stable boy. He confronts Priscilla and she gives up Nehemiah, although, she feels really awful about it. To break up the courtship, her wicked father arranges to have the boy exiled to the colonies on some fabricated reason." Dory opened a can of Coke and offered it to Jake.

Jake continued, "Next thing Nehemiah knows, he winds up at Quahog

Bay as a fisherman. Time goes on and his heart longs for Priscilla. He's illiterate, so he can't try to send a letter home. And after being shang-haied, he doesn't trust anybody to carry the message for fear of reprisals from evil Lord Flashy Pants. It's a real brain-squeezer for him. So—what Nehemiah decides to do is, every chance he gets, he climbs to the top of England Point and whips out his flute. He plays a tune and prays he'll see his Priscilla again."

"Ahh… what a sweet guy," Dory said.

"There's more to the story." Jake took a pull from the Coke. "Nehemiah faces ol' England and keeps praying and playing the sorry song over and over. The westerly winds carry his music to Priscilla's ears in England. She's still madly in love with him. She wondered every day what happened to Nehemiah. Priscilla can't contain her excitement when she recognizes Nehemiah's flute music. She runs away from home and boards a ship bound for the Americas. Tragically, the ship she's on goes down with all hands in a bad easterly gale somewhere up around the Grand Banks."

"That *is* a tragic ending," Dory said.

"Hold on," Jake said. "Meanwhile, Nehemiah starts to realize he'll never see her again. It weighs so heavily on his heart, he writes a very somber song. Nehemiah played his woeful song up on top of England Point whenever the wind was out of the west—sometimes he played for hours. He must have been pooped from fishing all day, climbing up there to the top of the Point and gigging all night. The wrap-up of the story is—and this is where it gets a little weird." Jake tilted his head back and gulped more of the cola. "Priscilla was hearing that sad song in her watery grave for so long she knew it by heart. She taught the song to the wind and the waves. Now, every time you go to England Point, if the wind is out of the east, which almost always brings nasty weather here, the elements play Nehemiah's song back to him. It whistles and moans through the rocks. When the east winds blew, Nehemiah ignored the wicked weather, and hiked up there to listen for her response." Jake took a long pause. "The funny part is, Pastor Simvasten tells me, that in the Bible, the book of Nehemiah says prayer and hard work can accomplish impossible things when a person determines to try to trust and obey God. I guess Nehemiah's hard work and prayers really never were answered.

Maybe he didn't trust and obey."

Jake turned to Dory and could see her eyes tearing up as she spoke. "Well…maybe his prayers were answered," she said.

"How do you mean?"

"She was able to send the song back to him. That's worth something if you can't show up."

"I suppose you're right. Not a Sisyphean effort after all, eh? "

"Have you ever climbed to the top of England Point, Jake?"

"I have."

"Did you cry out for your love lost at sea from up there?"

"Yeah…I did," Jake said, and then became quiet.

Jake knew he was madly in love with Dory, but didn't know how to express it. He wasn't afraid of her rejection of him. He realized that he didn't want to be in a position again to cry out for a lost love. The thought of that pain and the lonely days that followed were too much to relive. For the time being, he felt safe.

Dory stepped up beside him, draped her arm over his shoulders and hugged him. "It's okay," she said. "Sometimes we need that." She decided to change the subject. "So, tell me—what's it like to live aboard a houseboat?"

With the sun still high in the late June afternoon sky the *Sea Horse* chugged toward the village of Harmony Bay with Jake at the helm. Dory never left his side for the rest of the voyage. James awoke as Jake docked the boat.

Chapter 19

Fourth of July always saw Harmony Bay swell to its peak population for the year. Surely the annual tourism business and summer residents swelled the ranks, but moreover, it was the events of the day that drew an additional layer of visitors to the town. Memorial Day weekend was the official kickoff of the season but it was commonly agreed the Fourth of July was *the* start.

Like thousands of other American small towns, Harmony Bay started the day with a parade that was a tourist attraction by itself. Nobody seemed to know for sure why it was able to draw a bigger crowd than much larger towns. Being able to go to the beaches or go fishing or boating afterward was considered a factor. Harmony Bay's Fourth of July parade and festivities were in some ways about the same as any place else. Harmony Bay's events of the day were delivered with so much joy, sincerity and enthusiasm, it was hard not to pay attention. Harmony Bay was so Americana, so small town, and so charmingly quaint it could not be ignored. In addition to the parade, other activities throughout the day included the craft fair that the not-for-profit organizations in town relied on to raise funds, the clam chowder cooking contest, the whaleboat brigade races reenacting the events during the American Revolution at Harmony Bay and the customary fireworks display over the water.

Today would be exceptional. There was not a cloud to be seen in the sky or on any weather report. Accompanied by a full moon, a high-pressure system ushering in clear, cerulean blue skies with a daytime high of seventy-six degrees was forecast. Light winds and low humidity, with no chance of pesky late day thunderstorms, made the day perfect to be outdoors. This was guaranteed to liven the step of parade marchers who were outfitted in costumes or uniforms. Charter boats were out on the water today, but the commercial fishing boats, who considered it bad luck to fish on Independence Day, stayed firmly lashed to the dock. It was probably more a case of the men wanting to be home with their families to enjoy the festivities that kept them ashore.

James and Dory heard all about the upcoming events from the locals who encouraged them to participate. Harmony Bay's library had an entry in the parade and a booth at the fair selling lemonade, fudge and donated books. Dory was happy to participate. James was invited to march with The Sons of Liberty. Later on, this group would row whaleboats up Patriot's Creek for the reenactment competition. It was a competition, but a friendly one to be sure. It awarded nothing more than bragging rights until the next Independence Day. However, there were usually a few side bets placed at Molly's bar. James was excited about his role. His mother had sewn him a dark brown vest, removed the lower third of the legs from a pair of almost outgrown tan jeans, and affixed silver buckles made from cardboard and aluminum foil to his shoes. With white socks pulled up over his calves, he looked every bit the part of a young Patriot in the late eighteenth century. The Sons of Liberty Committee provided him with a tri-cornered hat and a genuine looking drum. A long-sleeved white shirt with the collar removed rounded out his costume. Other youngsters were given the assignments of carrying drums or yellow Gadsden flags emblazoned with coiled rattlesnakes above the motto *Don't Tread on Me*. Those who knew how to piped Yankee Doodle on recorders. Grown men with more elaborate outfits carried muskets or swords. James dreamed about the day when he could carry one himself.

To avoid the traffic snarls, Dory and James arrived early. Parking their car at the library, they walked over to the assembly area for the parade. Crowds had already begun to gather on the slab granite sidewalks with children sitting on the curb. Morning coolness caused many to clutch cups of hot coffee poured from thermoses. Doc Tollenson was one of the parade organizers. He'd been doing the volunteer job for decades. He greeted Dory and James heartily when they arrived. Doc complemented Dory on her costume and gave them their starting position numbers.

Dory was bedecked in an 1890's bicycle suit that Angelina had sewn for her. Mrs. Lanscome, who would ride a bicycle built for two with Dory, had a matching outfit. All of the other women from the library had similar outfits. They all wore white cotton bloomers fitted at the waist, a jacket with large puffy sleeves, six blue buttons side-by-side up the front and a billowing red bow around the neck. Dory tied her hair in pigtails with red ribbons. Dory and her library group were near the beginning. This allowed them enough time to make it to their lemonade booth before the parade ended. James and his fellow Sons of Liberty were at the tail end of the parade.

Mayor Vinny Pesce arrived at the parade check-in table. He was an odd, short, rotund man with narrowly set eyes who sweated profusely in the fresh morning air. The mayor looked like a comic book character. He wore white shoes, a pinky ring, polished fingernails and drove a big, shiny, black Lincoln Town Car. These were all items men in Harmony Bay didn't own or want. Pesce's family owned a lot of the commercial real estate in town. When competition moved in and threatened the family holdings, all sorts of things happened at Village Hall. Permits for new buildings were lost for months. Variances and zoning appeals took years to complete and some new projects never saw the light of day. While the board of Village Trustees managed to keep him in check, most town folk barely tolerated him. Others loathed him. Pesce was duplicitous and cunning.

Pesce was reelected every two years primarily because no one else, even those more qualified, didn't want the job. He either ran unopposed or against a novice opponent. It was recognized that the aggravation of the job wasn't worth the part-time paycheck that came with it. Pesce did it to fuel his ego and protect his family's empire. He was a professional politician and did everything he could to get his picture in the paper by attending ribbon cuttings, new boat launchings, school plays, community concerts, senior citizen functions, and parades.

Harmony Bay was generally a healthy town, but it bled from a thousand small cuts. Old-timers recognized it. As good as things were, it wasn't like the old days. The sharp drop in shellfish stocks, greedy slumlords who took advantage of depressed real estate prices and maneuvers by a slick local politician were beginning to turn the blood trickle into a hemorrhage. Harmony Bay was bare faced and transparent; a place where you saw everything for what it was. There were no false pretenses. The place had a good sense of humor. And—it didn't suffer fools gladly.

Pesce shook hands with Doc Tollenson, slapped him on the back, and smiled incessantly. "Great job as always, Doc! I new you could pull this off. You're an old pro at parades," the mayor said with affection. Still grinning, he held his clammy hand out to Dory. "My dear, you look absolutely stunning! It is such a pleasure to have you grace our library." Pleased that he didn't attempt to hug her as he usually did, Dory grimaced then politely shook his hand. "Thank you, Mr. Mayor," she said. Turning toward James, he stuck out his hand again. "How we doin' there, little fella?" James wanted to kick him in the shins.

Edmund *Fishhook* Cutsciko rolled up to the check-in station in his Model T pickup truck and joined them. Mayor Pesce stated the obvious, "Well look who's here now. It's good ol' Cutsciko! As always, a mighty fine showing for the parade, that Tin Lizzy of yours." Fishhook stepped out onto the running board then to the ground, the old-fashioned springs gasping in relief as they were freed of his bulk. Sizing up the situation, and not wanting to spend an extra minute with her landlord, Dory asked Doc Tollenson if James could wait with him until the other Patriots arrived. She was going to look for the bicycling librarians.

Doc chuckled, and then responded. "Sure, he can help me hand out these number cards. We're going to need some new, young organizing volunteers in the upcoming years. I'll start training him now." James liked Doc. He was always friendly and had a no nonsense approach. Doc's thin frame was decorated with a wide-brim white straw hat with a red, white and blue band, a red string tie and blue sleeve garters.

Mr. Mayor threw an arm around Fishhook while thanking him profusely for his participation in Harmony Bay's parade. "You know, after all, Big Ed, its people like you who make the event a success! We know we can always count on you! Isn't that right Doc?" the mayor gushed. Doc Tollenson was visibly annoyed and James wanted to give the landlord a kick in the shins as well. The mayor babbled on, "Ooh—ee, yes siree, look at the shine on this baby. Great job, Ed."

Cutsciko fancied himself a country gentlemen and real estate tycoon. In reality, he inherited most of his wealth, although he did manage to build his inventory of rental properties by snapping up foreclosures at auction on the steps of Village Hall. These bankruptcies were often the result of bay families who had one bad year after another on the water, or had lost their breadwinner at sea. Harmony Bay inhabitants tagged him with the moniker *Fishhook* because of his unsavory practice of hooking a tenant in at a low rental price and promising to fix up the property as part of the deal. Once the lease was signed and the tenant moved in, the only home improvements they ever saw were the ones they performed themselves. Fishhook was also known for substantial rent increases in subsequent years once a family was settled into their jobs or had kids established in the schools. This made moving an uncomfortable option.

Harmony Bay folks did not take kindly to greed and meanness. They always rallied around the families that were displaced. Many opened their homes to them or helped the families find a new affordable place to live. No questions were asked and no one ever expected compensation. For hundreds of years the coastal residents learned that the next hurricane, nor'easter or bad luck on the fishing grounds could render them homeless. They all looked after each other.

Fishhook was beefy, the byproduct of too many free luncheons in the company of the mayor. Round-shouldered, Fishhook always wore a sour face. His plump, flaccid jowls and full moustache drooping sadly at the corners of his mouth gave him the appearance of a walrus.

The two least liked citizens of Harmony Bay strolled off arm-in-arm to politic, leaving James and the doctor alone. Cutsciko was in search of a driver for his second parade entry, a 1922 Model T roadster. Pesce was in pursuit of votes.

"Is he *always* like that?" James asked about the mayor.

"More than usual. Next year is an election year," Doc said.

James was learning at a tender age what made slimy politicians slimy.

James and Doc Tollenson looked over the Model T truck. The morning sun reflected off its black fenders. It glittered like a polished gem. Body panels appeared white from the brilliance. James took notice of the wood-staked rear bed with a bulging picnic hamper covered in a red and white checked cloth. It was in reserve to provide a post parade lunch for Cutsciko and his cronies. The cab was finished in a matching polished wood grain. Displayed on each side was a wooden sign with gold-leaf lettering displaying the name of Cutsciko's real estate company. There was a hand crank in front of a brass plate stating *1919 Ford Motor Company*, skinny tires mounted on twelve spoke wooden wheels that tapered where they fit together at the flange, and solid brass headlamps. Each of them stuck their heads into the side entry openings. Doc explained to James, "The Model T was the best selling vehicle in its day. By 1918, half of the cars on the road were Model T's. It sold very well. Henry Ford didn't even have to advertise it. Mr. Ford invented the moving assembly line. It only took them an hour and a half to build these cars. It's very tricky to drive by today's standards. Yes, really very tricky." He went about explaining the controls. "There's the clutch, reverse and brake pedals on the floor and two levers on the steering column. The left lever is for the spark advance and the other is for the throttle. That floor lever on the driver's left is for neutral when it's in the upright position. If you push the left pedal all the way to the floor it engages first gear, half way out is neutral and with the floor lever thrown forward, all the way out is second gear. Depressing the middle pedal engages reverse. The brake pedal is on the right. You can understand why not too many folks know how to drive these anymore." James really didn't understand, but he didn't let on. He figured if Henry Ford had sold that many cars, somebody must have figured out how to drive them.

Cutsciko returned without the mayor or a volunteer to drive his 1922 model. He spoke in a low, patronizing tone. "Say Doc, you know about these Model T's. Waddaya say to taking the '22 for a spin in the parade?" Doc folded his arms across his chest, taking pleasure in delaying his response for as long as possible.

"Gee, Ed, I'll have to think about it for a while," he said. Doc unfolded his arms and stuck his hands in his back pockets. "Looks like you're doing a little advertising there, Ed." Doc pointed to the signs.

"Oh yeah, those little signs. They're nothing really, they're so small."

"Well, you know the parade rules, Ed. No advertising or commercial vehicles allowed."

"Bu, bu, but, those little signs? You mean to tell me you're not going to allow this beautiful historic piece in the parade because of those little signs?" he stammered.

"The rules are the rules. Same way it's been for as long as you've been entering your vehicles in the parade. You can withdraw if you like. But if you're staying in—the signs have to come off."

"If I remove the signs will you drive the '22?"

Doc shrugged. "Let me think about it, Ed. Either way, the signs have to come off if you want to be in the parade."

"I can't believe you're being so petty."

James noticed Billy and Angus approaching and stepped back to let them join the men's discussion. Billy interrupted the standoff by shaking hands with the doctor and nodded toward Fishhook. "Good morning, Ed," Billy said. Angus moved forward then took several steps back. He let out a low growl and glared at Fishhook.

"Hi there, Billy. Are you ready to sell me those acres next to your place up on Pencil Hill?

"No, I do not think so."

"Well, waddaya asking for it?"

"I am not asking."

"Be reasonable, Billy. Everything is for sale. Everything has a price. Name a price."

"I am thinking of holding on to that land. You never know. I may have children at some point in the future. It would be rather nice to leave it to them. Wouldn't you agree, Doc?" The doctor laughed heartily. The slumlord fumed and a befuddled expression contorted his walrus face.

"Say Billy, wouldn't you love to drive a mint condition 1922 Model T Ford Roadster in the parade?" Cutsciko said.

"I will have to think about it."

"Everybody has to think about it. What's to think about! You know how to drive it."

"That is true. I surely do know how to drive it. If I must say so, probably better than you do," he said, and then directed a subtle wink at James.

"It's an opportunity that doesn't come along every day."

The debate continued and James and Doc stepped back facing Billy, Cutsciko and the antique truck. James watched Angus circle around the far side of the truck and warily approach its rear bumper. Billy and Cutsciko still had their backs turned toward the vehicle. Angus looked both ways and leapt onto the bed of the truck. In a single motion, as Billy and Cutsciko continued the animated verbal exchange, Angus moved to the picnic basket and pulled off the checked cloth with his mouth. He stuck his face in the basket and devoured its contents. James looked up at Doc who stood watching the whole caper unravel. Once again, Doc folded his arms across his chest. He leaned over to James and whispered in his ear, "Sometimes it's just better to stand back and let things happen."

After finishing off the edibles in the basket, Angus quietly retraced his steps around the blind side of the truck and returned to his spot a few paces behind Billy. If ever there was a spiteful act by a dog, this was it. Lying down, he licked his front paws and the drool from his lips as though nothing had ever happened. James couldn't believe what he had witnessed and tried not to laugh. He poked Doc with his elbow. The doctor poked back. James giggled.

Now Cutsciko was begging Billy to drive his prized collectible in the parade, with or without the real estate signage.

"C'mon, waddaya think?" Cutsciko pleaded.

"I am thinking that Harmony Bay needs a new scholarship program to send more of our deserving children to college."

"What are you talkin' about? There's student loans for that kinda stuff. We already pay a lot of taxes here." He looked around for Mayor Pesce to confirm his statement.

"It is not the same. I am thinking that some of the local businesses could set the pace with a sizeable donation to get things rolling."

"Okay, okay, I get the picture. Cutsciko Real Estate will contribute fifty bucks. You'll drive then—right?"

"That is quite magnanimous of you. However, I am thinking five hundred dollars is a good place to start."

Cutsciko began to stammer again. Wild eyed and red faced, the bristling whiskers twitched.

"Fa fa five… hu hun hundred bucks? You've got to be kidding me!"

"My dear, Ed… I am not kidding. Furthermore, I do not appreciate your bellicose behavior. And yes, for a five hundred dollar donation I will pilot your flivver."

"This is blackmail!"

Billy stroked his beard and attempted to mollify Fishhook. "No, it is a donation. After all, everything *does* have a price. Right, Ed? Fully tax deductible, I assure you. I will trust you for the check. Angus and I will pick it up at your office on Tuesday." Angus let out a growl that ended with a bark. "A deal then?"

"Okay, okay. You win. The car is parked around the corner at my office. Doc, give him his starting position."

Cutsciko fumed. He turned to the truck and wrenched the hand crank to start the engine. He jumped into the cab and gunned the motor, leaving in a cloud of dust. In his hostile wake, the red and white checkered cloth floated to the ground.

Doc stood with his arms still folded. He addressed James and Billy, "He's *the* wealthiest man in town, maybe even the county. You'd swear by his version of the story that he's on the brink of bankruptcy and can't survive until his next paycheck. Imagine the good he could do with some of that money if he redirected his thinking. He's such a tightwad—it's pitiful."

James watched the Sons of Liberty assemble in front of Doc Tollenson's table. Jake's crew consisted of Luke Hewes the Police Headquarters dispatcher, Molly's brother Liam McDuff, Joe Ciamariconi an avid sport fisher who was called *Sea Macaroni* by the crew, Rory MacNish a veteran bayman, who was a researcher at the lab, and another member, one of Jake's strapping college student interns. The officers, minutemen, pipers, drummers, and whaleboat crews started to arrive in two and threes. Members of the opposing team harassed Jake saying, "Hey that young guy—he's a ringer."

"Oh, hey now, you're just going to have to rely on your good looks to even up the score!" Jake shouted to a pair of burly, musket toting baymen in minuteman dress. Jake looked dashing for the occasion. He wore the blue jacket of an officer in the Continental Army with a wheat colored vest and pants. Black boots came to his knees, a scabbard hung from his hip holding an ornate sword. A tri-cornered hat sat atop his blond head. Jovial bickering and bantering continued among the participants until all of the *Sons* arrived. Stirring themselves into a frenzy, they all joined together in a rousing chorus of *Yankee Doodle* as they went to the sideline of the parade. James sang right along with the crew while keeping a steady cadence on his drum. They were last in the line-up so James had the opportunity to watch from the curb. He took up an observation post alongside Jake.

As it had for over a century, Harmony Bay's Fourth of July parade stepped off at nine a.m. sharp. It was corny by some standards, but traditions absolved all issues. Police Chief Dooley proceeded slowly on the parade route in his patrol car with red roof lights flashing and an occasional blast of the siren, clearing the streets of those wandering into the path of the oncoming marchers. The United States Coast Guard Color Guard led off the event with flags flying and sparkling bayoneted rifles. James learned in school that the Coast Guard had been around longer than the Navy. Folks on the coast were beholden to the Coast Guard for the service they provided. The honor had always been bestowed on them to be the first entry.

Mayor Pesce followed the color guard in his brother's black Cadillac convertible. Magnetic signs on the doors told the crowd the car contained Vincent T. Pesce, Mayor, Harmony Bay. Actually, the question never came up as to who was mayor, or what his name was. It was nothing more than a chance for him to put his name in front of the voters one more time. Pesce grinned like an oily jack-o-lantern as he waved to everyone and called out to him or her by name if he knew it. Laying on sugary accolades and well wishes, he schmoozed everyone that he could of voting age.

Next in line was the Harmony Bay Volunteer Fire Department displaying two of its fire engines and a contingent of firefighters in dress blues. James returned the volunteer's wave who greeted the crowd from the tops of the trucks and from their perches on the tailgates. Following close behind was the diminutive fire department marching band supplemented by several non fire department civilians to fill out the ranks.

Dory and the staff from the library filled the street pedaling brightly festooned bicycles. Red, white, and blue crêpe paper was woven through the spokes, and each was fitted with a thumb-bell, which the riders chimed continuously. They all waved in their coordinated outfits, steadying their bikes with one hand. A tall girl with long dark hair called out as Dory and Mrs. Lanscome made zigzagging progress. "Hey, Mrs. McDonough. Hey Dory, we love you!" Mrs. Lanscome leaned forward from the rear seat of the bicycle and said, "That's Kaelin. She will be starting college in September to become a nurse, thanks to the help she received with her applications and all from Jake and the others. She's a little nervous about going away to school. Perhaps you can chat with her some time. And, yes my dear, the kids really do think you are grand. Honestly, they do." Dory smiled and waved back at Kaelin and her family.

Maureen Donnelly marched in the parade with Riley, her golden retriever. Miss Donnelly wore a simple tee shirt that read, *United We Stand*, red sneakers and blue jeans, Riley wore the stars and stripes around her neck. Unleashed, the dog performed tricks on command for the onlookers from simple hand signals given by Miss Donnelly. Roll over, play dead, dance on two legs, sit up and beg, walk backward, sneaky dog crawl, and bow. Riley loved to do her routine. When she finished her act, she faced Miss Donnelly and they bowed to each other. Applause flowed from the sidewalks.

Dave Small's tow truck was next with a huge American flag hung from the tow boom. Dave complied with the parade committee's wishes for no commercial advertising by covering the lettering on the doors of the truck with *God Bless America* signs.

Winton drove Billy's red pickup truck behind the tow truck. In the bed were James' friends. Katie was dressed as the Statue of Liberty, Steven was costumed as Abraham Lincoln and Raymond played the part of George Washington.

James' jaw dropped when he saw what followed behind them. Mr. Stanley Dzjankowski, wearing a complete Rough Riders uniform, rode into view on Chloe. He wore a campaign hat, a brass-buttoned jacket with dark epaulets, a black leather belt, which was wrapped around his middle and fastened with a U.S. Cavalry buckle, leather gauntlet gloves, riding boots, an authentic Colt revolver on his hip and he brandished a silver saber. Standing high in the saddle and waving the sword, he yelled at the top of his lungs, "Remember the Maine! Bully!" He bellowed other memorable Teddy Roosevelt quotes including, "Let us speak courteously, deal fairly, and keep ourselves armed and ready." Chloe hammed it up right along with her rider by pawing the pavement and whinnying in acknowledgement of each quote delivered.

After legions of Boy Scouts, Girl Scouts, cheerleaders and service clubs came Angus. Led by the stately Pastor Simvasten, Angus towed a miniature wagon that carried a life-like replica of the Liberty Bell. It was exact in every detail from the crack to the inscription, *Proclaim liberty throughout all the land unto all the inhabitants thereof—Lev. XXV, v. x.* The good pastor wore the garb of a member of the Continental Congress. He sported a gentlemen's burgundy frock coat, vest, ruffled bib, white stockings to the knees, a white wig and the ubiquitous tri-cornered hat. James thought he looked rather dignified, but couldn't discern which signer of the Declaration of Independence he was. James thought maybe Pastor Roger was supposed to be Thomas Jefferson or John Adams. Possibly, it was Lyman Hall from Connecticut or John Witherspoon from New Jersey who were both ministers like Pastor Roger. Or perhaps, William Floyd the land speculator from Long Island, New York, Francis Hopkinson the lawyer and musician from Philadelphia or John Hancock the wealthy merchant with good penmanship from Massachusetts. It didn't matter too much. He figured any one of fifty-six signers would be okay, but he'd ask Jake later. Jake knew everything about Harmony Bay and everybody in it. Secretly he wished Jake was the mayor instead of smarmy Mayor Pesce.

Fred Lanscome drove a fully restored World War II Army Jeep. It pulled a small flatbed trailer carrying a sound system. It pumped out the music of Tommy Dorsey, Glenn Miller, and Benny Goodman from the Big Band era. Mr. Lanscome wore the U.S. Army khaki uniform of the Second World War. Following behind the music, and similarly dressed in period costume, were Sheryl the cop, Frank the ambulance driver, Buzzy and Chester from the post office, along with their wives, Susan the volunteer nurse EMT from Harmony Bay's rescue crew and Dan Kelly from the pharmacy, who all jitterbugged to the swing music in a well-choreographed routine.

I love parades, thought James. Everybody he knew was here and they were all having fun. His patriotic gear didn't disguise him as well as he thought. One by one the paraders picked him out and called out to him as they passed.

Kenny Clarke strode down the center of the street juggling a set of belaying pins. Kenny stuck to his nautical background by wearing a Jack Tar's uniform, a brass-buttoned, fitted blue jacket veeing down to a red cummerbund, black and white horizontally striped crew neck shirt and white bell-bottoms. A flat topped, wide-brim black leather hat banded with a black and gold silk ribbon streamer with USN boldly embossed on the front was on his head. He moved toward the curb as he juggled. "Ahoy, James! Would you like to juggle these, Mon?"

"Not me," James replied.

"No problem, Mon." He never missed a beat or dropped a pin.

Several antique farm tractors passed by, emitting popping noises from their exhaust stack. James didn't care for these. They were noisy and smelled of thick diesel fumes. Mr. Hirsh followed with a team of four horses pulling a Conestoga style wagon. He was holding the reigns and Mrs. Verdi was beside him behind the buckboard. They were dressed like early American pioneer settlers, he with a ten-gallon Stetson and she with a bonnet. The canvas cover of the prairie schooner was removed to allow members of the high school Glee Club to ride in the back. The girls wore blue denim prairie dresses and the boys wore loose fitting blue denim shirts and white cowboy hats. When the wagon reached predetermined points on the route, it stopped and the teens stood and erupted into song. They entertained the spectators with *This Land is My Land*, *My Country 'Tis of Thee* and *She's a Grand Old Flag.*

Dozens more exhibits rolled or walked by and it was almost time for James and the Sons of Liberty to take up their position at the end of the parade. Before he stepped off the curb, James saw the Model T truck driven by Fishhook Cutsciko go past. Closely following was the 1922 Model T Roadster with Billy behind the wheel. Billy tooted out a hello to James on the a-ooh-gah horn and waved animatedly. James returned the wave and laughed aloud as Billy went by. Without a doubt, the Cutsciko Real Estate signs were gone from the vehicles. Now, the '22 sported a handmade poster board sign on the back. It was held in place with duct tape and simply stated, PLEASE SUPPORT OUR SCHOOLS. A smiley face completed the artwork.

Chapter 20

Jake, James, Luke, Liam and the college guys fell in line. James lined up with the other drummers, flautists and boys carrying flags. "Give us a marching beat, boys!" Jake hollered. The two teams, the *Tide Runners* led by Jake and the *Bay Privateers* under the command of Roland Rutledge joined the ranks of the parade. Each crewmember pulled their whaleboat, which would later be used in the reenactment and competition, with thick manila lines drawn over their backs. They pulled and cussed and shouted out the slogans of the Revolution— *No taxation without representation, The British are coming, One if by land, two if by sea* and *Don't shoot until you see the whites of their eyes*! After each exclamation, all of the men yelled in chorus, "*Huzzah! Huzzah! Give me liberty or give me death*!"

Pointed at each end, the replica whaleboats were nearly thirty feet in length and six feet wide. Each sat in its own cradle that rode on heavy wooden wheels. Six men made up each crew. Four oarsmen rowed the boats with the twenty-foot long oars. A helmsman handled an oar held over the stern to act as a rudder. Each team captain stood in the bow to give orders to the crew.

It was now a challenge of strength and stamina. Pulling the boats along the street was relatively easy. The crews were buoyed by the cheers of their fans and fueled by donuts and coffee from Shea's Bakery. At the conclusion of the parade, the boats were pulled to a spit of beach next to the commercial dock. The hard work began here. Each crew pushed the boats off their dolly then dragged them on the sand to the water's edge. They'd row out into the bay to a point where a Bay Patrol launch was anchored. This marked the starting point for the first leg of the race. When an air-horn sounded from the Bay Patrol, each crew started rowing toward the north end of the peninsula where Patriot's Creek emptied into the bay. Their backs, along with every muscle in their body, were put into each stroke. The whaleboats would make their way across the open water to the peninsula's point. After rounding the point, each continued to row up the creek to an inland spot where the contest judges waited. It was always much easier if it was a rising tide. They wouldn't have to row against the strong current flowing out of the creek.

The parade ended and the crews dragged their whaleboats across the short beach and launched them stern first. This allowed the captain, who boarded last, to throw the painter in and give the final push-off. Katie, Steven and Raymond still in their Miss Liberty, Washington and Lincoln costumes, joined James to watch the boats enter the water. Excitement filled James' eyes as he watched from the shoreline. The men rowed backward, then turned 180 degrees, aiming their bows toward the Bay Patrol launch. It was a leisurely pace at this point. There was no sense in rushing. Every oarsman was conserving his strength for the race ahead.

Over two hundred years ago, dedicated Yankee rebels rowed in the ocean along the coast and turned in at Osprey's Gut. Under the cover of darkness, they rowed completely across Quahog Bay, and then made their way to Patriot's Creek, a distance of more than twenty miles. All the while, the Patriots knew if they were captured, they'd most likely be hanged. Once the boats were beached, they sprinted overland on foot to their objective. After they carried out their mission of pillaging, sabotage and arson against his Majesty's military targets, they'd return to their boats before the sun rose. Timing their departure on an outgoing tide, the raiders quickly evacuated from the creek and were out into open water. Their intimate knowledge of the local shoals, currents, ledges and hiding places always helped them evade capture. Raiding parties along the coastal waters wreaked havoc on the British forces during the Revolution. Today's exercises were considered politically incorrect and internationally insensitive by some of the city folk. For the boat crews, it was all about tradition and honor. Harmony Bay residents hailed the reenactment as if it was 1776 and the British were still camped in their town.

Redcoat sentries were silently and permanently removed from their posts with cutlasses or tomahawks during the Revolution. The British horses were commandeered by the best horsemen in the gang to initiate swift delivery of the Patriot's mission to burn hay barns and sabotage cannons. Afterward, the captured King's horses were turned loose to roam free on the countryside. In the interest of safety for the participants, the modern day reenactment segued from the accounts of the original Quahog Bay raids.

⟞⟝

Jake's and Roland's boats arrived at the Bay Patrol motor launch moored two miles offshore. They circled it and faced northwest toward the distant shore on the peninsula's point. There they'd turn southwest at Patriot's Creek. Jake started as an oarsman when he first came to Harmony Bay and inherited the coveted position in the bow a few years ago after Fred Lanscome stepped down. Fred said the years were catching up to him and this was a job for the young and courageous. Jake, and all those who went before him knew—that even with favorable weather and tides, it was a backbreaking chain of events for the men.

Rowers hunched over oars that were straddled by simple, crude, heavy wooden pegs in the gunwales acting as oarlocks. Their oar blades were at the ready inches above the water's surface, their hands firmly wrapped around the rough handles, prepared to dig in on command. James, who stood two miles away on the beach, could hear the discharge from the air horn. With his fingers crossed, the words formed on his lips, "C'mon Tide Runners."

"Yo! Heave ho! Full ahead!" yelled Jake. The sudden acceleration knocked him toward the stern as Liam, Rory, Joe and the college apprentice's oars grabbed the top layers of the bay, each causing its own whirlpool in the water.

Jake's Tide Runners moved into an early lead. Roland's team of Bay Privateers were bearing down and caught up by Roland urging them to increase the rate of their strokes. It was now high noon and the brilliant sun made it easy to pick out the white clapboard whaleboats that were making way and constantly trading positions toward land. The Bay Patrol followed in their wakes in the event of a man overboard or an injury.

On the beach by the docks, James' friends urged him to come with them. There wasn't much that could be seen until the boats landed and the match continued at the high school's football field. They convinced James there was plenty of time to visit the clam chowder contest for samples. Also, they could get lemonades, and perhaps a fudge brownie or two from his mom at the library's booth. James was hungry. The idea appealed to him very much.

The whaleboats were side-by-side as they approached the turning point. Jake shouted to his crew, "Glory goes to the winner, boys! Let's give 'em a race!"

Roland countered with, "Heave-ho! Let's go Privateers. Pull hard. Let's win for the Republic!"

Jake, not to be outdone, delivered the most inspiring message to his crew. "Remember, boys—if you win, I buy the beer!" There was quite a bit of honor in being on the winning team.

Jake's boat was on the inside when they reached the point to turn southwest. Therefore, he'd have to make a tighter radius turn. He commanded his starboard oar men, Rory and the student, to lift oars. This maneuver sent them toward the competition's boat. It forced Roland to take evasive measures. Pushed even farther outside of the turn, Roland had to reduce his speed to prevent running his Privateers aground.

"Give way or be broadsided, Mr. Rutledge!" Jake yelled to Roland. "Wicked good! Nicely done, men!" Jake shouted to his crew. He ordered Liam on the port side to lift, his starboard oars to heave hard, and then called back to Luke at the helm, "Hard rudder to port." The boat turned smartly to the left. Executing the 180-degree turn, Jake's boat headed straight down the middle of Patriot's Creek. They were now well ahead of Roland, whose boat was crowding the Spartina grass on the right bank. Roland's problems became complicated when one of his rowers, Hank, who was added to the team for his equestrian skills, got his port and starboard mixed up during the tight-quarter maneuvers. Jake, who was familiar with the heat of battle, anticipated that the same problem could occur with his own crew. To avoid confusion, the day before the race, he tattooed *Port* and *Starb'd* on the appropriate oar handles with an electric wood-burning pencil.

Roland suffered a further setback. A starboard oar wedged into the muddy embankment during the near collision, causing one of the wooden oarlock pegs to shear off. They were designed to do that. If a rower's oar jammed, neither would he shatter his oar nor would he be catapulted from the boat. Roland scrambled over the bench seats and dropped a spare peg in its hole, but it cost them additional yardage. To maintain their lead, Jake kept the crew on a steady pace. He gave a spirited salute toward the port side shore as they passed Dory's house. The judges welcomed them as they landed at the designated point, a clearing in the bulrushes marked with a Union Jack. They were easily a hundred yards ahead of the Privateers.

"Jake, once again, you win!" Mr. Kelly the pharmacist called out.

"It looks like the Tide Runners are still in good hands. Well done, men!" Fred Lanscome yelled. The crews were exhausted. As sweat streamed down their backs, they slumped over their oars with blistered hands.

Roland arrived a moment later and heckled Jake. "Hey, Jake, that was cheatin'."

"Cheating? My good man, that was good seamanship by a worthy crew," Jake said.

"We're gonna knock you off in the next round."

"Fat chance."

"You may have won this battle but you haven't won the war."

Jake's boat overflowed with hysterical laughter. He turned to see Liam McDuff standing in the boat—mooning the Bay Privateer's crew and their captain.

Liam bellowed, "Hey guys—salute the new rear admiral!"

Jake handily won the first round and now it was time for the teams to enter the second phase of the competition that retraced the Patriot's land route to attack the original British encampment. Part of this path was on Bay Road. Bay Road was called King's Road during colonial times. After being humiliated by several successful Yankee raids on the bay town, the British located an observation post with a garrison and cannon on high ground. It had a commanding view of the bay in hopes of thwarting any more attacks. Patriots invoked the name change to Bay Road after the Revolution. This leg of the contest created an interesting race between the teams. The team that arrived at the finish line with all of their members first won that round. Over the years, event organizers added a few twists to the format. Each crew now had to roll a sixty-gallon wine barrel, whimsically relabeled *RUM*, over the course. It contained twenty-five gallons of water that added over 150 pounds to the already heavy oak barrel. To make it even more challenging, as the water sloshed back and forth, the barrel had to be lifted over a series of split rail fences set up along the way.

With onlookers lining the route cheering on their favorite team, off they went, huffing and grunting as they rolled, pushed and lifted the kegs all the way to the high school. The school was conveniently in a histori-cally correct location, being less than a quarter mile from the site where the original Quahog raids took place. For a multitude of reasons, includ-ing Jake's student crewmember spraining his ankle, Roland's team rolled onto the field first.

Scoring for the whaleboat competition was worth two points. The barrel race only scored one point. Roland's team could even up the score in the horsemanship contest. It was worth one point. Each team selected their best rider to run the length of the football field on foot, knock a mannequin dressed as a redcoat sentry off a wooden horse with a bayo-neted reproduction musket, then mount a horse tethered to the goalpost and ride back up the field. There the horseman was handed an unlit torch by his teammates and was required to ride back to the opposite goalpost and re-secure his horse. After doing so, he'd jog out of the end zone where he was met by yet another teammate who'd light his torch with a flint and steel. Once the torch was lit, it was used to ignite a miniature barn that was constructed out of cardboard and filled with hay. Each barn flew a Union Jack. Both riders had to snatch the British colors off its post before razing the barn, return to their mounts and thunder the hundred yards back to the starting point, delivering the captured flag.

All of the tourists and townspeople filled the school's bleachers for the arrival of the teams and to watch the equestrian barn-burning event. Dory and James took front row seats and were disappointed to see Jake's team literally limp to the finish line. Doc Tollenson attended to the injured Tide Runner college intern who had sprained his ankle and the team captains presented their man for the next segment of the contest. Luke was representing the Tide Runners while the Bay Privateers put forward the young man who had miscued in the boat. Henry, or Hank Klunkergarten, or *Klunk* as he was known locally, worked as an insurance adjuster. Although he worked in the Harmony Bay area, Hank grew up farther to the north just outside the town of Catacoot, primarily an agricultural community. Unknown to Jake, Klunk was a ringer. Klunk had been a high school track star and could ride a horse before he could ride a bicycle. The playing field became uneven. By comparison, Luke should have been a spectator. Luke rode horses a few times at Boy Scout camp as a kid, but that was the extent of his experience.

The two opponents stepped up to the line and the crowd began to cheer and whistle. A small cannon was fired and the contest began. By the time Luke reached the fifty-yard line, Klunk was swinging his musket like a baseball bat, whacking the dummy off the sawhorse. He was at the goalpost in a flash, untying his assigned chestnut mare. Luke arrived to harpoon the stuffed guard with his bayonet as Klunk took off in a clatter of hooves. "See ya," Klunk called out. His stallion broke into a full gallop down the field.

While Hank Klunkergarten arrived to grab his torch from an outstretched hand, Luke was still trying to get up into the saddle. Some spectators broke out in a peal of laughter. Finally succeeding, Luke pointed his horse in the right direction and charged off. Holding the unlit torch high while on his way to meet Roland in the opposite end zone, Klunk passed Luke at midfield. Klunk dismounted and retied the horse to the goalpost and ran with his torch to rendezvous with Roland who was set to light it. Roland was botching the job with the flint and steel. He tried to set fire to a small wad of dried grass, striking the flint time after time to no avail. He and Klunk were becoming impatient and flustered. Luke grabbed his torch from his teammates and was now approaching the far end at a steady gallop, ready to meet up with Jake to have it lit. Luke and the horse made it to the goalpost and Luke wrapped his reigns around it. Roland still fumbled in the end zone. Luke held out the torch wrapped in char cloth and Jake stuffed dead grass in its folds. On the first strike, sparks fell from Jake's flint and the tinder flamed. He blew on the dry grass clippings and the torch burst into flames. Simultaneously, Roland and Klunk got their torches going. Now it was a close race to the finish as they snatched the flags from their staffs, tossed their torches into the hay-barns and ran back to their horses. Klunk tripped and fell as he rushed, allowing Luke to gain an advantage. Those assembled in the grandstands came to life as they saw fire and smoke billow from the cardboard barns and the sight of Klunk face down in the dirt. Klunk got back on his feet and sprinted to his horse. Both men were saddled up in equal time but Hank Klunkergarten's superior horsemanship won the round, finishing ahead of Luke by twenty yards. It added one point to their score. Each team was now tied with two points apiece.

A marksmanship contest was the final round using smooth bore, black-powder *Brown Bess* muskets. A watermelon placed on hay bales sixty yards away was the target. During the Revolutionary War, due to the inaccuracy of the guns, human targets didn't have too much to worry about at a range of seventy- five yards. At this distance, it was a challenge for an untrained musketeer to hit the bull's-eye. Members of the Harmony Bay Gun Club were in charge of reloading the muskets between rounds. Every man from each team drew a number that determined his firing order. Each team started with six points. For each shooter who missed, one point was deducted from the score. If all six points were used, the count started back at six. If both marksmen scored on the same round, the tab was reset to six. The point in the sequence when the two teams hit the target resulted in the total amount of points. If the Bay Privateer's second shooter hit, then the Tide Runner's fifth shooter scored, four points would be awarded to Roland's team and one to Jake's team. With the present team scores, only one point by either team was needed to break the tie. It could go through a couple dozen rounds before a winner was determined. Today, hitting the watermelon first ended the challenge. Jake drew third position for the Tide Runners.

The first round resulted in a miss for both teams. Both were down to five points. Round two produced the same results. Luke was the number two entry causing Jake to comment, "If Harmony Bay does have any criminals they could rest comfortably tonight."

Jake was handed his musket. "Hey Lukey, they should've put a bag of free donuts up there. You couldn't find the target—but you would've found those," he said. Now it was four points apiece. Jake recalled a historical side note. During the Civil War soldiers were instructed to aim their muskets low to hit high. Jake calculated the guns were shooting high. He'd aim at the hay bale before pulling the trigger, allowing the .69 caliber musket ball to arc up to the target. His opponent fired first and missed. Jake removed his topcoat and tri-cornered hat. He wiped his forehead with the back of his hand and held his breath. Squinting down the barrel, he braced himself and squeezed the trigger. The watermelon sprayed its green envelope and pink guts for yards beyond as the lead exploded dead center into the target. Everyone in the stands cheered. Jake handed his weapon off to a gun club member and met his crew who still had enough energy left to hoist him up on their shoulders. Dory and James poured out of the bleachers and raced to Jake. Dory gave him a peck on the cheek after he was safely back on the ground. James gave him a high-five.

"That was amazing! I'm proud of you, Jake Kane," she said.

"Aw shucks, Miss Dory. It weren't nothin'. Them thar redcoats is on the run now. Dory playfully punched his arm.

"Hey, easy. Ouch!"

"Perhaps we shall have you ordered to sick bay, Commander Kane?"

"I'm starving. I'm thinking about grilling up some hot dogs and burgers before we head down to the boardwalk for this evening's award ceremony and to celebrate the Tide Runner's victory. How about you and James swing by the houseboat?"

"Not until I change out of this silly outfit."

Jake nodded toward James. "I'll bet he's starving too. He's probably drummed himself into a feeding frenzy."

"A girl gets hungry too."

"Then we could all stick around for the fireworks tonight. We can watch them from the roof of the houseboat. Best seats in town."

"Okay, how about five bells. Does that work for you?"

"Aye-aye. Five it is."

Beneath the moon, the stars and the fireworks, Dory and James wrapped up the Fourth of July in the company of Harmony Bay's hero. The radiance of the pyrotechnics and the luminosity of the full moon paled in comparison to the glow emanating from within Dory.

Chapter 21

When Dory's phone rang at seven a.m. Angelina Verdi was on the line speaking in a hoarse voice. "Angelina, you don't sound good. You okay?" Dory said.

"Gee, Dory, I've got a terrible cold and a sore throat. I shouldn't be around James today—or anybody for that matter."

"Okay, I understand. I'll take him with me to work today. I'm going to check in on you at lunchtime to make sure you're all right."

"Grazie, grazie, Dory. Don't worry, I'll be okay."

"Just the same, I'll look in on you and make sure you're comfortable."

"I'm taking apple cider vinegar and honey. That'll do the trick. Capisce?"

"Io capisco. I understand." Dory was well aware of the old Yankee home remedy, extracted from Native American's pharmaceutical knowledge of herbs and plants, for everything from the common cold to arthritis. "I'll be there a little past noon."

"Ciao."

"Ciao, Angelina."

Dory woke James with the bad news. He'd have to spend the day at the library. He wasn't happy about it, but understood. With no alternative, she felt badly for him. It was the plight of many single parents. Tomorrow she could come up with another plan. For today, Dory knew they were both going to have to deal with it.

"Don't you think it's time you started calling me Mel?" Mrs. Lanscome said to Dory. "You've been here almost six months. You're part of the library family." Every word that came from Margaret Lanscome sounded like an order rather than a request. Dory learned it was only the library director's style. She meant nothing by it.

"Well, I suppose I could, Mrs. Lanscome. I mean—Mel," Dory said. "If that pleases you."

"It would please me very much. I have a thought, well, more of a plan actually."

"What is it?"

"I'm taking the afternoon off. I'm putting you in charge."

Dory's eyes widened, her brows arched upward. "Okay—but, I need to stop by Angelina Verdi's house at lunchtime. She's not feeling well and I want to see if she needs anything."

"Not a problem. I'll wait until you get back before I leave. And—I have another thought."

"Is it part of the same plan or is it a new plan?"

Mrs. Lanscome laughed in her pinched way. "Dory, you are very quick. I'm thinking, if it's all right with you, I'll take James out for lunch and then take him up by Mill Pond to go berry picking." Because James was growing more restless, Dory was delighted to hear this. She wasn't about to let on that James' lunch was in her backpack.

"That'll be great, Mrs. uh—Mel."

"Fine then. It's twenty minutes before twelve. Why don't you scoot now? It will give you a chance to eat your lunch and see Mrs. Verdi. After lunch I'm going to swing James by your house to get him long pants. We'll be out in the berry brambles." Dory wondered what the director was going to wear. No one had ever seen her in anything but a dress.

"Thank you, Mel. I'll let James know the plan." Mrs. Lanscome's high-heels click-clacked across the floor as she departed the reference desk.

Mrs. Lanscome pulled her car onto the dirt road that rose up Pencil Hill. She opened the trunk and pulled out four pails. "Here we go, James. Two buckets each for black raspberries," she said.

They hiked up the trail past where the old mill once stood. "There's a lot of history in this part of town, James."

"Yeah, I know about the old mill," he said. They started to pluck berries, each landing in the empty pails with a soft ping.

Mrs. Lanscome pointed to the end of Patriot's Creek. "That's where the Yankee whaleboats landed for the raids during the Revolution. There was a lot of spying and espionage in this area. It was a very treacherous time." Her dress snagged on a bramble thorn.

"Why was it like that?" James questioned.

"Around here, people were divided into three groups. One third, the Loyalists, remained faithful to the king. Another third, the Patriots, fought however they could for independence, including supplying the war effort through Harmony Bay. The last third were citizens who sat on the fence waiting to see what happened so they could ride the coattails of the victor."

"It must have been crazy. The shooting and all. And not knowing who to trust," James said. He pitched a fistful of dark, plump berries into his bucket.

"Yes, James, no wars are good wars, but they all do result in something. If it wasn't for the valiant men, boys, and women who courageously fought in the Revolution, this great country never would have been founded."

"So they were all heroes?"

"They certainly were. There'd be no American history and all of the wonderful things that Americans have done for people around the world since 1783 never would have happened. We owe them a debt of gratitude."

After skirting the pond, Mrs. Lanscome led James deeper into the woods. This put them in a meadow between Ezra's Pond and Mill Pond, overrun with wild black raspberry canes and swarms of butterflies. "In colonial times people used black raspberries to make dyes for clothing. Black raspberries or thimbleberries, as they are sometimes called, are quite healthy for you. They're loaded with antioxidants." She held one up to the sunlight between her thumb and forefinger. James shrugged. "They're wonderful for pie, cobbler or even black raspberry ice cream. Even great for a snack. Here try one." She plucked a ripe berry and offered it to James.

It is almost three in the morning. Eerie wisps of ground fog float above the marshes. Clouds shroud the moon as a small craft, propelled by a lone occupant working a long pole in the bottom mud, moves stealthily through the still air. Ballasted by its heavy cargo, the boat sits precariously low in the water. Approaching the waterwheel at the end of the creek, the pilot has an errant thought about shell fishing in the creek bed at some time in the future. That had to wait. Tonight is a clandestine mission and fishing provides a convenient alibi for his operations. He is well aware of the redcoat detail posted on the overlooking hill to his right. He reckons his whaleboat, which he skillfully tacked across the bay with its overload, will not raise suspicion with only himself aboard. His boat smells of the sea and smoke. It emanates up from beneath layers of sailcloth. If intercepted, it is an easy explanation warranted by the barrels and bins of smoked fish. The sailor dropped the boat's single sail when he entered the creek and now only relies on the pole and the flooding tide to carry him inland. He hears the distinct creaking of the mill's wheel as clouds disappear; allowing the moon to cast it's borrowed light on the mill house. He doesn't see, or expect, the three British regulars who are hidden within the mill.

Nearing his destination a voice calls out, "Who goes there?"

"Only a fisherman, my friend."

"How many of ye aboard?"

"Only me-self. A lone fisherman."

Landing alongside the mill, the three sentries quickly encounter him. Bayonets pierce the darkness. They order him to make his boat fast and show his hands.

"Excuse me," he says, "this must be some sort of mistake."

"State yer business or be run through."

"I've come to barter some of my catch for some fresh grist. The remainder of the load I'll be bringing to the market tomorrow."

"Any weapons on board, mate?"

"No. Only my haul of fish. It's lovely smoked fish. Might you care for some?"

"Aye, it's the King's fish. We'll be having it all."

"Are ye a rebel or loyal to the crown?"

"Ah, I'm glad you asked. A Tory, to be sure." He lied.

"State yer name."

"Carroll. Christian Carroll."

"What're ya doin' sneakin' aboot in the middle of the night Mr. Christian Carroll?"

"Given my heavy load, I needed to take advantage of the incoming tide to float me upstream with ample draft."

"Arrrgh. There's a high tide in broad daylight tomorrow. Why aren't ye floatin' on that un?"

"My good man, as I'm sure you will agree, I'm a working man and need to be out on the water in daylight." Seeing that he is not convincing them he adds, "And—I want be the first one on the miller's steps so I may be on my way to the market early to get top price for this load."

"You're aboard a whaleboat, the very same as ye rebels use for attackin' an' creatin' havoc."

"Right, it is true. She's a whaling boat indeed. I salvaged her off a wreck that ran aground out on the Gut. This boat needed quite a bit of repair, I might add. Patched her up myself, I did. I don't fathom that she'd be up to the rigors of war, serving the needs of a full crew and such."

"Hmm—just the same—it's a whaleboat."

Things don't add up for the interrogators. It's too suspicious. They hope it isn't a diversion or an advance scout for a rebel raiding party. In the past, they were caught off guard. It would be their necks if they let Mr. Christian Carroll slip through and something happened. A heated discussion breaks out among the three soldiers about what to do with the captive. The first argues to let him go. The second makes the case to search the boat—in case Mr. Carroll is running guns for the rebels. The third, and most vociferous of them, insists they march the prisoner up the hill to their commanding officer for questioning. It will be first light in a couple of hours. The soldiers can search the boat then. If it all checks out, Carroll can be on his way.

They decide two of them will escort Mr. Carroll to the base camp while the third stands guard on the whaleboat.

"Mr. Carroll, if ye decides ta run, I'll put a round through yer spine sure as ye're standin' thare," says the outspoken one. Christian Carroll carefully considers what a .75 caliber musket ball would do to him. He and the two soldiers ascend the escarpment surrounded by a chorus of bird noises as the sun nips at the lower edges of the horizon.

Christian Carroll stands facing Lieutenant Oliver Stockbridge. Stockbridge is anything but a soldier. He whines to himself incessantly about being bivouacked on this observation outpost, confounded daily by mosquitoes, poison ivy and the lack of brandy. Lieutenant Stockbridge is a dandy who'd much rather be attending balls or the theater in New York, Boston, or Philadelphia. Or more so, in London. His men thoroughly despise Stockbridge. He has put them on short rations, but they still follow his orders. Initially he is annoyed at being awoken early by the reports from the patrol and the taking of a captive. But now he realizes a sudden delight in the interrogation of a prisoner that will be a pleasant distraction from his routine military duties. Before Stockbridge finishes his breakfast he gives orders to send a detail to the creek to seize the stores on board the boat for his majesty's troops. He begins his questioning in a cordial manner. After all, the man professed himself as a loyalist. The circumstances were suspicious and the whole episode puzzles Stockbridge. Never since the establishment of his post has anyone had the audacity to come up the creek at night. However, Carroll's story seems plausible enough. Stockbridge decides to detain him until the boat is searched and Carroll's story can be checked out with the miller and others.

Stockbridge feigns a smile. "Mr. Carroll, are you any relation to Charles Carroll of Carrolton?" The prisoner hesitates then answers. "Not to my knowledge, sir."

A tent flap opens, interrupting the interrogation. Stockbridge's aide enters and asks for the lieutenant's presence outside. The stuffy commandant exits then returns moments later.

"Mr. Carroll, in addition to a passel of smoked fish that will feed them well for the next few weeks, my men uncovered a vast cache of gold coin and bars along with certain precious jewels stowed in your boat. This is most unusual for a lowly fisherman. What say *you*?"

Mrs. Lanscome and James filled their pails. It was time to go. She had been bending over for a while to pick berries and was slow getting up. Dizzy, in fact. The library director wondered about her autumnal years getting the best of her and took a deep breath. *Maybe it's only the summer heat*, she speculated.

Chapter 22

Thick fog ascended from the warmth of the bay as a cold front rolled in from the north. It blurred all images and cloaked everything it touched in pearlescent wetness. Dampness permeated the muted morning light, adding surreal fringes to everything it feebly painted. Its smoky veil muffled the senses. Visibility was only possible up to fifty yards, less in some low pockets, or perhaps as much as a hundred in places that held an extra degree of dew point raising warmth. After a cool night, fog was not an uncommon or welcome visitor during this time of the year, but it always departed with a warming sun. When cold air advanced over the warm bay water during the summer months, advection fog occurred as water from the surface evaporated into the cold air. Locals called it pea soup or *sea smoke*. Hampering navigation, fog was nobody's friend on the water.

A mysterious shroud at its best, fog could be a sinister enemy at its worst. At times, it arrived fast and dense in the blink of an eye. Otherwise, it smoldered slowly, its moist breath increasing in reluctant, small gasps. This morning the bay's beach, displaying inky stones uncovered by the tides retreat, was devoid of visitors except for some noisy plovers and James and Angus, who waded through the low tide foam. James was on the sand attempting to skim flat stones for more than three consecutive hops over the seaweed-laden water. The heavy fog was not enough to suppress the dank, fishy smell of low tide and there was not enough breeze to flush it from the air.

Dory gazed out the kitchen window for the limited distance that she could, lamenting it was *another bad hair day*. Humidity would transform her otherwise flowing locks into tight ringlets. It was Sunday, a day entirely to herself to relax, therefore she didn't mind very much. The sun had yet to disclose its presence as the clock showed it was not quite eight.

Bacon popped and crackled on the stove while she opened the kitchen door and called out for James to come home for breakfast. Although he acknowledged her, being all too familiar with his distractions, she waited until he crossed the threshold before cracking the eggs and dropping them into the frying pan with the bacon.

James and Angus arrived at the door. Dory instructed her son to leave the dripping dog outside. Angus seemed to understand, but James protested. "Not when he's wet," Dory said. Dory and James joined hands as they prayed before the meal. After giving thanks, James devoured everything before him.

Dory studied her son's face. She decided to ask him the question she had been holding back. "James, how do you feel about Jake?"

James knew why she was asking. "Jake is the greatest, Mom. It's okay you're with him. I like him a lot."

Internally, Dory sighed in relief, even though she knew the answer before it was delivered. She should have asked for James' approval earlier. It was important to her. Everything was going smoothly. It hardly seemed necessary.

When they finished eating, James fidgeted in his seat. He couldn't wait to get back outside. Dory instructed him to stay put as she moved to the stove and single-handedly cracked two eggs on the side of the cast iron skillet, setting them to fry along with two strips of bacon. She removed a bowl from the cupboard that was reserved for visiting canines and scooped the skillet's contents into it. She presented the bowl to James saying, "Here's a snack for your friend. You can join him outside while he eats." James snatched the bowl and bounded across the kitchen to the door. Angus met him with a furiously wagging tail. Placing the bowl on the ground, James told the dog to sit and stay. Angus obliged. He looked at James with pleading eyes and an increased rhythm of his tail. After what seemed like an agonizing amount of time, James snapped his fingers and said, "Okay!" Angus wasted no time downing the contents of the bowl. When he finished, the dog held the bowl in place with his front paws, licking every drop of yellow yolk and flavor from it. Angus nudged James with his head and then grasped James' skinny forearm softly in his mouth as a sign of approval. The metronome tail increased to full tempo.

Dory, James and Angus didn't pay much attention to the barking coming from across the creek behind the house. Fog handily disguised the owner of the noise. Loose dogs were not unusual around Harmony Bay. Local dogs were seldom seen on a leash. Bay dogs might take off after a rabbit or chase birds, but they were never far from home and easily found their way back. They didn't bother anybody except for trying to mooch a free lunch during their walk-abouts. City folks and tourists brought their unusual array of dogs. Most of the dogs were unsuitable for the bay or the beach. The locals took it in stride. If a dog was in the control of their owner, by leash or otherwise, they let it be. Sometimes the owner was harder to bridle than the pet.

Angus' ears perked up when he detected a growl interspersed with the distant barks. There was a daunting tone in the growls, making his forelegs as stiff as pilings. Growls became more frequent as they grew closer and the barking became more frantic. The curtain began to lift, revealing the actor on the other side of the creek. It was a German shepherd dog, a large male that probably belonged to a vacationer because Angus didn't recognize him by sight or smell.

Dory stood with her hands on her hips, starring across the divide, wondering if the creek provided enough of a moat to keep the stranger away. An ebb tide didn't provide as much of a barrier as had existed some six hours earlier. She did realize, even at low tide, the creek's swift current was still about four feet deep at its midpoint. James stood beside his mother. His pulse increased in intensity. The growls became snarls. "Maybe we should all go in the house for a while," Dory said.

The intruder paced back and forth on the opposite shore with its head down. If they could have seen through the persisting fog, they might have noticed the hackles standing up on the shepherd's neck. Angus lowered his head and let out a growl of his own. It was the sort of deep warning he reserved for those he didn't like or trust. The growl didn't emanate from his muzzle or his throat, but from a place deep within and included his whole being. This growl was the one he usually set aside for Fishhook Cutsciko since no other being on the bay was that evil. Now he had found one other.

The villainous dog's devil horn ears stood straight up. He continued to flash his teeth and snap toward the trio across the water. Dory wondered what would make a dog behave that way. Perhaps he was hungry and the smell of bacon in the thick air enticed him. City people often dumped their dogs at the beach when they no longer wanted them. They were left to forage or rely on handouts. Harmony Bay didn't have a dogcatcher. It could be another refugee. In any case, she didn't like it and considered calling the police before the brazen dog could get enough courage up to cross the creek. Now that the fog was starting to lift, families with their children would soon be on the beach.

In a flash the foe plunged into the water, only being slowed when his paws no longer touched bottom. This was the only provocation Angus needed to react physically and bolted toward the creek. Everyone knew Angus was a gentle giant that could withstand any outward annoyance. His rapid departure made Dory gasp. "Angus, stay!" James screamed. Angus was not going to stop for anyone—his mission was clear. His adversary exhibited hostility toward his extended family. It needed to be silenced and exiled. His job was to protect and serve his masters at all costs, whether it was Billy, James or Dory. His opponent was ferocious, but Angus didn't worry a bit. He was more than double the size of the Shepard dog and certainly much more cunning. Even though he wasn't a fighter by nature, Angus occasionally had to quell a battle between two rivals in the forest. Here it was a question of keeping the peace by dealing out swift justice to protect Dory and James.

At the sight of Angus bounding headlong into the water the scoundrel retreated to the shore, but did not run and hide. Standing his ground at the high water mark he continued to snap and snarl with his ears laid back, black eyes glistening and his tail rigid. His actions did not thwart Angus' advances as the big dog easily swam across the current. Angus emerged from the shallows and the shepherd mounted an attack. Angus stood fast downhill at the water's edge allowing his opponent to be front heavy, which threw him off balance. Hackles high, he went for the Newfie's throat. Angus fearlessly sidestepped like a crafty boxer and watched the other dog splash into the water in a heap. The shepherd scrambled to his feet and launched another reckless sortie by trying to sink his teeth into Angus' shoulder. It was to no avail. Angus whirled, lowered one shoulder and swung his enormous paw against him. The broadside rolled him over twice before he could regain his footing. Angus didn't fret. Nevertheless, he was becoming concerned that it was going to take a little more effort on his part to send the shepherd packing. Still snarling violently, the dog attacked and tried to snatch at Angus' underbelly without success as the water dog's double-layered coat repelled the attempt. *Enough was enough* thought Angus. It was time to put the culprit in his place. With the shepherd's next surge, Angus slapped him over again on his back and pounced on him with his full weight. Now he was on his back and struggling to get out from beneath the larger dog. Angus deftly clamped his jaws around his throat, applying only enough pressure to send a message, although not with enough force to pierce the skin. He could have ended the evil dog's life with a single devastating bite. Intimidated, the opponent became still and acquiesced as Angus backed off. Slowly and warily placing his tail between his legs, the vanquished got his paws back under himself. Sullen-eyed, he trotted off into the marsh with his head down. He never looked back. Satisfied that the job was done, Angus wagged his tail and paddled back across the creek.

Chapter 23

Dory sat at her desk musing about Mr. Christian Carroll. Her intuition told her something in the story didn't make sense. It didn't add up. She was going to get to the bottom of it and satisfy her curiosity. Weekday mornings at the library were quiet. The senior citizens were coming in for their mahjong games in the afternoon, so other than the anticipated event, she could count on some free time to see what she could find out about Mr. Carroll of Carroll's Landing fame. Today, Jake took James with him to go out and check the long-lines and do *guy stuff* as Jake called it. This probably meant they were going fishing at some point. Jake promised to return James to her before she finished for the day.

Dory tilted her computer monitor away from the sun glare that streamed in over her shoulders. She typed *Christian Carroll* into the search bar. The screen displayed page after page of unusable information, mostly linked to social networking sites. She delved further adding Harmony Bay to the search, which narrowed the results. Information came up about the naming of Carroll's Landing and Carroll Way. Dory tapped her pencil on the desktop several times and clicked on the links. It seemed Christian Carroll was somewhat of an obscure Patriot hero. He was arrested by the British military for attempting to aid and abet the enemy through financial contributions.

Her pulse began to quicken as she read archived historical vignettes of the Revolution and Harmony Bay. Once again narrowing her search with Boolean operators, she researched *Carroll* plus *American*

Revolution. Results with matches numbering nearly a half-million appeared. Dory had forgotten about Charles Carroll of Carrolton, signer of the Declaration of Independence. Of Irish ancestry and one of the wealthiest men in America at the time of the Revolutionary War, Charles Carroll outlived all of the other signers. She continued to read about how Carroll, the only Roman Catholic signer, was harassed by members of the Continental Congress who felt he should not be allowed to sign because of his religion. As a Catholic, he was excluded from practicing law, entering politics, and—voting.

That was hardly fair, Dory thought. *After all, wasn't the country founded on freedom of religion*? She rolled her chair closer to the screen and scrolled through the accompanying facts. Members of Congress illegibly scratched their names on the documents. Once they signed their name they became outlaws. If caught, they would be hanged for sedition. The Declaration of Independence was their death warrant. Charles Carroll clearly signed his name, instigating several who had already endorsed the Declaration to comment, "Easy enough for Charles Carroll to write his name boldly. Carroll is such a common name the British will never know where to look or who they're looking for." The outward comments by men who were supposed to be his brothers-in-arms caused Charles Carroll to return to the podium and add *of Carrollton* after his name.

Her further research revealed that historians believed the First Amendment to the Constitution was written by his judicious peers in appreciation of Charles Carroll's generous financial support during the Revolution, regardless of the denial of his civic rights due to his Catholicism.

Dory rubbed her temples and crossed her legs at her ankles before moving the mouse again. *Financial support during the Revolutionary War.* The words struck her as her thoughts sprang back to Christian Carroll. Were Christian and Charles Carroll related? It was a possibility, but the records showed Carroll was indeed a common name. She checked the population records. In 1776 there were around two and half million people in the thirteen colonies. Unless there was a traceable family tree, it was going to be hard to prove. Many records were destroyed by fire back in the day, some were only entries in a family bible, and others were never documented at all.

Dory now worked at a feverish pace, the only distraction she allowed was an occasional phone call from a patron who needed help. She hunted for relationships between Christian Carroll, American Revolution, plus money and being arrested. Her jaw dropped as she pulled up the results and read an excerpt from the diary of a British Sergeant named Randall Stone-Bayard.

In the predawn of 18 July 1777, whilst on patrol we confronted a sole boatman with a great cargo of smoked fish. Mostly finfish, but eels and oysters as well. The hour of his arrival raised our suspicion. He stated he was a loyal Tory subject, identifying himself as Christian Carroll. We did not ask, nor did he give, his residence. He declared his occupation as fisherman. Our suspicions caused me to send him up the hill to be questioned further by Leftenant Oliver Stockbridge. With many spies and double agents in these parts, we could not release him on his word. Our hilltop position is now fortified with two six-pound field artillery pieces and a three-pound galloper. We could not afford them captured by the rebels.

With my two men off to Leftenant Stockbridge with Carroll, I stood guard over the boat awaiting daylight and further orders.

At two hours past sunrise, a detachment of four dragoons, two horse drawn drays driven by known loyalist civilians and six regulars arrived. Orders came to search Carroll's boat and its cargo be declared contraband.

Emptying the boat's contents, the dried fish were loaded onto the two wagons. Whilst unloading, Corporal Smyth discovered false bottoms in several fish-holds. Prising off their covers with bayonet, Smyth made a startling discovery of bullions of solid gold and silver, gold doubloons and varieties of jewelry with valuable stones contained in leather pouches marked with peculiar double C insignias. I could fathom no reason why a fisher might have such grande treasures.

I inventoried the precious stores and metals. One dragoon was ordered at full gallop to Leftenant Stockbridge with news of the find. I ordered the mill house surrounded and the miller and his family taken at gunpoint. They were turned over for interrogation as well.

On the day following, a loyalist informant suggested prisoner Carroll was providing a layover point for the privateers and whaleboat raiders somewhere out on the bay. In addition, we were told the miller and his wife were both Yankee scoundrels who were also complicit in affording refuge and sustenance to the raiders.

It was becoming clear to Dory why Christian Carroll ended up being a Harmony Bay hero. He was helping fund the Revolution with the loot he scavenged off wrecks at England Point. There were still some unanswered questions. What happened to the gold? And, what became of Mr. Carroll? She started her search again, this time including the name Leftenant Oliver Stockbridge along with Christian Carroll. After agonizing over page after page of historical documents, Dory pieced the whole story together. She categorized all of her findings into one word document, hit print and loaded the pages into a large manila envelope.

It was almost closing time when Jake and James showed up at the library. Dory could tell by James' face that he was beyond exhausted and probably starving to boot.

"Where have you guys been? I thought you'd be back hours ago," Dory said. She gathered her personal belongings along with the envelope. She was very glad to see both of them, but was annoyed by Jake's indifference in sticking to the schedule. His easy-going nature sometimes spilled over into absentmindedness.

"We were doing guys stuff...but we come bearing gifts," Jake said.

"Oh, really? I love a surprise."

"How does lobster sound for dinner? That is—if I can invite myself."

"What's the special occasion?"

"Oh nothing. I traded bivalves for lobsters with one of the lobster boys."

"Sounds good to me. I'll stop by George's farm stand and pick up zucchini and corn for grilling. I'm glad you're coming by, there's something I want to talk to you about."

"Really? On my way I'll pick up a bottle of wine. Why don't you take James home with you now? I want to stop home and get cleaned up."

They departed the library, agreeing to reconvene at Dory's house an hour later.

She got out the lobster pot, filled it with water from the bay, added a quartered lemon and set it on the kitchen stove to boil. She took another large kettle, filled it with tap water, put in the corn on the cob to soak, sliced the zucchini lengthwise in quarters, then seasoned them with salt and freshly ground black pepper. Dory set three places at the table on the screened porch. Jake arrived and started the barbeque grill. He placed the corn on the grill first. It would take the longest. Carrying the lobsters in a cooler, he brought them to the kitchen and dropped them in the boil. Dory arranged the vegetable spears on the grill while Jake uncorked the wine. It all came together at once and they dined. Now with a full belly, James was bleary-eyed with exhaustion. Dory sent him to the shower— followed by bed.

It was still early evening and long before dusk and the arrival of the mosquitoes. Dory pulled the wine bottle from the refrigerator, picked their wine glasses up off the table with her free hand and invited Jake outside to the Adirondack chairs facing the bay. She clenched the manila envelope under her arm.

"Jake," Dory began, "you now how I always thought there was more to the story about Christian Carroll and Carroll's Landing?"

"You're still going on about that, eh?"

"Well, yes. Now I think I've got the whole story. Here." She dropped the packet on his lap. Jake read the printed information, sporadically raising his eyebrows.

"Wow. This seems like a story that was long forgotten."

"But wait, there's more," she said. "Christian Carroll, along with the miller and his wife, Arthur and Rebecca Bell, were all charged with high treason in an impromptu trial and sentenced to hang. Since the Patriots were anxiously awaiting the delivery of the gold, they immediately determined what happened. Their worst fears were corroborated by a couple of redcoats in a local tavern who imbibed a little too much rum and bragged about the capture, and—upcoming executions."

She admired the glint of her wine glass in the lowering sun. After taking a sip, she continued. "The Patriots organized a daring rescue sometime after midnight on July 21 to free the three of them. The sentries were hit over the head and only one shot was fired. It was only after the single shot was heard did the Brits realize the prisoners escaped. Guess who the musket ball hit? It was the commanding officer Lieutenant Stockbridge. Stockbridge was shot in the head at close range and killed. The speculation is that he was shot by his own troops… since the Patriot rescuers and the prisoners were already long gone. It was a covert rescue attempt. The Patriots wouldn't have announced their arrival, or departure, by firing a shot. If the Yanks were going to shoot, to take out the guards and the garrison—there'd have been a skirmish."

Jake leaned forward in his chair. "What happened to the gold?"

"Well, if they needed horse and wagons to bring it up the hill, there was no way the jail breakers could have carted it off. Sergeant Randall Stone-Bayard inventoried the cargo when it was discovered. But that's the last record of it. No mention of it being used by the British or that it was sent back to merry old England."

"So, maybe since Carroll and his cohorts were gone, the redcoats had no reason for a formal explanation of the charges or a reason for the execution. Hmm…can we assume Lieutenant Stockbridge was bumped off by his own troops, who hated him anyway, so they could split the loot?"

"Maybe. At least it makes Sergeant Stone-Bayard suspect. He was the only one who had an exact accounting of the treasure. Remember—it was a small camp. The next in command would have seen to it that the gold got sent to headquarters," Dory said and drained the remainder of her wine.

Jake tilted his head back looking to the heavens for guidance. "Maybe not. And what if, just maybe, they reported to their commanders that the loot *was* spirited off with the prisoners. It would've been the best way to explain the missing treasure. *And*—they had a dead lieutenant to show as evidence of an attack. You have to remember the Royal Army was getting their collective butts kicked out here by a bunch of fishermen and farmers in rowboats. They would've flogged the whole garrison with a cat-o-nine-tails if they were suspected of stealing the King's gold. There was no such thing as plunder. Everything that was in the colonies, no matter where it came from, was considered property of the crown. Anything could be taken—homes, livestock, or treasure in support of England's war effort."

"Good point, Jake, pass the wine please. However… by that time, the redcoats had three cannons on the hill to protect against an attack."

"It wouldn't have mattered. They could have claimed a rebel inland commando raid up the unprotected west slope in the middle of the night. That would've been plausible."

"Jake, I still think there may be some evidence, or artifacts, out at Carroll's Landing." She reached behind him and ran her fingers through his hair. "C'mon, Jakey boy. What do you say?"

"By the way, whatever became of Christian Carroll?"

"Never heard from again. Maybe he was in the colonial witness protection program or something."

"How's Sunday?"

"Perfect." They clinked glasses.

Chapter 24

Early on Sunday morning Dory called Jake before leaving for town. "Everything is going to be okay," Jake assured her. "We'll stay on the lee side of the point. We can search the cove beach and the cave first. The sea side of the point can wait for another day. The storm is still more than 250 miles down the coast. We'll keep an eye on it."

"Jake, we shouldn't be out treasure hunting with a major storm brewing," Dory said. She was furious. "I can't believe you're being so cavalier. Whatever was out there will be there after the storm...let's just wait."

"That's exactly the point," Jake said. "Whatever *is* out there may not be there later. Beach erosion is one of the worst things about a hurricane."

Churchgoers were making their way through the village for early services as news from the hometown station crackled on Dory's car radio. She and James were headed to the lab's dock where Jake was to pick them up. The weather forecast made her tense.

Dory decided not to tell James why they were going. A boat ride was explanation enough. The radio churned out static and a report from a meteorologist. Dory slapped the dashboard above the radio. It didn't improve the reception. "*Small craft advisory on the bay beginning later this afternoon. Gale warnings in effect for this evening depending on the track of the storm.*" The storm, Belinda, was a hurricane.

Belinda's eye sat 250 nautical miles southeast of Harmony Bay sucking up warmth and power from the Gulf Stream. She could ricochet off a Canadian high-pressure system racing south across Quebec Province, or continue on a collision course with the bay. Barreling north at fifteen miles per hour, she'd hit the bay by midnight, if she chose. Computers belched out one scenario after another. For waterfront communities, it was a role of the dice. At sea, Belinda packed sustained winds of 125 miles per hour and wave heights of fifty feet or more. It was formidable for any craft. Water weighing almost 1,700 pounds per cubic yard can move almost anything it wants, anywhere it wants to. Driving rain and spray reduced the visibility to zero. Belinda was a strong category three hurricane. The hysterics and stern warnings from the radio continued. *"The storm surge will be in excess of fifteen feet. All low-lying areas should be prepared to evacuate. Secure all loose outdoor objects. Fill your bathtub with water."*

Dory pulled up to the old sail maker's shop that housed the lab. She always noticed the stark contrast of the exterior of the building with its inside. The outer shell was badly beaten from bayside living. The inside was pristine, methodical and scientific. *Hmmm—just like Jake*, she thought.

The *Sea Horse* was already tied to the dock with a Boston Whaler, equipped with a small Evinrude outboard, tethered behind her. Dory knew the skiff was for going out to the *Sea Horse's* mooring. It was a utilitarian boat, just big enough to get the commuting job to the anchorage done. On the *Sea Horse's* deck were a couple of gray plastic lockers held closed with nylon web straps and plastic snap-buckles. She cautioned James to stay away from the edge of the dock. Even with Belinda out in another time zone, she was already beginning to introduce herself. Her affect was already noticeable on the bay. Water bounced the boats up and down like slow motion horses on a merry-go-round.

Jake stepped from the lab building with Rory and Joe. They were reviewing instructions for what to do if Harmony Bay drew the short straw with Belinda. Jake held bright yellow rain gear under his arm. "It's only a fifty-fifty chance we'll get hit, but we gotta go through the drill. Move whatever can be moved into the building, lash everything down that can't be moved," Jake said. This was making Dory nervous as she walked down the dock to meet him.

"Jake, do you *really* think it's a good idea to be heading out today?"

Jake absentmindedly looked at the lab building. "Oh yeah, and go ahead and board up the windows." He handed Dory and James each a squall jacket as he greeted them. "Here, stay dry. Put these on."

"Jake, I asked you a question," Dory said.

"Oh yeah, we'll be fine. *If* Belinda hits, and that's a big if, it won't be until late tonight. We'll go out to Carroll's Landing and look around. You'll be back home way before then."

"Yes—but look at the weather now!" A stiff breeze steadily beat a halyard's hardware against a flagpole.

"Low pressure system, a little breeze, a little chop. Yeah, it'll do that." Dory took his attitude to be aloof. After she considered it for a while she realized it was Jake's confidence speaking. He wasn't worried a bit. "Hey now, where's your sense of adventure?"

"My sense of adventure is safely stowed with my common sense and protective mothering instincts."

"If I didn't think you'd be safe, we wouldn't be heading out."

"I trust you, Jake. I don't know why, but I trust you."

"But you *are* nervous?"

"Only liars and idiots would say they aren't."

The boat left the dock with Led Zeppelin screaming from the sound system. "Jake, I like *Communication Breakdown* as much as the next girl, but do you think we could have something, uh, *less stimulating?*" Dory said. He punched a button on the console and the tracks changed to Beatles music. After leaving the dock, he turned on the display screen for the autopilot. After clicking on the coordinates slightly north of Carroll's Landing, a line appeared on the screen for the boat to follow. Plotting a more northerly course then east would help avoid the onslaught of nasty weather moving through Osprey's Gut. Next, he flipped on the surface radar and overlaid the radar screen image on the autopilot display. The radar showed several boats scurrying toward port from the sea. Jake pushed the *Sea Horse* easily through the swells while keeping watch for the other crafts that showed on the screen. They now were fifteen minutes off of Carroll's Landing. Dory braced herself each time green water buffeted the hull. James took it all in stride, for him it was as much fun as a roller-coaster ride.

Dory was delighted that Carroll's Landing lagoon was as tranquil as they had left it two months earlier. The perimeter barrier of hulking boulders held back the waves and the wind and noise of the bay. Fifty yards off shore Jake checked the depth gauge and decided he was in a good position to anchor. He dropped the fore anchor and set its flukes. Once completed, he also opted to set a stern anchor to minimize the boat's swing in any wind that might come up. This would also provide a more stable platform to board the skiff.

James grew impatient. Jake settled him down by telling him about the plan to go exploring. Jake asked James for help with the ladder and hauling in the Boston Whaler's tether line. Jake unshackled a locker box on the deck and withdrew the electronic equipment.

"What's that?" James asked.

"It's a pulse induction metal detector," Jake said. "It'll allow us to search for stuff in the sand. Even in this highly mineralized sand that probably contains some amounts of iron."

"Are we going treasure hunting?"

"Let's just say we're going relic hunting. If we find some treasure— that wouldn't be too bad. Go scoot and pull out a few flashlights and a couple of those waterproof lanterns. Oh, yeah—and three vests." Jake tied the Whaler's painter to the *Sea Horse*. Climbing aboard the smaller boat, he fastened the stern line to it, throwing the whip end to Dory on the *Sea Horse*. "Tie her on to a cleat," he said. She complied, making the two boats parallel. "Start handing me down the gear." Alternately, Dory and James handed the gear to Jake. "Don't forget the lunch."

"Right," Dory said. She lowered an insulated bag with sandwiches and bottled water overboard.

"Hold on a minute. I'm checking the National Weather Service one last time before we go ashore," Jake said while loading the gear.

"Now you're thinking," Dory remarked. She glanced up at the top of the cliffs where Belinda's twenty-five mile per hour easterly fringe winds swayed the trees. The weather service reported Belinda's northerly track. What way she might veer was anyone's guess.

Jake commented, "We don't have a lot of time today. Let's search the cave first."

"It'll be the most likely place to find artifacts if it had been occupied," Dory said. The three huddled in the cramped quarters of the Whaler as it covered the short distance to the beach. Jake tilted the motor up as they landed, jumped out, and dragged the boat to dry sand. Dory and James handed the metal detector, backpacks with folding shovels, pickaxes, waterproof lanterns, flashlights, cameras, a hand-held weather radio and their lunch overboard. "Let's search the cave first. If there's nothing, we'll eat lunch, check the weather, and then decide if we should look further," Jake said.

Jake switched on a lantern as he entered the cave. Dory studied the walls illuminated with the high-powered flashlight she held. The craggy walls offered no information. Jake formulated a plan to scan the cave's sand floor in a grid pattern with the metal detector, working from the mouth to the back wall. He instructed James to draw parallel, then vertical lines in the sand with a stick at approximately two-pace intervals.

"We'll scan the whole grid first. If we get a tone we'll mark the box or boxes then dig after we're done," Jake said. The cave, although narrow at its entrance, mushroomed out to a twenty-foot wide chamber. Jake sent James out to collect clamshells to use as markers. He turned to Dory. "Is this scaring you?" Jake asked.

"It's a little creepy, but I'm not afraid," she said. James returned with an armful of clamshells. "I guess you're expecting to find a lot," Dory quipped. Jake donned the headphones and began to sweep the floor in 180-degree arcs. One grid square after another revealed nothing. James grew anxious. Dory hoped the whole trip wasn't an exercise in futility. Dory and James lit the way with their lamps and Jake worked his way toward the back of the cave. He stopped, continuing to pass the sensor over the same grid spaces. Narrowing the pass to two adjacent boxes, he held his finger to his lips. Dory and James became quiet. Jake used the same finger to point to the two squares. "Mark these two," he said. James laid a clamshell at the center of each. Jake finished scanning the remainder of the grid with no further results. In the bluish artificial light, the three stood around the two shells. "Can we dig?" James asked. Jake responded, "Yeah, but we have to move slowly and carefully. It could be fragile."

"I hope it's not just a rusty old chowder pot," Dory said.

Jake unfolded a shovel and began to scrape away the sand. Scraping became digging. It was easy to dig. The sand was neither compacted nor wet. At a depth of three feet, the shovel stopped with a thud. "Oh, no. A rock," Dory said.

"I'm not sure about that," Jake replied. "It feels more like driftwood." Jake returned to scraping. By the time he finished alternately digging and scrapping the dry sand, a very large piece of flat wood was uncovered.

"I think it's a door," James said. At the outer boundary, Jake dug deeper.

"I think it's a crate of some sort," Jake said. It was slightly more than six feet long, three feet wide and as deep as it was wide, and made of fitted thick boards with perpendicular cross braces.

"It looks like an old sea chest," Dory said.

"I think the meter picked up the iron in the hardware," Jake said.

"Maybe there's treasure in there," James blurted. None of them wanted to admit they were nervous about opening it.

Jake ran his hand across the top of the box. "The lid is held on with pegs. You don't see that anymore. This thing must be very old," he said. It occurred to Jake—the metal detector's tone he heard wasn't from any hardware holding the crate together. "I'll see if I can pry it off." He reached for the pickaxe. Forcing the point between the lid and the box, he pulled up on the handle. After several tries the wooden pegs emitted a cracking sound as the cover broke lose. Dory held the light over Jake shoulder, directing its beam on the box top.

"Okay, here we go." Jake inserted a shovel blade into the crevice created by the pickaxe and lifted the entire top in one motion. Dory screamed. She dropped her lamp and scrambled for the cave's entrance.

Now holding his own lantern above the box, bathing the excavation in a pool of light, James was the first to speak. "Jeepers creepers—take a look at that."

"Stay here. Don't touch anything!" Jake yelled and bolted after Dory.

"I'm okay," she said. Visibly shaken, Jake put his arm around her. "It's okay, I'm over the shock. I guess we found Mr. Christian Carroll."

"How can you be so sure?"

"Did you see the belt buckle with the CC monogram? Same as that one." She pointed to the stone wall outside of the cave. It bore the double C brand that Jake showed them in June.

"I'm going back in to have a closer look and take some pictures." Jake pulled a digital camera from his pocket.

198 | TOM GAHAN

"Are we grave robbers?" Dory asked. Her face showed deep concern.

"No. We're not taking anything. As long as you aren't *intentionally* disturbing human remains, there's no violation. Do you want to come back inside or stay here?" Dory looked at the boiling sky that was now changing to slate gray.

"I'm okay, I'm coming in. I'm worried about James."

"Don't worry about him. He's the least scared of all of us."

They entered the cave where James still stood holding the lantern high above the full, well-preserved, human skeleton. Anything cloth on the body was badly decomposed, but a few items of leather, a belt, boots, and a vest, although blackened, stayed reasonably intact. As Dory had mentioned, the belt around the corpse's mid-section held a scabbard carrying a buckle with the distinctive double C logo. The hilt of a full-length sword protruded from the sheath. Inscribed on the underside of the coffin lid was MDCCLXXXII.

"I guess the buckle and the sword gave him away," Jake said.

"Why does he have a sword in there with him?" James questioned.

"I'm not sure exactly why. He must have been a man of considerable importance and rank. I do know Viking warriors were buried with grave goods—swords, spear points and so forth. Up in Labrador, the Inuits buried their people the same way. Whatever happened, we can assume this is Christian Carroll and that he didn't put himself in this coffin, pull a sword in with him and peg the top shut. I'd say he was given a burial with all of the military honors. It was also unusual to bury someone with their boots on. Boots and shoes were hard to come by in those days."

"It's too bad he never got to see his dream come true," Dory said.

"What do you mean?" James asked.

Dory pointed at the numerals. "1782. I'm assuming that's the year he died. Or, at least, he wasn't buried after that date. He died a year before it was all over. The American Revolution didn't end until the signing of the Treaty of Paris in September of 1783. The last of the British troops shipped out of the colonies in November 1783."

Jake said what he was thinking aloud, "He was probably buried out here to hide him from the redcoats. I'm sure we're looking at the remains of one of the founders of covert operations for the Sons of Liberty."

"May he rest in peace," Dory said.

Jake took command of the moment. "Yeah, let's get some pictures, put this back together, and skedaddle outta here. It's getting nasty outside. Once we get back, and Belinda has settled down, I'll call Chief Dooley and have him contact the State Police and the coroner's office. That's what you're supposed to do when you find human remains. I'll call the archeology and American History departments at the university, too. They'll want to weigh in on this." Jake snapped off two dozen pictures. "Both of you—promise me you will not say a word about this to anyone until the authorities can get out here. We don't need any thrill seekers or souvenir hunters disturbing him." Dory and James swore themselves to secrecy.

"Can we keep the sword?" James asked.

"Sorry, James. This was found on public property. So…we don't get to keep any of it."

Outside, wind gusts swept debris from the peak of the cliffs, raining it down on the beach below. On their return to the *Sea Horse* they were pitched about in what was otherwise a normally safe harbor. Dory looked back to face Jake.

"Jake, I looked up the meaning of the name Belinda. In Old German it means—*crafty.*"

Chapter 25

Belinda was beginning to make her presence known in the cove. The Whaler skidded about in the turbulence on its way back to the *Sea Horse*. Jake could hear the two-way radio crackling as they neared. Due to the wind, he couldn't discern the message or whose voice it was.

"Come in Sea Hass, come in. Ah you they-uh Jake? Come in."

The *Sea Horse* dwarfed the smaller boat as Jake skillfully pulled alongside. He stood, reached up to the gunwale of the bigger boat and pulled the two crafts tightly together. Dory clung to the ladder, inching her way up. Once on deck, she reached out to James. He scrambled aboard without trouble. Jake tied a line to the *Sea Horse's* stern and hefted the gear up to Dory. Each boat rode up and down in an independent rhythm.

The two-way came alive again. *"Come in Sea Hass, come in Sea Hass."*

Jake recognized the thick New England accent of Ben Hathaway, the Bay Constable and grabbed the mic. "Come in, Ben, this is the *Sea Horse*. Over."

"Geez, fellah, I've been tryin' to reach ya. You okay?"

"Yeah, were fine. Doing a little pleasure cruisin' is all."

"Hey now, ya picked a hell of a day fah it." Jake watched Dory roll her eyes.

"What's yah location?" Jake gave Hathaway his coordinates. "Ahl right then. We got a May Day from out that way. A sail boat up on the rocks aff England Point. Three abarhd. Two men, one woman. Hah name is the *Real Rewahd*. The Coast Gahd is steamin' aftah a long-linah that's taking on wa-tah 200 miles out. The choppahs went out to a freightah. A crewman has appendicitis—they have to get him in befah it bursts. The *Real Rewahd* thinks it'll be done-in long befah dahk. The stahm is still tracking fah us. The Coast Gahd doesn't know if they can make it to the *Real Rewahd* by then. Twenty minutes ago we lost radio contact with *Real Rewahd*." Jake thought about the name *Real Reward*. There was a familiar ring to it, but he couldn't place it. It didn't matter for now.

"We'll try to reach her from here. The static in front of the storm might be blocking your signal, Ben. Maybe she's lost her antennae." Jake thought to himself, *she might be upside down.*

"Can ya pick hah up?"

"Roger wilco. Have you got numbers for me?" Hathaway responded with the longitude and latitude. Jake punched the coordinates into the autopilot and wrote the numbers on a white board with a marker. "We can handle that, Ben. *Sea Horse* is on her way—over and out."

Dory was livid. Her eyes spoke before her lips did. "Jake, look at this weather. Are you nuts? Going after that boat, we could be the next one in trouble. Where are they?"

"Dory, it's the rules of the sea. If a boat is in distress—you go."

"But—*where* do we have to go?"

"Out through the Gut, turn left. Not far from there."

"Oh my God, Jake. I've seen Osprey's Gut in good weather. Going out there with a hurricane bearing down is crazy!" Jake gripped her by the shoulders.

"We're going to be fine. *And*, I need your help. If I don't think we can do it—we'll turn around. I'm not going to put you and James in danger."

"Gee whiz, when I signed on as a librarian in a waterfront town I never thought it would include this."

"It's time for us all to get our floatation vests on. Give me a hand with the anchors. *Please*, we don't have a lot of time."

Jake took the confused sea head-on and pushed the *Sea Horse* through Osprey's Gut. Green water deluged over the bow as the boat broached another wave. Cresting each wave, they slammed down into another trough, only to be met by another wall of water. Dory thought about how

202 | TOM GAHAN

bad conditions were with the eye of hurricane still over 150 miles out. She was glad they skipped lunch, mostly due to the compression of time. A full stomach certainly would've ended up overboard. Sea foam blew in from the east combining with storm-generated mist, making visibility difficult. When the boat slid down into a trough, any horizon, visible or not, ceased to exist.

Jake hollered above the wind as water gushed from the fore deck to the stern. "Once we get through the narrows, things will calm down a bit. It'll be tough going—but we can handle it. We're going to track into the sea, then turn 180 degrees around and head west with the wind behind us. That'll keep us from being broadsided and laid over." Dory watched the water drain back to the sea through the scuppers…and prayed.

James had never been beyond England Point and La Plage de Sable Rouge to the open waters, only the confines of Harmony Bay. He was amazed that the waters calmed as Jake had predicted. The wind picked up in intensity, delivering fresh fusillades of froth and spray. James saw it as an exciting adventure that he couldn't wait to tell Gramps about. In James' mind's eye, they'd never believe he was involved in a rescue mission.

Jake got to the turn around point and spun the wheel fast and hard. He throttled into the face of a wave. Turning the boat before it reached the crest, it rode down the slope and chugged up out of the trough. Now they faced west and looked into the face of England Point. A terrifying seascape rebuffed Belinda's assault. Ledges as big as freight trains lurked just beneath the surface while elephantine boulders hunkered down in the water. Waves breaking on the beach were clearly audible. Jake tried the *Real Reward* on all frequencies. Nothing. He hoped they weren't too late. Suddenly, James sounded an alert. "Look!" he said as he pointed toward shore. Every time the *Sea Horse* rose up on a wave, it offered a vantage point. Jake could make out the green hull of the sailboat lying on its side. Three crewmembers were hanging over the side, holding onto to the toe rail at the edge of the deck. Every time a wave washed over the *Real Reward*, they disappeared from view.

"Let's roll," Jake said. Still not being sure if this was a rescue or recovery mission, he opted not to call Ben Hathaway with the news.

He checked the depth gauge and glanced at the display screen of the sounder. It showed the contour, and obstacles, on the sea floor as a visual exhibit of wavy lines. Repeating the turnaround procedure, he nosed the boat into the wind and waves. Jake showed Dory how to watch the display and how to maneuver to avoid hazards. "You've been at the helm before, Dory. You'll know what to do," Jake said over the wind. "Keep her nosed into the wind and about forty-five degrees to the oncoming water. If a big one comes through, throttle up into it." With those words, Jake disappeared below deck. He returned to the companionway a minute later wearing a neoprene wet suit and had a scuba mask on top of his head.

"Jake, why the wet suit?" Dory probed.

"It's only in case I have to go in the water after somebody." He also knew it would help protect him against abrasions from the rocks and hypothermia if things didn't go well.

"Here, hold these," Jake said, handing Dory his eyeglasses.

"How are you going to see?" she said.

"My eyeglass prescription is ground into the lens," he said, tapping the glass of the dive mask. Jake strapped on a bright orange life vest over the wetsuit. He went to the starboard side, grasped the boom of the crane-hoist, and locked it into place perpendicular to the boat. Jake pushed the yellow button on the remote control box and pulled out nine yards of cable from the spool. Grabbing another life vest, he snapped it to the hook on the end of the cable.

"Okay, crew—here's the plan. I'm going to attach this hook to the stern of the Whaler. This extra vest will keep the end of the line afloat if it becomes detached, or if the Whaler comes apart in the shoals."

"Jake, please, this is too dangerous," Dory argued.

"We've got to get them out of there. I don't know how much longer they can hang on. I'll be okay. Boston Whaler's hulls are filled with floatation material. Even if you cut one in half, it'll still float." Jake's voice was straining against the wind. "If the skiff goes over you can reel me in like a big fish." Jake showed James and Dory the controls for the hoist. "Yellow is neutral. You can let slack out that way. Green pulls the line in, red stops the line and locks the spool. Whatever happens—don't let the line go slack—we don't want it fouling the propeller. Leave it in neutral as I go in. If you need to tension the line, push the red button. Use green for the return trip. *And*, stay off the back deck. If the cable sweeps across the deck it will throw you overboard." James helped Jake with the ladder. Jake retrieved the Whaler by its towrope and pulled it alongside. He threw in a pair of swim-flippers, a mesh vest with a flashing emergency beacon and a life ring with a hundred feet of line attached. He lowered himself in and attached the tow cable as the outboard sputtered to life. James never took his eyes off the Whaler.

The outboard was hardly necessary. Wind and the waves pushed the motorboat toward shore at an alarming rate. Jake bounded up and down in the waves steering ever closer to the *Real Reward*. As he got closer he could see the sailboat was laid over on her starboard side. Her keel was sheared off. Obviously, that was where the trouble began. If she had sheets up it would have easily rolled over or at least been very difficult to maneuver. The rocks could easily do their handiwork after that. It was now apparent the main mast was snapped cleanly off and the buoyant contents of the boat had already washed ashore. Three life-jacketed mariners were face down on the side of the boat, hanging from the toe rail, which offered even less protection against the pounding surf that cascaded over the partially submerged hull. One of them, the largest, was inside a life-ring as well. Jake was sure they had ingested a lot of salt water by now. Not a good thing. Nevertheless, they were alive.

A wave receded and the survivors turned at the same time to see Jake arrive. Jake was taken aback when he realized who the unlikely trio was: Hank "*Klunk*" Klunkergarten, Maureen Donnelly and Ed Fishhook Cutsciko. Fishhook was wearing the life-preserver ring. Jake knew it wouldn't be easy to load them aboard in the surf. His action strategy was simple. It was going to be women first. Besides, Maureen would be easier to pull on board than Hank. With the two of them on the skiff, Jake could position their weight to counterbalance Cutsciko's. They still might have enough strength left to help lug him over the side. Jake thought, *After all, the captain is the last one to abandon ship.* With the outboard now burbling in neutral, Jake got up as close as he could and called out to Miss Donnelly to let go of the rail. She released her grip and slithered down the *Real Reward's* lubricious hull into the wash. Being in good athletic shape, she paddled the short distance to Jake and boosted herself over the gunwale.

"Are you okay?" Jake asked. The wind tried to slap down his voice.

"Yeah, fine. Just cold. Let's grab the other two."

Hank let go next. Miss Donnelly and Jake helped him aboard. Their combined weight on one side dipped the boat to an unstable angle. Hank was in bad shape. He had hit his head on the deck when the boat went over. Once overboard, the constant bashing against the hull bloodied his face. Having swallowed a lot of water, Hank wretched over the side. Jake realized that Hank, as strong as he was, wasn't going to be much help in getting Cutsciko on board. Jake ordered the slumlord to let go. Cutsciko refused. Jake repeated the order, and sternly added, "Let go and get in this boat or I will leave you here." At last, Cutsciko slid down into the frenzied water. He made no forward progress as he flailed his arms. The wind and the water started to carry him shoreward.

"He'll get killed in the rocks if we can't get him in," Jake shouted.

"Maybe that wouldn't be a bad thing," the schoolteacher said. Her choice of words surprised Jake.

Jake watched Fishhook's corpulent body float away. He knew they were safely tethered to the *Sea Horse* by the winch cable and wouldn't be sucked into the pounding surf—as long as Dory remembered to lock the spool. He also understood that he didn't have many options. "Maureen, take care of Hank. I'll be back." She watched in astonishment as Jake slipped the flippers on his feet and rinsed the scuba mask out. Jake wrapped the life-ring's line around the bench seat and tied a quick knot. "You might have to help pull us back," Jake said, gesturing to the yellow propylene line. Holding the ring, he let himself fall backward over the side away from the hull of the floundering *Real Reward*. He kicked toward his target. Cutsciko was hysterical by the time Jake reached him.

"Shut up and listen!" Jake screamed above the storm's howl. "Lock your arms through this," Jake said. He pushed the ring toward him. Cutsciko obeyed and Jake rolled him over on his back as torrents of rain began to rake the rescue. Looking skyward, the victim gasped as the rainwater now mixed with the sea to flood his face. Aided by a life vest and two life buoy rings, he floated effortlessly. Jake pushed him toward the Whaler as he signaled to Maureen to pull on the safety line. Getting him in the little boat presented a daunting task. In the face of the drama, Jake laughed inwardly as he thought about the idea of towing Cutsciko behind the Whaler to the *Sea Horse*.

Cutsciko flopped around like a Sea World exhibit, his face contorted by stress. Miss Donnelly held fast to the line, keeping her captive cinched up against the boat. Jake pulled himself aboard and removed his flippers. Working together, they tried to haul Cutsciko's dead weight aboard. Cutsciko made no effort to extricate his gluttonous mass from the water and continued to rant. Hank recovered enough to grab the life-ring around Cutsciko's middle and made the final difference in landing the big fish. Now curled into a ball on the floor of the boat, Fishhook alternately sobbed and breathed heavily through his mouth. "My beautiful boat! My *Real Reward*. There's nothing left," Cutsciko cried.

Jake reached over the transom and unhooked the cable. Moving forward he snapped it into the anchor mounting eyelet on the bow. He was concerned. The boat was reaching its limit as the waves sawed at the hull as relentlessly as a school of sharks feeding on a slab of beef. He sized up the situation. They very well might capsize. Everyone was wearing a floatation device, and Cutsciko had three. The tow cable still had the life vest attached. If the boat broke apart, as long as they stayed together, Dory could winch them in. In any event, the hull would float. In the water, Cutsciko would be a liability and Hank was weak and disoriented and wouldn't last long. Jake suspected a concussion.

"Listen up!" Jake yelled. "There's a chance we might go over. If that happens, grab the bow line and stay together." Cutsciko began to sob again. The behavior disgusted Jake.

"Aye-aye," said Miss Donnelly.

"Got it," Hank said and nodded his battered head. Because the sea was no longer rinsing his face, blood now clotted his hair and features.

Jake fired up the outboard and tried to turn into the waves. The overload and low horsepower were no match for the volleys that Belinda sent. The Whaler, frozen in place, wasn't budging and the *Sea Horse* was still a hundred yards out from Jake. It seemed like the *Sea Horse* might as well have been on the dark side of the moon. He hoped Dory or James comprehended that they were trying to make their way back. Visibility was a problem. There was no prearranged signal for the haul back. Suddenly, the boat started to move slowly eastward toward the *Sea Horse*. Somebody on board was pushing the green button.

"How am I doing, Mom?" James called out.

"You're doing great, honey. Don't let go of that button until I tell you to or until Jake is back in the boat," Dory said. She had her hands full. Piloting the *Sea Horse* on a sunny day across the bay was far from what she was being asked to do now. Dory felt she was in way over her head. Every time an ominous wave approached, she nudged the gearshift from neutral to forward to keep the boat in position. An hour ago, waves peaked at twenty-five feet. Breaking crests formed, sending spindrift and airborne spray over their heads. Streaks of foam blew from the east in the gale winds. Dory knew she could not let the boat parallel the incoming waves, which could roll them over. She fought the wheel, watched the depth-sounder and kept a steady eye on the GPS. It was either them or the sea, and she wasn't going to let Belinda win the battle for her son.

James wrapped his arms and legs around the post that supported the aft edge of the cockpit roof. He kept pressure on the green button of the remote control with his thumb and hoped Jake would be back soon. He was getting very tired.

"How much longer, Mom?"

"Soon. Very soon."

"My hand hurts."

"You're doing great. Hang in there. I know you can do this for me."

"Hey, I can see them!" Dory looked behind her to see the intermittent pulse of the emergency locator beacon Jake brought with him.

"Hold that button down, James. Don't let go!" Dory noticed a change in conditions. Although the blinding rain persisted, streaks of wind driven foam no longer coursed through the water. The wind didn't whistle through the cockpit and rattle the windshield as it did earlier, the wave crests ceased to break, and longer, less frequent, waves formed. It was a strange, yet welcome change.

The Whaler continued to buck forward. At times, the tow cable completely submerged. Water sloshed into the boat. Hank, Miss Donnelly, and Jake bailed as best as they could. Cutsciko cowered down, blocking the spray with his hands.

Almost there, thought Jake. *Another fifty yards and we're good.* Jake noticed the wind's decreased intensity and what had been ski slopes of seawater, now looked more like rolling pastoral hills.

The Evinrude continued to push them forward, aided by James' thumb on the green hoist button. Dory slipped the *Sea Horse* into neutral as they approached. She pulled a boat hook from the storage rack and reached out to Jake. Once connected, James pushed the red button as Jake killed the outboard and threw a line to the *Sea Horse*.

Jake surveyed the Whaler crew. The rain and spray worked to reopen Hank's head wounds. Blood ran down his temples and onto his life vest. Maureen was shivering from exposure to the elements. Her freckled skin took on a gray pallor, her lips showed twinges of blue. Harmony Bay's real estate mogul remained in a catatonic state. Jake knew he'd need James and Dory's help getting them up the ladder in the undulating sea. Jake motioned to Miss Donnelly to go first. Weak-kneed, seasick, and exhausted, she didn't have the strength to make it over the top. Dory reached over and slid her hands up under Miss Donnelly's arms. Leaning back, Dory managed to pull the smaller woman aboard by letting her own weight fall back. She dragged Miss Donnelly to the safety of the cockpit.

"James, get her a dry towel," Dory said.

Hank was next up. Dory was well aware that she couldn't heft him over the side like the schoolteacher. Hank was groggy but made it to the top step and was losing his balance. Jake reached up and placed his hand in the small of Hank's back so he wouldn't fall backward into the skiff. James returned from below. He helped his mother steady Hank as they each took an arm and eased him over the gunwale.

Jake stared at Cutsciko and shook his head in disgust. "Hey Ed, are you going to make it aboard or do you want to stay here in the Whaler?" Jake asked.

"Oh, don't leave me! Don't leave me!" His walrus moustache flickered up and down as he shuddered.

"Looks like you're in the best shape of everybody on your crew. Get moving!"

Literally, Fishhook could not pull his own weight. His every attempt to board the *Sea Horse* failed. It was embarrassing. When he did manage to get his foot in the first rung, he sagged down like a sack of potatoes. After the fifth try, Jake became impatient. "That's it—you're staying in here. We have to get moving," Jake said. "You're not even trying."

Fishhook look down at his feet. The water in the Whaler was now well above his ankles. His shirt buttons strained against the wet cloth in a hopeless effort to contain his enormous belly. The look of bewilderment returned to his face.

"B, bu, but," Fishhook mumbled.

"No buts about it. I've got four other people that I'm responsible for. I'm getting them back to dry land right now. Stay in the boat. You've got three floatation devices. If you fall overboard I'll harpoon you and snatch you up with the winch."

James' jaw dropped when he heard the exchange. He couldn't imagine Jake spearing his landlord and dragging him behind the *Sea Horse* like a trophy fish.

"Waddaya mean! I'm begging you!" He now held his hand together in a prayerful position.

"One last chance—that's it. Get going," Jake seethed.

Fishhook grabbed the uprights of the ladder and let out a mighty groan as he pulled himself up.

"Atta boy—keep going," Jake said.

"Bu, but you helped the others up." Tears streamed down his cheeks into the trembling gray whiskers.

"In case you didn't notice, one's a woman, the other is injured. Keep moving."

Fishhook made it to the top as a swell passed beneath the old lobster boat. Thrown off balance, he fell face-first into the boat with a dull thump. With his life-ring still around his middle he flopped around like a mackerel. Jake mounted the ladder and came aboard, joining the others as they circled Cutsciko.

"Ed, what were you thinking bringing these two as crew?" Jake scoffed. "I know Maureen has *some* sailing skills, but *Klunk* doesn't even know port from starboard."

"B, b, but." Fishhook gurgled from his sprawled position.

"It was the stupidest thing I've ever done," Miss Donnelly said. She stabbed a finger at Cutsciko. "He told me he was looking for crew to bring his sailboat up from Hilton Head. We were in trouble before we even left the dock. He said all I needed to do was pay my airfare down there. I figured it would be a fun, free sail up the coast. Until I found out, with no place to escape, what a repulsive, lecherous, cad he is. He's a pig."

"Hank, what about you?" Jake asked.

Hank shrugged. He gazed over the sea through blackened eyes and rolled his thumb toward Miss Donnelly. "I heard she was coming," Klunk said. Dory shook her head. It seemed as though Harmony Bay's favorite schoolteacher was in popular demand.

"Well, you *almost* made it," Jake said and gestured toward the rocks where they were rescued from.

"*Almost* is right," Miss Donnelly said. "We missed the turn in for Osprey's Gut. I had to handle the *Real Reward* on my own. Our *captain* was scared out of his wits when the hurricane started chasing us. He was below deck downing cocktails while his crew was topside trying to save his precious yacht."

"He was drunk?" Jake probed.

"Probably. If nothing else, he abandoned his crew," Miss Donnelly said. Cutsciko covered his ears with his hands. Dory decided it was best if she steered clear from the conversation.

"Hey Cutsciko, do you remember I told you to hire Kenny Clarke to sail your boat up?"

"Bu, but he wanted to be paid *money*," responded the sniveling slumlord.

"That's exactly right. Look how much you saved by being cheap. Kenny Clarke could sail your boat through the eye of a needle in a full gale. Kenny would have gotten you up here in one piece. The *Real Reward* will be a total loss by the time the surf finishes with her, *and*, you almost got two good people killed. As for you, well, that's another story. You're lucky to be alive."

"We've been through a disaster. My beautiful boat is destroyed and this is how you're speaking to me?" sobbed Cutsciko.

"I'm not worried. You probably have it insured for more than it's worth. I wouldn't doubt it if you called your insurance agent at the first sign of trouble to file a claim. Eh?"

Jake gave out orders. "Dory, take Maureen below and find her some dry clothes. James, get a towel with some ice for Hank's noggin. Find a dry place in the cockpit and prop him up. I don't want him keeling over.

Ed, take the life ring off. You look ridiculous." Jake switched on the radar and weather screen and let out a hoot. "Looks like Belinda might be turning away from us. We'll still have our hands full running the rapids through Osprey's Gut, but we'll be okay after that. Pull up the ladder and let's get outta here."

He turned on the radio and spun the dial to a familiar frequency. "*Sea Horse* to Bay Constable—do you copy? Come in, Ben."

"Eee-yup, Ahm righ-ut hee-ah, Jake. Have ya found the *Real Rewahd*?"

"Roger that, Ben. All hands saved—the boat is a total loss. Please advise the Coast Guard."

"Eee-yup. Rawjah-wilco. Good jawb, Jake. You'll be pleased to know hahricane Belinda was downgraded to a categawrhy one hahricane. Prawbably be a trawpical stahm by suppa time. She's made a shahp righ-ut and she's blowin' out to sea."

"That's good news, Ben. Have the Harmony Bay Emergency Response Unit meet us at the dock with an ambulance. Our ETA is under an hour. Once we get through the Gut I'll crack the throttle wide open. I'll call when we get close. I have one survivor with head injuries, possible concussion. One with hypothermia. And one with hysteria and a badly bruised ego."

Hurricane Belinda only dealt a glancing blow to Harmony Bay. The town was spared from a storm's wrath—for the time being.

Chapter 26

Harmony Bay's newest celebrity pedaled along North Road. His head spun with the glorious tales of finding buried historical bones, rescues on the high seas, and the Harmony Bay Gazette's headline: Treasure Hunters Perform Rescue—Scientist, Librarian and Boy Save Lives. Interviewed and photographed for his part in the hair-raising adventure, he now saw himself as a super-star. There were quotes from the Coast Guard about how the daring rescue was above and beyond the call of duty. Archeologists and historians marveled at the astounding discovery of Christian Carroll's remains. James knew he was famous, at least for the moment, in every corner of Harmony Bay. Sure, Mom and Jake were involved, but he was without a doubt the only kid on the expedition and rescue. The new school year would begin in a couple of weeks. James was ready to strut in the door as a celebrated explorer, hero, and the only ten-year-old Little Leaguer in anyone's memory who had slugged a game winning, walk-off home run.

He worked his bike toward the rendezvous with his school friends Katie, Steven, Raymond and Peter. They all agreed to meet in the tree house on Mill Pond at one o'clock. James promised them the gut wrenching, inside details about digging up a body and scraping the bloody remnants of the *Real Reward's* crew off the rocks.

James climbed over the gnarled, twisted roots of the old tree and scaled the crude ladder to the hideaway. His friends were already there. The first to greet him was Steven who slouched in the corner. "I think you made up the whole story. Finding some dead guy isn't such a big deal," he said.

"It is so true," Katie interrupted. "It was in the newspaper. The Coast Guard said the boat was wrecked near England Point. Did you read what Miss Donnelly said about the rescue? She'd never lie and the newspaper wouldn't lie either."

"Forget what Steven says," Peter said, in awe of the storyteller. "Tell us about the dead guy. Were his eyes oozing out? Did he stink?"

"Everybody shut up and let him talk," Raymond said. "I want to hear about this."

James stayed silent for a few, awkward moments. He pondered how much he could embellish the story. Then he remembered his mother once told him, "A lie is the hardest thing to remember." They could check his story. If he got tripped up in the details, they'd be onto him. Steven wouldn't think twice about going to the library to grill James' mother about the facts to catch him in a fib. Besides, the story was true and spooky enough. Finding a skeleton and rescuing his teacher off a shipwreck was a sufficient tale. It didn't need exaggeration. Although, he reckoned he could jazz the yarn up a little. The more James thought about it, the more he considered holding onto the story for a dark, dreary night. It couldn't wait that long. He was the center of attention. He relished the limelight.

"Christian Carroll's bones were in good shape," James began, "there were no guts, eyeballs, or anything like that. Only his crusty old bones covered in dust." Katie gasped and took a step back. "It sure was creepy, though. That old wooden box was buried this deep in the sand." James stretched his arms out to illustrate the depth. "Jake Kane says the archeologists told him the coffin was made out of teak. It's some kinda tree that grows in jungles. They found 1,000 year old coffins and sacrificial altars and stuff made from teak in perfect condition in Asia."

"Well, there's no jungles around here," Steven said, his voice syrupy with sarcasm.

"Shush! Let him talk," Raymond urged.

"That's exactly right," James said. "They believe the coffin was made from the teak parts of a ship that crashed out on England Point. In those days, they used teak a lot to make ships. Teak is full of something called silica and natural oils. It makes it real waterproof. Termites won't eat it either. That's why the box wasn't rotted. It had 1782 carved into the lid in

Roman Numerals… just like a tombstone. Like I said…real creepy."

"They can't prove it was made from an old ship," Steven snickered.

"Well, the stuff in between the coffin boards was called oakum. It was mixed with pine pitch. That's the same stuff they jammed in between the boards of ship's hulls back then to make them watertight. Whoever built the box, knew how to build boats. Anyway, it kept ol' Christian Carroll high and dry for over 200 years."

"Did you get to hold the sword?" Peter asked with an air of diplomacy.

James felt the urge to stretch the truth—and did. Looking each in the eye, he lowered his voice to a whisper, "I couldn't—even if I wanted to."

"Why not, were you chicken?" Steven said. He defiantly crossed his arms in front of his chest and stepped closer.

"Heck, I ain't chicken." James was up to the challenge. "Carroll had a death grip around the handle of his sword. I would've had to bust his bony fingers off to get it out. Besides, Jake told me it's a crime to disturb a burial site—so we couldn't."

"How could he be gripping the sword if he was dead?"

"That's the point. Maybe he was buried *alive*." James' audience stood wide-eyed. The only sound was the rustling of maple leaves outside the tree house. James knew he had them with that line. They wouldn't dare question his veracity again.

"What about the rescue?" Katie asked. She blinked twice and stepped back farther.

"Yeah, it was wicked dangerous out there. The water was crashing over our boat. I thought we all were gonna drown. It was awful. Water was everywhere. The wind was howling like a monster. Their sailboat was bashed up to smithereens. Miss Donnelly was near dead and that guy Klunk from the whaleboat races was bleeding so bad, sharks started circling around. Old man Cutsciko was crying like a baby. To shut him up, we threatened to harpoon him. I had to reel in those grownups like they were riding on the back of a humongous striped bass. You know— even way bigger than the ones *I've* caught. I hauled 'em in till my hands ached."

"Geez," she said, "what about Jake?"

"Jake was the only brave one in that little boat. He had to go in the drink after them with his scuba gear and all. Those three on the sailboat would've been goners if it wasn't for Jake."

"Wow. We're you scared?" Raymond said.

"Nah. I just kept pulling in that skiff. There were a couple of close calls though. You know, like near tidal waves and all."

"Oh man, that's crazy! It's unbelievable," Katie said. James silently agreed. Katie now saw James in a whole new light. More like an intrepid explorer, brilliant scholar, or a courageous, swashbuckling sailor, not like the shy boy who came from the city only six months ago. Now she adored him.

It was the most sensational event to take place on Harmony Bay for the last couple of years. James figured he'd ride it for all it was worth. It put a little swagger in his step.

James scrambled down the rickety ladder and over the maple's knobby knees, possessed by an undeniable sense of victory. It was still early. He had a standing promise with Mrs. Verdi that he could go out bike riding as long as he stayed out of the water. Fair enough, he thought. After his stunt in the rowboat last winter, he wasn't about to test the limits. His friends had all scattered. In the case of Steven and Raymond, it was from the jealousy of James' accomplishments. Peter had heard enough about buried bones for one day. Katie was the last to leave, hoping to engage James in further conversation. She even tried to cajole him with an invitation to try new games on the laptop she had received for her birthday. He decided to ride his bike up the hill to Billy's house. Even if Billy wasn't home, he could visit with Chloe, or Angus, if he was around. He plunged into the cooling shade of the maples that lined the dirt road. Pedaling the bike became more difficult as the surface turned to loose sand.

He arrived at Billy's cabin sweating and breathing heavily. Billy emerged from the barn to see James sprawled out on the grass. "It looks as though you have given yourself quite a workout, young man," Billy said.

"Oof, yeah. It was harder to get up here than I thought."

"Does your mother or Mrs. Verdi know you are up here?"

"Mrs. Verdi only knows I'm out. Not exactly where. I have permission. But I have to be home by five."

"I see. Take a break. I will be right back." James liked Billy a lot. He was like a grandfather. Unlike his own Gramps, Billy was more intellectual. Even though Billy lived a simple life, he always had an answer for everything. Billy returned with two glasses of cold water. He handed one to James and they moved to a bench on the porch. Angus joined them, curling up on the dusty porch boards. Billy took two short pieces of rope, two bars of soap, and two pocketknives from his overall pockets.

"I'm not allowed to play with knives." James said.

"Yes, I know. I have permission." Billy produced a whetstone from another pocket. "The first order of business is to sharpen our knives. A sharp knife is a safe knife." Billy taught James how to hone the blade. "There is always a proper procedure for everything." They continued to sharpen and Billy spoke, "James, you had several successes this summer. An exemplary homerun, you made a remarkable discovery at Carroll's Landing, you were involved in a heroic rescue at sea, and you have become a proficient fisherman."

"Yep. I did," James said. He thumped his chest. "What's your point?"

"How we handle those successes is how we develop our character. Exaggerating or being boastful can lead to false pride." James sat up erect, then squirmed in his seat. He wondered if Billy was listening outside of the tree house to his slightly overblown story. "When folks brag, it can make others feel inferior. It is not a good way to be." James thought about Raymond and Steven leaving the tree house.

"You mean bragging like Mayor Pesce?"

Billy chuckled and tugged his beard. "Well, indeed. He does ramble on a bit about his accomplishments, however mundane they may be," he said. "James, to be a true hero, we must let our actions speak louder than our words."

"My father was a hero."

"Yes, I do know that."

"My mom told me that. We never got to meet each other. He was killed overseas just after I was born. He never got to tell me he was a hero."

"Yes, I know that as well. So you see—although you know he was a hero, you never heard it from him directly. That is owning the reputation of good character."

"Do you mean people should be more like Jake?"

"Yes, Jake leads by example."

"Yeah, he does cool stuff and never brags about it."

"Yes, however, people do know of his good deeds, don't they?"

"If you really did something, is it bragging?"

"James, dealing with success can be complicated. It is all in the delivery. It is called humility. A good thing to remember is, always be quick to give praise and slow to take it."

"What else do you have to do if you're a hero?"

"Hmmm. God gave us two ears and one mouth. Perhaps that should tell us to listen twice as often as we speak. Sometimes, all we need to do to be a hero are the little things, like listening and putting others before ourselves."

Having thoroughly sharpened their knives, Billy held out a soap bar. "We will practice by carving on this soap."

"Why don't we just carve wood?" James asked.

"All in due time. Learning is a natural sequence of events. Have patience."

They used Angus as a model. When finished, James was amazed at how accurately Billy was able to carve the likeness of the dog.

"It is time to learn how to tie some knots, young man." Billy pulled two short lengths of rope from his pocket. "If you are going to live in these parts, they will come in handy." Billy stood and stretched one of the pieces of rope with his thick hands and approached a porch post. "This is called a bowline. It is particularly good if you want to moor a boat to a post or a ring. It makes a secure loop in the end of a piece of rope. Under load, it will not slip or bind. Without a load it can be untied easily." Billy demonstrated tying the knot twice. "Here, James, you give it a try."

James tied the bowline knot on his first try. "This is fun," he said.

"All right, good show. Yes, it is fun. Keep practicing until you can do it with your eyes closed." On his third try, James did it with his eyes closed.

"Let's have a look at another knot. This is called a *round-turn with two half-hitches*. Once again, it is good for attaching a line to a post. This knot is better if you are working with a heavy load. The *round-turn* is really two wraps around the post. These wraps or turns take the initial strain while you finish the knot. If you are handling a very heavy load, you can wrap it around an extra time or two. These turns allow you to control the load while you complete the two half-hitches. Here we go." Billy told James to hold one end of the line. He slapped the other end around the porch post twice. "Give it a tug," Billy said. James yanked on the bitter end as Billy held the other end and saw that it did not free itself from the post. "Keep pulling," Billy said and added two half-hitches. "Go ahead and pull all you want. You will neither loosen the knot, nor will you pull down the porch." James pulled as hard as he could and laughed.

Billy made James practice this knot several times. He practiced it until he could do it with his eyes closed.

"Why do I have to do it with my eyes closed?" James asked.

"There are two reasons. Firstly, it tells that you know the knot. Secondly, you will always be able to tie it, even in the dark of night, or in a fierce gale that does not allow you to open your eyes. Take your piece of line home and practice. We will learn some new knots another time. Practice makes perfect. Have you been practicing your guitar, James?"

"Yes sir, I have."

"It is getting late and time for you to start heading home. I do not want to be in trouble with your mother *or* Mrs. Verdi."

James didn't want to leave. He moved like his feet were cast in cement as he moved toward his bike. Billy filled the bike's two water bottles for the ride back. He placed his hand on James' shoulder. "Take a break on the way back. It is still considerably hot out," he said. James mounted the bike, rode off, and thought about his visit with Billy. Billy was wise without being overbearing. That suited James. Although he didn't consciously recognize it—he needed direction, not bossiness. James worried about Billy being alone. It was past four o'clock as James struggled on the sand road. The steep downhill slope of Pencil Hill eased his travel. Clearing the maple's deep purple shadows, he broke into sunlight. Clouds battled with the sun above the trees. In James' estimation, the sun was winning. Its late afternoon heat poured down on his neck.

James crossed the culvert pipe that drained Mill Pond. He saw Peter Dyson sitting on the end of the pipe. Peter's legs dangled over the end, his feet were in the cool, bubbling water that discharged. "Hey, Peter," James called out. Peter raised his hand in a wave without turning around. James thought Peter looked lonely sitting by himself. Like James, Peter didn't have siblings. Peter's father worked for the power company and his mom worked at County General Hospital. James knew that Peter was often orphaned by shift hours. Dropping his bike by the side of the road, he joined his friend. James figured he wouldn't be breaking Mrs. Verdi's rule about staying out of the water if he only soaked his feet. After all, he wasn't swimming. "Watcha doin', Peter?"

"Checking out the snappers. Wish I had my cane pole with me," Peter said. He pointed into the creek. The creek teamed with scores of silver snappers chasing minnows and anything else that was edible.

"Cane pole?" James asked.

"Yeah. That's all you need for these. They'll bite anything. You don't even need bait. Sometimes those baby blues even bite a shiny, bare hook if you drag it through the water. This looks like a great spot to fish from."

"Peter, when we met up at the tree house today, the questions about Christian Carroll and the hurricane came at me fast. I didn't have a chance to congratulate you about winning the summer art contest at the library."

"Gee, thanks, James. I didn't think anybody noticed."

"I saw your name in the library newsletter and in the Harmony Bay Gazette. My mom says they're going to keep all of the winners on display until like Thanksgiving or something."

"Wow. They'd keep my picture up that long?"

"Sure, why not. It's good."

"Thank you, James. I didn't think anybody cared."

"Peter, what do you say you and me come down here tomorrow with our poles and see how we can do with these snappers?"

"You'd fish with *me*? Really? I thought you'd only be fishing out at England Point and Sable Rouge and going after sharks and stuff. And—."

"Sure, I'll fish here with you, Peter. It will be fun."

"School will be starting up again in less than two weeks."

"Yeah. We get to pick our own seats this year. We can keep them as long as we don't get caught fooling around. Can I sit next to you?"

"Next to *me*? Why would you want to do that? You got that homer. You found the skeleton. You saved Miss Donnelly's life." Peter chucked

220 | TOM GAHAN

a rock at the fish.

"None of that stuff lasts forever. Your artwork will last much longer. Anybody could have done it. Just glad I could be a part of it. You're cool, Peter. You're as cool as any other kid in the class, and—you won the art contest."

"Wow, James. Thank you. That would be really great."

"Hey, want to come to our house for supper?"

"You really mean it? I'll have to call my mom at work and ask permission." James hadn't asked permission either. He was sure his mom could not deny the company of one of Harmony Bay Library's favorite artists.

"C'mon. I'll ride you on the handlebars. We need to get there by five."

James knew Peter Dyson needed a friend. He was willing to stand by him when things weren't going well. James wondered if this was part of being a hero.

Summer, and the swelled population of Harmony Bay, was getting ready to say goodbye. Before long, as the seasons changed, the snappers would leave the estuaries for the open sea. The start of school, followed by the foliage's change to a glorious palette of gold, scarlet and browns, was only a matter of weeks away. November brought brutal winds. Bay folks didn't question them, or fight them, they just let it happen. Winter laid its icy blanket down sometime long after Thanksgiving. The bay held enough warmth to moderate the autumn temperatures at the expense of a cold, lengthy spring.

Chapter 27

The weather remained true to the forecast and landed hard on Harmony Bay. Trees burdened with autumn foliage that genuflected to the growing winds whistling across the bay last night now heaved in the moderate gale. Anything not tied down found a new resting place that wasn't according to any plan. Sands shifting on the beach were confronted and slowed by the sentinel rows of snow fencing and their ancillary reinforcement of beach grass. Shore birds took refuge deep within the tidal marshes or up in the surrounding hills where all there was quiet with the animal kingdom. The only sounds were from the onslaught of wind driven rain and the occasional falling limb. Crimson and golden leaves swirled in a great display of color, contrasting against the wine bottle green pines.

Dory heard the locals talk about the nor'easters of the past. The storms took a heavy toll on the infrastructure of Harmony Bay by collapsing roads from the undermining washouts and the downing of power lines. Past storms redrew the maps of the bay itself. Years ago, Osprey's Gut, the mouth of the bay between England Point and Sable Rouge, was widened by several hundred yards from a fall storm pushing in from the North Atlantic. The removal of the sand barrier beach resulted in even more exposure to the ocean and protection from subsequent gales that tried to push themselves down the throat of Harmony Bay.

Her concerns for her son continued as the wind and rain began to intensify. She wondered why school wasn't cancelled. Dory voiced her concerns to the others in the library. Since no patrons came in all day, she posited that they might all be better off at home to look after their houses and kids. Shirley, Louise and the others on the staff decided if Dory thought it was a good plan, she should present it to Mrs. Lanscome. The wailing wind and relentless rain challenged Dory's knock on Mrs. Lanscome's office door. Dory paused, then knocked again as the door opened abruptly.

"Oh, hello, Dorothy," Mrs. Lanscome said. The library director always called her Dorothy when she was trying to make a point. "Quite the storm isn't it? I was on the phone with Police Chief Dooley. I asked about the road conditions and so forth. *And*—if he thought I should close early. He told me he didn't *think* it was a good idea, he *knew* it was a good idea. Truth is, he's already called the school and recommended an early dismissal there. He told me North Road was in danger of flooding over. It's best that you get going. Are you two going to be okay out there on the peninsula, Dory?"

Jake left two days ago for a conference and wasn't due back until tomorrow at the earliest. Dory wondered about what might happen to his houseboat, or the *Sea Horse,* in the storm. Most of the other boats put out to open water to ride out the storm so they wouldn't be bashed against the bulkheads. Then she started to worry about James and herself. Their cottage was little more than a boat on the bay.

Dory was relieved that she didn't have to ask her boss about closing early. At the same time, she was alarmed about the mounting weather conditions and the possibility of the only access road to the cottage becoming impassable.

"You don't say," Dory said almost inaudibly. In the same moment, the lights flickered off and on. "I hope we'll all be okay, Mel, but I am worried about being out there and being swept out to sea."

"Not to worry, Dorothy. Harmony Bay is good strong community. They will all keep an eye on you." Dory noticed Mrs. Lanscome was breathing heavily.

Was it because of the excitement about the storm? Dory pondered.

Mrs. Lanscome led Dory to the front desk. In her shrill voice, Mrs. Lanscome made the announcement. "Ladies, it's time to abandon ship!" Dory and the others took a moment to shut down and unplug the computers and move them off the floor to the relative safety of the check out counter. Winton Hector had stopped by earlier in the morning and placed large X's of masking tape over the plate glass windows in the lobby. He left the small six over sixes to fend for themselves. If the small panes were broken by the wind or flying debris, they wouldn't result in large shards of broken glass. Mrs. Lanscome instructed Dory not to set the alarm. "If it goes off this evening it will only be because of the storm. Dooley's boys will be busy enough without having to answer a false alarm. The only reason we added an alarm was to please the insurance company. Crime has never been a problem here and with all of this rain, I don't think we have to worry about a fire. To be sure, let's shut off the main power supply before we leave," she said.

They finished all of the storm preparation. With the lights blinking madly, it was agreed that it was time to go. Mrs. Lanscome went to the utility room, shut down the electric service, and emerged with a powerful flashlight. Although daylight, the overcast dimmed the sun and Dory's spirits. Knowing it was senseless to try to open her umbrella in the wind, Dory pulled her collar up and kept her head down as she dodged the puddles in the parking lot. *I really should stop at the market and pick up extra milk and bread for James on the way home*, Dory thought.

She pulled out of the library parking lot with the small car's windshield wipers working furiously. Fallen leaves clogged the storm drains. Rain filled the gutters and spilled over the curbs in some places. The white line became indiscernible. Dory tried to stay in the middle of the street as best she could. She noticed that Hirsch's Hardware took all of the merchandise usually displayed on the sidewalk, wheelbarrows, rakes, push brooms, wagons and doghouses, and sent them to safekeeping in the shed behind the shop. Harmony Bay's post office and Shea's Bakery taped over their windows in large crisscrossed patterns as was done at the library. When Dory passed the Harmony Bay Volunteer Fire Department, she noticed they were at the ready. The Chief's car stayed parked in front and a number of volunteers' cars were in the firehouse parking lot. A rather unusual sight for an early weekday afternoon. Harmony Bay Fire House, with its Second Empire Victorian styled architecture, featured a mansard roof with dormers and tall arched windows with decorative cornices. Elaborate braces and knees supported the eaves. Dory always wondered, in a comical sort of way, why they painted the firehouse trim green. After all, the fire trucks were all red, why shouldn't the firehouse trim match? Something caught her eye through the rain-spattered windshield. Seagulls, perched on the knee braces, took up refuge from the storm under the eaves. The broad firehouse, with its back to the wind, offered a safe haven for the birds to ride out the worst of it. Later, they'd take advantage of everything tossed up on the beach by the unrelenting surf. *I guess nobody is taking any chances*, Dory said to herself.

Dory parked close to the door of Dzjankowski's grocery in the otherwise empty lot. Opening her car door, she was pelted by hard rain and greeted by a gust that pulled the door from her hand, springing it wide open. She scurried to the market door where Mr. Dzjankowski greeted her. He held open the front door to the store.

"Well you certainly are adventurous, Dory," he said.

"Thank you, Jank," Dory said.

"What brings you out in a storm like this?"

"They shut the library down early—and the school, too. I'm sure James is already home. I want to be sure to have enough in the house over the next few days."

"I see. You can be assured we've got a couple more days of heavy weather. Nor'easters always come in three days at a time. I hear North Road is already in bad shape, Bay Road will be next, and we're still not up to high tide. That won't hit for another couple of hours or so. The full moon is going to make it worse."

Dory put her hand basket with milk, bread, butter and eggs on the counter. Jank rang up the groceries that included chocolate chip cookies and a box of large milk bone dog biscuits.

"Ah, chocolate chips are the perfect comfort food for a stormy day. James will enjoy these," he said.

"I will, too," Dory said.

"How about the dog biscuits?"

Dory giggled. "You never know when you'll have company," she responded.

"Let me carry this out to your car, Dory."

He opened the front door with his free hand. "Dory, please do me a favor. Give a call here when you get home. Let us know you're all right. I'll stay open as long as the electric stays on. Even if it goes out,

I think I'll stick around to keep an eye on the place. Have you got your cell phone on?" Dory nodded yes. Dory agreed and felt a warm feeling inside. It was the kind of feeling she'd get from her dad when she was a young girl. She thought back to the times when she could put all of her worries into his hands and they'd go away.

"You okay there, Dory? Seems like you drifted off on me for a moment."

"Thanks, Jank. I'll be sure to call when I get home."

The grocer gripped the door and braced himself against the buffeting. He stepped aside as two Harmony Bay policemen dressed in yellow rain slickers and knee high boots entered. Water dripped from their visors and coats, pooling effortlessly around their well-protected feet.

"Thanks, Jank," Sam, the taller, and senior of the two cops said. "Heck of a blow we've got comin' in. I hear it's a brutal one. Coast Guard is on full alert. Some of the boys sailed out to ride out the storm. I'm just happy to be standing on dry land."

"Me, too," Cliff said. Cliff, a robust young cop with a roundish face and square shoulders, was born and raised in Harmony Bay. Everybody knew him and he knew everybody. Cliff had been the captain of the High School football team and nearly all mothers figured him to be the most eligible bachelor in the county. He went away to college and returned to Harmony Bay to serve the community. With little or no crime, the most that cops like Cliff usually had to do was write parking tickcts to tourists during the season and occasionally visit Molly's when a heated argument over the size of a day's catch got a little out of hand. Chief Dooley partnered Cliff with Sam, a thirty-year veteran of Harmony Bay's police force. Sam started his police career in the city and opted to move to Harmony Bay to be closer to good fishing, lower taxes and his family.

Sam and Cliff warmed themselves with the coffee poured by Dzjankowski. They told him a roof was already lost up on Pencil Hill and a derelict boat washed up on the beach, apparently broken loose from its moorings. Sam quoted the National Weather Service forecast. Within a short time, the presiding strong winds moved to a whole gale with occasional gusts of sixty miles per hour. Sam knew from experience that those winds were enough to undo more than a few roof shingles, snap off limbs and uproot trees. Cliff brooded over the fact that Harmony Bay wasn't really a wealthy community, except for some of the seasonal folks who owned summer homes here. The damages could be costly to some and devastating to others, depending on how unforgiving this nor'easter was.

Dory settled down in the car, fastened her seatbelt, turned on the wipers and headlights and then turned on the car radio in an attempt to get the latest weather forecast. She spun the radio dial with her right index finger while the windshield defroster removed the fog from the glass.

Tuning to the local hometown station Dory was met with a burst of static mixed with intermittent gibberish that became all too taxing. *Oh nice—a hometown storm and no hometown information*, she thought. She clicked the radio off. Dory figured it was better to concentrate on driving and not be distracted by a radio station that could hardly broadcast beyond Main Street. She'd never listen to it on the way to work because of the rude, obnoxious morning deejay, Cal Terry and his endless airplay of outdated songs.

She headed out of town on Bay Road past the tackle shops and boat yards, and then past the marina, which was virtually empty. Once around the marina inlet, she guided the car on the narrow roadway that dissected open marshlands and the small tributaries that ambled through them. Dory was disturbed by how close to the roadway the feeder creeks had overflowed as she turned up North Road. The rain hadn't let up a bit and the wind was worse than ever, driving branches and debris intermittently in her path. Wind raked the cord grass making ever-changing kaleidoscope patterns as phragmites danced in time to an unusual beat.

Gripping the wheel even tighter, her knuckles whitened. She was worried about James and tried not to be afraid. She hummed a child's song to herself. *Rain, rain go away. Come again some other day*. Around the bend was the next obstacle. The tiny North Bridge was barely wide enough for two cars to pass over at a time. It traversed a tidal creek that fed directly into the bay on Dory's right. The small waterway emptied and filled the marshlands twice a day, supplying nutrients to its inhabitants and carrying the newborn out into deep waters. It seemed the bridge was sturdy enough with concrete anchors on both banks. An ironwork frame spanned the gap. It supported a lattice of bulky, well-weathered planks. Strength or support of the old bridge wasn't the problem. It was its elevation. The bridge's road height was about the same as the roadway leading up to it and trailing away. An incoming full moon tide combined with the storm surge swelled the water above the roadbed level. Water now flowed under, over, and through the bridge. Dory nudged the car forward slowly in the hubcap-deep brine. She wished Jake was with her.

Dzjankowski stood behind the store counter and watched the storm through the foyer windows. Buzzy the postmaster burst in. Buzzy, a very thin man, wore thick, rain-coated bifocals. He had on a yellow slicker. Harmony Bay Post Office was stenciled on the back, stating the obvious. Atop his head was a Gloucester styled rain hat. Its chinstrap just cleared his bobbing Adam's apple.

"Jank, Jank! Chester called. He can't deliver out to Bay Road. The road is wiped out. North Road is out too and the water is over North Bridge. The phone at the post office is out. He called me on my cell phone." Buzzy spilled out the information as fast as his lips could move.

"Okay, okay. Buzzy, calm down. Does Chief Dooley, Sam or Cliff know about this?" Dzjankowski said.

"I told Chester to call them straight away," the postmaster replied. "Dooley said he didn't know how they could get out there if the road is gone."

"If the water isn't too deep, how about maybe a four-wheel-drive?" Jank questioned, his brow furrowing deeply. He drummed the counter with his fingers. "*Dory and James*," he said. The postmaster understood immediately. Dzjankowski went to his phone book where he kept all of his customer's home, work and cell phone numbers for a multitude of reasons. They were filed by first names first. He flipped the book open to D and ran his finger ran down the column of listings, stopping at Dory's name. Jank picked up the phone. "Bully, a dial tone," he commented to his audience of one. He dialed Dory's cell number and got her voice mail. "Oh no," Dzjankowski hollered. "Get over to the firehouse—see who you can get hold of and get out there!"

Dzjankowski's frown, and the furrows in his forehead, deepened. "Bully. Just bully," he said.

Chapter 28

Buzzy sloshed at a half-run through the ankle-deep water to the firehouse. Jank began to dial as many Harmony Bay folks as he could think of who could help with the mission. Buzzy arrived at the firehouse to find the other volunteers huddled around the short-wave radio, monitoring it for distress calls. They learned from Chester about the dire consequences out on North Road and that Bay Road was awash. The rescue crews figured they were going to be called to action at any moment.

"It's about Miss Dory and James out on the peninsula. Jank can't get her on the phone and she left over an hour ago," Buzzy said. Buzzy was still panting from his sprint against the wind.

One of the volunteers in a turnout coat and red suspenders spoke. "Yeah, we know. Dooley radioed in. He took a ride up there. Most of the planking on North Bridge washed away." He looked at the others, read their expressions and continued in a grim tone, "The road farther north of the bridge is already collapsed. It's impassable." Buzzy was visibly shaken. "Dooley already tried the Coast Guard. It'll be hours until they can get here. Seems there's some maritime disaster down coast a ways." Buzzy nodded that he understood, not that he approved.

Dory had already made it past the bridge and sat terrified, watching the river of water pass from her left to right directly in front of her. Buckets of rain hammered the car's windows. Storm surges ate away the roadbed allowing the macadam to collapse in large chucks. Some of the pieces of roadway were swept away with the currents, others stood up-ended. Dory could see the brackish water had also eroded the sand around the base of the telephone pole to her right. The wind was working to push the pole to a prone position in front of her. Her first impulse was to escape from the vehicle and run to James at the cottage. It was still a very long way away. She didn't know how much worse it might be on foot if she was caught in a flood. Fretting about what to do next, her heart raced as her mind dizzied. *C'mon Dory, you're a smart woman. You can figure this out*, she murmured. She opened the car door and looked down to see the water was almost up to the doorsill, shut it quickly and started to panic. *What if the roadway beneath her started to collapse?* she thought. Dory had seen pictures on the news of cars being carried away in a flood. Perhaps she might meet the same fate? Dory rested her hands at the ten and two o'clock positions on the steering wheel with her head at noon.

Although it seemed like an eternity, in actuality, it was only moments later when Dory sensed something outside. Maybe it was a noise, or possibly a muffled voice that jolted her from her daydream. The car was still running as she looked down to see that the radio was turned off. She was startled to look out her left window too see what were unmistakably the legs of a horse beside the car. Her astonishing realization was followed by the distinct sound of a horse's whinny and someone calling out her name.

"Dory, Dory! Are you in there?" the voice called out, followed by thumping sounds on the roof. Although the deep voice was muffled by the wind, she instantly recognized that it belonged to Billy. In the same moment, she realized it was Chloe alongside her. "Roll down the window," Billy said. Dory lowered the window, allowing in a rush of cold damp air. Billy crouched down to speak with Dory face to face. "Let's get you out of here," he said.

"How are we going to get through this mess?" Dory asked.

Billy pointed at the mare. "That is why I brought our friend along," he responded. Dory rolled her eyes and tried to imagine how it was going to work.

"Haven't you ever ridden a horse?" Billy said. He chuckled through his soaked whiskers. Dory knew she hadn't been on a horse since she was a little girl and probably had more experience on an amusement park ride than a live animal. Billy told Dory, "North Bridge behind us is out."

She knew the road ahead was not drivable.

"What about my car?" Dory asked. "I have to get to James."

"Your car is going to have to stay here for now. We can deal with it later. James is at home and is fine. We will be there shortly," Billy said in soothing voice. Dory tried to call the house from her cell phone to no avail. Apparently the storm affected the overland phone lines all around Harmony Bay.

Billy helped Dory out of the car and fit what he could of her groceries in his saddlebags. The large man hefted himself onto the back of his horse and settled in the saddle, leaving Dory feeling very small as she looked up at him on the colossal horse. Her thin trench coat was already soaked through and her boots only offered moderate resistance to the water. Being cut too low, water was apt to spill into them at any time. She shuddered and told herself she had to hold on for James.

"Are you just going to leave me here?" she said. Panic strained her voice.

"No, my dear. Here is what you need to do. Put your right foot in this stirrup and hold on to my arm with both hands. When I lift, you push up with your foot." Dory followed the instructions by lifting her right foot up and into the stirrup. It was a big stretch for her but she pulled her knee to her chin and leaned forward. She was tall enough to manage a toehold. Billy lowered his right arm down to her and she grabbed it tightly. Billy lifted her effortlessly off the ground, hoisting her up like a derrick. She swung her left leg over the animal and straddled it.

"Hold on tight," he yelled. Dory placed her arms loosely around his midsection. To reinforce what he said, Billy tugged her arms toward each other then placed his strong hands over her hands and squeezed. Dory got the message and hooked her hands together in front of his belly. The horse shifted from hoof to hoof to adjust to the weight of the additional rider, pawing the wet roadway several times to test its strength to support all three of them. Billy let out a short, shrill whistle and snapped the reigns to move Chloe forward.

Well aware of the potholes and pitfalls, Chloe went forward slowly and deliberately. She forded the stream that crossed the roadway with the water surging over her fetlocks. Now and then, the water climbed halfway up her cannon bone. Undaunted, she stood firm against the currents.

This wasn't the horse's first experience with a coastal storm. The wind, spray and water didn't faze her at all.

Billy coaxed her on and she complied. When the ground beneath her hooves was stable, she picked up the pace, steadily moving toward the destination of Dory's cottage. In the deeper sections the water reached the horse's belly. Dory now understood why Billy made her leave her car. On the un-flooded stretches of North Road, seashells and crustaceans, along with pieces of driftwood and jetsam, crunched beneath the iron shoes. Shells of scallops, mussels, oysters, razor clams, hard shell quahogs and soft-shelled steamers, which the storm washed up on the road surface, were now fragmented into coarse grit. Chloe turned her head away from the gale to prevent her eyes from being stung by the salt. This did not alter her gait or the interpretation of the signals that Billy sent through the reigns. She lowered her head and canted into the wind during heavy blasts, absorbing the onslaught with her hindquarters. Passing tightly shuttered beach houses, closed up since the end of the season, she intermittently whinnied and shook her head and white mane. It did nothing to upset her riders.

Billy was always very good to her so she was faithful to her master and his commands. For Chloe, this was just another opportunity to please him. She'd be rewarded by a warm, dry stall in the barn, plenty of oats, hay and apple treats.

They reached a rise on North Road where on a clear day they'd be in sight of the cottage. Dory, wracked with anxiety, hunkered down behind Billy, her knees tightly pinched in against the animal's sides. Gusts of wind were strong enough to pull her off the horse and would've if it weren't for her firm grip around Billy. Plodding along briskly, it still took another ten minutes to reach Dory's front door.

Roof shingles began to lift up through the air in unorganized arcs as they arrived. The outer porch screen door blew open and shut with each blast. Billy steered Chloe to the back of the house and out of the direct wind. Panicked by the spiraling shingles, Dory was anxious to dismount. She wanted to get inside to see James and make sure he was all right. Billy lowered her down in the opposite fashion he had lifted her. She looked across the creek behind the house. It now bulged to the very pinnacle of its banks well above the high tide marks. On the opposite shore, she saw Jake's red Jeep. Jake stood beside it in chest-waders and a bright yellow squall jacket with a tight fitting hood.

"What are you doing here and how did you get there?" Dory called out. Her voice was drowned out by the wind. She was briefly jealous of his efficient storm gear. Now soaked to the bone, she was bordering on hypothermia. Her teeth chattered. She decided to worry about it later. With her feet now on the ground, she ran to the kitchen door. She threw it open to find James sitting at the kitchen table in the dimness.

"Hi, Mom. You okay? You look wet. The electricity went out right after I got home. I ate the last of the ice cream. I figured it was going to melt. I hope you're not mad—." Dory flung herself across the room and hugged James with all of the energy left in her body.

"Thank God. You're okay!"

Billy appeared in the doorway. "It is time to evacuate. Grab what you think you will need for tonight and let's go," he said. Dory instructed James to get his toothbrush and heavy sweatshirts and warm socks. She did the same.

"How are we all going to get on Chloe?" Dory said.

"No—not, Chloe. I have another way. However, we need to move quickly before we lose the roof. Wait out of the wind around back by Chloe," Billy said in a firm, yet rushed, manner.

Dory and James gathered their belongings and packed them into large, black plastic bags. James put his baseball glove and his copy of *White Fang* in the bag. He snatched up Winton's guitar in its leather case. From his viewpoint, it was essential not only to bring along these things, but also not to lose them. Mother and son followed Billy's instructions and went out through the kitchen door to the back of the cottage. There they watched Billy retrieve and right the dinghy that had blown off the sawhorses.

Billy took his whittling knife from his pocket and cut the anchor line free from the boat. At the garden's edge, he knelt down and pulled a softball size stone from beneath a beach rose bush. James watched in amazement as Billy quickly used the free end of the half-inch anchor line to fashion a monkey's paw knot around the stone. Billy's bulky fingers moved swiftly as he laced the line around the stone, loop after loop.

He took the opposite end of the line that was still attached to the anchor and cut it free. He stripped off a twelve-foot section and allowed it to drop to the ground. Billy tied the other end of the long line with the stone attached to Chloe's saddle horn sitting high atop her withers. Billy went to the boat, pulled one of the bronze North River style oarlocks free and loosened its cross pin while he walked back toward his horse. Billy snatched up the twelve-foot length of line lying on the ground and deftly wrapped the mid-point of the rope once, then twice, around the oarlock in a round turn leaving two six-foot pieces dangling down toward the ground. Once done, he placed the oarlock up under the line that led to the saddle horn. Its two upright prongs straddled the wet rope. Billy reinserted the cross hasp and tightened it securely. Grasping the twin six-footers, he stepped toward the dinghy. He took one of the loose ends and laced it through the port oarlock hole. Once the rope cleared the hole, he pulled it through, tying it to the end of the other six-foot piece. He pulled on the new knot with all his might to be sure it wouldn't slip.

Billy spoke for the first time since emerging from the cottage. "Stand back and away. Get back farther," he told James and Dory.

"What's going on?" an exasperated Dory asked through trembling blue lips.

"We are making a zip line. It will be fun," Billy said. Billy then turned toward Jake on the other side of the canal, "Jake! Jaaaake," he yelled as loud as his big voice could while waving his arms over his head, "here we go." Billy removed his outer coat and grabbed the end of the line with the rock tightly attached. Paying out four feet of free line, he began to swing the rock around over his head at increasing speeds and finally let the weight sail free toward the opposite side of the canal with the line following behind. It would have been an impressive feat on any day. Given the swirling wind and rain, the projectile almost making it across the entire span was miraculous.

The stone splashed into the water several feet in front of Jake, who waded into the turbulent water to retrieve the rope. Walking backward to dry land, he gave an acknowledging wave to his audience. Billy used body language by kneeling down on one knee and making a wrapping motion and pointed to the Jeep. Jake shook his head up and down. He squatted down by the Jeep's trailer hitch, wrapping the line several times around the hitch and then on itself in two half-hitches.

Once secured, Billy went to Chloe and displayed the back of his hand with his fingers pointing upward. She understood the silent command and obediently started to pace backward into the wind, taking the bight out of the sloping line. The former anchor line was now attached to the horse, located on high ground beside the cottage, and to the Jeep's hitch where Jake stood on the opposite shore at sea-level. Chloe's stature and her position on higher ground gave the line a slight downward angle. The dinghy was now effectively tethered to the zip line by the six-foot rope sections that were attached to the oarlock that encircled the zip line.

Dory and James helped Billy shove the boat down to the water's edge.

"Where are we going, Mom?" James demanded.

"Don't worry, James. Just do as Billy says. We'll be okay." Dory wasn't sure if they were going to be okay or not. She had to trust.

"It's kinda funny, Mom. This is the boat Angus and me fell out of last winter," he said. That's not what Dory wanted to hear and grabbed James' hand.

Billy tossed their bagged belongings and the guitar in the bow of the boat and went to Chloe's saddlebag to retrieve Dory's groceries, a drop line, several heavy lead sinkers and a large bobbin. Billy placed the groceries in the boat with their baggage and set about stripping arm lengths of the heavyweight Dacron line off the spool of the drop line. He tied several lead sinkers to the end and placed the red and white bobber about four feet up the black line from there. Billy's fishing tackle was the practical type used for lifting hefty doormat fluke from the bay floor and cod from the bottom of the ocean. It wasn't pretty, but he thought it could stand up to the job. Again, Billy instructed Dory and James to stand back, and as he did earlier to create the zip line, twirled the fishing line and sinkers over his head. He let out a sharp whistle to alert Jake. All at once, the lead, the line and the bobbin arched over the canal. Just as last time, the tackle almost made it across. Jake waded out to waist deep water to capture the floating bobbin.

Billy ushered his two refugees into the boat and tied the fishing line to the bow-ring where the anchor line had been fastened. "Hold on and keep your heads down," he warned. Returning to the stern, Billy pushed the little boat into the current. Hand over hand, Jake slowly pulled on the fishing line attached to the boat. His gloves prevented the heavy fishing line from cutting into his fingers. The rowboat, joined securely to the zip line overhead, made its way gradually across the creek, buffeted by the winds and strong currents.

Dory lifted her head to see Jake on the shore carefully working the boat toward him. The weathered line had seen many fishing excursions in Billy's hands. Now it was being put to a crucial test. Dory watched Jake suddenly fall back, the line slack in his fingers. Billy's old fishing gear couldn't withstand the strains put on it by the weight of the boat and the nor'easter. "Hold on. You'll be okay," Jake yelled to them. The boat stopped farther out than the bobbin had landed earlier. Jake wasn't sure if the water level there would be up and over the top of his chest waders. If his boots filled with water, he'd likely be pulled under by the current. Jake reached into the chest waders to his belt, groping for his sheath knife. If the boots did fill, he could use the knife to cut the straps and pull them off. Even if he dropped the fishing knife, it would float. But he couldn't take the chance it might be carried away. He withdrew the knife and held the butt end in his teeth.

Slogging into the water, Jake held the zip line to support and guide him; he never took his eyes off the prize. He edged his way forward through the rushing water with his right hand on the line and took careful steps as he went out farther, not wanting to step into a sinkhole or get his boots caught in the rocks. At a distance six feet shy of the bow, the water was about three inches from the top of his waders. The tail wind was almost enough to push the boat forward, but the tension on the zip line didn't allow it to move.

An idea came to Jake. With the scales of the knife still clenched in his teeth and his eyeglasses flooded with salt spray, he reached up to the zip line with both hands and pulled down with all of his might. This created a new low point allowing the heavy, bronze oarlock to slide toward him. By pulling the line down and releasing it, the oarlock inched forward a little more each time. The wind nudged the boat forward.

The boat was now spinning on its single connection to the tether line. It did not impede the forward progress. Jake had the starboard side within his reach. Stretching his fingertips to the boat, they were met by Dory's outstretched fingers. Jake welcomed her hand, but knew they weren't finished with the rescue mission yet.

"Hang on. Hang on tight," he said.

"I'm never letting go of you," she replied.

Working quickly in the chest-high water, Jake turned the boat's bow toward shore and began the slow retreat by walking carefully backward. The water level lowered to his hips, then to his knees, and finally, it only covered the tops of his boots. He heaved the boat up on to the sand and helped Dory and James over the side. She held him and started to shake. The chill and the whole ordeal had taken its toll. Dory turned to wave to Billy, only to realize that she could not see him or Chloe anywhere. The zip line, once suspended above, now lay slack and floated across the water. "Where's Billy?" she gasped.

"Don't worry about him, he'll be okay," Jake said. "You and James get in the Jeep and start it up. Get the heater on—she's already warmed up. I'll finish up here."

Jake pulled in the slack line, untied it from the back of the Jeep and tied it to the eye ring on the boat's bow. He walked along the shoreline, came to the old bulkhead pilings and tied the line to a bollard. It allowed more than enough slack for the boat to rise and fall with the changing of the tides. They could deal with it after the storm. Exhausted, he returned to the Jeep and climbed into the driver's seat.

"How are we going to get out of the marsh?" Dory asked.

"A long time ago, Billy showed me a narrow trail leading down from Pencil Hill to the flats. It's just wide enough for us to fit through," Jake said. "The thick, matted vegetation here drains really well. It'll give enough support to carry us back to high ground."

Jake, Dory and James crossed the flats with little incident. Jake found the sandy road that wound its way up Pencil Hill, where they welcomed the safety of Billy's cabin. Angus greeted them at the door and led them to the warmth of the fireplace.

Chapter 29

Dory entered the cabin and peeled off her wet coat. She excused herself to go change into dry clothes. James started rummaging through their bag of belongings and the few groceries that had made the trip. The package of chocolate chip cookies was crushed beyond recognition, its contents, crumbs. Jake and James sat at the kitchen table, working on ferreting the bits from the package. Dory returned in a gray sweat suit. "Not very stylish," she said. "At least it's dry." She sent James to change out of his wet clothes. She turned to Jake. "Thank you for being there. We wouldn't have made it without you," she said.

"Now there you go again," he said, "thanking me for something that I'm glad to do for you."

"Just the same, if it weren't for you and Billy, I don't know what would've happened to us."

"No worries," he said.

"You must be starving. Chocolate chip crumbs isn't a healthy dinner. Let me see what I can find in here." She wondered, and worried, where Billy was.

The front door swung open admitting Billy with a gust of wind and a flurry of wet leaves. "Sorry that I am late. I hope you have made yourselves feel at home. I had to dry Chloe off and put her in the barn," Billy said. He carried two bulging burlap bags.

Dory was relieved. She surveyed the cabin. The interior was exceptionally large for one person. It was manly. Overstuffed leather couches paralleled the huge fireplace. An antique musket hung above the mantel. Fully stocked bookcases lined the walls, which pleased her. There were no family pictures. A simple braided rug covered the living room floor. Although Spartan, he allowed a few luxuries such as electricity, an old-fashioned record player, a chainsaw and power tools. Billy built everything himself. There was no phone.

"I have gathered up some provisions. I will prepare a nice, hot dinner. All of you go sit in front of the fire with Angus and get warm," Billy said. Dory and Jake offered their help. Billy protested. They chose to remain in the kitchen.

Billy dumped the bags on the refectory table in the cavernous kitchen. His garden, which provided fresh produce, was as large as everything else about him was. Whatever was left at the end of the growing season either went into the root cellar or was canned for the winter. Prudence the cow and two goats supplied all of his dairy needs. During the warm months, Billy bartered produce and fresh eggs for staple items: flour, rice, sugar, salt and coffee. He stopped making his own sea salt years ago. It was too labor intensive. The land and the bay provided almost everything he needed.

One sack contained carrots, tomatoes, potatoes, onions, celery and parsley. The other held clams, mussels, crabs and a sizable striped bass. "I went out and got these last night before the storm started. I did not know how long it might be before I could get back out," Billy said.

"You must be dead tired. Are you sure you want to cook?" she said. "There's only four of us. Are you expecting anyone else?" Dory added.

"Hmm. You never can tell. Oh, there will be five for dinner," Billy said and looked toward Angus. "It is not a problem. It's not often that I get to entertain company." Billy chopped the vegetables. After adding them to a large chowder pot, he set it to boil on the gas stove. "This is going to take a while. We can have something to hold us over. He took out a loaf of homemade bread and a jar of Margaret Lanscome's blueberry preserves. After spreading the jam on slabs of bread, he placed them on plates. Taking four mugs from the cabinet, he filled them with fresh apple cider that simmered on the stove. After placing a cinnamon stick in each, he winked at Jake and produced a bottle of dark, bartered rum. Dory was content enough and declined. Billy poured two ounces of the liquor into two of the cups, handed one to Jake and kept the other for himself.

Billy waved his hand toward the living room. "Please have a seat," he said. They joined James in the living room, who was lying on the floor and using Angus as a pillow. James hungrily ate the bread and preserves and licked the jam from his fingers. Surrounded by people he loved, James was happy. Billy, Dory and Jake sat on the couches and soaked in the heat from the fireplace. Rain battered the old windows. The warm cider was an added welcome relief.

"What a lovely home you have," Dory said.

"Thank you. It is a lot of space, a lot of land, and a lot of work for one person. However, there is only me to clean up after," Billy said.

"Quite a library." Dory looked at the rows of books surrounding the living room.

"Yes indeed. Many of those books are very old."

"What's the story with the gun hanging up there?" James wanted to know.

"That is a Brown Bess from the Revolutionary War. It's been handed down through the generations," Billy said.

"Was it from the British or the Americans?" James asked.

"Those were typically British weapons. Either army could have used it. Weapons were captured from the other side by both forces all the time. The story that goes along with it is—it was found right up here on Pencil Hill. A lot of history took place in these hills."

"Wow, really? Miss Donnelly said the same thing," James said.

"What same thing?" Jake asked.

"There's a lot of history in these hills," James answered.

"She knows, because her family, on her mother's side— fought in the Revolution in these hills," Billy said. "They were Patriots."

"How come she didn't say that?" James countered.

"Perhaps she did not want to seem as though she was bragging," Billy replied. "Her ancestors were the Bells. Arthur and Rebecca Bell operated the old mill before British soldiers arrested them and torched the mill. The Bells were with the Sons of Liberty. Their descendants had already lived by Quahog Bay for over a hundred years before that. Arthur and Rebecca were never seen again after their arrest and escape from British forces. They may have moved to another colony. Some of the other Bells returned here after the war."

It explained a lot to Dory. The woman's name who she replaced at the Harmony Bay Library was Mrs. Bell. Then it occurred to Dory why Maureen Donnelly was attracted to the teaching job at Harmony Bay. Miss Donnelly had roots here that were as deep as any long entrenched townie. The conversation turned to the discovery of Christian Carroll's remains, the mystery surrounding the night of his capture, and the unaccounted for treasures.

"I spoke with the Archeology Department this week at the university," Jake said. "They're finished with their study of Christian Carroll and will be turning his remains over for a proper interment. I called the congressman's office. He's going to arrange for a burial with full military honors at the National Cemetery."

"Ah, yes," Billy said. "Local lore, folk tales, oral traditions, and many, many rumors. Let us see what we can see." Billy got off the couch and went to a bookcase. Scanning numerous volumes, he pulled a worn leather bound book from the shelf and handed it to Dory. In relatively good condition, it showed only a few watermarks and dog-eared pages. She flipped open the first few pages of the fragile book, stopping at the publication date. It read 1876. The title page stated, *One Hundred Years of Liberty—Reflections on the Revolution. Accounts of the British Occupation at Quahog Bay.*

"This was way before the internet," Dory said. She wondered what information the other books held.

"Yes, I am sure it is now out of print," Billy said and gave a smirk.

Outside, the storm continued to rage as Dory read the book. "I'd say it's still a mystery," she said. "There's a full account of Christian Carroll's arrest and his daring escape. The same British characters are mentioned. Lieutenant Oliver Stockbridge, Corporal Smyth, spelled here with an *e* as *Smythe*, and Sergeant Randall Stone-Bayard." Dory thumbed through a few more pages as the lights began to flicker. "Okay, it also mentions Arthur, Rebecca, and Christian Carroll, were tried in absentia after their escape for acts of sedition."

"Didn't you find some info on-line that mentioned the three were tried at Stockbridge's camp? Then were sentenced to hang immediately after being taken prisoner?" Jake asked.

"Yes, I did. We don't know whose version of the story that was. If they were tried after their escape, Stockbridge was already dead," Dory said.

"What if the Americans leaked a story that there was going to be a summary execution without a fair trial to stir up their underground forces. That might've moved them to enact a covert raid on Stockbridge's encampment and free the prisoners."

"The previous accounts said the hangings were confirmed by two redcoat soldiers in a pub."

"Sure—*so they say*. It could've been a complete fabrication."

"That's true, Jake. In 1770, although five were killed at the Boston Massacre, it wasn't quite a massacre. British soldiers were called out to quell a riot that turned ugly. It started with some young men throwing snowballs and insults at British occupying forces. One thing led to another. Radicals brandished clubs and swords." A tree branch crashed against the house, emphasizing her point. "Somebody on the British squad got nervous and opened fire, followed by some of the other soldiers. In the end, radicals used the Boston Massacre as a propaganda tool to promote their agenda. It worked. So…if we go back to the case of Christian Carroll, it may well have been that the rumor mill was working overtime creating a smokescreen to stir up the rebels."

"Sounds like the founding fathers of the CIA," Jake said. He threw another log on the fire.

"Hmm, good point," Dory said. "Hype worked after the Boston Massacre and other events to fuel the revolt. By the time of Christian Carroll's arrest, making fellow Americans *think* there'd be an execution without a trial would've moved them to action. In any event, Carroll and the Bells would've been hunted down and killed if recaptured. The crown assigned hit squads to track down and assassinate the signers of the Declaration and the Sons of Liberty. They'd have added the *Quahog Three's* names to the list."

"They wouldn't have stood a chance at a trial anyway," Jake added.

"Exactly," Dory said. "The Yankees were well aware of the cruel and ruthless treatment of captives held by the British. If they weren't killed by the gallows, their demise would have certainly been at the hands of their jailers."

"Now you can understand why Carroll was buried in a hidden grave out on England Point," Jake concluded.

James was sprawled wide-eyed on the floor. Billy sat hunched forward on the couch soaking in every word along with the rum and cider. Angus sensed the tension in the room and stirred. Dory continued to read from the dusty book.

"Apparently, later on after Quahog Bay, Randall-Stone was given a field promotion to the rank of Sergeant Major. *That* is curious. His camp lost three prisoners and boatload of gold. And he was given a promotion? It doesn't make sense. When I get back to work I'm going to see what I can find out about Smyth with an e and Randall Stone-Bayard as a Sergeant Major. Maybe we can find out who promoted him. That might tell us something."

The nor'easter took charge and the cabin lost power. Billy lit several candles and two lanterns. "Lucky for us that I have a gas stove," he said. Working by candlelight, he filleted the fish and cut it into cubes. He added it, along with the shellfish, to the boiling pot. The crabs went in last. He tasted it for seasoning and ground in pepper. Billy declared, "Dinner time!"

Dory set the table and they sat down to eat. Ingredients from Harmony Bay and Pencil Hill, prepared by Billy, provided a sumptuous seafood stew. After dinner, James practiced his guitar in the dark. The strain of the day, full stomachs and the warmth of the fire brought on sleepiness. James yawned.

"Dory, you and James will sleep in my room tonight. Jake, you and I will take the couches," Billy said. "By tomorrow, the storm surge will be gone. Jake and I will go check on your house, Dory. If everything is okay, you can return there. If not, you are welcome to stay here for as long as you need to."

"I'll check out your car," Jake said. "Assuming it didn't get submerged, I'll have Dave Small pick it up and check it over."

Chapter 30

Dory and James were able to return to their cottage. The storm surge licked at the foundation of their home, but did not enter. Fishhook Cutsciko sent two repairmen to replace the roof shingles and a window that was broken by flying debris. Luckily, the landlord had found a warm place in his dark heart to make speedy repairs. Cutsciko's recent near death experience and rescue from the rocks endeared Dory and James to him. Nobody could guess how long the feeling might last.

With the storm long gone, James decided to patrol North Road by bike after school to see what might have washed up. He worked his way along the shore and the roofer's hammering drifted away. Barking replaced the worker's noises. Angus ran toward James at full speed. James stopped his bike. He was always glad to see Angus. Angus skidded to a stop in the sand beside James and bounded up, licking James' face. He grabbed a coat sleeve, tugging it furiously.

"Angus, stop pulling!" James ordered. "I'll play with you—but don't knock me over." Angus began dragging James and the bike along the road. "Stop it!" James yelled. The tug of war only ended for a moment. Angus began to cry and yodel. He raced forward twenty feet or so, then stopped and turned toward James.

"Oh, you want me to follow you? What did you find, boy?" Angus bolted and ran like a scalded dog. James pedaled in pursuit. Angus, panting laboriously, lumbered the length of the road and over the freshly repaired North Bridge. At the intersecting dirt road that led to Mill Pond, and eventually to Pencil Hill, he turned west. James had trouble keeping up on the muddy road littered with slippery leaves and tracts of standing water. They passed Mill Pond and the empty tree house. He was already winded as the dog kept forging up the hill. The storm had uprooted several trees. Fallen branches and an occasional tree littered the path, but didn't block it completely.

James and Angus were mud splattered and breathing heavily as they crested the hill and passed Billy's house. The trail narrowed to the width of a single car, then billowed into a large clearing. Billy's trusty pickup was parked there. James leaned his bike against the open tailgate of the truck and called out for Billy. The only response was the dog's frantic bark at the far end of the clearing. Still trying to suck more air into his lungs, James scrambled toward the dog hidden by the thicket. James' eyes sprang open as he reached the edge of the forest. Billy was lying on the ground with his leg pinned under a fallen tree. His chainsaw was at the base of the newly cut, dead tree. James' heart raced when he saw the stream of blood coming from Billy's forehead. It was apparent what had happened. Billy always cut dead trees for firewood. It was evident that Billy was cutting all day, given the stack of firewood. An old oak caught Billy off guard in response to being unbalanced by the chainsaw's swipe, throwing him to the ground and pinning him squarely. A thick branch hit him in the head as he fell.

"Billy. Billy! Open your eyes!" James begged. "Talk to me." Billy groaned. His eyes flickered slightly, then drooped tightly shut again. James swallowed the panic that was tightening his throat. He didn't know how long Billy was unconscious and debated whether he should ride his bike to the village or home for help. Either would take too long. It would be dark soon and he couldn't leave Billy alone in this condition. He knew Billy was in a great deal of pain. James tried to lift the fallen tree to no avail.

Think, James McDonough, he said to himself. *What would Jake do?* James tried to think of a practical way out of the quandary. He needed a plan and he needed help. James wished his friends had decided to hang out at the tree house after school. Peter would help him. Even crazy Raymond could have been a help. If Katie were there, she'd help him figure this whole mess out.

James ran to the truck at the other end of the clearing. In the truck bed, along with an axe and red gas cans for the chainsaw, was a long, sturdy rope. He thought about using the axe to chop away the tree trunk. It would take too long and he feared, if he miscued, Billy's leg might get hacked. James didn't know how to start the chainsaw.

James rolled his bike aside, grabbed the coil of rope and jumped in the driver's seat. He didn't know how much trouble he was going to get into for doing it—he figured he'd worry about that later. Reaching underneath the seat, he positioned it all the way forward and checked if he could reach the pedals. Vision over the dashboard was limited, even if he sat up straight. It was enough. He turned the key with the clutch pushed in. The engine coughed to life. His driving lessons from Winton Hector, and careful observations of Billy's and Jake's driving, assured James that he knew enough to get the job done.

James recalled Winton Hector's words from his first lesson, "*Jes think of it as a big 'ol letta H on da floor.*" James prodded the shifter into first gear. "*Heeya's first gear. Dat's fo gittin' started .*" The truck rolled forward as he slowly let out the clutch. He swung the truck in a wide arc. With the front facing away from Billy's position, he snaked the gearshift through the neutral gate and found reverse with a grinding clunk. Looking over his shoulder, he backed across the open ground. "*When y'all need to park ya push in the clutch an slip 'er into first, then shut off da motor.*" James pushed in the clutch, shifted back to first and turned the motor off.

The boy hopped out of the cab with the rope and flew into action. Every word from Billy's knot tying lesson came back to him. "*...a round-turn with two half-hitches ...it is good for attaching a line to a post. This knot is better if you are working with a heavy load. The round –turn is really two wraps around the post.*" He wrapped the rope end twice around the tree trunk that was holding Billy down and added two half-hitches. With the remaining coil, he tied a stout stick to the other end and threw it like a spear, up and over a limb of a nearby towering maple with brilliant yellow foliage. The projectile landed, pulling the rest of the rope with it. James untied his impromptu javelin. At the rear of the truck he wound the line around the rusty trailer hitch several times and finished off the knot with half-hitches. James was breathing hard again, his heart pounded. He checked on Billy, whose chest was rising and falling sporadically. "Don't worry, Billy. I'll have you out of here in a minute," he whispered. Angus paced about nervously and whimpered.

James slid behind the wheel, restarted the engine and let out the clutch as gently as possible. Inching forward, he watched over his shoulder. The limp line pulled through the overhead bough and tightened. All of the slack was taken up and the tree on the ground offered resistance causing the pickup to buck. James deftly worked the clutch in and out and the oak lifted from Billy's leg. James jammed the shifter in first gear, killed the motor and pulled hard on the handbrake. *"Pull back on this here hand brake too so's ya don't roll."*

James jumped out, grabbing one of the empty five-gallon metal gas cans from the back. He wedged the square can under the log that now dangled from the maple.

Billy started to stir. Although Billy's leg was freed, James now tried to figure a way to move him. Every time a breeze moved the maple the fallen oak moved with it. James locked his arms under Billy and pulled with all of his might. Billy only moved about an inch. James called Angus. Angus shoved his muzzle into his master's face and licked it vigorously. Billy awakened and propped himself up on his elbows. He was delirious, yet strong enough to assist with his extraction. Billy pushed with his good leg while James and Angus tugged, moving him a safe distance from the felled tree. James took the axe from the truck and chopped a branch for Billy to use as a crutch.

"Hang on, Billy. Don't try to move till I get back," James said.

"Do not worry, James. I am not going anywhere," Billy said.

James backed the truck up to just behind Billy. This released the tension on the rope and the weight of the downed oak crushed the steel gas can. The tree trunk now teetered on this new fulcrum point. With the aid of the crutch, James was able to get Billy off the ground and eased him onto the tailgate. James and Angus jumped on board and slid Billy into the truck bed. Billy grimaced, then slipped back to unconsciousness. James peeled off his jacket and placed it under Billy's head. He left Angus in the back of the truck and slammed the tailgate shut. The axe severed the rope where it was tied to the tree. It only took one swing. He tossed the rope in the truck bed. "Take care of him, Angus. Keep him comfortable," James said. The dog curled up beside his master.

Shadows reached their longest point as the little red truck rattled down the hill. James tried to decide where to go. Trying to make it to the inland county hospital was insanity. Besides, he had no idea how to get there. Dave Small's repair shop was closest, but probably already closed for the day. He didn't want to waste any time chasing to Dave's for nothing. He knew today was Jake's day to be at the university and wouldn't be back in Harmony Bay until late this evening. The library was an option, but he didn't know how he was going to explain this to his mother. Thinking about it further, James decided to go to Doc Tollenson's office. Billy needed medical attention. Doc would take care of him. He continued to drive and hoped there wouldn't be any other cars, or that he wouldn't drive off the road into a ditch. James tried not to think about being scared.

Weaving on the road as he shifted, James negotiated the turns and was able stop and start smoothly. Lights were on in the village when they arrived. Pulling up to Doc's, James' heart sank. The office was closed. James looked over his shoulder at his precious cargo. He'd have to do something right now and considered going to the Harmony Bay Police station, even though he feared being arrested for driving without a license or the ability to see clearly over the steering wheel.

Down the block, the lights were on in Mr. Kelly's pharmacy. A flood of emotion overcame James as he coasted to a stop in front of the store. Tears filled his eyes as he ran into the pharmacy. He called out and entered, "Mr. Kelly! Hey, Mr. Kelly!" James was surprised to see Dan Kelly in casual conversation with Doc Tollenson. "James, my boy. What's wrong?" Mr. Kelly said.

"You're never going to believe it! Billy is out in the truck and I hope he's still alive." The two men shot glances at each other and ran to the street.

Doc Tollenson reached over the side of the truck and checked Billy's pulse. In the dim light of the streetlamp, Doc could see the blood pooled on James' jacket beneath Billy's head and that Billy's leg was, without question, broken. "Dan, I don't want to move him. He's in shock. I suspect a concussion. We need an ambulance. Call the police department," the doctor said. "Tell the ambulance crew I'll ride with them to County General Hospital." Mr. Kelly sprinted back to his store, called the police, and then called Dory.

"Don't worry, James. Billy is going to be okay. He'll have a head-ache and might be on crutches for a month or two – but he's okay," Doc said. James sighed in relief. Doc took James' trembling hand. "Tell me, James, did you drive Billy here?"

 James remained speechless. "If you did, it was a very brave thing to do," Doc said as he squeezed James' shoulder.

"Yeah – I did it. I'm very sorry. I didn't know what else to do. I was all alone."

"Tell me what happened. I promise you won't be in trouble. I'll see too it."

James unraveled all of the details about Billy getting pinned by the tree, his secret driving lessons from Winton Hector that made him able to drive the truck, and the knot skills taught by Billy that enabled him to rig the line around the tree, over the branch and to the truck.

"It was really nothing, though. Anybody could have done the same thing. Just glad I was around. Billy would've been out there all night. Or—maybe forever. Something else. His chainsaw is still out there. We should pick it up tomorrow. And—who's going to take care of Angus?" James said.

"Don't worry about it, my boy. You've already done enough. There's more than a few good people around to take care of everything," Doc said. A Harmony Bay patrol car, followed by the Emergency Response Unit and Dory McDonough, rolled up.

"James, what happened?" Dory said.

Doc held his hand up. "Everything's okay. James was a hero," he said.

"How is Billy?" she asked.

"He's pretty badly banged up. He'll need surgery on that leg." Doc said.

"He has no insurance, and I don't know how much money he has saved."

"There'll be no charges for any of my services. I'll speak with the hospital. We'll work something out. Billy has been a blessing to the com-munity. It's the least we can do. Right now I want to get him out of here and into surgery."

The telephone lines of Harmony Bay began to glow with warmth as the village spun into action. Dave Small would get Billy's truck back up the hill to the cabin and pick up the chain saw. Molly McDuff volunteered to bring Billy some non-hospital food meals and pick him up at County General when he was discharged. Jake Kane and Kenny Clarke agreed to spend alternating nights at the cabin looking after Billy. Buzzy the postmaster arranged for Chester the mailman to drop Billy's mail at the cabin so Billy wouldn't have to come to his Post Office box to pick it up. Since Roland Rutledge was up well before dawn to start at Shea's Bakery, he'd stop by Billy's and milk Prudence and the goats. Hank *Klunk* Klunkergarten, the horseman from Catacoot, arranged to exercise, feed and brush Chloe, and muck her stall several times a week. Lenny Hirsh and Winton set about making plans to build a handicap ramp at Billy's cabin. Labor and materials compliments of Hirsch's Hardware. Angelina Verdi readily agreed to tend to Billy during the day, clean his house, and fix the meals and such until James got home from school. Chief Dooley and Sheryl the woman police officer, along with her fellow cops Sam and Cliff, put their names in to do the shopping. Stanley Dzjankowski refused to accept a dime for any groceries that went to Billy. Bay Constable Ben Hathaway spoke to Rory MacNish and Joe *Sea Macaroni*, telling them to get Billy whatever he wanted from the bay. Maureen Donnelly's class, as well as the other classes at Harmony Bay Elementary, were going to start making get well cards the next day. Fred and Mel Lanscombe worked out a car pool schedule to chauffer folks to visit Billy if they needed transportation. Pastor Roger Simvasten offered prayers and added Billy's name to the church's prayer concerns list. Dory called the library staff and asked them to compile a list of reading materials and classic movie DVDs. She asked Jake to set up a DVD player at Billy's house. James wanted to look after Angus for as long as necessary.

Chapter 31

Dory had a busy day lined up. She signed up to help with the community children's Christmas show. This afternoon was the first day of rehearsals. James was scheduled to perform a guitar solo Christmas song. Today was mentoring day and the library would be full of high school kids—which always kept Mrs. Lanscome and the library staff on its toes. Dory didn't mind a bit. She looked forward to the day. The high school students always helped decorate the library for the holidays. Dory couldn't wait too see what they had in mind for Thanksgiving ornaments. After last evening's upset from Billy's grisly accident, Dory was relieved she didn't have to open the library today. It afforded her the luxury of some time to herself before the day started, although, she would have to work late.

Dory flashed a smile in the entryway, waiting to dole out pleasantries to the staff. Something was wrong. Shirley and Louise sat at the circulation desk below the spinning fish. They were grim faced. Their eyes were red and swollen, Louise dabbed at hers with a tissue. Doc Tollenson stood behind them with his hands in his pockets. His expression was more than sad and it showed signs of exhaustion.

"Oh, no! Billy! Please God, no! What happened?" Dory said. Tears welled up in her eyes also.

The doctor shook his head no and moved out from behind the counter, putting his arm around Dory. "Dory, I am so very sorry. It's Mel Lanscome," he said. Her knees began to buckle as his words sunk in. Doc steadied her and moved her to a seat along with the other two women. Shirley handed her a tissue.

"Doc what happened? Mel was here all day yesterday. She seemed fine," Dory said. She sobbed.

"Her heart, Dory. Mel had problems over the years, but she always kept it to herself. Dory, I want you to know she didn't suffer. She passed quietly in her sleep early this morning. Fred called just as I was getting back from County General and taking care of Billy."

"Poor Fred, he must be devastated." Dory wiped her eyes again.

"I sent Jake and Kenny Clarke over there so he wouldn't be alone. Are you okay?"

"I'm shocked. Last night with Billy's accident—now this."

"Billy is okay. He has a concussion. They put a couple of pins in his leg; it's in a full-length cast. He'll be on crutches for about seven weeks. He's resting comfortably in stable condition. He's very strong—he'll be fine."

"What should we do, Dory?" Louise asked. It was obvious to Dory that Louise and Shirley were not good in a crisis.

"We owe it to the public to stay open today. We'll take turns on the desk and ask the pages to pitch in with returns and checkouts. When I get myself pulled together, I'm going to call on Fred and see what help he needs with the arrangements. We are going to have to hold it together and get through," Dory said.

"I'll come with you," Doc said.

"You look like you need some rest, Doc."

"I'm a small-town physician. I'm used to this."

"Okay, you know what's best for you. Please call Pastor Simvasten and ask him to join us."

"Sure. I don't know if Pastor Roger has heard yet. I'll take a ride over there and tell him personally."

"Breaking the news to the others will be hard. I'll handle it. Once we know the details of the funeral service, I think the library should close for half a day to give everyone the opportunity to attend." Her shoulders heaved up and she let out a sigh. "If we inform the patrons and the board —I don't think anyone is going to object. I'll call the radio station and the Harmony Bay Gazette." Louise and Shirley bobbed their heads in agreement. They were glad somebody else was taking the leadership role. Dory accepted it as her duty. Louise worked at the library almost as long as Mel Lanscome did. Shirley had been there twenty-two years. It was too much for them to cope with.

Dory went to her desk and started a list of things Mel did on a daily, then weekly, basis. The staff had to cover those tasks as best they could. She went to Mrs. Lanscome's office and slowly opened the door, almost expecting Mel to be sitting at her desk. It didn't occur to Dory how much Mel Lanscome meant to her. She had to be strong and help the others through the crisis. Opening the director's appointment book, she checked the calendar to see if there were any pressing matters or appointments that needed to be cancelled. Dory started to make the calls then hesitated and dialed Jake's cell phone. She needed to hear his voice.

Sitting at the director's desk, Dory took in the mementos in the room. Garden Club awards, a proclamation from the Governor for meritorious service, a national award for librarian of the year, her diploma for Library Science from the university, and a stuffed bear wearing a red sweater with bold letters that said, *Words Explain Everything*. There were photos chronicling her years of service. Dory's eyes stopped on the gold framed picture on the credenza. It was Mel and Fred on their wedding day. He was in his Army uniform; she was in white. *What a happy marriage they had*, thought Dory. The tears returned.

Slumping in the chair, her mind wandered back ten years to her only other experience with death. It was surreal. A flag-draped coffin and military honor guard contrasted with the new life she held in her arms. Dory was told to be brave and accept what happened. It was part of being a soldier's wife. She felt so cheated. First it was the long periods of time and distances that separated the too-young newly weds. Then death arrived at her doorstep, announced by an officer and a chaplain. The hugs and well meaning words from people in uniforms wore off all too soon. Thankfully, she had Mom and Dad to pull her through. She thought about them now, and, how much she missed them. She dreaded the day the call would come from far away, signaling it was time to grieve again.

Dory could hear voices in the library and left the office to greet the employees and patrons. She went to break the news. Later, she would call her mother.

James took the news hard. He never dealt with the death of someone close to him before. Dory embraced her son as he wept. Dory, Jake, Miss Donnelly, and Pastor Roger all would work with James to help him overcome his grief. Loss was foreign to him. After a while, he would begin to understand that death was part of the process of life, and that Mrs. Lanscome was now in a far better place. After a while, his pain would start to subside.

A week of healing went by and Harmony Bay returned to everyday small town life. Fred Lanscome established a college scholarship fund in his wife's name. "She would've liked that," Fred said. The first contributor was none other than Fishhook Cutsciko. He voluntarily set the pace with a $2,500 contribution. Many townsfolk figured that Fishhook being bounced around on England Point's rocks finally knocked the skinflint's wallet open. They didn't care what the motivation was. It was long overdue. Billy came home from the hospital to the unconditional love and care of Harmony Bay. He wasn't used to folks making such a fuss over him. Nonetheless, he was deeply appreciative.

Dory stood at the kitchen sink doing the dinner dishes. There was a knock at the front door. She flipped on the porch light to see Stanley Dzjankowski holding his Rough Rider hat in his hand. "Sorry to come by unannounced, Dory," he said. "May I come in?" Dory was puzzled by the unexpected appearance of the grocer.

"Sure, Jank, come in. I just put a pot of coffee on. James is visiting Billy. Jake said he would drop him back here by eight. What's up?" Dory said as she made her way to the kitchen. "Care for a slice of pie? Angelina baked it."

"Coffee and pie sounds outstanding," he said from the far end of the kitchen table. "Dory, I'll get right to the point. The library board held a special meeting this afternoon. They sent me up here figuring that I knew you the best. Margaret Lanscome was an institution here and those are darn hard shoes to fill." He paused and rubbed his forehead was his index finger and thumb. "However, we need a new director as soon as possible.

Things have been going well and the board doesn't want to see the library lose momentum. But—there's still a lot of room for improvement. They want somebody who can take the lead for the next several decades. Somebody who is up-to-date with computers and modern technology. A new director needs to be somebody who can relate to our young people, start new programs, and improve the existing ones. They want somebody who is part of the community and understands its strengths and weaknesses." Jank pushed his chair back, waiting to see Dory's reaction.

"I understand. You want me to help with the candidate search."

"Not exactly. Dory, the board wants you as the new director."

Dory's hands shook as she put down her coffee cup. "Me? Why me?"

"Eeee-yup. We see you as all of the things I just stated. Besides, your academic credentials are impeccable. Everybody in this town has come to love you like their own. Our young people worship you. Sure there might be a couple of old-timers, and that idiot on the radio station, who might think an old townie should have the job. Don't worry about them. I'll straighten them out. Nobody else has your spunk. You've already been doing Mel Lanscome's job—but you didn't know it."

"Jank, I am truly flattered. I don't know what to say."

"We're hoping you say yes. The board voted unanimously for you to have the position—if you want it."

"This is coming as very big surprise. What will the other staff members think? I had no idea…"

Jank interrupted, "Forget about it. The staff, the pages, the volunteers all adore you and respect you. Of course, you understand that you'll set your own hours and be on a set salary. It'll be a very substantial increase over what you're earning now. You'll have paid leave time too. If you wish to continue your education further, the board will subsidize your schooling."

Visions of not working weekends, a new car, and being able to cover the rent without working two jobs flashed through Dory's head. "Jank, I'm blown away by this…"

"Tell us how you want the director's office redecorated and we'll get started on it in the morning. We have it in the budget. We'd also be open to considering any other ideas you have for the place."

"I haven't said yes yet."

Jank drummed his fingers on the table and looked Dory in the eye. "Dory, you're sharp and you lead by example. We like that here. I'll wait for your answer."

"When would you want me to begin?"

"Tomorrow. We already have a statement prepared for the newspapers and the radio. If you say yes, my next stop is back to my store to fax it to them." He reached into his coat pocket and put the press release printed on the library's letterhead in front of Dory to read. His fingers drummed on.

"Okay, Mr. Dzjankowski. Thank you. I accept the position." Dory jumped up from her seat and hugged him. "Bully," he said.

Chapter 32

Jake delivered James home at eight o'clock. Dory met them at the door with news of her promotion. After hearing the news, James danced around the room. Jake squeezed her. "I think this calls for a celebration," Jake said. "Since tomorrow is Saturday, let's all go to dinner at Molly's."

They greeted Kenny Clarke when they arrived at Molly's. "Congratulations, Miss New Library Director!" Kenny bellowed from behind a toothy grin. "Ya—this calls for a celebration. Dinner tonight is on me. No problem, Mon. No problem." Kenny directed them to the booth where Jake and Dory sat during their first date. Molly McDuff arrived at the table a moment later, placing menus in front of each of them.

"Ah, hey now! I trained you too well, Dory. Working here all of those Saturday mornings has got you moving up in the world," Molly said, unable to control her laughter. "Congratulations, sweetie. You deserve it. The first day you walked in the door here, I told you it was probably the first and last time I'd be waiting on you. Like I said— probably. Tonight I want the honor of serving you. And, I'll be fighting with Kenny over the check."

"Gee, I feel like some kind of celebrity," Dory said.

"You and your son are the finest gust of wind that has blown into Harmony Bay in many a year. Maybe he was the last one before that," Molly said as she looked at Jake. Molly took their drink orders and departed.

"I guess the news is all over town," Dory said.

"I was up at Billy's this morning. We had the radio on. That irritating little man—Cal, *The Mouth,* Terry was rattling on about your promotion," Jake said.

"What did he say?"

"The usual nonsense. You know how Calvin is. He was vaccinated with a phonograph needle. He just doesn't know when to shut up."

"He thinks I didn't deserve the promotion?"

"Sort of. It doesn't really matter. He had six or seven call-ins who came to your defense and set him straight. One of them was Stan Dzjankowski. Jank really blasted him. Nobody called the station to say they agreed with *The Mouth.*"

"Yes, Jank said he'd do that. Cal Terry should remember—I was offered the position. I didn't ask for it."

"Maureen Donnelly phoned in too."

"I guess I owe her." Dory placed her elbows on the table and cradled her chin in her hands.

"No, I think she still believes she owes you for rescuing her from Belinda. No matter, Maureen spoke highly of you."

"Anybody else we know?" James inquired.

"Well, let me think," Jake said. "Some ornery, scallop crazed, marine scientist called to defend your mother's honor. He told *The Mouth* to grow up, stop hiding behind his microphone and get a real job." James laughed at Jake's feeble attempt to shield his identity.

"Anybody else?" James asked again.

"That goofy clam man turned the phone over to an old timer from around here named Billy. Billy dressed Calvin down real well. You know how Billy uses terms like 'now see here my good man', and, 'the facts speak clearly for themselves.' Billy never let up. It really made Cal Terry stammer and stutter," Jake said. James was thrilled to hear about everyone sticking up for his mother.

"Okay, let's change the subject," Dory said. "Jake, Mr. Dzjankowski also said the library board was open to considering any other ideas I might have for the library. You know...I've wanted to put on a Dickens Festival. It's already been done in other towns around the country. It could be a gold mine for the town in the off-season. Everyone dresses in nineteenth-century costumes. I could put Angelina in charge of costumes. She'd absolutely love that. The library could present a reading of *A Christmas Carol*. At the end of the festival there would be a big Christmas parade. Think about how many people come out for the Fourth of July parade. Imagine what a boon it would be to the bed and breakfasts and the mom and pop shops right before winter sets in. The weather is still fairly mild here until Christmas, isn't it?"

"Great idea," Jake said. He was only half listening. His thoughts drifted back to his first date with Dory at their table. "Tell me more."

"The church choir could perform *Handel's Messiah*. Vendors selling roasted chestnuts, hot cider and fish and chips. I'll work with the school to develop a suggested reading list of Dickens and other works to get kids interested in the classics. James, you and the kids could dress as chimney sweeps, streetwise scalawags and whatever else we can dream up. We could start small and build it up. If we hurry, we could get something started this year. I have dozens of ideas. It will be fun."

"Speaking of gold mines, how's your research been going on the Christian Carroll caper?"

"Jake—were you listening?"

"Eh, yeah."

"Okay, I'll stop rambling on about my Dickens idea for now. Since you asked, it was quiet in the library yesterday."

"Mom, it's supposed to be quiet in the library every day." James said as he stirred his Coke with his straw. Dory was losing her audience.

"Yes, James. That's true. Anyway, I had some time to do more research. And—I received an e-mail reply from the British National Archives in Surrey, England about my inquires on Sergeant Major Randall Stone-Bayard and—Corporal Smythe with an *e*.

Jake hunched forward. "Wow. Really? I want to hear all about this," Jake said. Dory now had Jake and James' full attention.

"From what I can determine, Stone-Bayard and Smythe, along with the light dragoon unit stationed at Quahog Bay, were sent to serve under the command of Lieutenant Colonel Banastre Tarleton, nicknamed *Bloody Ban*."

"Why, *Bloody Ban*?" James asked.

"Well, son, his tactics against the Patriots and civilians certainly earned him the reputation of being a cruel, ruthless man. At the Waxhaw Massacre near Lancaster, South Carolina, he ordered his troops to open fire on a column of American soldiers who had surrendered. Even worse, Tarleton's men used their sabers to hack the wounded Patriots who were lying on the ground."

"Oh man. That's horrible."

"Tarleton was hated by everyone in the south. His archenemy was none other than Francis Marion, better remembered as *Swamp Fox.*"

"Hey, I remember the story about Swamp Fox. Everybody liked him," Jake interjected. "What were Tarleton's tactics against civilians?"

"This is all terrible stuff. Are you sure you want to hear it?" Dory said. James and Jake urged her to continue. "Tarleton took civilian's cattle and supplies, burned their houses and tortured them. In one instance, he forced the widow of a Patriot officer to feed him dinner. When he was done, he ordered the house, barn and crops burned and the remains of her deceased husband dug up."

"That's crazy," James said. He clutched his head.

"On the other hand, when Francis Marion and his men requisitioned supplies, or sabotaged weapons to render them useless to the British army, they gave the owners receipts for the stuff. After the war, the new state government redeemed most of the receipts.

Swamp Fox and his men were experts at guerilla tactics. Marion's men knew the swamps down there like the backs of their hands. They lived off the land and provided their own horses and arms." Dory pushed her menu aside. "They were a renegade bunch who never really were a part of the recognized Continental Army. Swamp Fox drove the British crazy with lightening fast raids, and then disappeared into the swamps to hide and fight again."

"What happened to Smythe and Stone-Bayard?" James asked, his eyes widening.

Dory continued, "This is interesting. At the Waxhaw Massacre, only five British were killed. Corporal Smythe was one of them. By comparison, there were 113 Americans killed outright, and 150 wounded. Many of the wounded died later. As I mentioned—the redcoats slaughtered the wounded while they were helpless on the ground. I should note—the British don't refer to this event as a massacre, but rather, as the Battle at

Waxhaws. As for Stone-Bayard, he was promoted to the rank of Sergeant Major while under Tarleton's command. The question we have to ask is *why* was he promoted."

James fidgeted in his seat. "Okay, so *why* was he promoted?" he said.

"Apparently, Stone-Bayard honed his blood-lust skills in the company of evil Colonel Tarleton. In plain sight of his regiment, Stone-Bayard shot and killed a civilian. It was a musket shot to the head at close range. When his commanding officer moved to arrest him, the Sergeant-Major drew his sword and swiped at the officer, wounding him slightly. He likely would've been hanged for his war crime anyway, even in comparison to Tarleton's unspeakable actions. Murder of civilians and rape were the only punishable capital crimes for British troops, but striking an officer in front of witnesses sealed his fate."

"Ye're onto somethin' here, Dory. Eh, let's see," Jake said. "Stone-Bayard's actions, a head shot at close range, were consistent with the murder of Lieutenant Stockbridge at Quahog Bay. That and the attempted murder of a superior officer in South Carolina matches his modus operandi for violence toward an officer, and, killing Stockbridge."

"Okay," Dory said, "...this seems to confirm our suspicions of Stone-Bayard killing Stockbridge. At the same time, this discounts the theory that Stockbridge was shot because his troops hated him. Although, killing him would have satisfied many men, whether or not it was to eliminate him as a partner in splitting the gold. What else?"

"Let's think about his promotion to Sergeant Major," Jake said. "It couldn't have been in reward for valiant service. He was camped out on a mosquito infested lookout post in the middle of nowhere. Besides, he held rank at an encampment that let three prisoners escape. Promoting him to Sergeant Major would put him in a close relationship with his Commanding Officer, probably Tarleton. That would make Stone-Bayard a confidant to Tarleton."

"Maybe Stone-Bayard squealed about the gold," James said.

Jake leaned closer as he spoke, "Maybe Tarleton's motivation for promoting Stone-Bayard was greed. Let's assume Stone-Bayard spilled the beans about the loot to Tarleton. We can also assume that others stationed at Quahog Bay knew about it. Maybe the Sergeant Major was willing to trade some of the treasure for preferred treatment and the privilege of rank. Benjamin Franklin said, '*Only three men can keep a secret if two of them are dead.*' With Smythe and Stone-Bayard dead, maybe the only one with the treasure map was Tarleton."

Dory picked up her menu and spoke from behind it, "That's even if they told Tarleton exactly where the gold was. After the war, Tarleton returned to England and ran for public office. I'd think if he knew where the gold was, he'd have dug it up and retired a very wealthy man. Tarleton was in the House of Commons until 1812 and was an outspoken supporter of slave trade in Liverpool. He became well known for antagonizing abolitionists. He never had any children. If he did have a fortune, there was no one to leave it to."

"It would be interesting to know what happened to the rest of the garrison on Pencil Hill," Jake said.

"I wondered the same thing," Dory offered. "So, I also made that inquiry with the British Archives. After extensive research, it was determined that all of the men who were sent from the Pencil Hill garrison to serve under Tarleton were killed at the Battle of Cowpens in South Carolina, a resounding victory and turning point for the American forces in January, 1781." Dory pushed up her sleeves and flipped back her hair. "Those few who were left behind on the hill at Quahog Bay died of yellow fever in August of 1783. They were all buried here. The camp was disbanded and the war ended the following month."

"Yellow fever? Jake questioned.

"Yes, yellow fever is typically a tropical or sub-tropical disease that is carried by mosquitoes," Dory said. "Insects carrying the virus could have hitched aboard any of the many ships that came up here from the south. This region suffered from an unusually hot, wet summer in '83. It was prime weather for breeding mosquitoes. There is no cure for yellow fever. In those days, there was no vaccine, and without any kind of medical intervention—they were goners. Later on in 1793, there was a massive epidemic of yellow fever in Philadelphia. Thousands died. The outbreak was so dreadful, George Washington and the new American government fled the city."

"So…the gold must still be around," James said.

"That's a very good point, son. There are no inventory records, recorded diary entries, ship's manifests, or bills of lading mentioning anything about a quantity of gold or treasures coming out of Quahog Bay during that time. Tories may have spirited it off in small amounts or it could be a buried treasure somewhere along the coast."

Molly approached the table, pulling an order pad from her apron to take their dinner order. "Somebody talking about buried treasure?" Molly boomed. "Are we talking about the Quahog gold?"

"Yeah! How did you know?" James exclaimed.

"Well, hey now," Molly said. "That topic comes up around here every now and then. I can remember my grandpa telling me stories about how folks used to come out from the city for digging parties. There were so many craters in beaches and countryside around here, it looked like the face of the moon. Nobody ever found anything. I strongly doubt there's anything out there. If anybody did find a fortune, they never came here to spend it." Molly threw her head back and cackled.

"I think they missed the point," Jake said. "There's tons of treasure buried in the sand around here." Molly, James and Dory all stared at Jake.

"Why didn't you tell us?" James asked.

"I have. Think about how much money shellfish brings in when things are going right. It's equal to a king's ransom." Jake pointed to the price of bay scallops on the menu.

"I see your point," Dory said.

"Everybody makes a buck. The guys on the boats, the marine mechanics that keep 'em going, the seafood market. Even scallop shuckers get paid two bucks a pound during the season. A veteran shucker goes through fourteen or fifteen pounds of scallops per hour."

"They keep you in business, too, Jake," Dory countered.

"Ye're exactly right. And *my* happiest day will be when all those little clams, oysters, and scallops can reproduce in huge numbers by themselves without my help."

"Enough talk about the critters. I'm starving. Let's eat," James said.

Jake closed his menu. "All righty then, let's order. After that, Dory, tell me more about the plans for your Dickens Festival."

Chapter 33

Dory was thankful for everything Harmony Bay brought to her and her son. Even though the cottage was small, she decided to have Thanksgiving dinner for as many friends as she could fit that didn't already have plans. She and James went into town to assemble the remaining groceries. They would stop at Dzjankowski's and at George's farm stand for the produce they couldn't get from Billy's garden. It was the last day George was open for the season.

"Mr. Hirsch wants us to stop by the hardware store," Dory said.

"Why?" James replied.

"He didn't say why. He only said to come by around two o'clock. Maybe he wants to wish us a Happy Thanksgiving. Let's get everything else done. We'll stop there last."

"Okay, Mom." James was excited at the prospect of having so many guests for dinner in their home. In the past, the most people they ever had for Thanksgiving were Gram, Gramps, and Mom. This was going to be special. All of the people coming to his house for dinner were like family. They were just like aunts, uncles, and cousins. In addition to the adult guests, James invited his friend Peter whose parents had to work shift hours on Thanksgiving Day. They weren't having their turkey until a week later.

James pushed the door open. The sleigh bells dangling from the knob jingled their welcome to Hirsch's Hardware. "Hey there, young fella, we've been waiting for you," Lenny Hirsch said. He slid a pencil in the top pocket of his coveralls and shuffled from behind the counter.

"Hi, Mr. Hirsch. Is Winton here, too?"

Winton appeared from the stock room. "I am right here," he said.

"Hello Lenny, hello Winton. Happy Thanksgiving to both of you," Dory said.

"Why did you want to see us?" James asked as Angelina Verdi walked from the back room carrying a large package wrapped in brown paper and tied up with twine.

She placed the package on the counter. "James, I know how hard you've been practicing your guitar playing," Mrs. Verdi said. "I must say, you have made astonishing progress. The Christmas concert is next weekend and I'm looking forward to hearing you play. I've decided to give you your Christmas present early to help you out with the concert. This belonged to my husband, many, many years ago." Mrs. Verdi pushed the package across the counter toward James. "Go ahead, open it." James looked up at his mother who gave an approving nod.

"Let me help you with that string," Mr. Hirsch said and flicked open a penknife to cut the cords. James tore the paper off the box and opened it, revealing a guitar.

It was an electric model and a collector's item. James examined the mahogany's swirling grain that converged like the confluence of russet streams. The double cutaway model, with its delicate f-shaped violin sound holes, was handsome in every way. James pressed down on the strings, noticing how little effort it took. Every bit of chrome, every piece of wood gleamed. "Thank you, Mrs. Verdi. Thank you so much. This is awesome," James said. Speechless, he looked each adult in the eye.

"You're very welcome, but you also have to thank Lenny and Winton. That guitar was in very bad shape from sitting in the attic all these years. They completely restored it. There's something else," Mrs. Verdi said. "Winton, please lift it up here."

Winton Hector picked up an electric guitar amplifier and put it on the counter. "It's not a lot of watts but it sure kin git the job done. It's a classic. She's got a real sweet sound," Winton said.

"James, it was in the attic, too. Mr. Lanscome and Jake got it working. I think they rewired some things and changed tubes or something. I don't know much about that sort of thing," Mrs. Verdi said.

Covered in blond colored fabric, with a brown tweed grille in front of the speaker, it reminded Dory of an old-fashioned television set. "James, I think you have a lot to be thankful for and a lot of people to thank," she said.

"Plug it in. Check it out, James," Winton said. Dory noticed there was something different about Winton. She couldn't put her finger on it. Winton plugged in the amp and James played a few chords. He was amazed by the sound the glassy strings offered.

"We'll need to get a good carrying case for that guitar," Dory said. "Thank you to all of you. James, we need to get moving along. Tomorrow is a big day."

Jake brought the rowboat's sawhorses into the house from the yard. He pulled the hinge pins from James' bedroom door and removed the doorknob. Placing the door across the horses created a dining table. This, added to the kitchen table, made enough space for the dinner guests. Dory covered it with a tablecloth borrowed from Mrs. Verdi. Jake excused himself and left to pick up Billy.

Dory considered herself a good cook, but she counted on Angelina Verdi's help. The others offered to bring a dish as well. In addition to Dory's turkey, stuffing, turnips, green beans, roasted Brussels sprouts and creamed white onions, Jake traded scallops for a lobster salad first course. Rory MacNish was on the bay during the morning pulling up oysters to share. Joe Ciamariconi smoked striped bass and prepared a sauce from sour cream and horseradish. Maureen Donnelly was mashing potatoes and baking cookies. Kenny Clarke lined up bottles of Champagne, Sauvignon Blanc and Pinot Noir. Winton Hector bought an assortment of dinner rolls at Shea's Bakery. Fred Lanscome went to his cellar and retrieved the last of his wife's blueberry preserves from the summer, adding it to his contribution of whole cranberry sauce and vanilla ice cream from Jank's grocery. Peter's mother sent a bowl of sweet potatoes. Billy's cow, Prudence, provided the fresh cream that would be whipped and placed on top of the pumpkin and apple pies that Mrs. Verdi baked.

"Good afternoon, Jake Kane and Happy Thanksgiving to you," Billy said as Jake arrived at the door. After spending the morning with Billy, Angelina left to go home to bake the pies. Jake helped Billy into the Jeep and loaded his crutches in the back.

"Splendid day, don't you agree, my good man?" Billy said and settled into the seat.

"Eh, yeah, I couldn't agree more." Jake shifted into gear. "Let me check on Chloe and Prudence before we go."

"Not to worry. Winton was here and took care of it. He will meet us at the McDonough residence."

"All righty. Then we have plenty of time."

"Yes indeed, we do."

Jake drove down Pencil Hill past Mill Pond and onto North Road. It was a brisk and brilliant day. Dry brown leaves scattered in the wake of the Jeep. "It is certainly a pleasure to get out of the house for a while," Billy said. He patted his belly. "I am looking forward to this magnificent meal. Jake, we are ahead of schedule. Would you mind terribly if we drove down by the water for a bit? I have not set my eyes on the bay in quite some time."

"Sure, no problem. Jake's Tours at your service." Jake turned off the road, shifted into four-wheel-drive and crossed the beach to the waterline.

"Hmm, yes. Would you mind stopping so that I may roll down the window and enjoy some fresh bay air?" The Jeep rolled to a stop. Billy rolled down his window. "Ah yes, delightful." They watched spiraling gulls fill their wings with fresh breeze. Wintering ducks bobbed on the bay. Billy reached inside of his parka and removed a thick, yellowed envelope.

"Jake, as you are aware, my family goes back to the original founders of Harmony Bay in the mid-seventeenth century. Back to when it was Quahog Bay, of course. It looks as though I am at the end of the line of caretakers for all of those acres on the hill. I do not want to see it fall into the hands of an unscrupulous developer after I am gone."

"C'mon now, Billy. You're going to be around here for a long time."

"Possibly. However, accidents do happen. The current Lord of the Manor had that nasty accident with a tree and is now on crutches. If it was not for the actions of a noble dog and James, who is to say what might have happened. Do you see my point?"

"Billy, I see your point. What are you driving at?"

"Most people do not know that I was married for a short time. I built my house on the hill for her. I built it big because we were looking forward to having a family." Billy paused and bit his lower lip. "She died giving birth. The baby, my son, died as well. I have neither a Will nor any heirs. I want to put things in order in the event of another accident. Give me a dollar, Jake." Jake was taken aback by Billy's comments. Fishing in his pocket for a dollar, he found one and handed it to him.

"What's the dollar for, Billy?"

Billy handed the fat envelope to Jake. "Here is the deed for ten of those acres adjacent to mine on top of the hill. I want you to have that property. You are not getting any younger and some of us are worried about you living on that houseboat. If you choose to build a home up there, I assure you that you will have the help of the entire community."

"Billy, I can't accept this. There's no way…"

"Surely you can. Here, take it."

"Billy, why me?"

"You've always been like a son to me, Jake. Moreover, you have been like a father to the bay. Please accept this with my blessing."

"Ten acres? That's a lot of land to look after."

"Yes it is—you are the perfect man for the job."

"How many more acres do you own up there?"

Billy smiled and patted his beard, casting a furtive glance toward Jake he said, "More than enough, I would say. My family owned everything from the edge of the bay to the top of Pencil Hill and west beyond Ezra's Pond. Beautiful day, Jake, isn't it?"

"Billy, this is beyond beautiful. That property on the hill with its water view is worth a fortune."

"The money is inconsequential to me. I have everything I need except good neighbors."

"Billy, how can I say thank you?"

"Simply say thank you and pay it forward. You have always done the right thing in the past." Jake thought about that. He wondered how he could ever pass along such a generous gift.

"Thank you, Billy. Thank you very much. Happy Thanksgiving."
They shook hands.

"You are very welcome, young man. All of the paperwork, the survey, the title and deeds are all in this package and have been signed over to you for the sum of one dollar. It is all one hundred percent legal. Welcome to the neighborhood."

Jake was in a state of bewilderment as he drove the rest of the way to Dory's. He backed the Jeep up to the kitchen door and helped Billy into the house. There were no steps there, which made Billy's entry easier. After getting Billy in and comfortable, Jake went back out to the Jeep and returned with a dozen red roses for Dory that he purchased the day before. "These are for the hostess," Jake said. He gave her a warming hug along with the bouquet.

"Never, ever, has anyone given me flowers before. Let alone a dozen roses. Thank you, Jake! They're beautiful," she said, giving him a kiss.

"I guess we all have a lot to be thankful for today." Jake turned away and cast his eyes downward. Jake decided to keep his new land ownership quiet for a while. He was going to try to persuade Billy to change his mind.

"Amen to that," Dory said. She placed the long-stemmed flowers in water.

Everyone arrived by three o'clock and took their places at the table. They joined hands in prayer, each offering thanks for their individual blessings. They were as varied as they were plentiful. The conversation became lively while passing the dishes. Dory talked about the upcoming Dickens Festival and Christmas show.

"I've been giving it some thought," she said. "Jake, Rory, and Joe, do you think you could get some of the boat owners to decorate their boats with Christmas lights to add to the festivities of the *Holiday* parade? It could be quite a spectacle."

"Sure, you can count on it," Joe said.

"I'll start on the *Sea Horse* and Jake's houseboat in the morning," Rory offered.

"No problem. I can run some lights up the masts of my sailboat," Kenny said.

"I'll give Ben Hathaway a call tomorrow. We can go around and visit the boat owners and ask them to participate," Jake said. "Pass the cranberries, please," he added.

"This will be so much fun," Dory said. "There's something else that's been on my mind. I want to ask everyone's opinion…since you all represent different aspects of the community."

"Well, go on," Billy said from the other end of the table. "I am listening." The others nodded in agreement.

"It's about the parade," Dory said. "Does anyone see why it can't be called the *Christmas* parade instead of the *Holiday* parade?"

"Who says it can't be called a Christmas parade?" James uttered.

"Well, son, Mayor Pesce said it wouldn't be politically correct to use the word Christmas for a village sponsored parade. It might upset people and affect tourism."

Billy spoke next, "Hmm, it seems to me that this is a classic question of the chicken and the egg. If there was never a Christmas, there would not be a holiday."

"I say go with Christmas," Jake said. "Pesce is only thinking of his vote count."

"After all," Miss Donnelly chimed in, "we don't call the Fourth of July parade a *Summer Holiday* parade."

"There's no way I'd let *that* happen," Jake replied.

"Have you asked anyone else's opinion?" Billy asked.

"Yes," Dory said, "I spoke with Pastor Simvasten. He told me he couldn't get involved directly in a public argument about church and state. Although, privately he supported my thinking. He did go on to say almost eighty percent of the population in America is Christian in some form or other— and I should let that be my guide. He did add that he'd pray about it."

Fred Lanscome entered the discussion, "I'm all for calling it the Christmas parade. Right along with putting a nativity scene on the front lawn of Village Hall again. Freedom of religious expression is what this country was founded on. Think about all of the veterans who gave their lives to defend that freedom."

Kenny Clarke raised a toast, "I say, let it be Christmas, Mon. No problem. Here's to Dory, her beautiful Thanksgiving dinner, her Dickens Festival and Christmas parade!" Everyone raised their glass and voiced their approval.

"Buon Natale! It should always be Christmas," Mrs. Verdi exclaimed.

"Well then," Billy said, "it appears a vote of the representative aspects of the Harmony Bay community has been taken. The results show a unanimous vote yes to approve using the word *Christmas* for the parade. Dory, I do not want you to end up in a political conflict. Jake, if you would be so kind as to take me to Village Hall tomorrow morning, I will inform Mayor Pesce that he will change his mind about the matter. After all, who in their right mind would argue with Santa Claus?" They all laughed.

The dinner dishes were cleared and Dory asked Jake, James and Peter to start a fire in the fireplace. Coffee, along with a fine assortment of pies, a mountainous bowl of freshly whipped cream, and desserts made their way to the table.

"Now is as good a time as any to make an announcement," Fred Lanscome said, the words floating over his coffee cup. "The administration at the university has been talking to me. They're in need of a full time professor for marine sciences up there. They're looking for somebody with hands-on experience. Someone with applicable successes would be preferred. Jake, your name came up. It came up because I brought it up." Fred nestled his cup back in its saucer. "You were right under their noses the whole time. The selection committee discussed it thoroughly and brought it to a vote." He picked up his cup, took a sip and paused. "It didn't take much convincing. Everyone agreed—they want you. The position is yours if you want it."

Jake was bowled over by the two gifts bestowed on him in one day. "Thanks, Fred. But, I don't have any teaching experience. I'm a field scientist, not an academician."

"You'd be a fine lecturer, Jake. I'll teach you the ropes. I've watched you in action mentoring those high school kids and the interns. You're a natural born teacher. You've been paying it forward all these years. It's time to share your skills and talents with a wider audience. It would only be three days a week up at the campus. It's not a bad commute. Especially when you can come home to the bay at the end of the day. The rest of the time, you can still be out here on the water. You'll have the summers and holidays off. You can still do your research. There's benefits included too."

"Ye're twisting my arm a little too tight. Ouch."

"Do you need the weekend to think about it?"

"Well, no."

"All righty then, as you would say—welcome aboard."

Dory jumped up from the table, wrapped her arms around Jake, and kissed him squarely on the mouth. Her eyes were wet. "Congratulations! I am *so* happy for you."

"Thank you, Fred. Thank you, Dory. I sure do have a *lot* to be thankful for."

James wasn't entirely happy for Jake. The new job would take him away from Harmony Bay several days a week. James would miss him. He struggled with feelings of jealousy for Jake's new job.

Winton was unusually quiet all day. Dory couldn't help but notice how good Winton's table manners were. She was sure he hadn't learned them in the backwoods or the Army's mess halls. Breaking his silence, he addressed Jake. "Congratulations, mistuh Kane. I always admired you at the library working with those kids."

A light went on for Dory. Winton had shed his boondocks speech pattern for a noticeably more refined vernacular. "My goodness, Winton. It seems like you're growing into a Harmony Bay accent," she said.

"Not growing into it. I am learnin' it from Billy. Since he's been home restin' up, he has been teaching me proper speaking. He told me people judge you by how you're speakin'. He taught me to listen to my words before I spoke them. Billy says it will make a difference if I ever go out into the world away from Harmony Bay."

"That's wonderful advice. One day you will have a car with a pernundle and see the world. You're a wonderful guy. Doors will open for you."

"Thank you, Dory. I still got lots of work to do—but I'm on my way. I don't have my leg and I can't change that." He tapped his prosthetic leg to make his point. "But, still, there's lots 'o things I kin change to make me a better person. There's still a lot I don't understand. I need to learn how to work from my abilities, not my disabilities. I think I can achieve a lot."

Chapter 34

On Friday morning, with Thanksgiving Day's excitement behind them, Jake headed into town with Billy and James. School was closed for the weekend, the library and Village Hall were open. Hard frost covered the ground and glazed windowpanes. James shoved his hands deep in his jacket pockets for warmth.

Harmony Bay's government resided at Village Hall. The ocher clapboard, gray trimmed building, featuring a columned front porch, steeply pitched roofs and cupola was built before the Civil War. It was originally heated with a potbelly stove. During World War I the building housed the Selective Service headquarters for the area. It served as the village courthouse, mayor's office and offices for Harmony Bay's various public officials and their subordinates. It was old school. It was cramped. A red brick box annex jutted off the back. This contained two jail cells for holding prisoners awaiting trial in by-gone days. Not much had changed except for the wood stove and the scant few crooks that Harmony Bay did have were now detained at police headquarters.

Visitors entered through the double wooden front doors beneath the porch and directly into the courtroom. The courtroom doubled as the place for Village meetings. Department offices were located on the second floor, the mayor's office sat behind the courtroom on the ground floor. Many believed this layout allowed the mayor to see town employees who were trying to leave work early by sneaking down the squeaky stairs.

James ran into the courtroom and boldly sat at the dais in the mayor's seat. "It will be a few years until you can run for mayor, James," Billy said as he made his way past the jury box on his crutches.

"James! C'mon now. Get out of there before Mayor Pesce comes out and finds you in his seat. He'll stick you in one of those jail cells," Jake said in a loud voice. The words left his lips and the mayor came out of his office.

"Stay right there, little fella!" the mayor chortled. "Who am I to kick Harmony Bay's youngest hero out of that seat. We're going to have to make you mayor for the day!" Pesce turned to Jake and Billy, who both realized the mayor was working for a vote eight years in advance. "What brings you to our humble seat of village government on this fine day?" he said, thrusting his pinky-ringed hand forward.

"Good morning, Mr. Mayor. May I have a word?" Billy said.

"Absolutely. How's the leg coming along, Billy? Sorry I haven't been up to visit. You know, the demands of government and all. Would you be more comfortable here in the courtroom or can I invite you into my office?"

"Your office, I suppose. James, you can wait out here and practice running the town."

"I want to come with you," James replied and leapt from the platform.

Mayor Pesce led Jake and Billy to his office, offering seats in front of his ornate walnut desk. James leaned against the wall behind the chairs. Jake couldn't help noticing the overly large portrait of Pesce on the wall.

"Coffee, gentlemen? How's about a candy cane for you little fella?"

"No thank you. This will not take long," Billy said. He steepled his fingers in front of his beard. Pesce shrugged.

"What's on your mind, boys?" Pesce said. Jake eased back in the overstuffed chair.

"Mr. Mayor, as you are aware, Mrs. McDonough, our new library director…"

Pesce interrupted with a growl and an exaggerated wink. "Yeah, great gal, that Dory," he said.

Billy continued, "…has planned a Dickens Festival to heighten the awareness of a fine classic author, along with a parade to augment tourism in the off-season."

"Yes, yes! I've heard all about it! She has my complete support. What a worker that gal is!" Pesce winked again, harder this time. Jake leaned forward, his shoulders stiffened.

Billy touched his fingertips together again. A twinkle came to his eyes. "It is the parade that I want to speak to you about."

"I'd be delighted to lead the parade. I'll have my brother decorate his convertible for the occasion. Billy, you dress as Santa Claus and ride with me, okay? We'll be great! We'll get that little hero fella in there, too," Pesce blabbered. Jake was approaching the outer limits of his patience.

"I am flattered. Thank you, Mr. Mayor. However, there is something else."

"Sure—just name it!" Mayor Pesce grinned from ear to ear, picturing himself beside St. Nick and tossing popcorn balls to the crowd.

"It will be called the Harmony Bay *Christmas* parade. Not the *Holiday* parade." Billy let his words sink in.

"We, we ,we ca, ca, can't do that." Pesce now simpered while he stuttered.

"We *will* do that."

"It's not politically correct!" He thought about his vote plurality plummeting downward.

"For whom?"

"Some people will really get upset," the mayor shot back.

Billy was firm. "That is the point. Only *some* people. I have it on good authority that a vast majority, nearly eighty percent, will approve. Of the remaining twenty percent, there will only be a few outspoken malcontents."

"Yeah, that's my point! They'll go to the newspapers and call the radio station," Pesce shrieked.

"Let me remind you. Next Saturday's show at the library has been called the Christmas Show for as long as I have been around. Perhaps longer."

"Well, yeah. That's an old tradition. People are used to it, so they accept it."

Billy raised his voice. "Christmas is a tradition that is 2,000 years old. It has always been called *Christmas*." The glimmer in Billy's blue eyes evolved into an intense stare that pushed the mayor back in his seat.

Pesce's face reddened. Beads of perspiration formed on his oily brow.

"We can't have controversy over this nice parade."

"There will be no controversy, there will be no argument. There will be no political retaliation, sabotaging anyone's career, or their well being. It *will* be called the Harmony Bay Christmas Parade. *That* is final. If you do receive any complaints—and *you* cannot handle them— please refer them to me. I would be more than happy to give anyone a lecture about the true meaning of Christmas. Good day, sir." Billy rose. Pesce was visibly shaken. Jake fought to contain his laughter. James was in awe of Billy.

"Oh, by the way…" Jake said and took a calculated parting shot, "Fred Lanscome wants a nativity set out on Village Hall's lawn." Now in a state of shock, Mayor Pesce collapsed in his chair as his guests filed out.

Jake loaded his passengers back into the Jeep. "While we are in town, may we stop at Mr. Hirschowitz's hardware store? There are a few sundry items that I need," Billy said. James never heard anyone refer to Lenny Hirsch as Mr. Hirschowitz. He didn't know what sundry items were either. He asked Billy to explain.

"Ah yes, it was originally Leonard Hirschowitz many years ago. I believe he decided to use a shortened version so that it would fit on the sign over his door. It is sort of a nickname, I imagine," Billy said.

"Call him whatever you want," Jake interjected, "he's still a good guy."

James bounded up the steps and into the hardware store. He wanted to be the one to ring the sleigh bells hanging on the door.

"Good morning, Mr. Hirsch!" James hollered.

"Good morning, James. Good to see you. Here by yourself?"

"Nope," James replied as the door swung open again in a flurry of bells to admit Jake and Billy.

"Every time a bell rings an angel gets his wings," Billy said.

"What does *that* mean?" James inquired.

"It is a line from an old Christmas movie, *It's a Wonderful Life*. You will have to see it sometime."

"No kidding? Okay."

"It is a classic. After we are finished here, we will go to see your mother and borrow the movie from the library. We should all watch it together this evening."

"Hey now—good to see you guys. Hope you all had a fine meal yesterday," Hirsch said.

"Dory is a wonderful cook and hostess. I had a marvelous time. Jake received a full professorship position at the university. It was wonderful to celebrate with everyone," Billy said.

"Yeah, Winton told me he had quite a feed out at Dory's and told me the news about Jake. What can I help you with?" asked the hardware man.

"Oh, not much. I will hobble around and have a look." Billy navigated his crutches through the narrow aisles and made his selections. Jake stayed at the counter chatting with Hirsch. Billy returned to the counter. "Incidentally," Billy said to Hirsch, "have you heard about the idea to officially name next week's parade the Christmas parade?"

"Surely did. Pastor Roger was by and asked me my opinion. I'm all for it. One hundred percent."

"That is interesting."

"Anybody who's against it can kiss my butt," Hirsch said. James giggled from a hiding place in the fishing tackle aisle.

"Hey, Lenny… if you see Mayor Pesce around town, maybe you could ask him how he feels about it," Jake said. He cringed at the thought of the mayor on all fours puckering up to burly Lenny Hirsch.

"Look here," Hirsch said, "folks are entitled to their opinions, but the birth of Jesus changed the world. It changed people like no one else has ever done before or since. Later, He died for us. For that, I am forever thankful. The very least folks can do to show respect is keep the name Christmas." He paused as James approached the counter then continued. "I became a changed man a long time ago after attending the funeral of a Christian friend. That family of the deceased, who you'd think would be sobbing, grieving, and crying and all, were all happy and smiling. Same thing with their entire congregation. They showed nothing but love for one another and strangers too." Hirsch hooked his thumbs in his coveralls and looked at Jake and Billy. "I was curious, learned more, and became a believer. I'm not nearly half as ornery now as I was before then. Like I said, folks can have their own opinions. The way I see it— part of the beauty of Christmas is how we make each other feel. I think folks ought to act like it's Christmas everyday."

Billy broke the silence that followed. "Very well said, Mr. Hirsch. You may tally my purchases and get back to your business."

—◁▥◖◗▥▷—

Dory took pictures of the *Sea Horse* decorated with Christmas lights and wrote a brief story about the Harmony Bay residents asking the town to change the parade's name to the Christmas parade. She sent the photos and story via e-mail to the Harmony Bay Gazette and to the city newspapers.

The week passed quickly as Harmony Bay spun itself into a frenzy preparing for the Dickens Festival, the Christmas Show and the parade. It was all set to take place on the weekend following Thanksgiving. The magic of the small town came together. Many of the entries from the Fourth of July parade were redecorated in red and green Christmas themes. Dory ran off photocopies of instructions for Dickens character costumes. Removing the blades from ice skates created old-fashioned lace-up shoes. Attics were searched for old clothing that could be transformed into costumes. Mrs. Verdi worked non-stop, snipping, pinning and sewing. Top hats were rush-ordered. High school students made chimney sweep brushes. Chestnuts were purchased for roasting along with cases of hot chocolate mix. The church choir endlessly rehearsed Handel's *Messiah*. Everyone was reading Dickens' *A Christmas Carol* and those in Saturday afternoon's production of the play practiced their parts. James practiced his songs for the Christmas Show until his fingers ached. He was nervous.

On Friday evening, James and Dory sat at the kitchen table preparing for the events. James addressed his Mother, "Mom, I'm scared I'll make a mistake."

"I see," she said, "do you realize—the only one who can hear a mistake is you?"

"I'm not too sure about that."

"Trust me. You'll be fine. You have that wonderful new guitar and many people put their love into it. They wouldn't have done that if they thought you weren't capable."

"Do you think Dad will hear me playing?" Dory hugged her son for a long time.

"You know he will. He'll hear every note, and he will be very, very proud of you."

The next morning a sliver of light forced its way through Dory's bedroom window. Awakened by a knock on the kitchen door, she glanced at her alarm clock, somewhat annoyed. Six-fifteen. "Who could it be at this hour?" Dory said aloud. She no longer had to be up before dawn on Saturdays to work at Molly's. She pulled on her robe and stepped into her slippers. Jake was at the kitchen door.

"What's the matter?" she said.

"Oh, nothing. I brought you breakfast." Jake held up a bag from Shea's Bakery. "And, good news." There were several newspapers under his arm.

"Geez, Jake, I look a mess. You should have called first."

"Hey, don't worry about it."

She raked her hair with her fingers to untangle the bed-head snarls and tightened her robe. "What's the good news?"

Jake flipped the papers on the table. Selecting the fat, city paper he opened to the Arts and Leisure section. Dory saw an almost full-page color picture of Jake's *Sea Horse* decorated for Christmas beneath a headline that read, *Harmony Bay Sails Into Christmas.*

"Look at this," he said. The page displayed a feature article pointing out Harmony Bay's firm stand to keep the name Christmas in their holiday events. "Even our weasel mayor is quoted as saying that most people prefer calling it a Christmas parade." Dory read on. The story detailed all of the events taking place in the quaint town that weekend. "But, hey now, hold on," Jake continued, "there's more. The Harmony Bay Gazette has an editorial accusing Mayor Pesce of …trying to *sidestep Christmas* by calling it a holiday parade! All of the papers have a complete list of events taking place this weekend."

Dory waited until seven-thirty to wake up James. "Time to get up, young man! Jake brought your favorite—jelly doughnuts." That was all James needed to hear and rolled out of bed. "We've got a big day ahead. Time to get moving."

An hour later, Jake chauffeured them into town. During the drive, Dory noticed cars in the driveways of many of the summer homes. She was astounded by the traffic they encountered as they traveled farther. Cars were everywhere. Jake decided it was best to drop Dory and James off at the library since its parking lot was full. He decided to park by the lab and walk back. On his return, he saw every shop was decked out for Christmas. Town folk, including Dory, were dressed in mid-nineteenth century apparel. She wore a garnet taffeta hoop skirt and woolen shawl. She strolled up and down the narrow streets greeting tourists. Kids dressed as London street urchins and chimney sweeps roamed the narrow lanes of the village.

"My, you look fetching. You sure do look the part," Jake said as he wrapped his arm around her waist.

"Hmm—fetching," she said in a questioning tone. Dory looked down at her Victorian outfit touching the sidewalk and laughed.

"Dory, do you realize? All of these people all over town are here because of what you did? You pulled it all together in only a few weeks. You're amazing." He kissed her on the cheek.

"Thank you, Jake Kane. I had a lot of help from a lot of people. You're amazing, too. Your top hat and tailcoat is in my office. Go put them on. Don't you think we'll make a nice couple? I want to get a picture."

Kenny Clarke arrived in his antique Jack Tar sailor's outfit. "Kenny, you fit right into the theme. This is so much fun," she said.

"No problem, Dory, this is incredible. It's December. Not even noon yet, and every shop is full. Every bed and breakfast and motel is booked for the weekend," Kenny said. He now began juggling popcorn balls. "The town should be very thankful to you."

Everything went flawlessly. Members of the community presented *A Christmas Carol*, the choir performed *The Messiah* in the candlelit church, and in the evening, Harmony Bay's annual Christmas Show took place on the stage of the community room in the library. It was nearly the same as always. Children dressed as snowflakes, candy canes and snowmen were in choreographed skits. A variety of students performed piano pieces and gave dramatic readings. Just before the reenactment of the Nativity, complete with live farm animals, James was scheduled to perform *Greensleeves* on his guitar. He arrived on stage with Winton, who helped him carry out the guitar amplifier and get it plugged in. James stepped up to the microphone. The mic squealed and James jumped back.

"Good evening, ladies and gentlemen. Tonight I am playing *Greensleeves*, which was originally an English Folk song. Later on, a man named William Chatterton Dix added words to the music. This made it the song that you know as *What Child Is This?*" James pulled a small bell from his pocket. "Before I play, I want to remind you—every time a bell rings—an angel gets his wings." James rang the bell in front of the microphone and the room burst into applause. James was flooded with warmth and confidence as he sat center stage on a stool. Winton handed James the guitar. He played flawlessly and was met with a standing ovation.

Sunday afternoon's Christmas parade was an immense success. Some of the spectators took the initiative to dress in holiday theme costumes and entered the procession from the sidelines. Someone carried a sign, handwritten with red and green ink, *God Bless Harmony Bay. A Place Where Christmas Always Has a Home.*

Late autumn's early sunset cast darkness on the tiny village. The boats on the bay, all decorated with Christmas lights, turned the waterfront into a mystical sight. The colored lights shimmered on the water as the town settled down, awaiting the arrival of Christmas.

Chapter 35

A week before Christmas, Jake and James ventured into the hills west of town in search of a Christmas tree. They were successful in their mission, cutting down a perfect seven-foot evergreen. The tree now decorated James' living room. Its position in the window faced the front of the house so visitors could see the lights from the road and was far enough from the fireplace to keep it from drying out.

Christmas Eve dawned cold and cloudy. Dory was almost ready for the day; the library was closing at noon. There were a couple of errands to run on the way home. This evening's celebration of Christmas would be a much quieter, simpler affair than Thanksgiving. For dinner, it would only be Billy, Mrs. Verdi, Jake, and James. James' friend Peter Dyson was invited for Christmas Day. Once again, his parents had both pulled holiday duty. Everyone was attending Christmas services at church before dinner. After dinner, they'd all exchange gifts and reminisce around the fire about past Christmases.

Mrs. Verdi picked up Billy and brought him to church. Dory, James and Jake met them in the narthex and they all shared a pew near the front. It was well past sunset when the candlelight service ended. Temperatures dropped below freezing and snow flurries powdered the churchgoers as they left the church and shook hands with Pastor Simvasten on its front steps.

"A white Christmas!" Dory exclaimed as she wrapped her scarf around her neck. "How beautiful. What could be better?" It was beautiful. White lace covered the surfaces of Harmony Bay's village giving it the appearance of a Norman Rockwell Christmas card.

"The only thing missing is Santa Claus," Mrs. Verdi said.

"He is right here. Ho, ho, ho," Billy replied. He laughed and patted his belly. Billy had healed to the point of only needing a cane to walk. Nonetheless, Jake and Mrs. Verdi supported him on both sides to prevent him from slipping on the snow.

"Mom, can we make a snowman?"

"Well, James, let's see if it snows enough to do that. If it does, I'm all for it. Will you lie on the ground with me and make snow angels?"

"I'm all for *that*," Jake butted in.

Dory thought about Jake's remark and said, "Let's all get home for dinner. We'll have all day tomorrow for that."

Jake cleared the windows of the Jeep with a snowbrush. He did the same on Mrs. Verdi's car after helping Billy into her front passenger seat. Only a light dusting covered Harmony Bay's streets, so their drive out to the end of the peninsula would be easy. Jake shuffled though his CD collection and slid one into the player. He turned the volume up and Nat King Cole's mellow voice blasted from the speakers, "*Let it snow, let it snow, let it snow!*"

"Let everybody get home first. Then it can snow all it wants," Dory said.

"You may get your wish. The forecast is for three to four inches with accumulations beginning before sunrise on Christmas morning," Jake answered.

"The poor guys from the Village will be out plowing on Christmas Day," Dory pouted.

"Probably not. Probably won't be enough to plow, and once the sun comes up it'll melt really fast. If not, I'm sure some of them will appreciate receiving double-time holiday pay."

Christmas Eve dinner was magnificent. Jake cooked Oysters Rockefeller as a first course. Dory purchased Dzjankowski's best cut of roast beef, which steamed as it came out of the oven. Mashed potatoes, fresh green beans, gravy and assortment of condiments and breads filled the table.

They heard a scratching sound on the kitchen door. Dory opened the door. It was Angus. Snow encrusted his coat.

"Welcome, sir. Merry Christmas. Won't you please come in?" she said. The dog shook vigorously from head to tail to remove the snow. "We have room at the Inn." Dory retrieved his special bowl from the cupboard and added generous slabs of roast beef and a dash of gravy. "Seeing how it's Christmas and all, please join us at our table." She placed the bowl on the floor next to Billy's chair.

For dessert, Angelina Verdi baked a triple layer chocolate cake with homemade chocolate icing. This was in addition to the Christmas cookies she and James baked during the week. Although Dory brought many of them to the library's Christmas party, there were still dozens left. Pignoli cookies shared the tray with anise biscotti and Madeleines, oatmeal cookies, and chocolate chips. Pinwheel cookies fought for recognition among the gingerbread men and Christmas shape cookies—snowmen, angels, Christmas trees, Santa Clauses and reindeer. Billy unwrapped a bottle of thirty-year-old Tawny Port.

"I have been saving this for a special occasion," he said. "This is as special as it can be. Here is to good friends, good food, and good times."

Dory and Angelina shooed the men into the living room with their Port and a plate of cookies while they finished the dishes. James stretched out on the couch and stared at the twinkling lights on the tree. Angus curled up in front of the fireplace.

Jake put on his coat. "Where are you going?" James asked.

"I'm taking your mother out for a breath of fresh air."

Dory entered the living room. "Oh, are you?" she said. Jake handed Dory her coat and scarf.

"Just for a minute."

"Well then, I suppose…" Jake was already steering her toward the front door.

They walked to the water's edge. Dory looked up at the sky, letting the snowflakes catch her eyelashes. "It's so quiet, so beautiful, out here in the snow," she said.

"Not nearly as beautiful as you," Jake replied, holding her tightly. Neither of them felt the cold and dampness drifting in from the bay. "Dory, we haven't known each other for a long time. But that doesn't lessen how much I love you."

"Aw, Jake. This is romantic." She pulled away from his grasp and tilted her head back again. "Let's just enjoy the snow."

Jake's nerves began to get the better of him. He decided to switch his tactic. "Dory, Billy gave me ten acres up on Pencil Hill next to his place," he said. Dory looked up at him. Her eyes popped wide open. "Since I've been living like a hermit on that old houseboat for all of these years, I've been able to stow away a lot of money. And now, I have a new position starting at the university next month."

"That's wonderful, honey. That was extremely generous of Billy. What are you trying to say, Jake?"

"I am trying to say Billy won't take the property back, no matter how much I try to reason with him. I am trying to say how much I love you. I fell in love with you the minute I met you."

"Really? Was that at the hardware store or at Molly's?"

"Anyway, I asked an architect to draw up plans for a house. It will be up on the hill overlooking the bay and right into the sunrise. I spoke to Mr. Coaterie at the bank. Based on how much I've saved, and my new permanent teaching position, he told me I'd have no problem getting a construction loan for the balance. Mr. Coaterie said I could act as my own General Contractor and use whoever I want to build the house. Billy told me Kenny Clarke, Winton, Hirsch, Jank, Fred Lanscome, Dave Small, Chief Dooley, and pretty much everybody else in Harmony Bay will help build that house. Sort of like an old-time barn raising. Luke Hewes, Roland Rutledge, Joe and Rory will help too."

"Wow, that's great, Jake. I'm happy for you. I love you so much, and so does James. We'll help you, too."

"Well Dory, I kinda wanted to give you your Christmas present in private. That's why I asked you out here."

"It's warmer inside. Why don't we—."

"Close your eyes." She did. Jake placed a complete oyster shell, wrapped with red ribbon and tied with a bow, in her mittened hands.

"Okay, open." Dory opened one eye. "Hold on. Wait a minute. Not yet. Before you do—let me say this. Dory, I am so sure about my love for you that I want to be with you forever. That house I'm building is going to be a very big house. It needs more than just *me* in it. I want you, James, and me to be under the same roof, to always decorate our Christmas tree together as a family, and always be there for each other. And, I have never been more sure about anything else in my life. Dorothy McDonough, will you marry me?"

Salty rivers streamed down her cheeks, melting the snowflakes. "Mr. Jacob Kane, if I was ever shipwrecked on a desert island, the only man I'd want there is you. Yes, I will marry you and love you forever and always." They kissed long and hard.

"Aren't you going to open your present?" Dory looked at the oyster shell with a mystified expression.

"Gee—I almost forgot." Dory stopped sobbing long enough to untie the ribbon.

"Oysters are usually the guys who make pearls. This little guy had to work a little harder."

Dory separated the two halves. Nested in black velvet was a diamond engagement ring. "Oh Jake, it's gorgeous!" She pulled off her woolen mittens and Jake slid the ring on her finger. Dory held him tightly. Kissing him again, she said, "Merry Christmas, professor. I love you."

Her knees trembled as they walked back to the house. It wasn't from the cold. "After I tell James, I want to call my mother," she said.

Snow swirled into the kitchen as they opened the door. Angelina looked Dory in the eyes. "Bambina, have you been crying? Per piacere, tell Mamma Angelina what's wrong." Dory held her left hand up in front of Mrs. Verdi's eyes. "Congratulazioni, bambina. Buon Natale!" Angelina said. The two women didn't say another word. They hugged each other and danced around the kitchen. "Ssshh, I haven't told James yet," Dory said.

Dory, Jake, and Angelina filed into the living room. Jake poured himself and Billy another round of Port. Dory sat on the couch and asked James to sit next to her. "Are you okay, Mom?" he said. Dory's mascara was now dribbling down her face. "James, I've never been happier. You are the most important guy in my life. You know that, don't you?" James nodded yes. "After you, who do you think is the next most important?"

"Gramps."

"Well, uh, yes. Okay, after Gramps, who next?" Dory reached for Jakes hand and squeezed it to make a point.

"Jake?"

"Yes, you're right. You know what a good man Jake is, don't you?"

"You bet. Jake is the best at everything."

"Well, I agree. James, Jake has asked me to marry him. The three of us will be a family." James bolted up from the couch. Dory was startled not knowing what to expect. James jumped up and down on the couch like it was a trampoline, pumping his fists in the air. "Yes, yes, yes!" he shouted. James stopped jumping long enough to bear hug Jake. Billy pushed himself out of his chair and leaning on his cane, reached for Jake's hand. "I cannot think of a better family to have next door," Billy said. James gave a questioning look. "Allow me to be the first to congratulate you."

"Thank you, Billy. I'd like you to be my best man," Jake said.

"Without question. I am honored. I unconditionally accept. Here is a toast for the both of you." Billy picked up his glass. "It is never too late to live happily ever after. Bless you all."

"Amen to that," Angelina said, squeezing Billy's arm.

Jake explained to James the plans for the big house on the hill with plenty of room, even enough extra space for Gram and Gramps to have their own room when they came to visit. "At least we don't have to worry anymore about getting washed away in a storm if we're up there," James said.

Dory went to the kitchen and dialed the phone. "Hi, Mom. Merry Christmas. I have some wonderful news. Are you sitting down?"

"Well, dear, a very Merry Christmas to you, too. What's the news?"

"Jake asked me to marry him and I said yes." There was a long silence.

"I couldn't be happier for you. This is quite a Christmas gift for all of us." The call continued with the typical mother to daughter advice, the question if a date was set, the news of the new home, and such. Dory told her mother she didn't want to be rude to her guests. They'd speak again first thing in the morning.

Over the next few hours the flurries and the celebration continued. The time arrived to exchange gifts. As far as Dory was concerned, she had already received more than she could ever hope for. Jake was beyond content. Dory had said yes, and they'd be married and living in a new house on the hill.

In his woodshop, ignoring his need to recuperate, Billy made Angelina a sewing box, Dory a jewelry box, Jake, a rack for fishing rods, and for James, a music stand that folded up neatly. All of the gifts, made from the cedars that grew on Pencil Hill, were delicately carved and featured inlays of local black walnut and maple. Mrs. Verdi knitted red sweaters for all of them. Mrs. Verdi opened a diary book from Dory. "I think you should begin to write your memoirs," Dory said. "This past year alone could fill a book." Dory gave Jake a boxed set of classic rock CDs. She allowed James to open the package that came from his grandparents, telling him that Santa Claus would bring the rest tomorrow. James tore into the box to see a set of swim fins, snorkel, and dive mask.

"It'll be a little too chilly for a while to use those," Jake said. "Hang on until spring and I'll teach you how to use them." Jake and Dory excused themselves and went out onto the screen porch. He returned lugging in a large box wrapped in red foil; she held a smaller one wrapped in green. "Billy, these are from me, Dory and James."

"Well, my goodness. I thought that I had everything I needed," Billy said. "Apparently not." He unwrapped the presents. Wrapped in the red paper was a flat screen television. A DVD player was in the green box.

"We have an endless supply of DVDs at the library, Billy. All of the classics, too." Dory said.

"Splendid. This will be most enjoyable," Billy said. "Thank you and Merry Christmas."

Jake, Billy and Angelina headed home. Dory and James headed to their bedrooms.

Christmas Day crept into Harmony Bay with a sunrise that lit the bellies of clouds from below. Now emptied of snow, the gray, violet veined clouds made their way out to sea. It was quiet. Even the gulls decided to sleep in for the holiday. James thought otherwise. His feet hit the floor a moment after his eyes opened. "It's Christmas!" he hollered. He scrambled to the Christmas tree in the living room without giving notice to his mother. Her rule always was, nothing gets opened until everyone is up. James remembered the rule and returned to bang on his mother's door. "Mom! Wake up! It's Christmas." He was about to knock again as the door swung open. Dory knelt down and held him close. "Let's get started," he said.

"Give me a minute, I'm still half asleep." Dory shuffled toward the living room, stopping to look out the kitchen window on the way. "Nice," she murmured. "Very nice." Everywhere she looked the ground was coated in white. Crystal finger icicles hanging from the eaves caught the nascent light. Steady drips clung to their tips before falling and making way for another. Looking down at her left hand, Dory realized the prism effect her diamond had on the morning sun hitting it. Rainbows danced on the walls.

"C'mon, Mom. I can't wait any longer."

Dory sat down on the couch and authorized James to begin. "Where should I begin?" he asked aloud.

"Wherever you want," she replied. "Do you hear something?" James stopped shaking the boxes and listened.

"It sounds like something is crying out on the porch," James said. He went to the living room door and flung it open, allowing in a rush of cold air. "Mom, come quick! Look at this!"

Dory pulled the collar of her bathrobe up and walked to the open front door. On the porch's floorboards, directly in front of the door, was a large cardboard box with three large round holes on each side. Written in large blocky letters was: FOR JAMES. MERRY CHRISTMAS. SANTA CLAUS. It differentiated from all of James' other packages. This one whimpered, rattled and shook by itself.

"Well, go look in there, son," Dory said.

James opened the box to reveal a yellow Labrador retriever puppy tangled in several thick towels. "Mom, it's a dog!" James said as he scooped the fuzzy puppy out of the box.

"Let's get him inside. It's chilly out here."

"Can I keep him, Mom?" The dog licked his face frantically. "Can I keep him? *Please?*"

"Sure, you can keep him. I don't want to disappoint Santa Claus. You're old enough to have a dog. At least once, every boy deserves to have a dog to call his own. You'll be in charge of him, James. He's your dog. "

"Thank you, Mom!"

"When he gets a little bigger, you might have a hard time keeping him out of the water."

"Don't worry, Mom. He can go snorkeling with me and Jake."

"*That* should be interesting. Remember something, James…there is nothing better than a good dog, and there's nothing worse than a bad dog. You'll need to train him well."

"Mom, this is the best Christmas ever!"

"I couldn't agree more. Next Christmas, it will be you, me and Jake, and this little guy, in a house on the hill. Are you thinking of a name for him?"

"Yeah—Dewey." The dog now chewed on James' pajama sleeve.

"Dewey?"

"Yeah, like Dewey decimal system. He's going to be the smartest dog on Harmony Bay."

"Why don't you have Dewey help you unwrap the rest of your stuff? Then you can feed him."

For James, Dory and Dewey, it was a perfect Christmas in every way.

Chapter 36

Dory spent the entire day in the village making wedding preparations. She met with Pastor Simvasten and then with the church organist, Verna Jervis. Verna, with butterfly eyeglasses that had gone out of style when Elvis was king, was getting on Dory's nerves. Every time they discussed a possible song for the ceremony, Verna repeated in a shrill voice, "This will be so beautiful. This will be *so, sooo* beautiful. This *wedding* will be so beautiful." Dory started to wonder even if she suggested the theme song from the Three Stooges, Verna would think it was *so beautiful*. Dory caught herself and thought, *Dory, don't sweat the small stuff.* It was prenuptial jitters.

Molly McDuff was closing her Harbor Front restaurant to the public for the occasion. "Hey now, what the heck. It's the off-season and it's the least I can do for the two of you," she told Dory. "Jake saved the shellfish businesses, and you've prettied up this sleepy town in more ways than one. Everybody in this town owes the both of you. You go on and have your wedding reception here. Any out-of-towners snooping around for some grub will have to snoop a little farther that day." Molly found this to be very amusing and roared with laughter.

They decided to have the wedding as soon as they could. "It took us this long to find each other," Dory said to Stanley Dzjankowski at her last stop before heading home. "We don't want to delay it any longer."

"You're a couple of mature, level headed people. I don't see a problem with that," he said as he bagged her groceries.

Dory's mom and dad arrived three days before the wedding and had the chance to spend time with Jake's parents and his sister who flew in from California.

On February 2, Ground Hog's Day, Dory McDonough, baptized Dorothy O'Toole, became Mrs. Jacob Kane. Jake found humor in the date. He kidded Dory, "Every year on our anniversary, if you wake up and see my shadow, it means we're married for another year." Dory took his twisted sense of humor in stride.

Verna was correct. It was a fairytale wedding and the most beautiful wedding Harmony Bay had seen in a long time. Dory dispensed with many of the formalities. If you knew her, Jake or James, you were invited. The floor of the old sanctuary groaned as it reached capacity on the wedding morning. Lenny Hirsch and Jank shut down their business for the morning. A skeleton crew of volunteers and pages manned the library. Mail delivery was delayed until later that afternoon allowing Buzzy and Chester to attend. Baymen's boats were off the water for the day, dutifully tied to the town dock. Their captains were glad to sacrifice a day's haul and make their way to the church. A note on the front door of Shea's Bakery said, *We are busy building a wedding cake—please see us after lunch.* The sign on the door of Molly's Harbor Front Restaurant was more succinct, *Closed for family wedding.* Everybody in town who was anybody was in the church.

Tears of joy fell like raindrops on the creaky church floor. When Pastor Roger announced to the groom, "You may now kiss the bride," thunderous applause reverberated off the high, tin ceilings and shook the stained glass with hurricane force. James fidgeted in his seat next to his grandmother. He couldn't wait for the party to begin at Molly's.

Molly spared no expense. Dory and Jake begged her to accept some kind of payment for the reception. "Hey now, won't hear a word of it. Just take care of tippin' the help. Everything else is a wedding present," Molly said.

In the following days, Jake, Dory and James squeezed into the tiny beach house on the peninsula while they awaited construction to begin on the new house on the hill. "Think about it this way," Jake said, "there's more room here than on the boat, but close enough for all of us to get to know each other really well."

"Is this how I'm going to find out about your bad habits?" Dory joked.

"My only bad habit is you," he said.

Harmony Bay enjoyed a mild winter and an early spring. The new home's foundation was poured in early March and work began on the framing. James, watching the men build the stud walls on the ground and then push them up into place, was amazed at how quickly the house took shape. Folks from Harmony Bay, and beyond, came to help. They descended like seagulls on a dumpster as Jake liked to say. Work continued at a feverish pace. Jake was so well liked, and owed by so many, most tradesmen wouldn't accept payment, or only enough to cover the cost of materials. The Harmony Bay regulars, from Billy, to Chief Dooley to Joe Sea Macaroni wouldn't accept a dime. They would only shake their heads and tell the newlyweds, "It's no big thing," or, "It's a wedding present," or, they'd recall something Jake did for them over the years, or more recently, that Dory did.

Kaelin was the high school waitress who worked at Molly's. Dory and Jake helped her get into nursing college. Her father was a plumber. "When my daughter graduates college, I'll be very thankful. I'm just considering this being part of the tuition," he said. "Just take care of paying for the pipe."

When it came time for the wiring, James' friend Peter Dyson, whose father worked at the power company, pulled in favors from electricians. "You and Dory have been wonderful to our son," Mr. Dyson told Jake. "It's the least I can do to return the favor. Some of these guys owe me big time for getting them out of tight spots. Like when they wanted the power shut off on a weekend or a holiday. What comes around goes around. If you feel obliged, you can buy them lunch. Since we are already delivering power to Billy's house next door, we can have electric up here in a snap."

Mr. Coaterie from the bank sent an inspector to see that the bank's loan money was being spent wisely and that everything was being done to meet the building code. The next day, Saturday, Mr. Coaterie came to the job site himself.

"I'm flabbergasted," he said to Jake. Jake couldn't remember the last time he heard anyone use the word flabbergasted.

"*Flabbergasted?*"

"I'm flabbergasted because my inspector was flabbergasted. Every piece of lumber, every single specification, all of the plumbing and all of the wiring, does not meet the building code."

Jake was horrified. "Does not meet the building code," he repeated. Dory joined Jake. After hearing the banker's remarks, she looked over the completed work. Ladders and sheets of plywood paraded by them. The air was full of hammering, the whine of power saws and the smell of sawdust. Dory put her fingers to her lips, inhaled, then whistled loud enough to be heard over the drone of the generators.

"Whoa! Everybody stop!" she yelled. Every hammer, saw and drill on the job came to a standstill.

"That's right. It does not meet the building code," Coaterie said. "It *exceeds* the code. This job, this home, exceeds regulations by a wide margin. My man has never seen anything like it. What's more, he's never seen a job move along this fast. You and your family could be in your new home in a matter of weeks!"

"Whew," Jake said. Jake and Dory looked at each other in bewilderment.

"Okay, everybody," Dory hollered. "You're all knocking off early today. Please be our guests at Molly's at four o'clock. Jake is buying!" Dory poked Jake and a collective cheer went up from the men. "That means you too, Mr. Coaterie!" she said.

—◦◦◦◦◦◦◦—

James threw sticks for Dewey to chase as Jake worked in the yard of their completed new home. "What are you doing?" James asked.

"A year ago on our first date, your mother told me she's always wanted a garden. I'm going to clear out this area with its southern exposure in full view of the kitchen window and give her the garden she wants. I guess we can figure out how to grow more than scallops, eh?"

"I want to help," James offered.

"The soil is fairly sandy here. We can add composted leaves from the woods, along with some manure from Chloe to get things going."

"Yuck, I don't want *that* job."

Jake and James worked together clearing brush and cutting saplings. Dewey worked on chewing things he shouldn't. "What are we going to do about these big rocks?" James asked. Three large stones stood in a row where the center of the garden would be. The center stone was easily the size of a bushel basket; the other stones flanking it were smaller.

"I figured we'd roll 'em down to the end of the driveway by the mailbox," Jake said. Jake used a long handled shovel to pry one of the smaller stones loose. It began to roll as Billy rode up on Chloe.

"Good morning, gentlemen. May I be of assistance?" Billy said.

"That's mighty neighborly of you, sir." Jake replied. "Once we get these rolling down the hill we should be okay. Let's get the two smaller ones. Then we can all heave ho on that big one." The three of them moved the smaller stones to the edge of the road.

Billy returned to the garden spot. "Let me see that shovel for a moment, young man," he said. James handed Billy the shovel. Billy took a length of tree trunk and placed it beside the rock to use as a fulcrum. Inserting the shovel blade under the rock, and laying its handle across the stump, it now resembled a crude catapult. Billy stood on the free end of the shovel and the rock budged loose. Working together, they managed to roll the rock several yards. Dewey started sniffing at the spot where the rock had stood.

"Dewey—quit goofing off," James said. James went to grab the dog's collar and noticed a hole in the ground. "Hey, it's a sink hole, run for your life!" he called out. Jake and Billy joined the boy and the dog. They all now stared at a square black hole where the rock rested a moment ago. Jake took a large pebble and dropped it in the opening. It landed with a barely audible click. He then took a four-foot length from a volunteer sapling and tested the hole. "Billy," he said, "do you know if anybody ever capped a well up here?" The young tree didn't touch the bottom.

"Not that I am aware of." Jake used a push broom to clear the sand away from the hole. Several inches below the sand, the surface was hard and smooth. After shoveling and sweeping, they cleared a round, perfectly flat stone, five feet in diameter with peculiar flutes radiating out from the square hole. It was at least several inches thick.

"I know what this is," James said. Billy and Jake looked at each other, then at James. "It's a millstone. Last year Miss Donnelly taught us about water mills and millstones and stuff."

"Well, I'll be darned. There used to be a mill up here," Jake said.

"I disagree," Billy said. "I would know about it if there was one."

"Maybe it's covering a cesspool."

"I do not think that is the case either. This section of the property was never built on."

"Well…it's hollow under there. If we could move this, which I'll have to do anyway if Dory wants to garden here, we can see what the story is."

"We will require a sizable contingent of men to move this, or…" They all turned and looked at Chloe. "Hold on. I will return shortly." Billy came back with a long length of thick rope and a three-foot crow bar. He laced one end of the rope around Chloe's saddle horn and tied the other end around the middle of the bar. Billy lowered the steel shaft into the square hole. Once the bar disappeared, he tugged on the rope. The crow bar now straddled the opening from below. Giving a signal to the mare, she eased forward. The line tightened. Nothing happened.

"Hold on," Jake said. He used a shovel and cleared the dirt away from the leading edge of the millstone. James and Billy followed suit. With the dirt cleared, Billy laid several maple sprouts on the ground to act as rollers.

"It worked for the ancient Egyptians," Billy said. He gave a whistle and urged his horse forward. Dewey barked and nipped at Chloe's hooves. Chloe threw her head back and her muscles rippled as they strained against the load. The massive slab rolled forward uncovering a deep, stone lined chamber.

"Holy mackerel! Look at that," Jake uttered.

Dory called from the kitchen window, "Are you guys ready for lunch? I'll bring it out if your shoes are dirty."

"Honey, I think you better come have a look at this. There's more growing here than petunias. Dewey—get away from that hole." Inside the eight-foot deep hole were stacked oblong, piano bench size, wooden boxes. Dory rushed out from the house. Jake went to the garage for a ladder. Billy untied the rope from Chloe and then stood pensively pulling his beard. James grabbed Dewey's collar.

"I'm going to check this out," Jake said.

"Please, be careful," Dory pleaded. Loose sand spilled from the rim into the chamber. He lowered the ladder into the hole. Lying atop the crates were flintlock carriage pistols, several muskets, and a saber. Pulling on the box handles, they sheared off in Jake's hands.

"Throw me down the crow bar." Jake used the pry bar to remove a box's padlocked lid. "Oh man. Geez…this is incredible. Ye're not going to believe this!" he said. Inside the box were solid gold bars. A search of the other crates revealed, dozens of gold bars, tarnished silver ingots, and a blackened, fragile leather satchel containing jewels. It was stamped with the insignia… CC.

They all stood around the pit with their hands on hips and looked in. Silence fell over them as the stunning affect took hold, then capitulated to a state of shock then complete jubilation. Jake clambered up the ladder, folded his arms and took a deep breath. "Billy," he said, "you're rich."

"You are incorrect, Jake Kane. *You* are rich. The treasure trove laws clearly state that any valuables found on private property, whose ownership cannot be traced within the last hundred years, belongs to the property owner. You, young man, and your lovely bride, hold the title and deed to this land."

"Billy, that's not fair. It's been in your family for centuries."

"What am I possibly going to do with that much money? There are millions of dollars worth of gold in that hole."

James jumped up and down screaming, "We're rich. We're rich!" Dewey barked excitedly and ran in circles. Dory hugged Jake and wiped tears from her eyes. Jake let out a howl that echoed off the trees of Pencil Hill. Billy tugged his beard and then gave a deep belly laugh.

"Well, Billy," Dory said, "we insist on splitting it with you. What you do with the money is up to you. Money is not evil, it's what you do with the money that counts. In the meanwhile, we need to keep this quiet. When word about Christian Carroll's treasure being discovered gets out, we won't be able to protect it. We'll be overrun with media people and thrill seekers." Billy coaxed Chloe to drag the millstone back into place.

Exhausted and excited, they sat on the back steps of the house looking out over the bay. "Everything is in fairly good condition," Jake said.

"The southern exposure, sandy soil and that millstone, obviously looted from the Mill Pond watermill after it was burned, protected the stuff from the elements."

"I'm guessing Sergeant-Major Randall Stone-Bayard and Corporal Smythe were in charge of burying the loot," Dory said. "Whether or not Lieutenant Oliver Stockbridge gave them the order to do it is hard to say. If he did, it may well have been the reason that led to Stockbridge's murder. I think we can safely assume they probably figured England would be victorious, and the plan was to return to Harmony Bay after the war to retrieve the gold. The rest of the garrison—if they were even told what was in the hole—was probably ordered to guard the cache with their lives. Which they did until they died of yellow fever."

"They may have been told it was ammunition storage magazine. A place to hide it from American raiders," Jake conjectured. "Those are ammo crates. They have dimpled bottoms for holding canon balls. We know they had artillery pieces up here. Whoever schemed this up likely tossed in the pistols and muskets for effect. I want that stuff to go to the university for study— then maybe to the Smithsonian. I'll speak to Mr. Coaterie privately about stowing the rest of the treasure in his bank vault until we can figure this all out."

"Are we going to be heroes again?" James asked.

"I guess so, my son. We've solved another mystery," his mother replied.

James looked down the hill toward the water. It was spring. New life was returning. Sunlight tinged clouds, stenciled with a formation of geese, scudded out to the sea. As had been done since a time, not long after the dawn of time, the tides flowed in and out of Harmony Bay.

Epilogue

In the following months, Fishhook Cutsciko, baptized by his life-threatening ordeal on the rocks at England Point, donated land to the town at the edge of Harmony Bay for regulation-size Little League ball fields. Billy used his gold proceeds to equip the fields with sod, bleachers, scoreboards and lighting for nighttime play. He started another scholarship fund, enough to award twelve Harmony Bay students every year with ambitions in history, marine science, library science, music and other subjects. Billy also bought Winton a car with a pernundle. Winton visited his mother and was received in his hometown as a hero.

Miss Donnelly began dating Dave Small the auto mechanic.

Fred Lanscome grew tired of sitting home alone and started a fishing charter business that catered to older, single adults.

Kenny Clarke was chosen to skipper the United States entry in the America's Cup yacht race.

After an investigation by the FBI, Mayor Vinny Pesce was indicted for the misappropriation of public funds.

Jake legally adopted James and now called him son. The Kane family discovered that it truly was never too late to live happily ever after.

Breinigsville, PA USA
06 April 2011
259307BV00001BA/2/P